Stay Close

HARLAN
COBEN

About the author

HARLAN COBEN is the #1 *New York Times* bestselling author of twenty-two previous novels, including the popular Myron Bolitar series. *Seconds Away*, his second novel for young adults, was published in September 2012. The winner of the Edgar®, Shamus, and Anthony Awards, he lives in New Jersey.

CONNECT ONLINE
www.harlancoben.com
facebook.com/harlancobenbooks
twitter.com/harlancoben

DIRECTION DE LA PUBLICATION : Carine Girac-Marinier

DIRECTION ÉDITORIALE : Claude Nimmo

NOTES EN MARGE : Natalie Pomier

RÉVISION DES NOTES : Marianne Mouchot

RELECTURE : Joëlle Narjollet

INFORMATIQUE ÉDITORIALE : Philippe Cazabet, Marie-Noëlle Tilliette

CONCEPTION GRAPHIQUE : Uli Meindl

MISE EN PAGES : Cynthia Savage

FABRICATION : Rebecca Dubois

Remerciements à Stephanie Carey et Marie Gabiache

Mot de l'Éditeur

Vous aimeriez lire en langue originale, mais le vocabulaire, les expressions figurées ou la syntaxe vous arrêtent parfois ?

Cette collection est faite pour vous !

Vous trouverez en effet, en note dans la marge, une traduction de certains mots et expressions qui vous permettra d'avancer facilement dans votre lecture.

Nous n'avons pas cherché à vous donner une traduction littéraire de l'ouvrage et nous nous sommes parfois écartés du sens littéral pour vous fournir celui qui convient le mieux à l'histoire. Aussi les mots sont-ils traduits dans le contexte du texte original.

Les expressions figées anglaises sont, bien entendu, rendues par une expression équivalente en français.

Les allusions à des réalités culturelles du monde anglo-saxon sont expliquées également dans la marge, pour vous aider à mieux comprendre la trame de l'histoire.

Vous aurez ainsi, en regard du texte original, tout le savoir-faire d'un dictionnaire rien que pour vous et adapté à ce livre !

Notre objectif est de vous mener jusqu'au mot FIN en vous donnant les clés nécessaires à la compréhension du récit.

Laissez-vous gagner par l'angoisse, l'humour et le suspense qui règnent chez les maîtres de la littérature anglo-saxonne.

Lire en VO ? You can indeed!

This one is for
Aunt Diane and Uncle Norman Reiter
and
Aunt Ilene and Uncle Marty Kronberg,
with love and gratitude.

Acknowledgments

The author wishes to thank Ben Sevier, Brian Tart, Christine Ball, Diane Discepolo, Lisa Erbach Vance, Chris Christie (I'm skipping titles[1]), Linda Fairstein, Ben Coben (who enjoyed "researching" the ruins, Lucy, and the boardwalk[2] equally), Anne Armstrong-Coben, and Bob McGuigan.

This is a work of fiction. That means I make stuff up[3]. That said, the Korean War Memorial on the boardwalk in Atlantic City, the ghost towns/ruins in the Pine Barrens, and Lucy the Elephant are all real and worth visits[4]. You can learn more about them at harlancoben.com.

I'd also like to give a quick shout-out to[5] Erin Anderson, Guy Angiuoni, Samantha Bajraktari, Howard Dodds, Jaime Hatcher Hemsley, Missy Malek, Rick Mason, and Barbara and Anthony Reale. These people (or their munificent loved ones[6]) made generous contributions to charities in return for having their names appear in this novel. If you'd like to participate in the future, please visit harlancoben.com for details.

1. j'omets leurs titres
2. le front de mer [et ses casinos]
3. que j'invente des trucs
4. méritent une visite
5. saluer
6. des proches très généreux

Coup de pouce pour vous aider à bien comprendre le début de l'histoire...

Depuis que sa vie a basculé, Ray Levine ne mitraille plus pour des photoreportages mais pour des gens riches avides d'une célébrité même factice, le temps d'une fête.

Pourquoi est-il agressé à la sortie d'une bar-mitsva ? Pourquoi est-il obnubilé par des images de sang ?

Un jeune homme vient de disparaître. La disparition serait-elle un nouveau jeu de hasard à Atlantic City ?

Well now everything dies, baby that's a fact.
But maybe everything that dies, someday comes back.

—Bruce Springsteen, "Atlantic City"

1

1. pendant la
fraction de
seconde où

2. prenait une
photo

3. que la lumière
stroboscopique
de son flash
faisait
disparaître le
monde autour
de lui

4. le fruit de son
imagination

5. parfois

6. baisser

7. appareil photo

8. regarder
attentivement
le sol

9. ce paumé de
première

10. que vous
avez devant
vous

11. accablantes

12. bien réveillé

13. pris par ce
que certains
esprits
sarcastiques
appelleraient son
boulot

14. Heureuse-
ment, les visions
s'atténuèrent

15. de derrière
son objectif

16. C'est de
qui, ce que tu
portes ?

SOMETIMES, in that split second when[1] Ray Levine snapped a picture[2] and lost the world in the strobe from his flashbulb[3], he saw the blood. He knew, of course, that it was only in his mind's eye[4], but at times[5], like right now, the vision was so real he had to lower[6] his camera[7] and take a good hard look at the ground[8] in front of him. That horrible moment— the moment Ray's life changed completely, transforming him from a man with a future and aspirations into this Grade-A loser[9] you see in front of you[10]—never visited him in his dreams or when he sat alone in the dark. The devastating[11] visions waited until he was wide-awake[12], surrounded by people, busy at what some might sarcastically dub work[13].

The visions mercifully faded[14] as Ray continuously snapped pictures of the bar mitzvah boy.

"Look this way, Ira," Ray shouted from behind his lens[15]. "Who are you wearing?[16] Is it true Jen and Angelina are still fighting over you?"

1. donna un coup
de pied dans
2. le tibia
3. fronça les
sourcils
4. se cacha
5. s'avança
néanmoins
6. garder
l'équilibre
7. Sales
8. leva les yeux
au ciel
9. ne recula pas
10. d'en chasser
l'image
11. sur le
déclencheur
12. au ralenti
13. tomber plus
bas
14. Ben non
15. au crâne rasé
16. écarta Ray
17. d'un mou-
vement de son
bras énorme
18. Il y était allé
franco
19. le renversant
20. interrogea
Fester
du regard
« qu'est-ce qui
te prend ? »
21. s'excusa en
silence
22. propriétaire
23. à louer
24. ne traquait
pas
25. des clichés
26. journaux à
scandale
27. des gens
rêvant de
célébrité
28. une haute
idée d'eux-mêmes
29. des pro-
blèmes d'érection

Someone kicked[1] Ray's shin[2]. Someone else pushed him. Ray kept snapping pictures of Ira.

"Where is the after-party, Ira? What lucky girl is getting the first dance?"

Ira Edelstein frowned[3] and shielded[4] his face from the camera lens. Ray surged forward undaunted[5], snapping pictures from every angle. "Get out of the way!" someone shouted. Someone else pushed him. Ray tried to steady himself[6].

Snap, snap, snap.

"Damn[7] paparazzi!" Ira shouted. "Can't I have a moment of peace?"

Ray rolled his eyes[8]. He did not back off[9]. From behind his camera lens, the vision with the blood returned. He tried to shake it off[10], but it would not go. Ray kept his finger pressed down on the shutter[11]. Ira the Bar Mitzvah Boy moved in a slow-motion strobe[12] now.

"Parasites!" Ira screamed.

Ray wondered if it was possible to sink any lower[13]. Another kick to the shins gave Ray his answer: Nope[14].

Ira's "bodyguard"—an enormous guy with a shaved head[15] named Fester—swept Ray aside[16] with a forearm the size of an oak[17]. The sweep was with a bit too much gusto[18], nearly knocking him off his feet[19]. Ray gave Fester a "what gives" look[20]. Fester mouthed an apology[21].

Fester was Ray's boss and friend and the owner[22] of Celeb Experience: Paparazzi for Hire[23]—which was just what it sounded like. Ray didn't stalk[24] celebrities hoping to get compromising shots[25] to sell to tabloids[26] like a real paparazzo. No, Ray was actually beneath that—Beatlemania to the Beatles—offering the "celebrity experience" to wannabes[27] who were willing to pay. In short, clients, most with extreme self-esteem[28] and probably erectile dysfunction issues[29], hired paparazzi to follow them around, snapping pic-

16

tures to give them, per[1] the brochure, the "ultimate celebrity experience with your very own exclusive paparazzi."

Ray could sink lower, he supposed, but not without an extreme act of God.

The Edelsteins had purchased[2] the A-List Mega-Package[3]—two hours with three paparazzi, one bodyguard, one publicist, one boom-mike handler[4], all following around the "celebrity" and snapping pictures of him as though he were Charlie Sheen[5] sneaking into a monastery[6]. The A-List MegaPackage also came with a souvenir DVD for no extra charge[7], plus your face on one of those cheesy-fake gossip magazine covers[8] with a custom-made headline[9].

The cost for the A-List MegaPackage?

Four grand[10].

To answer the obvious question: Yes, Ray hated himself.

Ira pushed past and disappeared into the ballroom. Ray lowered his camera and looked at his two fellow paparazzi. Neither one of them had the loser L[11] tattooed on their forehead because, really, it would have been redundant[12].

Ray checked his watch. "Damn," he said.

"What?"

"We still have fifteen minutes on the clock."

His colleagues—both barely bright enough to[13] write their names in the dirt[14] with a finger—groaned[15]. Fifteen more minutes. That meant going inside and working the introduction. Ray hated that.

The bar mitzvah was being held[16] at the Wingfield Manor, a ridiculously gauche[17] banquet hall that, if scaled back a tad[18], could have doubled as[19] one of Saddam Hussein's palaces. There were chandeliers and mirrors and faux ivory and ornate woodwork[20] and lots and lots of shimmering gold paint[21].

The image of the blood came back to him. He blinked it away[22].

1. selon

2. payé pour

3. le top du top

4. teneur de micro

5. [star à la vie tumultueuse]

6. entrant en douce dans un monastère

7. sans supplément

8. fausses couvertures de revues people un peu cheap

9. la une personnalisée

10. 4 000 $

11. le L de « loser »

12. superflu

13. à peine assez fûtés pour

14. par terre

15. grognèrent

16. avait lieu

17. de mauvais goût

18. en un peu plus sobre

19. aurait pu passer pour

20. des boiseries ouvragées

21. de doré

22. fit un effort pour la chasser

The event was black-tie.[1] The men looked worn[2] and rich. The women looked well kept[3] and surgically enhanced[4]. Ray pushed through the crowds[5], wearing jeans, a wrinkled[6] gray blazer, and black Chuck Taylor Hi-Tops[7]. Several guests stared at him[8] as though he'd just defecated on their salad fork.

There was an eighteen-piece band[9] plus a "facilitator[10]" who was supposed to encourage guest frolicking of all sorts[11]. Think bad TV-game-show host.[12] Think Muppets' Guy Smiley. The facilitator grabbed the microphone and said, "Ladies and gentlemen," in a voice reminiscent of a boxing ring announcer[13], "please welcome, for the first time since receiving the Torah and becoming a man, give it up for the one, the only[14] … Ira Edelstein!"

Ira appeared with two … Ray wasn't sure what the right terminology was but perhaps the best phrase would be "upscale strippers[15]." The two hot chicks[16] escorted little Ira into the room by the cleavage[17]. Ray got the camera ready and pushed forward, shaking his head. The kid was thirteen. If women who looked like that were ever that close to him when he was thirteen, he'd have an erection for a week.

Ah youth.

The applause was rapturous[18]. Ira gave the crowd a royal wave[19].

"Ira!" Ray called out. "Are these your new goddesses[20]? Is it true you may be adding a third to your harem?"

"Please," Ira said with a practiced whine[21], "I'm entitled to my privacy[22]!"

Ray managed not to vomit. "But your public wants to know."

Fester the sunglassed Bodyguard put a large mitt[23] on Ray, allowing Ira to brush past him. Ray snapped, making sure the flash worked its magic. The band exploded—when did weddings and bar mitzvahs start playing music at a rock-stadium decibel[24]?—into the

new celebration anthem[1] "Club Can't Handle Me."
Ira dirty-danced[2] with the two hired helpers[3]. Then
his thirteen-year-old friends joined in, crowding the
dance floor[4], jumping straight up and down like pogo
sticks[5]. Ray "fought" through[6] Fester, snapped some
more pictures, checked his watch.

One more minute on the clock.

"Paparazzi scum[7]!"

Another kick to the shins from some little cretin.

"Ow, damn it[8], that hurt!"

The cretin scurried away[9]. Note to self[10], Ray
thought: Start wearing shin guards[11]. He looked over
at Fester as though begging for mercy[12]. Fester let him
off the hook[13] with a head gesture to follow him toward the corner. The corner was too loud[14] so they
slipped through the doors.

Fester pointed back into the ballroom with his enormous thumb[15]. "Kid did a great job on his haftorah
portion[16], don't you think?"

Ray just stared at him.

"I got a job for you tomorrow," Fester said.

"Groovy[17]. What is it?"

Fester looked off[18].

Ray didn't like that. "Uh-oh."

"It's George Queller."

"Dear God."

"Yes. And he wants the usual."

Ray sighed[19]. George Queller tried to impress first
dates[20] by overwhelming and ultimately terrifying
them[21]. He would hire Celeb Experience to swarm[22]
him and his date—for example, last month it was
a woman named Nancy—as he entered a small romantic bistro. Once the date was safely inside, she
would be presented with—no, this was for real—a
custom-made menu that would read[23], "George and
Nancy's First Date of Many, Many" with the address,
month, day, and year printed beneath[24]. When they
left the restaurant, the paparazzi for hire would be

1. chant
2. fit quelques
pas de danse
suggestive
3. les deux
extras
4. prenant toute
la piste de danse
5. des échasses
à ressort
6. fit mine
de passer le
barrage de
7. Saleté de
paparazzi !
8. Oh, putain
9. détala
10. À se noter
11. des protège-
tibias
12. comme pour
demander grâce
13. le libéra
14. trop bruyant
15. désigna
de son énorme
pouce la salle de
réception
16. a très bien lu
son extrait de la
Haftarah
17. Super
18. détourna le
regard
19. soupira
20. ses nouvelles
invitées
21. en leur
faisant une
cour irrésistible
mais finalement
terrifiante
22. pour qu'ils se
pressent autour
de
23. où était écrit
24. au-dessous

there, snapping away[1] and shouting at how George had turned down a weekend in Turks and Caicos with Jessica Alba for the lovely and now-terror-stricken[2] Nancy.

George considered these romantic maneuvers a pre-quel[3] to happy-ever-after[4]. Nancy and her ilk[5] considered these romantic maneuvers a prelude to a ball gag and secluded storage unit[6].

There had never been a second date for George.

Fester finally took off[7] his sunglasses. "I want you to work lead on the job[8]."

"Lead paparazzo," Ray said. "I better call my mother, so she can brag to her mahjong group[9]."

Fester chuckled[10]. "I love you, you know that."

"Are we done[11] here?"

"We are."

Ray packed away[12] his camera carefully, separating the lens from the body, and threw the case over his shoulder[13]. He limped[14] toward the door, not from the[15] kicks but the hunk of shrapnel in his hip[16]—the shrapnel that started his downward slide[17]. No, that was too simple. The shrapnel was an excuse. At one time in his miserable life, Ray had fairly limit-less potential. He'd graduated from Columbia University's School of Journalism with what one professor called "almost supernatural talent"—now being wast-ed[18]—in the area of photojournalism. But in the end, that life didn't work out for him[19]. Some people are drawn to trouble[20]. Some people, no matter how easy the path they are given on the walk of life, will find a way to mess it all up[21].

Ray Levine was one of those people.

It was dark out.[22] Ray debated whether he should just head[23] home and go to bed or hit a bar so seedy it was called Tetanus[24]. Tough call[25] when you have so many options.

He thought about the dead body again.

The visions came fast and furious[1] now. That was understandable, he supposed. Today was the anniversary of the day it all ended, when any hope of happy-ever-after died like … Well, the obvious metaphor here would involve the visions in his head, wouldn't it?

He frowned. Hey, Ray, melodramatic much[2]?

He had hoped that today's inane job[3] would take his mind off it[4]. It hadn't. He remembered his own bar mitzvah, the moment on the pulpit[5] when his father bent down and whispered in his ear[6]. He remembered how his father had smelled of Old Spice, how his father's hand cupped Ray's head so gently[7], how his father with tears in his eyes simply said, "I love you so much."

Ray pushed the thought away. Less painful to think about the dead body[8].

The valets[9] had wanted to charge him[10]—no professional courtesy[11], he guessed—so Ray had found a spot three blocks down[12] on a side street. He made the turn, and there it was—his piece-o-crap[13], twelve-year-old Honda Civic with a missing bumper[14] and duct tape holding together a side window[15]. Ray rubbed his chin. Unshaven[16]. Unshaven, forty years old, piece-o-crap car, a basement apartment that if heavily renovated might qualify as a crap hole[17], no prospects, drank too much. He would feel sorry for himself, but that would involve, well, caring.

Ray was just taking out his car key when the heavy blow landed on the back of his head[18].

What the … ?

He dropped to one knee. The world went dark. The tingle ran up his scalp.[19] Ray felt disoriented. He tried to shake his head, tried to clear it.

Another blow landed near his temple[20].

Something inside his head exploded in a flash of bright light. Ray collapsed[21] to the ground, his body splayed out[22]. He may have lost consciousness—he

1. Les images se bousculaient

2. on verse dans le mélo

3. le boulot stupide

4. lui changerait les idées

5. sur l'estrade

6. s'était penché pour lui parler à l'oreille

7. avait posé une main délicate sur sa tête

8. cadavre

9. voituriers

10. lui faire payer le parking

11. pas de gratuité pour les professionnels

12. une place trois rues plus loin

13. tas de ferraille

14. un pare-chocs en moins

15. la vitre d'une portière qui tenait avec du Scotch

16. Mal rasé

17. un taudis

18. il reçut un grand coup derrière la tête

19. Un pico-tement envahit son crâne.

20. tempe

21. s'effondra

22. de tout son long

1. qu'on lui
tirait l'

2. resta inerte

3. lui faisait
atrocement mal

4. Roule-toi en
boule

5. On faillit lui
déboîter l'épaule
en tirant à
nouveau très
fort.

6. alors, Ray
comprit et ouvrit
les yeux

7. nouvelle
fonction d'envoi
électronique

8. se soulever
et la bride lui
glisser du bras

9. gagne-pain

10. lien

11. il ne l'aban-
donnerait pas
sans se battre

12. son
agresseur

13. dollars

14. qui tournait

15. les genoux
tremblants

16. de se jeter
sur

17. de les bloquer
entre ses bras

18. n'y
parvint pas
complètement

19. le bruit
métallique

20. espéra très
fort qu'il ne
venait pas de
bousiller

21. rouvrir les
yeux

22. les entrouvrir

23. ramper

24. qui lui
glacèrent le sang

wasn't sure—but suddenly he felt a pulling in his[1] right shoulder. For a moment he just lay limp[2], not able or wanting to resist. His head reeled in agony[3]. The primitive part of his brain, the base animal section, had gone into survivor mode. Escape more punishment, it said. Crawl into a ball[4] and cover up.

Another hard tug nearly tore his shoulder out.[5] The tug lessened and began to slip away, and with it, a realization made Ray's eyes snap open[6].

Someone was stealing his camera.

The camera was a classic Leica with a recently updated digital-send feature[7]. He felt his arm lift in the air, the strap running up it[8]. In a second, no more, the camera would be gone.

Ray didn't have much. The camera was the only possession he truly cherished. It was his livelihood[9], sure, but it was also the only link[10] to old Ray, to that life he had known before the blood, and he'd be damned if he'd give that up without a fight[11].

Too late.

The strap was off his arm now. He wondered whether he'd have another opportunity, whether the mugger[12] would go for the fourteen bucks[13] in his wallet and give Ray a chance. Couldn't wait to find out.

With his head still swimming[14] and his knees wobbling[15], Ray shouted, "No!" and tried to launch himself at[16] his attacker. He hit something—legs maybe—and tried to wrap his arms around them[17]. He didn't get much of a grip[18], but the impact was enough.

The attacker fell down. So did Ray, landing on his stomach. Ray heard the clacking[19] of something falling and hoped like hell that he hadn't just shattered[20] his own camera. He tried to blink his eyes open[21], managed to get them into slits[22], and saw the camera case a few feet away. He tried to scramble[23] toward it, but as he did, he saw two things that made his blood freeze[24].

The first was a baseball bat on the pavement[1].

The second—and more to the point[2]—was a gloved hand picking it up[3].

Ray tried to look up, but it was useless. He flashed back to the summer camp[4] his father ran[5] when he was a kid. Dad—the campers all called him Uncle Barry—used to lead a relay race[6] where you hold a basketball directly over your head and spin as fast as you can, staring up at the ball, and then, dizzy beyond words[7], you had to dribble the length of the court and put the ball in the basket[8]. The problem was, you got so dizzy from the spinning that you'd fall one way while the ball would go the other way. That was how he felt now, as though he were tumbling to the left[9], while the rest of the world teetered to the right[10].

The camera thief lifted the baseball bat and started toward him[11].

"Help!" Ray shouted.

No one appeared.

Panic seized Ray[12]—followed quickly by a primitive survival instinctive reaction. Flee[13]. He tried to stand, but, nope, that was simply not happening yet. Ray was already a weakened mess[14]. One more shot, one more hard blow with that baseball bat …

"Help!"

The attacker took two steps toward him. Ray had no choice. Still on his stomach he scrambled away[15] like a wounded[16] crab. Oh, sure, that would work. That would be fast enough to keep away from the damn bat. The asswipe[17] with the baseball bat was practically over him. He had no chance.

Ray's shoulder hit something, and he realized that it was his car.

Above him he saw the bat coming up in the air. He was a second, maybe two, away from having his skull crushed.[18] Only one chance and so he took it.

Ray turned his head so his right cheek was against the pavement, flattened his body[19] as much as pos-

---

1. trottoir
2. plus inquiétant
3. une main gantée qui s'en emparait
4. colonie de vacances
5. dirigeait
6. une course de relais
7. alors que vous aviez complètement le tournis
8. panier
9. titubait vers la gauche
10. vacillait vers la droite
11. vint vers lui
12. Ray fut pris de panique
13. Prends la fuite
14. dans un sale état
15. tenta de ramper hors de portée
16. blessé
17. connard
18. Il lui restait une seconde, voire deux, avant de se faire défoncer le crâne.
19. s'aplatit

sible, and slid[1] under his car. "Help!" he shouted again. Then to his attacker: "Just take the camera and go!"

The attacker did just that. Ray heard the footsteps disappear down the alley[2]. Friggin' terrific[3]. He tried to slide himself out from under the car. His head protested, but he managed. He sat on the street now, his back against the passenger door of his car. He sat there for a while. Impossible to say how long. He may have even passed out[4].

When he felt that he was able, Ray cursed the world[5], slid into his car, and started it up[6].

Odd, he thought. The anniversary of all that blood—and he nearly has a ton of his own spilled[7]. He almost smiled at the coincidence. He pulled out[8] as the smile started sliding off his face[9].

A coincidence. Yep, just a coincidence. Not even a big one, when you thought about it. The night of blood had been seventeen years ago—hardly a silver anniversary or anything like that. Ray had been robbed before. Last year a drunk[10] Ray had been rolled[11] after leaving a strip club at two A.M. The moron[12] had stolen his wallet and gotten away with a full seven dollars and a CVS discount card[13].

Still.

He found a spot on the street in front of the row house Ray called home. He rented the apartment in the basement[14]. The house was owned by Amir Baloch, a Pakistani immigrant who lived there with his wife and four rather loud kids.

Suppose for a second, just a split second, that it wasn't a coincidence.

Ray slid out of his car. His head still pounded.[15] It would be worse tomorrow. He took the steps down past the garbage cans[16] to the basement door and jammed the key into the lock[17]. He racked his aching brain[18], trying to imagine any connection—the slightest, smallest, frailest[19], most obscure link—between that tragic night seventeen years ago and being jumped tonight[1].

Nothing.

Tonight was a robbery[2], plain and simple[3]. You whack a guy over the head[4] with a baseball bat, you snatch[5] his camera, you run. Except, well, wouldn't you steal his wallet too—unless maybe it was the same guy who rolled Ray near that strip joint[6] and knew that he'd only had seven dollars? Heck[7], maybe that was the coincidence. Forget the timing and the anniversary. Maybe the attacker was the same guy who robbed Ray one year ago.

Oh boy, he was making no sense[8]. Where the hell was that Vicodin?

He flipped on[9] the television and headed into[10] the bathroom. When he opened the medicine chest[11], a dozen bottles and whatnot[12] fell into the sink. He fished into the pile[13] and found the bottle with the Vicodin. At least he hoped that they were Vicodin. He'd bought them off the black market from a guy who claimed to smuggle them in[14] from Canada. For all Ray knew[15], they were Flintstone[16] vitamins.

The local news was on[17], showing some local fire, asking neighbors what they thought about the fire because, really, that always got you some wonderful insight[18]. Ray's cell phone[19] rang. He saw Fester's number pop up on the caller ID[20].

"What's up?" Ray said, collapsing on the couch[21].

"You sound horrible."

"I got mugged[22] soon as I left Ira's bar mitzvah."

"For real[23]?"

"Yep. Got hit over the head with a baseball bat."

"They steal anything?"

"My camera."

"Wait, so you lost today's pictures?"

"No, no, don't worry," Ray said. "I'm fine, really."

"On the inside I'm dying of worry.[24] I'm asking about the pictures to cover my pain[25]."

1. l'agression de ce soir
2. un vol
3. tout simplement
4. On estourbit un mec
5. lui choure
6. cette boîte de strip-tease
7. Mince
8. il se racontait n'importe quoi
9. alluma
10. entra dans
11. armoire à pharmacie
12. de trucs divers
13. fouilla dans le tas
14. prétendait en rapporter en douce
15. Si ça se trouve
16. un cocktail de
17. C'était l'heure du journal régional
18. c'était toujours d'une grande aide pour mieux comprendre
19. Le téléphone portable
20. vit le numéro de Fester s'afficher
21. canapé
22. me suis fait agresser
23. Pour de vrai
24. Intérieurement, je suis mort d'inquiétude.
25. pour faire bonne figure

"I have them," Ray said.

"How?"

His head hurt too much to explain, plus the Vicodin was knocking him to la-la land[1]. "Don't worry about it. They're safe[2]."

A few years ago, when Ray did a stint as[3] a "real" paparazzo, he'd gotten some wonderfully compromising photographs of a certain high-profile[4] gay actor stepping out on his boyfriend[5] with—gasp[6]— a woman. The actor's bodyguard forcibly took[7] the camera from Ray and destroyed the SD card[8]. Since then, Ray had put a send feature on his camera— something similar to what most people have on their camera phones—that automatically e-mailed the pictures off his SD card every ten minutes.

"That's why I'm calling," Fester said. "I need them fast. Pick out five of them and e-mail them to me tonight. Ira's dad wants our new bar mitzvah paperweight cube[9] right away."

On the TV news, the camera panned over to[10] the "meteorologist," a curvy babe in a tight red sweater[11]. Ratings bait[12]. Ray's eyes started to close as the hottie[13] finished up with the satellite photograph and sent it back to the over-coiffed anchorman[14].

"Ray?"

"Five pics[15] for a paperweight cube."

"Right."

"A cube has six sides," Ray said.

"Whoa, get a load of the math genius[16]. The sixth side is for the name, date, and a Star of David."

"Got it."

"I need them ASAP[17]."

"Okay."

"Then everything is copasetic[18]," Fester said. "Except, well, without a camera, you can't do George Queller tomorrow. Don't worry. I'll find somebody else."

"Now I'll sleep better."

Marginal glossary:

1. le faisait planer
2. à l'abri
3. avait brièvement été
4. célèbre
5. trompant son petit ami
6. tenez-vous bien
7. avait arraché
8. détruit la carte mémoire
9. cube presse-papiers
10. la caméra glissa vers
11. une nana bien roulée en pull rouge moulant
12. Tout pour l'Audimat
13. fille canon
14. repassait l'antenne au présentateur au brushing impec
15. photos
16. admirez le génie en maths
17. fissa
18. tout baigne

"You're a funny guy, Ray. Get me the pics. Then get some rest[1]."

"I'm welling up from your concern[2], Fester."

Both men hung up[3]. Ray fell back onto[4] the couch. The drug[5] was working in a wonderful way. He almost smiled. On the TV, the anchorman strapped on his gravest voice[6] and said, "Local man Carlton Flynn has gone missing[7]. His car was found abandoned with the door open near the pier[8] ..."

Ray opened one eye and peeked out[9]. A man-cum-boy[10] with frosted tips in his spiky dark hair[11] and a hoop earring[12] was on the screen now. The guy was making kissy lips at the camera[13], the caption[14] under him reading "Vanished," when it probably should have read "Douchebag[15]." Ray frowned, a stray, vague concern passing through his head[16], but he couldn't process it[17] right now. His entire body craved[18] sleep, but if he didn't send in those five photographs, Fester would call again and who needed that? With great effort, Ray managed to get back to his feet[19]. He stumbled to[20] the kitchen table, booted up his laptop[21], and made sure that the pictures had indeed made it to[22] his computer.

They had.

Something niggled at the back of his head[23], but Ray couldn't say what. Maybe something irrelevant[24] was bothering him. Maybe he was remembering something really important. Or maybe, most likely, the blow from the baseball bat had produced little skull fragments that were now literally scratching at his brain[25].

The bar mitzvah pictures came up[26] in reverse order—last picture taken was first. Ray quickly scanned through the thumbs[27], choosing one dance shot, one family shot, one Torah shot, one with the rabbi, one with Ira's grandmother kissing his cheek.

That was five. He attached them to Fester's e-mail address and clicked send. Done.

1. repose-toi
2. Ta sollicitude me va droit au cœur
3. raccrochèrent
4. retomba sur
5. Le médoc
6. prit son ton le plus grave
7. a disparu
8. la jetée
9. jeta un œil sur l'écran
10. homme-enfant
11. des cheveux bruns aux pointes décolorées
12. anneau à l'oreille
13. une moue pulpeuse devant la caméra
14. légende
15. Pauvre con
16. un truc l'inquiétait vaguement
17. mettre le doigt dessus
18. réclamait
19. se lever
20. tituba jusqu'à
21. démarra son ordinateur portable
22. étaient bien arrivées à
23. le tracassait
24. sans importance
25. qui lui titillaient la cervelle
26. s'affichaient
27. parcourut les vignettes miniatures

1. se demandait
s'il n'allait pas
simplement
poser la tête sur

2. faire un petit
somme

3. Une extrême
tristesse
l'envahit

4. C'était débile

5. lui donnait,
sans qu'il sache
bien pourquoi,
un sentiment de
sécurité

6. sous cet angle
étonnamment
rassurant

7. sur son écran
d'ordinateur

8. Il fut saisi
d'un frisson

9. quand il
perçuta

10. ne cherchait
pas à mettre la
main sur

Ray felt so tired that he wasn't sure he could get up from the chair and make his way to the bed. He debated just putting his head down on[1] the kitchen table and napping[2] when he remembered the other photographs on that SD card, the ones he'd taken earlier in the day, before the bar mitzvah.

An overwhelming feeling of sadness flooded into his chest[3].

Ray had gone back to that damn park and snapped pictures. Dumb[4], but he did it every year. He couldn't say why. Or maybe he could and that just made it worse. The camera lens gave him distance, gave him perspective, made him feel somehow safe[5]. Maybe that was what it was. Maybe, somehow, seeing that horrible place through that oddly comforting angle[6] would somehow change what could, of course, never be changed.

Ray looked at the pictures he'd taken earlier in the day on his computer monitor[7]—and now he remembered something else.

A guy with frosted tips and a hoop earring.

Two minutes later, he found what he was looking for. His entire body went cold[8] as the realization hit him[9].

The attacker hadn't been after[10] the camera. He'd been after a picture.

This picture.

28

2

MEGAN Pierce was living the ultimate soccer-mom fantasy[1] and hating it.

She closed the Sub-Zero fridge and looked at her two children through the bay windows off the breakfast nook[2]. The windows offered up "essential morning light." That was how the architect had put it. The newly renovated kitchen also had a Viking stove[3], Miele appliances[4], a marble island[5] in the middle, and excellent flow to the family-cum-theater room[6] with the big-screen TV, recliners[7] with cup holders, and enough sound speakers[8] to stage a Who concert[9].

Out in the backyard[10], Kaylie, her fifteen-year-old daughter, was picking on[11] her younger brother, Jordan. Megan sighed and opened the window. "Cut it out[12], Kaylie."

"I didn't do anything."

"I'm standing right here watching you."

Kaylie put her hands on her hips[13]. Fifteen years old—that troubling adolescent cusp[14] between adult

1. menait l'existence idéale d'une mère dévouée

2. à travers le bow-window du coin-repas

3. cuisinière haut de gamme

4. de l'électro-ménager

5. un plan de travail central en marbre

6. un accès facile au coin-repas qui faisait aussi coin-télé

7. des fauteuils inclinables

8. et assez de haut-parleurs

9. pour assurer à un concert des Who

10. le jardin de derrière

11. houspillait

12. Arrête

13. les mains sur les hanches

14. transition

1. qui atteignent un point critique
2. d'un ton de défi
3. m'a traité de nul
4. son parti
5. avocat manqué
6. qui trouve des failles
7. s'acharnant sur les moindres détails
8. ton entraînement
9. pencha la tête de côté
10. s'affaissant
11. t'es engagée auprès de ton équipe
12. un milliard de fois
13. dit d'un ton geignard
14. se détourna
15. vautré
16. survêtement
17. déchu
18. se vantant
19. sans intérêt
20. qu'il avait emballées
21. conquêtes féminines
22. avait les yeux écarquillés d'un fou
23. visiblement shooté à un truc fourni par un médecin très complaisant

and childhood, the body and hormones just starting to come to a boil[1]. Megan remembered it well. "What did you see?" Kaylie asked in a challenge[2].

"I saw you picking on your brother."

"You're inside. You couldn't hear anything. For all you know, I said, 'I love you so much, Jordan.' "

"She did not!" Jordan shouted.

"I know she didn't," Megan said.

"She called me a loser[3] and said I had no friends!"

Megan sighed. "Kaylie …"

"I did not!"

Megan just frowned at her.

"It's his word against mine," Kaylie protested. "Why do you always take his side[4]?"

Every kid, Megan thought, is a frustrated lawyer[5], finding loopholes[6], demanding impossible levels of proof, attacking even the most minute of minutia[7].

"You have practice[8] tonight," Megan told Kaylie.

Kaylie's head dropped to her shoulder[9], her entire body slumping[10]. "Do I have to go?"

"You made a commitment to this team[11], young lady."

Even as Megan said it—even as she had said similar words a zillion times[12] before—she still couldn't believe the words were coming from her own mouth.

"But I don't want to go," Kaylie whined[13]. "I'm so tired. And I'm supposed to go out with Ginger later, remember, to …"

Kaylie may have said more, but Megan turned away[14], not really interested. In the TV room, her husband, Dave, was sprawled out[15] in gray sweats[16]. Dave was watching the latest fallen[17] movie actor bragging[18] in some tasteless[19] interview about the many women he'd bagged[20] and the years of scoring[21] at strip clubs. The actor was manic and wide-eyed[22] and clearly on something that required a physician with a loose prescription pad[23].

From his spot on the couch, Dave shook his head in disgust. "What is this world coming to?[1]" Dave said, gesturing at the screen. "Can you believe this jerk[2]? What a tool[3]."

Megan nodded[4], suppressing a smile. Years ago she had known that tool quite well. Biblically even[5]. The Tool was actually[6] a pretty nice guy who tipped well[7], enjoyed threesomes[8], and cried like a baby when he drank too much.

A long time ago.

Dave turned and smiled at her with everything he had[9]. "Hey, babe."

"Hey."

Dave still did that, smiled at her as though seeing her anew[10], for the first time, and she knew again that she was lucky, that she should be grateful[11]. This was Megan's life now. That old life—the one nobody in this happy suburban wonderland[12] of cul-de-sacs and good schools and brick McMansions knew about—had been killed off and buried in a shallow ditch[13].

"You want me to drive Kaylie to soccer[14]?" Dave asked.

"I can do it."

"You're sure?"

Megan nodded. Not even Dave knew the truth about the woman who had shared his bed for the past sixteen years. Dave didn't even know that Megan's real name was, strangely enough[15], Maygin. Same pronunciation but computers and IDs[16] only know spelling[17]. She would have asked her mother why the weird[18] spelling, but her mother had died before Megan could talk. She had never known her father or even who he was. She'd been orphaned young[19], grew up hard[20], ended up stripping in Vegas and then Atlantic City, took it a step further[21], loved it. Yes, loved it. It was fun and exciting and electrifying. There was always something going on, always a sense of danger and possibility and passion.

---

1. Où va-t-on ?
2. cet abruti
3. Quel naze
4. acquiesça d'un signe de tête
5. Connu bibliquement, même
6. en fait
7. donnait de bons pourboires
8. aimait les partouzes à trois
9. lui fit un grand sourire
10. comme s'il la découvrait
11. reconnaissante
12. dans ce petit paradis résidentiel
13. était bel et bien morte et enterrée
14. au foot

15. bizarrement
16. les papiers d'identité
17. l'orthographe
18. bizarre
19. perdu ses parents très jeune
20. avait grandi à la dure
21. avait poussé les choses un peu plus loin

31

"Mom?"

It was Jordan. "Yes, honey[1]."

"Mrs. Freedman says you didn't sign the permission slip for the class trip[2]."

"I'll send her an e-mail."

"She said it was due on[3] Friday."

"Don't worry about it, honey, okay?"

It took Jordan another moment or two but eventually he was placated[4].

Megan knew that she should be grateful. Girls die young in her old life. Every emotion, every second in that world, is almost too intense—life raised to the tenth power[5]—and that doesn't jibe with[6] longevity. You get burned out.[7] You get strung out.[8] There is a heady quality to that kind of action[9]. There is also an inherent danger. When it finally spun out of control[10], when Megan's very life was suddenly in jeopardy[11], she had not only found a way to escape but to start over completely anew[12], reborn if you will, with a loving husband, beautiful children, a home with four bedrooms, and a pool in the yard[13].

Somehow, almost by accident really, Megan Pierce had stumbled from the depths of what some might call a seedy cesspool into[14] the ultimate American dream. She had, in order to save herself, played it straight[15] and almost talked herself into believing that this was the best possible world. And why not? For her entire life, in movies and on television, Megan, like the rest of us, had been inundated with images claiming that[16] her old life was wrong, immoral, wouldn't last—while this family life, the house and picket fence[17], was enviable, appropriate, celestial[18].

But here was the truth: Megan missed her old life[19]. She was not supposed to[20]. She was supposed to be grateful and thrilled that she of all people, with the destructive route she'd taken, had ended up with what every little girl dreams of. But the truth was, a truth it had taken her years to admit to herself, she still longed for[1] those dark rooms; the lustful, hungry stares from strangers[2]; the pounding, pulsating music[3]; the crazy lights; the adrenaline spikes[4].

And now?

Dave flipping stations[5]: "So you don't mind driving? Because the Jets are on."

Kaylie looking through her gym bag: "Mom, where's my uniform? Did you wash it like I asked?"

Jordan opening the Sub-Zero: "Can you make me a grilled cheese in the panini maker? And not with that whole grain bread[6]."

She loved them. She did. But there were times, like today, when she realized that after a youth of skating along slippery surfaces[7] she had now settled into a domestic rut of dazzling sameness[8], each day forced to perform the same show with the same players as the day before, just each player one day older. Megan wondered why it had to be this way, why we are forced to choose one life. Why do we insist that there can only be one "us," one life that makes us up in our entirety? Why can't we have more than one identity? And why do we have to destroy one life in order to create another? We claim to long for the "well rounded"[9], the Renaissance man or woman inside all of us, yet our only variety is cosmetic. In reality we do all we can to smother that spirit out[10], to make us conform, to define us as one thing and one thing only.

Dave flipped back to the fallen movie star. "This guy," Dave said with a shake of head[11]. But just hearing that famous manic voice brought Megan back—his hand twined in her thong[12], his face pressed against her back, scruffy[13] and wet from tears.

"You're the only one who understands me, Cassie. ...."

Yes, she missed it. Was that really so horrible?

She didn't think so, but it kept haunting her[14]. Had she made a mistake? These memories, the life of Cassie because no one uses a real name in that world, had been kept locked up[15] in a small back room in her

1. *rêvait encore de*

2. *des regards concupiscents de ces inconnus*

3. *du martèlement de cette musique rythmée*

4. *poussées d'adrénaline*

5. *en train de zapper*

6. *pain complet*

7. *après une jeunesse sur le fil du rasoir*

8. *était désormais enlisée dans une routine familiale d'une incroyable monotonie*

9. *rêver d'une identité harmonieuse*

10. *pour étouffer cette liberté d'esprit*

11. *en secouant la tête*

12. *glissée dans son string*

13. *défait*

14. *ça continuait de la hanter*

15. *mis sous clef*

head all these years. And then, a few days ago, she had unbolted the door[1] and let it open just a crack[2]. She had quickly slammed it closed[3] and locked it back up[4]. But just that crack, just letting Cassie have a quick gaze[5] into the world between Maygin and Megan—why was she so sure that there would be repercussions?

Dave rolled off the[6] couch and headed for the bathroom, the newspaper tucked under his armpit[7]. Megan warmed up the panini maker and searched for the white bread. As she opened the drawer, the phone rang, giving off an electronic chirp[8]. Kaylie stood next to the phone, ignoring it, texting.

"You want to answer that?" Megan asked.

"It's not for me."

Kaylie could pull out[9] and answer her own mobile phone with a speed that would have intimidated Wyatt Earp[10], but the home phone, with a number unknown to the Kasselton teenage community, held absolutely no interest to her.

"Pick it up[11], please."

"What's the point?[12] I'd just have to hand it to you[13]."

Jordan, who at the tender age of eleven always wanted to keep the peace[14], grabbed it[15]. "Hello?"

He listened for a moment and then said, "You have the wrong number[16]." And then Jordan added something that chilled[17] Megan: "There's no one here named Cassie."

Making up some excuse[18] about the delivery people[19] always getting her name wrong—and knowing that her children were so wonderfully self-involved[20] that they wouldn't question it[21] anyway—Megan took the phone from her son and vanished into the other room.

She put the receiver to[22] her ear, and a voice she hadn't heard in seventeen years said, "I'm sorry to call you like this, but I think we need to meet."

MEGAN dropped off[1] Kaylie at soccer practice.

She was, considering the bombshell call[2], fairly calm and serene. She put the car in park and turned to her daughter, dewy-eyed[3].

Kaylie said, "What?"

"Nothing. What time does practice end?"

"I don't know. I might go out with Gabi and Chuckie afterward."

Might meaning *will*. "Where?"

Shrug[4]. "Town."

The nice vague teenage answer. "Where in town?"

"I don't know, Mom," she said, allowing a little annoyance in[5]. Kaylie wanted to move this along[6], but she didn't want to piss off[7] her mother and not be allowed to go[8]. "We're just going to hang out[9], okay?"

"Did you do all your homework[10]?"

Megan hated herself the moment she asked the question. Such a Mom moment. She put her hand up and said to her daughter, "Forget that. Just go. Have fun."

Kaylie looked at her mother as though a small arm had suddenly sprouted out of her forehead[11]. Then she shrugged, got out of the car, and ran off[12]. Megan watched. Always. It didn't matter that she was old enough to enter a field by herself[13]. Megan had to watch until she was sure that her daughter was safe.

Ten minutes later, Megan found a parking spot behind the Starbucks. She checked her watch[14]. Fifteen minutes until the meet[15].

She grabbed a latte[16] and found a table in the back. At the table to her left, a potpourri of new moms[17]—sleep deprived[18], stained clothes[19], deliriously happy, all with baby in tow[20]—were yapping away[21]. They talked about the best new strollers[22] and which Pack 'n Play folded up easiest[23] and how long to breast-feed[24]. They debated cedar playgrounds with tire mulch[25] and what age to stop with the pacifier[26] and the safest car seats and the back baby sling[27] versus the front

1. déposa
2. malgré le choc de l'appel téléphonique
3. les yeux humides
4. Haussement d'épaules
5. sur un ton teinté d'agacement
6. passer à autre chose
7. faire chier
8. perdre le droit d'y aller
9. traîner un peu
10. tes devoirs
11. jailli de son front
12. partit en courant
13. assez grande pour accéder au terrain toute seule
14. regarda sa montre
15. rendez-vous
16. se prit un café au lait
17. de jeunes mères
18. en manque de sommeil
19. les vêtements tachés
20. chacune avec son bébé
21. papotaient à qui mieux mieux
22. poussettes
23. se pliait le plus facilement
24. allaiter
25. au sol en caoutchouc
26. tétine
27. porte-bébé

1. on avait pu te faire une
2. maternelle
3. vitale
4. pour déjà le mettre sur les rails
5. covoiturages d'enfants
6. Le bonheur vire au tracas perpétuel
7. naguère compréhensif
8. ce couple qui allait faire l'amour n'importe où
9. n'a plus un regard pour la nudité de l'autre
10. une distance s'installe
11. les nounous
12. votre univers borné à votre progéniture
13. si uni
14. ça rend fou
15. ça étouffe
16. ça abrutit
17. ce côté sexy et rauque dû au
18. tout semblait dit en plaisantant à moitié
19. pas mal de sous-entendus
20. lui adressa un sourire en coin
21. mal teints en blond
22. une femme bien en chair et bien carrossée,

baby sling versus the side baby sling. One bragged about how her son, Toddy, was "so sensitive to the needs of other children, even though he's only eighteen months old."

Megan smiled, wishing that she could be them again. She had loved the new-mommy stage, but like so many other stages of life, you look back at it now and wonder when they fixed your[1] lobotomy. She knew what will come next with these mothers—picking the right preschool[2] as though it were a life 'n' death[3] decision, waiting in the pickup line[4], positioning their kids for the elite playdates, Little Gym classes, karate lessons, lacrosse practice, French immersion courses, constant carpools[5]. The happy turns to harried[6], and the harried becomes routine. The once-understanding[7] husband slowly gets grumpier because you still don't want as much sex as before the baby. You as a couple, the you who used to sneak off to do the dirty in every available spot,[8] barely glance at each other when naked anymore[9]. You think it doesn't matter—that it's natural and inevitable—but you drift[10]. You love each other, in some ways more than ever, but you drift and you either don't fight it or don't really see it. You become caretakers[11] of the children, your world shrinking down to the size and boundaries of your offspring[12], and it all becomes so polite and close-knit[13] and warm—and maddening[14] and smothering[15] and numbing[16].

"Well, well, well."

The familiar voice made Megan automatically smile. The voice still had the sexy rasp of[17] whiskey, cigarettes, and late nights, where every utterance had a hint of a laugh[18] and a dollop of a double entendre[19].

"Hi, Lorraine."

Lorraine gave her a crooked smile[20]. Her hair was a bad blond dye job[21] and too big. Lorraine was big and fleshy and curvy[22] and made sure that you saw it. Her clothes looked two sizes too small, and yet that worked for her. After all these years, Lorraine still made an impression. Even the mommies stopped to stare with just the proper amount of distaste[1]. Lorraine shot them a look that told them she knew what they thought and where they could stick that thought[2]. The mommies turned away.

"You look good, kid," Lorraine said.

She sat, making a production of it. It had been, yes, seventeen years. Lorraine had been a hostess/manager/cocktail waitress/bartender[3]. Lorraine had lived the life, and she lived it hard and without any apologies.

"I've missed you," Megan said.

"Yeah, I could tell from all the postcards."

"I'm sorry about that."

Lorraine waved her off[4], as if annoyed by the sentiment. She fumbled into her purse[5] and pulled out a cigarette. The nearby mommies gasped[6] as though she'd pulled out a firearm[7]. "Man, I should light this thing[8] just to watch them flee."

Megan leaned forward[9]. "If you don't mind my asking, how did you find me?"

The crooked smile returned. "Come on, honey. I've always known. I got eyes everywhere, you know that."

Megan wanted to ask more, but something in Lorraine's tone told her to let it be[10].

"Look at you," Lorraine said. "Married, kids, big house. Lots of white Cadillac Escalades in the lot[11]. One of them yours?"

"No. I'm the black GMC Acadia."

Lorraine nodded as though that answer meant something. "I'm happy you found something here, though, to be honest? I always thought you'd be a lifer[12], you know? Like me."

Lorraine let out a small chuckle[13] and shook her head.

"I know," Megan said. "I kinda surprised myself."

1. pour la fixer avec juste ce qu'il fallait de dégoût

2. qu'elles pouvaient aller se faire voir

3. serveuse de cocktails en salle et au bar

4. lui fit signe de ne pas s'en faire

5. fouilla dans son sac à main

6. sursautèrent

7. sorti un flingue

8. allumer cette clope

9. se pencha en avant

10. de ne pas insister

11. sur le parking

12. que t'étais coincée à vie

13. ricana doucement

"Of course, not all the girls who end up back on the straight and narrow[1] choose it." Lorraine looked off[2] as though the comment was a throwaway[3]. Both women knew that it was not. "We had some laughs[4], didn't we?"

"We did."

"I still do," she said. "This"—she eye-gestured toward[5] the mommies—"I mean, I admire it. I really do. But I don't know. It's not me." She shrugged. "Maybe I'm too selfish[6]. It's like I got ADD[7] or something. I need something to stimulate me."

"Kids can stimulate, believe me."

"Yeah?" she said, clearly not buying it[8]. "Well, I'm glad to hear that."

Megan wasn't sure how to continue. "So you still work at La Crème?"

"Yep. Bartending mostly."

"So why the sudden call?"

Lorraine fiddled with[9] the unlit[10] cigarette. The moms went back to their inane chatter[11], though with less enthusiasm. They constantly sneaked glances at[12] Lorraine, as though she were some virus introduced into their suburban life-form with a mission to destroy it.

"Like I said, I've always known where you were. But I would never say anything. You know that, right?"

"I do."

"And I didn't want to bug you now either[13]. You escaped, last thing I wanted to do was drag you back in[14]."

"But?"

Lorraine met her eye. "Someone spotted you[15]. Or I should say, Cassie."

Megan shifted in the chair[16].

"You've been coming to La Crème, haven't you?"

Megan said nothing.

"Hey, I get it[17]. Believe me. If I hung out with these sunshines all day[18]"—Lorraine pointed with her thumb at the maternal gaggle[1]—"I'd sacrifice farm animals for a night out now and again[2]."

Megan looked down at her coffee as though it might hold an answer. She had indeed returned to La Crème, but only once. Two weeks ago, near the anniversary of her escape, she had gone to Atlantic City for a mundane training seminar and trade show[3]. With the kids getting older, Megan had decided to try to find a job in residential real estate[4]. The past few years had been all about finding the next thing—there had been the private trainer and yoga classes and ceramics and finally a memoir-writing group, which in Megan's case had of course been fiction. Each of the activities was a desperate attempt[5] to find the elusive "fulfillment" that those who have everything crave[6]. In reality, they were looking up when perhaps they should have been looking down, searching for enlightened spirituality[7] when all along Megan knew[8] that the answer probably lay with the[9] more base and primitive[10].

If she were asked, Megan would claim that she didn't plan it. It was spur of the moment[11], no big deal[12], but on her second night down staying at the Tropicana, a scant two blocks from[13] La Crème, she donned her clingiest outfit[14] and visited the club.

"You saw me?" Megan asked.

"No. And I guess you didn't seek me out[15]."

There was hurt[16] in Lorraine's voice. Megan had seen her old friend behind the bar and kept her distance[17]. The club was big and dark. People liked to get lost in places like that. It was easy not to be seen.

"I didn't mean …" Megan stopped. "So who then?"

"I don't know. But it's true?"

"It was only one time," Megan said.

Lorraine said nothing.

"I don't understand. What's the problem?"

"Why did you come back?"

"Does it matter?[18]"

1. désigna du pouce le troupeau de mères

2. pour une soirée de liberté de temps en temps

3. pour un stage de formation et un salon professionnel assez quelconques

4. l'immobilier

5. tentative désespérée

6. « l'épanouissement » que n'atteignent jamais ceux qui ont tout

7. à la recherche de réponses métaphysiques

8. Megan avait toujours su

9. la solution était sans doute

10. primaire

11. Ça avait été sur un coup de tête

12. juste comme ça

13. à deux rues à peine de

14. avait mis sa tenue la plus moulante

15. que tu n'as pas cherché à me voir

16. On sentait un reproche

17. gardé ses distances

18. C'est important ?

1. un flic
2. est au courant
3. Il n'a jamais laissé tomber.

4. tu es venue me prévenir

5. ce que je veux avec qui je veux
6. Je ne me mêle pas des affaires des autres
7. éclairage
8. j'ai pu me tromper
9. si ça se trouve
10. entre toi qui es revenue

11. leva les yeux
12. avala sa salive

"Not to me," Lorraine said. "But a cop[1] found out[2]. Same one who's been looking for you all these years. He's never given up.[3]"

"And now you think he'll find me?"

"Yeah," Lorraine said. "I think there's a pretty good chance he'll find you."

"So this visit is a warning[4]?"

"Something like that."

"What else is it?"

"I don't know what happened that night," Lorraine said. "And I don't want to know. I'm happy. I like my life. I do what I please with whom I please[5]. I don't get into other people's stuff[6], you know what I'm saying?"

"Yes."

"And I may be wrong. I mean, you know how the club is. Bad lighting[7]. And it's been, what, seventeen years? So I could have been mistaken[8]. It was only for a second, but for all I know[9] it was the same night you were there. But what with you back[10] and now someone else gone missing ..."

"What are you talking about, Lorraine? What did you see?"

Lorraine looked up[11] and swallowed[12]. "Stewart," she said, fiddling with the unlit cigarette. "I think I saw Stewart Green."

3

1. s'approcha de la maison maudite

2. sonna à la porte

3. sans un regard

4. s'essuya les pieds

5. penaud

6. quitta son vieil imperméable

7. le replia sur son bras

8. L'éclairage encastré un peu démodé

9. en cuir

10. sur la cheminée

11. changées

12. laissé les chaussons de son mari près de

13. de passer à autre chose

14. les plafonds

15. étaient encore en deuil

16. peut-être est-ce l'impression qu'il avait

17. Ils ont besoin de pouvoir tourner la page.

WITH a heavy sigh, Detective Broome approached the doomed house[1] and rang the bell[2]. Sarah opened the door and with nary a glance[3] said, "Come on in." Broome wiped his feet[4], feeling sheepish[5]. He took off the old trench coat[6] and draped it over his arm[7]. Nothing inside the house had changed in all these years. The dated recessed lighting[8], the white leather[9] couch, the old recliner in the corner—all the same. Even the photographs on the fireplace mantel[10] hadn't been switched out[11]. For a long time, at least five years, Sarah had left her husband's slippers by[12] that old recliner. They were gone now, but the chair remained. Broome wondered if anybody ever sat in it.

It was as though the house refused to move on[13], as though the walls and ceilings[14] were grieving[15] and waiting. Or maybe that was projecting[16]. People need answers. They need closure.[17] Hope, Broome knew, could be a wonderful thing. But hope could crush you

41

anew[1] every single day. Hope could be the crudest thing[2] in the world.

"You missed the anniversary," Sarah said.

Broome nodded, not ready to tell her why yet. "How are the kids?"

"Good."

Sarah's children were practically grown now. Susie was a junior at[3] Bucknell. Brandon was a high school senior[4]. They had been little more than babies when their father vanished, ripped from this tidy household[5], never to be seen by any of his loved ones again. Broome had never solved the case[6]. He had never let it go either. You shouldn't get personally involved.[7] He knew that. But he had. He had gone to Susie's dance recitals[8]. He had helped teach Brandon how to throw a baseball[9]. He had even, twelve years ago and to his great shame[10], had too much to drink with Sarah and, well, stayed the whole night.

"How's the new job?" Broome asked her.

"Good."

"Is your sister coming in soon?"

Sarah sighed. "Yep."

Sarah was still an attractive woman. There were crow's-feet by the eyes[11], and the lines[12] around her mouth had deepened over the years[13]. Aging works well on some women.[14] Sarah was one of them.

She was also a cancer survivor, twenty-plus years now. She had told Broome this the first time they met, sitting in this very room[15], when he had come here to investigate the disappearance[16]. The diagnosis had been made, Sarah explained to him, when she was pregnant with[17] Susie. If it wasn't for her husband, Sarah insisted, she would have never survived. She wanted Broome to understand that. When the prognosis[18] was bad, when the chemo[19] made Sarah vomit continuously, when she lost her hair and her looks, when her body started to decay[20], when no one else, including Sarah, had any hope—that word again—he and he alone[1] had stuck by her[2].

Which proved yet again that there was no explaining the complexities and hypocrisies of human nature.

He stayed up with her. He held her forehead[3] late at night. He fetched her medicines[4] and kissed her cheek and held[5] her shivering[6] body and made her feel loved.

She had looked Broome in the eye and told him all this because she wanted him to stay with the case[7], to not dismiss her husband as a runaway[8], to get personally involved, to find her soul mate[9] because she simply could not live without him.

Seventeen years later, despite learning some hard truths, Broome was still here. And the whereabouts of[10] Sarah's husband and soul mate was still very much a mystery[11].

Broome looked up at her now. "That's good," he said, hearing the babble in his own voice[12]. "I mean, about your sister's visiting. I know you like when your sister visits."

"Yeah, it's awesome[13]," Sarah said, a voice flat enough to slip under a door crack[14]. "Broome?"

"Yes?"

"You're giving me small talk."[15]

Broome looked down at his hands. "I was just trying to be nice."

"No. See, you don't do just being nice, Broome. And you never do small talk."

"Good point[16]."

"So?"

Despite all the trappings[17]—bright yellow paint, fresh-cut flowers—all Broome could see was the decay[18]. The years of not knowing had devastated the family. The kids had some hard years. Susie had two DUIs[19]. Brandon had a drug bust[20]. Broome had helped both of them get out of trouble[21]. The house

1. lui seul
2. l'avait soutenue
3. lui mettait la main sur le front
4. allait lui chercher ses médicaments
5. serrait contre lui
6. tremblant
7. qu'il poursuive l'enquête
8. qu'il ne croie pas que son mari avait voulu filer
9. âme sœur
10. où se trouvait
11. restait un mystère entier
12. conscient qu'il trahissait son manque de conviction
13. merveilleux
14. sur un ton monocorde désespérant
15. Trêve de banalités.
16. Bien vu
17. Malgré les efforts apparents
18. à quel point la maison se détériorait
19. s'était fait choper deux fois pour conduite en état d'ivresse
20. Et Brandon, pour une histoire de drogue
21. les avait tous deux tirés d'affaire

still looked as though their father had disappeared yesterday—frozen in time[1], waiting for his return.

Sarah's eyes widened a little as if struck by a painful realization. "Did you find … ?"

"No."

"What then?"

"It may be nothing," Broome said.

"But?"

Broome sat resting his forearms on his thighs[2], his head in his hands. He took a deep breath[3] and looked into the pained[4] eyes. "Another local man vanished. You may have seen it on the news[5]. His name is Carlton Flynn."

Sarah looked confused[6]. "When you say vanished—"

"Just like …" He stopped. "One moment Carlton Flynn was living his life, the next—poof[7]—he was gone. Totally vanished."

Sarah tried to process what he was saying[8]. "But… like you told me from the start[9]. People do vanish, right?"

Broome nodded.

"Sometimes of their own volition[10]," Sarah continued. "Sometimes not. But it happens."

"Yes."

"So seventeen years after my husband vanishes, another man, this Carlton Flynn, goes missing. I don't see the connection[11]."

"There might be none[12]," Broome agreed.

She moved closer to him[13]. "But?"

"But it's why I missed the anniversary."

"What does that mean?"

Broome didn't know how much to say. He didn't know how much he even knew for sure yet. He was working on a theory, one that gnawed at his belly[14] and kept him up at night[15], but right now that was all it was[16].

"The day Carlton Flynn vanished," he said.

"What about it?"

1. figée dans le temps

2. les avant-bras appuyés sur les cuisses

3. respira profondément

4. tristes

5. aux infos

6. perplexe

7. hop !

8. essaya de comprendre ce qu'il était en train de lui dire

9. dès le début

10. de leur propre gré

11. le rapport

12. Peut-être qu'il n'y en a pas

13. se rapprocha de lui

14. qui le rongeait

15. l'empêchait de dormir

16. ce n'était qu'une théorie

44

"It's why I wasn't here. He vanished on the anniversary. February eighteenth—exactly seventeen years to the day[1] after your husband vanished."

Sarah seemed stunned[2] for a moment. "Seventeen years to the day."

"Yes."

"What does that mean? Seventeen years. It might just be a coincidence. If it was five or ten or twenty years. But seventeen?"

He said nothing, letting her work on it herself[3] for a few moments.

Sarah said, "So I assume[4], what, you checked[5] for more missing people[6]? To see if there was a pattern[7]?"

"I did."

"And?"

"Those were the only two we know for certain who disappeared on a February eighteenth[8]—your husband and Carlton Flynn."

"We know for certain?" she repeated.

Broome let loose a deep breath[9]. "Last year, on March fourteenth, another local man, Stephen Clarkson, was reported missing. Three years earlier, on February twenty-seventh, another was also reported missing."

"Neither was found?[10]"

"Right."

Sarah swallowed. "So maybe it's not the day. Maybe it's February and March."

"I don't think so. Or at least, I didn't. See, the other two men—Peter Berman and Gregg Wagman—could have disappeared a lot earlier[11]. One was a drifter[12], the other a truck driver[13]. Both men were single[14] with not much family. If guys like that aren't home in twenty-four hours, well, who'd notice?[15] You did, of course. But if a guy is single or divorced or travels a lot[16]…"

"It could be days or weeks before it's reported[17]," Sarah finished for him.

1. jour pour jour
2. abasourdie
3. lui laissant le temps d'absorber la nouvelle
4. je suppose
5. que vous avez vérifié
6. s'il y avait eu d'autres disparitions
7. s'il y avait un schéma récurrent
8. dont nous sommes sûrs qu'ils ont disparu un 18 février
9. lâcha un grand soupir
10. On n'a retrouvé ni l'un ni l'autre ?
11. bien avant
12. un vagabond
13. un camionneur
14. célibataires
15. qui va s'en apercevoir ?
16. voyage beaucoup
17. avant que ce soit signalé

"Or even longer[1]."

"So these two men might have vanished on February eighteenth too."

"It's not that simple[2]," Broome said.

"Why not?"

"Because the more I look at it[3], the pattern gets even tougher to nail down[4]. Wagman, for example, was from Buffalo—he's not local[5]. No one knows where or when he vanished, but I was able to trace[6] his movements enough to know that he could have gone through Atlantic City sometime in February."

Sarah considered that. "You've mentioned five men, including Stewart, in the past seventeen years. Any others?"

"Yes and no. Altogether,[7] I've found nine men who sort of very loosely could fit the pattern[8]. But there are cases where the theory takes a bit of a hit[9]."

"For example?"

"Two years ago, a man named Clyde Horner, who lived with his mother, was reported missing on February seventh."

"So it's not February eighteenth."

"Probably not."

"Maybe it's the month of February."

"Maybe. This is the problem with theories and patterns. They take time. I'm still gathering evidence[10]."

Her eyes filled with tears[11]. She blinked them away[12]. "I don't get it[13]. How did no one see this—with this many people missing?"

"See what?" Broome said. "Hell, I don't even see it that clearly yet. Men go missing all the time. Most run away[14]. Most of these guys go broke[15] or have nothing or got creditors on their ass[16]—so they start new lives. They move across the country[17]. Sometimes they change their names. Sometimes they don't. Many of these men … well, no one is looking for them. No one wants to find them. One wife I spoke to[18] begged me not to find[19] her husband. She had three kids with the guy. She thinks he ran off with some—as she put it[1]—'hootchy whore[2]',and it was the best thing that ever happened to her family."

They were silent for a few moments.

"What about before?" Sarah asked.

Broome knew what she meant, but he still said, "Before?"

"Before Stewart. Did anybody disappear before my husband?"

He ran his hand through his hair[3] and raised his head[4]. Their eyes locked.[5] "Not that I could find," Broome said. "If this is a pattern, then it started with Stewart."

1. selon ses propres termes
2. petite pute

3. se passa la main dans les cheveux
4. releva la tête
5. Ils se regardèrent droit dans les yeux.

4

THE knocks[1] woke Ray.

He pried open[2] one eye and immediately regretted it. The light worked like daggers[3]. He grabbed hold of his head on either side[4] because he feared that his skull would actually split in two[5] from whatever was hammering on it from the inside[6].

"Open up, Ray."

It was Fester.

"Ray?"

More knocks. Each one landed inside Ray's temple like a two-by-four[7]. He swung[8] his legs out of bed and, head reeling[9], managed to work his way to a sitting position[10]. Next to his right foot was an empty bottle of Jack[11]. Ugh. He had passed out[12]—no, alas, he had once again "blacked out"[13]—on the couch without bothering[14] to pull out the bed beneath it. No blanket[15]. No pillow[16]. His neck was probably aching too[17], but it was hard to find it through the pulsating pain[18].

48

"Ray?"

"Sec[1]," he said, because, really, he couldn't get more sounds to come out[2].

This felt like a hangover[3] raised to the tenth power[4]. For a second, maybe two, Ray didn't remember what had happened the night before, what had caused this massive influx of discomfort[5]. Instead he thought about the last time he had felt like this, back before it all ended for him. He had been a photojournalist back then, working for the AP[6], traveling with the twenty-fourth infantry in Iraq during the first Persian Gulf War when the land mine exploded[7]. Blackness—then pain[8]. For a while it looked as though he would lose his leg[9].

"Ray?"

The pills[10] were next to the bed. Pills and booze[11]—the perfect late-night cocktail. He wondered how many he'd already taken and when, and then decided the hell with it[12]. He downed[13] two more, forced himself to stand, and stumbled toward[14] the door.

When he opened it, Fester said, "Wow."

"What?"

"You look like several large orangutans made you their love slave[15]."

Ah Fester. "What time is it?"

"Three."

"What, in the afternoon?"

"Yes, Ray, in the afternoon. See the light outside?" Fester gestured behind him[16]. He took on the voice of a kindergarten teacher[17]. "At three in the afternoon, it is light out[18]. At three A.M., it is dark. I could draw you a chart[19] if that would help."

Like he needed the sarcasm. Weird. He never slept past eight, and now it was three? The blackout must have been a bad one. Ray slid to the side to let Fester in[20]. "Is there a reason for your visit?"

Fester, who was huge[21], ducked inside the room[22]. He took it in[23], nodded, and said, "Wow, what a dump[24]."

---

1. Une seconde
2. était incapable d'en dire plus
3. une cuite
4. carabinée
5. cet inconfort indescriptible
6. Associated Press
7. la mine terrestre avait explosé
8. Tout noir — puis très mal
9. on avait cru qu'il allait y laisser sa jambe
10. cachets
11. de l'alcool
12. puis décida de s'en foutre
13. en avala
14. tituba jusqu'à
15. t'étaient passé dessus
16. lui fit signe de regarder derrière lui
17. professeur d'école maternelle
18. il fait jour
19. Je peux te faire un dessin
20. s'écarta pour laisser entrer Fester
21. énorme
22. baissa la tête pour entrer
23. regarda autour de lui
24. c'est minable

"Yeah," Ray said. "On what you pay me you'd figure[1] I'd have a mansion in a gated community[2]."

"Ha!" Fester pointed at him. "Got me there!"

"Something you wanted?"

"Here."

Fester reached into[3] his bag and handed Ray a camera[4].

"For you to use until you can buy a new one."

"I'm touched," Ray said.

"Well, you do good work. You're also the only employee I have who isn't on drugs[5], just booze[6]. That makes you my best employee."

"We're sharing a tender moment, aren't we[7], Fester?"

"That," Fester said with a nod. "And I couldn't find anyone else who could work the George Queller job tonight. Whoa, what have we got here?" Fester pointed to[8] the pills. "So much for the not on drugs.[9]"

"They're pain pills[10]. I was mugged last night, remember?"

"Right. But still[11]."

"Does this mean I lost employee of the month[12]?"

"Not unless I find needles[13] in here too."

"I'm not up for working[14] tonight, Fester."

"What, you going to stay in bed all day?"

"That's the plan, yes."

"Change plans. I need you. And I'm paying time and a half[15]." He looked around, frowned. "Not that you need the cash or anything."

Fester left. Ray put the water on to boil[16]. Instant coffee. Loud Urdu-language voices were coming from upstairs. Sounded like the kids were coming home from school. Ray made his way to the shower[17] and stayed under the spray until the hot water was gone.

Milo's Deli on the corner made a mean BLT[18]. Ray wolfed it down[19] as though he feared it might try to escape[20]. He tried to keep his mind on the task at hand[21] without looking forward[22]—asking Milo how his back was holding up[23], reaching into his pocket for the money, smiling at another customer, buying the local newspaper. He tried to be Zen and stay in the moment[1] and not look ahead because he didn't want to think about the blood.

He checked the newspaper. The LOCAL MAN MISSING article featured[2] the same photograph he had seen on the news last night. Carlton Flynn made a kissy face. Classic asswipe. He had dark hair spiked high; tattoos on gym-muscled, baby-smooth skin[3]; and looked as though he belonged on one of those obnoxious Jersey reality shows[4] that featured self-obsessed[5], arrested-development[6] numb nuts[7] referring to girls as "grenades."[8]

Carlton Flynn had a record[9]—three assaults[10]. He was twenty-six years old, divorced, and "worked for his father's prominent supplies company."

Ray folded the paper[11] and jammed it[12] under his arm. He didn't want to think about it. He didn't want to think about that photograph of Carlton Flynn on his computer or wonder why someone had attacked him to get it. He wanted to put it behind him[13], move on with life, day at a time[14], moment at a time.

Block, survive—just as he had for the past seventeen years.

How's that been working for you, Ray?

He closed his eyes and let himself slip into a memory[15] of Cassie. He was back at the club, balmy from the booze[16], watching her give some guy a lap dance[17]—totally, positively in love with every fiber of his being—and yet not the least bit jealous. Cassie gave him a look over the man's shoulder, a look that could melt teeth[18], and he'd just smiled back, waiting to get her alone, knowing that at the end of the day (or night) she was his.

The air had always crackled[19] around Cassie. There was fun and wildness and spontaneity, and there was warmth and kindness and intelligence. She made you want to rip off her clothes[20] and throw her on the

1. *vivre l'instant*

2. *montrait*

3. *des tatouages sur une peau de bébé et des bras musclés*

4. *avait l'air de sortir d'une de ces émissions insupportables de télé-réalité*

5. *égocentriques*

6. *tarés*

7. *connards*

8. *traitent les filles de « thons ».*

9. *un casier judiciaire*

10. *agressions*

11. *replia le journal*

12. *le fourra*

13. *tourner la page*

14. *jour après jour*

15. *se laissa envahir par un souvenir*

16. *un peu éméché*

17. *faire une danse érotique à un mec*

18. *à vous faire fondre*

19. *pétillé*

20. *de lui arracher ses vêtements*

nearest bed, all while writing her a love sonnet. Sudden flashes, smolder[1], slow burn, hearth[2] warmth—Cassie could do them all at the same time.

A woman like that, well, something had to give[3], right?

He thought about that photograph by those damn ruins in that park. Could that have been what the mugger was really looking for? It seemed unlikely[4]. He ran through the scenarios and possibilities and made a decision.

He had hidden long enough. He had gone from the big-time photojournalist to that horrible rehab center[5] to the times of joy here in Atlantic City to losing everything. He had moved to Los Angeles, worked as a real paparazzo, gotten himself into another mess[6], moved back here. Why? Why move back to the place where he'd lost everything unless … unless something drew him back[7]. Unless something demanded he come back and figure out the truth[8].

Cassie.

He blinked her away[9], got back into his car, and drove to the park. The same spot he'd been using nearly every day was still open. Ray probably couldn't verbalize[10] what brought him here. So many things about him had changed, but one hadn't—his need for the camera. Many things make a photographer, but in his case, it was more about need than want. He didn't really see or process things unless he could photograph them. He saw the world through that lens. For most people, something doesn't exist unless they see, hear, smell, taste it. For him it was almost the opposite—nothing was real until he captured it on his camera.

If you took the path on the right corner, you could reach the edge of a cliff[11] that overlooked the Atlantic City skyline[12]. At night, the ocean behind it shone like a glimmering[13] dark curtain. The view, if you were

1. ardeur
2. du foyer
3. devait lâcher

4. peu probable

5. centre de rééducation
6. s'était encore laissé entraîner dans une embrouille
7. qu'il n'ait quelque chose qui le pousse à revenir
8. découvre la vérité
9. la chassa de son esprit
10. n'aurait pas su dire

11. bord d'une falaise
12. surplombait la ville d'Atlantic City
13. scintillant

willing to risk the trek through the underbelly[1], was breathtaking[2].

Ray snapped pictures as he started up the remote path[3], staying behind the camera as though it offered protection. The old ruins of the iron-ore mill[4] were on the edge of the Pine Barrens, New Jersey's largest track of wooded area[5]. One time, many years ago, Ray had gone off the path and deep into the woods[6]. He found a long-abandoned cement hut[7] covered with graffiti, some of it appearing satanic. The Pine Barrens were still loaded with[8] ruins from ghost towns. Rumors swirled of the deeper malfeasance[9] within the bowels[10] of that forest. If you've ever watched any cinematic Mafia portrayal[11], you've seen the part where the hit men[12] bury[13] a body in the Pine Barrens. Ray thought about that too often. One day, he figured, someone will invent a device[14] that will let you know[15] what is buried in the dirt beneath you[16]—differentiating between bones[17] and sticks[18] and roots[19] and rocks—and who knew what you would find then?

Ray swallowed and pushed the thought away. When he reached the old iron-ore furnace, he took out[20] the photograph of Carlton Flynn and studied it. Flynn had been standing over to the left, moving toward that path, the same path Ray had been on seventeen years ago. Why? What had Carlton Flynn been doing here? Sure, he could have just been another hiker[21] or adventurer. But why had he been here, in this very spot, seventeen years after Ray had been here, and then disappeared? Where had he gone from here?

No idea.

Ray's limp[22] was hard to notice anymore. It was still there if you looked closely[23], but Ray had learned to cover it up[24]. When he started up the hill so that he was standing exactly where he'd been when he'd taken the photograph of Carlton Flynn, the always-present twinge from his old injury[25] flared up[26]. The

1. si l'on était prêt à s'aventurer dans les broussailles
2. époustouflante
3. tout en s'engageant sur le chemin isolé
4. l'usine de traitement de minerais de fer
5. le bois le plus vaste
6. s'était écarté du sentier et enfoncé dans les sous-bois
7. cabane
8. regorgeaient encore de
9. Toutes sortes de rumeurs couraient sur la présence d'esprits maléfiques
10. au cœur
11. un film sur la Mafia
12. tueurs
13. enterrent
14. une machine
15. dira
16. sous vos pieds
17. les os
18. les bâtons
19. les racines
20. sortit
21. randonneur
22. boitillement
23. de près
24. à le cacher
25. le tiraillement de sa vieille blessure
26. se réveilla

1. ignorer la douleur

2. attira son regard

3. essaya de bien voir au bout du chemin

4. tout contre le bloc de roche

5. se pencha

6. tendit la main

7. la retira

8. une traînée de sang séché

rest of his body still ached from last night's attack too, but for now Ray was able to move past it[1].

Something caught his eye[2].

He stopped and squinted back down the path[3]. The sun was bright. Maybe that was it—that and the strange angle on this little hill. You wouldn't see it if you were on the path, but something was reflecting back at him, something right at the edge of the woods, right up against the big boulder[4]. Ray frowned and stumbled toward it.

What the … ?

When he got closer, he bent down[5] to get a closer look. He reached his hand out[6] but pulled back[7] before he touched it. There was no question in his mind. He took out his camera and started snapping pictures.

There, on the ground almost behind the boulder, was a streak of dried blood[8].

5

MEGAN lay in bed reading a magazine. Dave lay next to her, watching television, the clicker[1] in hand. For men the TV remote control[2] was like a pacifier or security blanket[3]. They simply could not watch television without holding one close, always at the ready[4].

It was a little after ten P.M. Jordan was already asleep. Kaylie was another story.[5]

Dave said, "Do you want the honors[6] or should I?"

Megan sighed. "You did it the last two nights."

Dave smiled, eyes on the television. "The last three nights. But who's counting?"

She put down her magazine. Kaylie's bedtime was a firm ten P.M., but she never went on her own, waiting until one of her parents insisted. Megan rolled out of bed and padded down the corridor[7]. She would yell out[8], "Go to sleep NOW!" but that was equally exhausting[9] and could potentially wake up[10] Jordan.

Megan stuck her[11] head in the room. "Bedtime."

1. télécommande
2. télécommande
3. un doudou
4. toujours une sous la main
5. Pour Kaylie, c'était une autre histoire.
6. À toi l'honneur
7. longea le couloir à pas feutrés
8. était tentée de crier
9. tout aussi épuisant
10. risquait de réveiller
11. passa la

1. ne leva même pas les yeux de l'écran

2. le quart

3. la lumière serait toujours allumée

4. privée de sortie

5. C'était toujours la même histoire.

6. à son aveu qu'elle n'était pas faite pour avoir des enfants

7. on le range dans un placard

8. on ne peut plus faire abstraction de la réalité

9. Il avait enlevé sa chemise

10. poitrine

11. léger ronflement

12. encore en forme

13. avec les années, il s'était un peu arrondi

14. Il commençait à se dégarnir.

15. bajoues

16. Il se tenait moins bien qu'avant.

17. avocat

Kaylie didn't even glance away from the monitor[1]. "Just fifteen more minutes, okay?"

"No. Bedtime is ten P.M. It is almost quarter after[2]."

"Jen needs help with her homework."

Megan frowned. "On Facebook?"

"Fifteen minutes, Mom. That's all."

But it was never fifteen minutes because in fifteen minutes the lights would still be on[3] and Kaylie would still be on the computer and then Megan would have to get out of bed again and tell her to go to sleep.

"No. Now."

"But—"

"Do you want to be grounded[4]?"

"God, what's your problem? Fifteen minutes!"

"NOW!"

"Why are you yelling? You always yell at me."

And so it went.[5] Megan thought about Lorraine, about her visit, about her not being cut out for kids[6] and those mommies in the corner at Starbucks and how your past never leaves you, neither the good nor the bad, how you pack it into boxes and put it in some closet[7] and you figure that it will be like those boxes you pack in your house—something you keep but never open—and then one day, when the real world closes in on you[8]—you go to that closet and open it again.

When Megan returned to her bedroom, Dave was asleep, the television still on, the remote control in his hand. He was on his back. His shirt was off[9], his chest[10] rising and falling with a light snore[11]. For a moment Megan stopped and watched him. He was a big man, still in shape[12], but the years had added layers[13]. His hair was thinning.[14] His jowls[15] were a little thicker. His posture wasn't what it once was.[16]

He worked too hard. Every weekday he woke up at six thirty, donned a suit and tie, and drove to his sixth-floor corner office in Jersey City. He worked as an attorney[17], traveling more than he should. He seemed to like it well enough[1], but he lived for those moments he could run home and be with his family. Dave liked coaching his kids[2] and attending the games[3] and he cared way too much[4] how well the kids performed[5]. He liked chatting up[6] the parents on the sidelines[7] and having a beer with the guys at the American Legion and playing in his old-man soccer league and doing an early morning golf round at the club.

Are you happy?

She had never asked him that. He had never asked her. What would she say anyway? She felt an itch right now[8]. Did he?[9] She was keeping it from him.[10] Maybe he was doing the same. She had slept with this man and this man only for the past sixteen years—and she had lied to him[11] from day one[12]. Would that matter to him now? Would the truth make any difference? He knew nothing about her past—and yet he knew her better than anyone else.

Megan moved closer to the bed, gently[13] took the remote control from his hand, turned off[14] the television. Dave stirred[15] and turned onto his side[16]. He mostly slept in the fetal position[17]. She moved into the bed next to him and slid into a spoon[18]. His body was warm. She put her nose up against his back. She loved the way he smelled.

When Megan looked at her future, when she saw herself old and living in Florida or some retirement village[19] or wherever she ended up, Megan knew that it would be with this man. She could not imagine anything else. She loved Dave. She had made a life with him and loved him—should she feel bad that she wanted something more or just different every once in a while?

It was wrong. The question was, she guessed, why was it wrong?

She rested her hand on his hip[20]. She knew that she could sneak[21] her fingers under the elastic waistband[22], how exactly he would react, the little groan[23]

1. Ça n'avait pas l'air de lui déplaire

2. aider ses enfants à s'entraîner

3. assister aux matchs

4. se préoccupait bien trop

5. des résultats des enfants

6. discuter avec

7. au bord du terrain

8. Ça la démangeait en ce moment

9. Était-ce pareil pour lui ?

10. Elle ne lui en avait rien dit.

11. lui avait menti

12. dès le premier jour

13. délicatement

14. éteignit

15. bougea

16. se tourna sur le côté

17. en chien de fusil

18. se mit en cuiller [derrière lui]

19. dans un village pour retraités

20. posa la main sur sa hanche

21. glisser

22. taille élastiquée

23. grognement

in his sleep. She smiled at the thought, but for some reason, she decided against it[1]. Her mind drifted back to[2] her visit to La Crème. It had been so wonderful to just be there, to just *feel* that much.

Why had she opened that closet door?

And the less abstract and philosophical question: Could Stewart Green really be back?

No. At least, she couldn't imagine it. Or maybe, when she stopped and thought about it, his being back[3] explained everything. Suddenly the excitement turned to fear[4]. There had been good times back then, vibrant[5] times, fun times. But there had also been very, very scary[6] times.

When you thought about it[7], didn't those go hand in hand[8]? Wasn't that part of the draw?[9]

Stewart Green. She thought that was one ghost[10] that had long been buried. But you can't bury a ghost, can you?

She shivered[11], put her hand around Dave's waist, and nestled in closer[12]. To her surprise, he took her hand and said, "You okay, hon[13]?"

"I'm fine."

Silence. Then he said, "Love you."

"Love you too."

Megan figured that sleep would never come, but it did. She dropped into it[14] as though off a cliff. At three A.M., when her mobile phone buzzed[15], she was still right up against[16] her husband, her arm still around his waist. Her hand shot out for the phone[17] without hesitation. She checked the caller ID[18], though there was no need.

Still half asleep, Dave cursed and said, "Don't answer it."

But Megan simply could not do that. She was already rolling out of bed, her feet searching for the slippers[19]. She put the phone to her ear. "Agnes?"

"He's in my room," the old woman whispered[20].

"It's going to be okay, Agnes. I'm on my way.[21]"

"Please hurry." The terror in her whisper couldn't have been more obvious if it came with a blinking neon sign[1]. "I think he's going to kill me."

BROOME didn't bother flashing his badge[2] when he walked into La Crème, a "gentlemen's lounge[3]"—a euphemism in so many ways—located two short blocks geographically[4] (but long blocks[5] in many other ways) from Atlantic City's Boardwalk[6]. The bouncer[7], an old-timer[8] named Larry, already knew him.

"Yo[9], Broome."

"Hey, Larry."

"Business or pleasure?" Larry asked.

"Business. Rudy here?"

"In his office."

It was ten A.M., but the place still had a few pathetic customers and even more pathetic dancers. One staff member[10] set up the always-popular, all-you-can-eat[11] ("food only"—ha-ha) buffet, mixing congealed[12] food trays[13] from Lord knows how many days ago[14]. It would be trite to note[15] that the buffet was a salmonella outbreak waiting to happen[16], but sometimes trite is the only sock in the drawer[17].

Rudy sat behind his desk. He could have worked as an extra on *The Sopranos*[18], except the casting director would deem him too much on type[19]. He was a big man, sporting[20] a gold chain thick enough to pull up a Carnival Cruise anchor[21] and a pinkie ring[22] that most of his dancers could wear around their wrists.

"Hey, Broome."

"What's happening, Rudy?"

"Something I can do for you?"

"Do you know who Carlton Flynn is?" Broome asked.

"Sure. Little pissant poser[23] with show muscles and a booth tan[24]."

"You know he's missing?"

"Yeah, I heard something about that."

---

1. était plus que palpable
2. ne prit pas la peine de montrer son insigne
3. club
4. sur le plan à deux rues à peine
5. à des lieues de là
6. front de mer [et ses casinos]
7. videur
8. un vieux de la vieille
9. Salut
10. employé
11. à volonté
12. à l'aspect douteux
13. des plateaux
14. datant de Dieu sait quand
15. une banalité de préciser
16. une épidémie de salmonellose en puissance
17. la banalité est le seul recours
18. [série télévisée]
19. l'aurait jugé trop stéréotypé
20. avec [autour du cou]
21. tirer l'ancre d'un paquebot de croisière
22. chevalière au petit doigt
23. Un petit merdeux
24. bronzage artificiel

1. *Que ça ne te mine pas, surtout.*

2. *J'ai plus de larmes*

3. *une petite bite*

4. *N'y touche pas.*

5. *Ça réduit les couilles en raisins secs.*

6. *Merci pour le conseil médical et pour l'image.*

7. *venir me casser les pieds*

8. *Rudy ouvrit de grands yeux.*

9. *ça fait un siècle*

10. *Faut dire qu'il n'avait pas tort.*

11. *papa dévoué*

12. *la compagnie de strip-teaseuses*

13. *avait une autre carte de crédit*

14. *dont les relevés arrivaient à son adresse professionnelle*

15. *en choisissant ses mots*

16. *la peine fugace*

17. *aime tout bonnement se rincer l'œil*

18. *se faire quelqu'un d'autre*

"Don't get all broken up about it.[1]"

"I'm all cried out[2]," Rudy said.

"Anything you can tell me about him?"

"The girls say he's got a tiny dick[3]." Rudy lit a cigar and pointed it at Broome. "Steroids, my friend. Stay away from them.[4] They make the cojones shrivel into raisins.[5]"

"Appreciate both the health advice and imagery.[6] Anything else?"

"He probably frequented a lot of clubs," Rudy said.

"He did."

"So why bug me[7]?"

"Because he's missing. Like Stewart Green."

That made Rudy's eyes widen.[8] "So? What was that, twenty years ago?"

"Seventeen."

"Long time ago. In a place like Atlantic City, it's a lifetime[9]."

Boy, did that make sense.[10] You live in dog years here. Everything ages faster.

And, yes, though it was not widely reported, Stewart Green, doting dad[11] of little Susie and Brandon, devoted husband of cancer-stricken Sarah, enjoyed La Crème's bottle service and the company of strippers[12]. He kept a separate[13] credit card with the bills coming to his office address[14]. Broome had eventually told Sarah about it, in as gentle terms as he could[15], and her reaction had surprised him.

"Lots of married men go to the clubs," Sarah had said. "So what?"

"Did you know?"

"Yes."

But Sarah was lying. He had seen that flash of hurt[16] in her eyes.

"And it doesn't matter," she insisted.

And in one way, it didn't. The fact that a man might be enjoying innocent ogling[17] or even getting his freak on[18] had nothing to do with the importance of locating him[1]. On the other hand[2], as Broome started to question[3] patrons[4] and employees of La Crème, a rather disturbing and lurid picture emerged[5].

"Stewart Green," Rudy said. "I haven't heard that name in a long time. So what's the connection?"

"Only two things, Rudy." Because, Broome knew, there was very little else Green and Flynn had in common[6]. Stewart Green was married, a father of two, hard working. Carlton Flynn was single, pampered[7], living off Daddy[8]. "One, they both went missing on the exact same day, albeit seventeen years apart[9]. And two"— Broome gestured—"this quality establishment."

In the movies, guys like Rudy never cooperated with the cops. In reality, they didn't want trouble[10] or unsolved crimes either[11]. "So how can I help?"

"Did Flynn have a favorite girl?"

"You mean like Stewart had Cassie?"

Broome said nothing, letting the dark cloud pass[12].

"Because, well, none of my girls are missing, if that's what you mean."

Broome still said nothing. Stewart Green did indeed have a favorite girl here. She, too, had vanished that night seventeen years ago. When the hotshot feds[13], who had taken the case from Broome and the ACPD[14] as soon as they thought it involved a high-profile, honorable citizen, saw this development, an obvious theory was rapidly formed and universally accepted:

Stewart Green had run away with a stripper.

But Sarah wouldn't hear of it[15], and Broome never really bought it either[16]. Green might be a narcissistic creepazoid[17] who wanted some side action[18]—but dumping the kids[19] and skipping town[20]? It didn't add up.[21] None of Stewart Green's accounts[22] had been touched. No money or assets[23] squirreled away[24]. No bags packed, nothing sold off, no sign at work that he had any plans to run. In fact, sitting at his tidy, methodically organized desk, nearly completed, was

1. le retrouver
2. D'un autre côté
3. interroger
4. les clients
5. un portrait dérangeant et malsain prenait corps
6. Green et Flynn n'avaient pas grand-chose d'autre en commun
7. choyé
8. et dépensait les sous de Papa
9. bien qu'à 17 ans d'intervalle
10. d'ennuis
11. ni de crimes non résolus
12. sans relever l'allusion au sombre passé
13. super agents du FBI
14. la police d'Atlantic City
15. ne voulait pas en entendre parler
16. n'y avait jamais vraiment cru
17. pauvre type
18. un peu de piment extraconjugal
19. larguer ses gosses
20. quitter la ville
21. Quelque chose clochait.
22. comptes en banque
23. ni capital
24. n'avaient disparu

1. des revenus
réguliers

2. était bien
intégré dans son
quartier

3. des frères et
sœurs

4. tout indiquait
plutôt le coup
de tête

5. qui
correspondaient
plus ou moins au
même scénario
de personnes
disparues

6. avait même
obtenu

7. fronça les
sourcils en guise
de réponse

8. Ouh là

9. feuilleta

10. Chômeur

11. Montre ces
photos autour
de toi

12. tous les
autres dossiers

13. la seule
affaire avec
disparition
d'une femme

14. avaient tous
décampé

15. dès qu'ils
avaient
su pour la
strip-teaseuse
disparue

the biggest deal of Stewart's career. Stewart Green had a steady income[1], a good job, ties to the community[2], loving parents and siblings[3].

If he had run, all signs pointed to it being spur of the moment[4].

"All right, I'll ask around. See if Flynn liked one girl in particular. What else?"

So far, Broome had been able to locate ten men who might roughly fit the missing-person pattern[5]. His ex-wife and partner, Erin Anderson, had even secured[6] photographs of three of them. It would take time to get more. He handed the pictures to Rudy. "Do you recognize any of these guys?"

"They suspects?"

Broome frowned away the question[7]. "Do you know any, yes or no?"

"Sheesh[8], all right, sorry I asked." Rudy shuffled through[9] the photographs. "I don't know. This guy might look familiar."

Peter Berman. Unemployed[10]. First reported missing March 4, eight years ago.

"Where do you know him from?"

Shrug.

"What's his name?"

"I didn't say I know him. I said he might look familiar. I don't know when or how. Might have been years ago."

"How about eight years ago?"

"I don't know, maybe, why?"

"Show the pictures around[11]. See if anyone recognizes any of them. Don't tell them what it's for."

"Hell, I don't know what it's for."

Broome had checked all the other cases[12]. So far—and it was early—the only one with a missing female attached to it[13] was, of course, Stewart Green's. Her name when she worked here had been Cassie. No one knew her real name. The feds and most cops scurried away[14] when the stripper entered the picture[15].

Rumors swirled[1], reaching the Greens' neighborhood. Kids could be mean[2]. Susie and Brandon had to hear the teasing from friends[3] about Daddy running off with an exotic dancer.

Only one cop—one probably very stupid cop—hadn't believed it.

"Anything else?" Rudy asked.

Broome shook his head[4], started for[5] the door. He looked up and saw something that made him pause.

"What's the matter?" Rudy asked.

Broome pointed up. "Surveillance cameras?"

"Sure. In case we get sued[6]. Or, well, two months ago, this guy rings up a tab for twelve grand on[7] his credit card. When his wife sees it, he pretends that someone stole his card or it's fraud, some crap like that[8]. Says he was never here. Demands his money back[9]."

Broome smiled. "So?"

"So I send him a surveillance photo of a double lap dance and tell him I'd be happy to send the full video to his wife. I then suggested he add on an extra tip[10] because the girls worked hard that night."

"So how long before you tape over?[11]"

"Tape over? What is this, 2008? It's all digital[12] now. You don't tape over nothing. I got every date in here for the last two years."

"Can I get whatever you have for February eighteenth? This year and last."

RAY drove to the FedEx Office in Northfield. He logged on to his computer[13] and printed off[14] the photograph of Carlton Flynn in the Pine Barrens. He knew that if he just sent the JPEG, the photo file could lead back to the originating camera[15]. So he printed out the photograph and made a color photocopy of the print.

He handled[16] everything by the edges[17], being sure to leave no fingerprints[18]. He used a sponge on[19] the

---

1. Les rumeurs s'étaient vite répandues

2. méchants

3. avaient subi les moqueries des copains

4. secoua la tête

5. et se dirigea vers

6. Au cas où on nous traînerait en justice

7. nous paye une ardoise de 12 000 $ avec

8. ou un bobard dans le genre

9. Exige qu'on le rembourse

10. un pourboire supplémentaire

11. Et combien de temps avant de réenregistrer sur la cassette ?

12. du numérique

13. ouvrit son ordinateur

14. imprima

15. avec le fichier image, on pouvait remonter à l'appareil photo

16. prit

17. par les bords

18. s'assurant de ne pas laisser d'empreintes digitales

19. une éponge pour humecter

63

1. simple
2. en majuscules
3. se vendit [en voiture] jusqu'à une boîte aux lettres

4. ce n'était pas la question
5. Quoi qu'on découvre
6. qu'avait-il à perdre
7. jeta
8. à la boîte
9. repartit

envelope, a plain[1] blue Bic pen, writing in all block letters[2]. He addressed the letter to the Atlantic City Police Department and drove to a mailbox[3] on a quiet street in Absecon.

The image of the blood came back to him.

He'd wondered whether this move was too risky, whether this could indeed come back to him. He couldn't see how, and maybe now, after all this time, that wasn't even the issue[4]. He didn't have a choice. Whatever was eventually unearthed[5], whatever unpleasantness came back to him, well, what did he have to lose[6]?

Ray didn't want to think about the answer. He tossed[7] the envelope into the mailbox[8] and drove off[9].

6

MEGAN pulled the car to a hard stop[1] and threw open the driver-side door[2]. She hurried through the lobby[3], past[4] the tired night guard[5] who gave her an eye roll[6], and made a left turn down the second corridor.

Agnes's room was the third on the right. When Megan opened the door, she heard a little gasp[7] come from the bed. The room was pitch-black.[8] Damn, where was the night-light[9]? She flipped on the switch[10] and turned to the bed and felt her heart break all over again[11].

"Agnes?"

The elderly woman[12] sat with the covers pulled up to her saucer-size eyes[13], like a small child watching a scary movie[14].

"It's Megan."

"Megan?"

"It's okay. I'm here."

"He was in the room again," the old woman whispered.

1. freina d'un coup sec

2. ouvrit sa portière d'un grand coup

3. l'entrée

4. passant devant

5. gardien de nuit

6. la regarda un peu hébété

7. cri de surprise

8. Il faisait tout noir dans la pièce.

9. la veilleuse

10. appuya sur l'interrupteur

11. se briser à nouveau

12. vieille dame

13. la couverture jusqu'aux yeux, ouverts grands comme des soucoupes

14. un film d'horreur

Megan hurried over to[1] the bed and pulled her mother-in-law close[2]. Agnes Pierce had lost so much weight[3] over the past year that it felt as though she were grabbing a bag of bones[4]. She felt cold to the touch, shivering[5] in her too-big nightgown[6]. Megan held her for a few minutes, comforting her[7] in the same way she'd comforted her children when they woke up with nightmares[8].

"I'm sorry," Agnes said through the sobs[9].

"Shh, it's okay."

"I shouldn't have called."

"I want you to call," Megan said. "If something scares you, you should always call me, okay?"

The smell of urine was unmistakable[10]. When Agnes calmed down, Megan helped her change the diaper[11]—Agnes refused to let Megan do it herself—and helped her back into bed[12].

When they were settled back in[13], lying side by side[14] on the big bed, Megan said, "Do you want to talk about it?"

Tears rolled down Agnes's cheeks[15]. Megan looked into her eyes because the eyes still told all. The signs of dementia[16] began three years ago with the customary forgetfulness[17]. She called her son, Dave, "Frank"—the name of not her late husband[18], but the fiancé who had left her at the altar[19] fifty years ago. Once a doting grandmother, Agnes suddenly couldn't remember the children's names—or even who they were. It scared Kaylie. Paranoia became Agnes's constant companion. She would think television dramas were real, worried that the killer on CSI[20]: Miami was hiding[21] under her bed.

"He was in the room again," Agnes said now. "He said he was going to kill me."

This was a new delusion[22]. Dave tried, but he had no patience for this kind of thing. During the last Super Bowl[23], right before they knew that she could no longer live on her own, Agnes had kept insisting that the game wasn't live[1]—that she had already seen it and knew who won. Dave began jovially enough, asking, "Who won? I could use a little betting money[2]." Agnes would answer, "Oh, you'll see." But then Dave wouldn't let it go. "Oh yeah, what's going to happen now?" he asked, his exasperation growing moment by moment[3]. "Watch," Agnes would say, and as soon as the play ended, her face would light up[4] and she'd say, "See? I told you."

"Told me what?"

Megan: "Let it go, Dave."

Agnes just kept nodding at her son[5]. "I've seen this game before. I told you."

"Then who won?"

"I don't want to spoil it for you[6]."

"It's live, Mom. You don't know."

"Sure I do."

"Then who won, huh? Tell me who won."

"And spoil it?"

"You won't spoil it. Just tell me who won."

"You'll see."

"You never saw the game, Mom. It's on live right now."

"Sure I did. It was on yesterday."

And on it went[7] until Dave's face turned purple and Megan stepped in and reminded him yet again[8] that it was not Agnes's fault. It was so hard to get that[9]. We get cancer or heart attacks[10], but mental illnesses are almost by definition beyond our grasp[11].

Now, for the past month or so, Agnes had a new delusion—a man was breaking into[12] her room and making threats[13]. Dave again wanted to ignore it. "Let the phone ring," he'd say with a tired groan[14]. "We need to move her to more controlled care[15]."

But Megan just couldn't. Not yet anyway.

Agnes, the doctors had warned her[16], was getting worse, almost ready for the "third floor[17]" where they put their full-on Alzheimer's patients[18]. To the out-

1. en direct

2. Un petit pari réussi serait le bienvenu

3. de plus en plus horripilé

4. s'éclairait

5. persistait à hocher la tête

6. te gâcher le match

7. Et ainsi de suite

8. intervenait en lui rappelant à nouveau

9. si difficile à admettre

10. des crises cardiaques

11. impossibles à saisir vraiment

12. faisait irruption dans

13. proférait des menaces

14. d'un grognement las

15. dans un service de soins plus encadré

16. les médecins l'avaient prévenue

17. étage

18. les patients à un stade avancé de la maladie d'Alzheimer

side world[1], it seemed a cruel place, but Dave was now a believer. Since there was no hope for a cure[2], the workers on the "third floor" did their best to make the patients comfortable, using "validation therapy,"[3] which basically meant, "if you believe it's so, it is." So if you believed, for example, that you were a twenty-two-year-old mother of a newborn baby[4], the caretakers[5] let you feed[6] and cuddle[7] an "infant" (doll[8]) and cooed at it like visiting relatives[9]. Another woman believed that she was pregnant[10] and so the nurses[11] kept asking how far along[12] she was, did she want a boy or a girl, stuff like that.

Megan looked into Agnes's frightened face. Agnes had been so sharp[13] just a few years back—funny and cutting[14] and wonderfully ribald[15]. One night, when the two women had enough to drink, Megan had even told her a little bit of the truth about her past. Not all of it. Just a hint that[16] there was more to it than met the eye[17]. Agnes had said, "I know, hon. We all got secrets." They had never spoken about it again. By the time Megan wanted to raise it again[18], well, it was too late.

"I'm okay now," Agnes said. "You can go."

"I have a little time."

"You have to get the kids off to school, don't you?"

"They're old enough to take care of themselves."

"Are they?" She tilted her head.[19] "Megan?"

"Yes?"

"What do I do if he comes back tonight?"

Megan turned her attention back to the night-light. "Who turned that off?"

"He did."

Megan wondered. Validation therapy. Why the hell not?[20] Maybe it would offer a terrified woman some comfort. "I brought something that might help." She reached into her purse and pulled out what looked like a digital alarm clock.

Agnes looked confused.

"It's a spy camera[1]," Megan said. She had bought it at a spy store online[2]. Sure, she could have just *said* that it was a spy camera—validation therapy was not about honesty—but why be deceitful when you don't have to be[3]? "So we can catch the bastard in the act[4]."

"Thank you," Agnes said, tears—maybe of relief[5]?— in her eyes. "Thank you so much, Megan."

"It's okay."

Megan set it up so it faced the[6] bed. The camera worked by timer[7] and motion detector[8]. Agnes's calls always came in[9] at three A.M. "What I'm going to do," she started explaining, "is to set the timer so that the taping[10] begins at nine P.M. and lasts until[11] six in the morning, okay?"

"Your hands," Agnes said.

"Excuse me?"

"They're shaking.[12]"

Megan looked down[13]. She was right. Her fingers could barely find the buttons[14].

"When he comes for me," Agnes said in a whisper, "my hands start to shake too."

Megan moved back to the bedside[15] and held her mother-in-law again.

"You too, right, Megan?"

"Me too what?"

"You're scared. You're shaking because you're afraid of him too."

Megan didn't know how to reply.

"You're in danger, aren't you, Megan? Is he visiting you too?[16]"

Megan started to say no, started to say something comforting about being fine[17], but she pulled up[18]. She didn't want to lie to Agnes. Why should Agnes think she was the only one who ever got scared?

"I … I don't know," Megan said.

"But you're scared he's come back to get you[19]?"

Megan swallowed, thinking about Stewart Green, about how it all ended[20]. "I guess I am."

1. une caméra de surveillance
2. sur Internet
3. pourquoi mentir quand ce n'est pas la peine
4. prendre le salaud sur le fait
5. soulagement
6. le positionna face au
7. une minuterie
8. un détecteur de mouvement
9. Agnes téléphonait toujours
10. pour que l'enregistrement
11. s'arrête à
12. Elles tremblent.
13. baissa les yeux
14. avaient du mal à trouver les boutons
15. revint près du lit
16. Est-ce qu'il te rend visite aussi ?
17. commença à la rassurer, lui disant que tout allait bien
18. s'interrompit
19. qu'il soit revenu se venger
20. à comment ça s'était terminé

"You shouldn't be."

"I shouldn't?"

"No."

Megan tried to nod. "Okay. Tell you what. I won't be scared, if you won't be."

But Agnes frowned and waved the patronizing deal away[1]. "It's different."

"How?"

"You're young," Agnes said. "You're strong. You're tough[2]. You've known adversity[3], haven't you?"

"Like you."

Agnes ignored that. "You're not an old woman confined to a bed[4]. You don't have to lie helplessly in the dark, shivering, waiting for him to get you."

Megan just looked at her, thinking, Wow, who's working—and who's receiving—the validation therapy now?

"Don't wait in the dark," Agnes said in an agitated whisper[5]. "Don't ever feel helpless[6]. Please? For me? I don't want that for you."

"Okay, Agnes."

"Promise?"

Megan nodded. "I promise."

And she meant it. Validation therapy or not, Agnes had spoken a universal truth[7]: Feeling scared was bad, but feeling helpless was far worse[8]. Megan had been toying with the idea of[9] making a big move since Lorraine's visit anyway. It might unearth the past[10], bring it back in a bad way, but as Agnes had pointed out[11], it was better than lying helplessly in the dark.

"Thank you, Agnes."

The old woman's eyes blinked, as though fighting back tears[12]. "Are you leaving?"

"Yes. But I'll be back."

Agnes spread her arms[13]. "Can you stay close[14] for a little while longer[15]? Not long. I know you need to

1. rejeta d'un geste ce marché condescendant

2. une dure à cuire

3. Tout n'a pas toujours été rose pour toi

4. clouée au lit

5. murmura Agnes d'un ton agité

6. Ne reste jamais à te dire que tu ne peux rien y faire

7. venait d'exprimer une vérité universelle

8. bien pire

9. avait caressé l'idée de

10. faire resurgir le passé

11. l'avait fait remarquer

12. comme si elle retenait ses larmes

13. ouvrit les bras

14. rester auprès de moi

15. encore un peu

be on your way[1]. But a few minutes won't make a big difference, will it?"

Megan shook her head. "It won't make any difference at all."

1. qu'il faut que tu partes

7

1. à visionner

2. sortir en titubant, un verre à la main,

3. des colliers de perles autour du cou,

4. des chapeaux de fête en carton

5. une fille à chaque bras

6. [Charme fauve]

7. leva les yeux au ciel

8. si vous voyez ce que je veux dire

9. le roi de la finesse

10. J'arrive.

11. un connard de la plus belle eau

12. C'est quoi ce bordel ?

13. se pencha sur lui

14. puait la bière

15. la sueur

16. le thon

Broome had just started going through[1] the surveillance videos, watching various idiots stumble out with drinks[2], beads[3], party hats[4], and girls[5], when Rudy from La Crème called him.

"Carlton Flynn had a favorite girl," Rudy said.

"Who?"

"Tawny Allure[6]."

Broome rolled his eyes[7]. "That her real name?"

"As real as anything else on her, if you get my drift[8]," Rudy said.

"Yeah, you're the master of subtlety[9]. When will she be in?"

"She's here now."

"On my way.[10]"

Broome was about to switch off the television when Goldberg, his superior and a dickwad of biblical proportions[11], said, "What the hell is this?[12]"

Goldberg leaned over him[13]. He reeked of beer[14], sweat[15], and tuna[16].

"Video feed of[1] La Crème the night Flynn vanished."

"Why you checking that?"

Broome didn't really want to get into this[2], but Goldberg wouldn't just let it go. Goldberg wore a beige button-down[3] dress shirt[4] that'd probably started life off as bright white. He snarled when he spoke[5], figuring that bluster[6] would hide the dim[7]. So far, it had worked for him.

Broome rose. "I'm seeing if there is any connection between Stewart Green and Carlton Flynn. Both men vanished on the same date."

Goldberg nodded as though in deep thought[8]. "So where you off to[9] now?"

"Back to La Crème. Flynn liked one stripper in particular."

"Hmm." Goldberg rubbed his chin[10]. "Kinda like[11] Stewart Green?"

"Maybe."

Broome ejected the flash drive[12] from the computer. Maybe he'd have Erin look into them[13]. She had a good eye for that kind of thing. He could drop them off on his way[14]. He hurried past Goldberg. As he turned the corner, he looked back, worried Goldberg would still be on his tail[15]. He wasn't. Goldberg was hunched over the phone[16], cupping the mouthpiece[17] like that did some good[18].

Twenty minutes later, after quickly dropping off the flash drive at Erin's, Broome sat across from Tawny Allure in La Crème's quietest booth[19]. Rudy stood behind her, arms crossed[20]. Tawny was all attitude and implants and daddy-didn't-love-me-enough self-esteem issues[21]. That was the cliché in a place like this, and truth was, most of the time the cliché applied. Tawny was young and brick-house built in a surgically enhanced way[22], but she had the kind of harsh face[23] that had already seen too many guys sneaking out at daylight[24] and then changing their cell phone numbers.

---

1. La sur-
veillance vidéo de
2. en parler
3. à col boutonné
4. chemise
5. parlait
toujours d'un ton
rageur
6. s'imaginant
que son ton
intimidant
7. sa bêtise
8. en pleine
réflexion
9. vous allez où
10. se frotta le
menton
11. Un peu
comme
12. la clé USB
13. qu'il
demanderait
à Erin de les
regarder
14. les déposer
en chemin
15. à ses basques
16. penché sur le
téléphone
17. la main
autour du micro
18. comme si ça
servait à quelque
chose
19. le box le plus
tranquille
20. les bras
croisés
21. un mix de
frime, de faux
seins et de
manque d'amour
paternel dans
son enfance
22. avec une belle
carrosserie aidée
par la chirurgie
esthétique
23. visage dur
24. filer au petit
matin

"Tell me about Carlton Flynn," Broome asked.

"Carlton?" She blinked with eyelashes so fake[1] they looked like dying crabs baking in the sun[2]. "Oh, he was a sweetheart[3]. Treated me like gold. Always a gentleman."

Tawny wasn't a very good liar. Her eyes darted about[4] like scared birds.

"Anything else you can tell me about him?"

"Not really."

"How did you meet?"

"Here."

"How?"

"He bought a lap dance," Tawny explained. "They're legal, you know."

"And then, what, he took you back to his place[5]?"

"Oh no. We don't do that here. This place is totally legit[6]. I'd never."

Even Rudy rolled his eyes at that one.

Broome sighed. "Tawny?"

"Yes?"

"I'm not vice[7], so I don't care if you bang monkeys for doughnuts[8]—"

"Huh?"

"And I also don't think you had anything to do with what happened to Carlton. But if you keep lying to me—"

"I'm not lying!"

Broome held up a hand for her to shut up[9]. "If you keep lying to me, Tawny, I'll nail you for it[10] and put you in jail[11], just for kicks[12]. I will frame you[13] and make it look like you murdered him because, really, I'm bored with this case and need to clear it[14]. So you can tell me the truth, or you can end up serving time[15]."

It was, of course, an idle threat[16]. Broome almost felt bad about it, what with[17] this girl who was too dumb to get out of her own way[18]. She glanced[19] behind her at Rudy. Broome wondered whether he[20]

74

should tell Rudy to take a hike[1], but Rudy nodded for her to go ahead.

Tawny looked down. Her shoulders slumped.[2] "He broke my finger."

She had been keeping her right hand under the table. There was a red glove covering it[3]—the color matched[4] her bra top[5]—and when she took it off, Broome could see that it hadn't been set right[6]. The digit was pointing to the side[7], the bone still nearly poking through the skin[8].

Broome shot a glare toward Rudy[9]. Rudy shrugged. "What, you think we got a good medical plan[10] here?"

A tear ran down Tawny's cheek. "Carlton is mean. He likes to hurt me. He said if I told anybody or complained[11] he'd kill Ralphie."

"Is that your boyfriend?"

She looked at Broome as though he had two heads[12]. "My poodle[13]."

Broome looked at Rudy. "You know about this?"

"What, you think I keep track of the girls' pets[14]?"

"Not the dog, dumb ass[15]. Carlton Flynn being a sadistic prick.[16]"

"Hey, if anybody hurts my girls, I tell them to take a hike. But if I don't know about it[17], what am I supposed to do, am I right? It's like that tree falling in the woods or whatever. Does it make a dent[18] if you don't hear it? If I don't know about it, I don't know about it."

Rudy, the gentlemen's lounge philosopher.

"Did he hurt you other ways?" Broome asked.

Tawny nodded, eyes squeezed shut[19].

"Can you tell me about it?"

"No."

"So you hated him."

"Yeah."

"And now he's missing."

Tawny's fake lashes flew open[20]. "You said you didn't think I had anything to do with that."

1. d'aller voir ailleurs
2. Elle se voûta un peu.
3. Elle était recouverte d'un gant rouge
4. de la même couleur que
5. sa brassière
6. qu'on ne lui avait pas remis l'os du doigt en place
7. Il partait vers le côté
8. l'os pointant presque sous la peau
9. regarda Rudy d'un air réprobateur
10. couverture médicale
11. si j'allais me plaindre
12. comme s'il avait deux têtes
13. caniche
14. que je fais attention aux animaux de compagnie de mes filles
15. eh couillon
16. Que Carlton Flynn ait été un salaud à tendances sadiques.
17. je ne suis pas au courant
18. Est-ce qu'il laisse une marque
19. les yeux bien fermés
20. Les faux cils de Tawny s'ouvrirent grand

"Maybe not you," Broome said. "Maybe someone who cares about you. Maybe someone who wanted to protect you."

Again she gave him the confused look.

"A boyfriend, a parent, a close friend[1]."

"You're kidding[2], right?"

Sadly her confusion was justified. She had no one, other than a poodle[3] named Ralphie. Dead end.[4]

"When did you last see Flynn?" Broome asked.

"Night before he, uh, left[5] or whatever[6]."

"Where did you two go?"

"Here first. He liked to watch me dance. He'd buy random guys lap dances[7] and he'd smile and watch and then he'd take me home and call me a slut[8] for dancing with them and hurt me bad[9]."

Broome tried not to show anything. You want to come here, get your rocks off[10], whatever, he didn't judge. But the thing they never tell people is, it's never enough. So Carlton Flynn started off as some two-bit player[11], getting some ass[12], but after a while, you crave more[13]. That's how it always works. Everything is a gateway drug to the next.[14] Broome's grandfather said it best: "If you were getting pussy[15] all the time, you'd want a second dick[16]."

"Did you make plans to see him again?" Broome asked.

"He was supposed to meet me the night he, you know, disappeared."

"What happened?"

"He called and said he'd be late. But he never showed[17]."

"Did he say why he'd be late?"

"No."

"Do you know where he went earlier that day?"

Tawny shook her head. The stale stench of hairspray and regret[18] wafted toward him[19].

"Anything you can tell me about that day?"

More head shaking.

"I don't get it[1]," Broome said. "This guy kept hurting you, right?"

"Yeah."

"It was escalating[2]."

"Huh?"

Broome bit back the sigh[3]. "Getting worse and worse."

"Oh. Right. Yeah."

Broome spread his hands. "How did you think it'd all end?"

Tawny blinked, looked away, considered[4] the question for a moment. "The same way it always does. He'd get tired of me[5]. Move on to the next thing[6]." She added a shrug. "Either that or he'd kill me."

1. Je ne pige pas

2. Ça s'intensifiait

3. retint un soupir

4. réfléchit à

5. Il se lasserait de moi

6. Passerait à autre chose

8

THE words "Law Office of[1] Harry Sutton" were stenciled into the pebbled glass[2]. Old-school[3].

When Megan gently rapped[4] on the pebbled glass, Harry answered with a resounding "Enter!"

She reached for the knob[5]. A few hours ago, she'd called home and told Dave that she wouldn't be home till late. He wanted to know why. She told him not to worry and hung up. Now here she was, back in Atlantic City, in a place she had known all too well[6].

Megan opened the door, knowing that doing so would probably change everything. The office was still a seedy one-room operation[7]—small-time with a lowercase *s*[8]—but Harry would have it no other way[9].

"Hey, Harry."

Harry was not an attractive[10] man. His eyes had enough bags under them to take a three-week cruise.[11] His nose was caricature bulbous[12]. His hair was a shock of white[13] that wouldn't come down without the threat of gunfire[14]. But his smile, well, it was bea-

78

tific. The smile warmed her[1]—brought her back[2] and made her feel safe[3].

"It's been too long, Cassie."

Some called Harry a street lawyer[4], but that wasn't really what Harry was. Four decades ago he had graduated[5] Stanford Law School and started on a partnership track[6] at the prestigious law firm of Kronberg, Reiter and Roseman. One night, some well-meaning[7] colleagues dragged the quiet, shy attorney down to Atlantic City for gambling[8], girls, and general debauchery. The shy Harry dived in[9]—and never left. He quit the big firm, stenciled his name upon this very office door, and decided to champion[10] the city's underdogs[11], who, in many ways, consisted of everyone who started out here.

Very few people you meet have a halo[12] over their head. They aren't beautiful or angelic or working for charities[13]—in Harry's case, he definitely preferred the sinners[14] to the saints—but there was just an aura of trust and goodness about them[15]. Harry was one of those people.

"Hello, Cassie," Harry said.

His voice was stiff.[16] He shifted in his chair.

"How've you been, Harry?"

His clear blue eyes looked at her in a funny way. This wasn't like him[17], but it had been nearly two decades[18]. People change. She started to wonder if coming here had been a mistake.

"Fine, thank you."

"Fine, thank you?"

"What's going on, Harry?"

His eyes suddenly brimmed with tears.[19]

"Harry?"

"Damn[20]," he said.

"What?"

"I promised I'd keep it together[21]. I'm such a wuss[22] sometimes."

1. la réconforta

2. lui rappela le passé

3. lui donna une sensation de sécurité

4. un avocat des pauvres

5. obtenu son diplôme à

6. était bien parti pour devenir associé

7. bien intentionnés

8. pour aller jouer de l'argent

9. s'y était mis sans hésiter

10. de défendre

11. les laissés-pour-compte

12. une auréole

13. des associations caritatives

14. les pécheurs

15. ils rayonnent de confiance et de bonté

16. Son ton était un peu froid.

17. Ça ne lui ressemblait pas

18. 20 ans

19. Il eut soudain les larmes aux yeux.

20. Bon sang

21. que je ne craquerais pas

22. une telle lavette

She said nothing, waited.

"It's just that … I thought you were dead."

She smiled, feeling relief[1] that, yes, he was the same overly emotional[2] guy she remembered. "Harry …"

He waved it away. "The cops came here after you vanished with that guy."

"I didn't vanish with that guy."

"You just vanished on your own?"

"Sort of."

"Well, the cops wanted to talk to you. They still do."

"I know," Megan said. "That's why I'm back. I need your help."

WHEN Tawny Allure first saw the smiling young couple standing near her doorway, she sighed and shook her head.

Tawny's real name was Alice. She had used it at first, going by the stage moniker[3] "Alice in Wonderland[4]," but her given name made it easier for those from her past to recognize her. Right now, with work behind her[5], she wore a loose, can't-tell-implants sweatshirt[6]. She'd traded in her stiletto heels for[7] low-top tennis shoes. She had scrubbed off the spackle-thick make-up[8] and thrown on a pair of celebrity-in-hiding-size sunglasses[9]. She did not, she thought, look anything like the exotic dancer she was.

The smiling couple looked as though they'd just wandered away from a Bible study[10]. Tawny frowned. She knew the type[11]. Do-gooders.[12] They wanted to give her pamphlets[13] and save her. They would have some corny catchphrase[14] like "lose the G-string[15] and find Jesus," and she would respond, "Does Jesus tip well?"

The smiling blond girl was young and pretty in a wholesome way[16]. Her hair was tied back in a cheer-leader-bouncing ponytail[17]. She wore a turtleneck[18] and a skirt that would normally work at the club for a schoolgirl fantasy number[1], complete with bobby socks[2]. Who wore that in real life?

The cute guy[3] with her had the wavy hair of a politician on a sailboat[4]. He sported khakis, a blue button-down, and had a sweater[5] tied around his neck.

Tawny was not in the mood[6]. Her finger throbbed and ached[7]. She felt weak, beaten, defeated[8]. She wanted to get inside and feed[9] Ralphie. Her mind was still on[10] that cop Broome's visit and, of course, the missing Carlton Flynn. The first time she met Carlton he wore a tight black T-shirt that read[11] "I'm Not a Gynecologist, But I'll Take a Look." Talk about a big-time "Keep Away" sign[12]. But stupid Tawny had giggled[13] when she read it. Sad when she thought about it now. Tawny had some decent attributes, but her asshole-dar[14] was always off when it came to men.

Sometimes—most times—Tawny felt as if bad luck walked two steps behind her, catching up every once in a while, tapping her on the shoulder, reminding her that he was there, her constant companion.

It hadn't started that way. She had loved her job at La Crème in the beginning. It had been fun and exciting and a dance party every night. And, no, Tawny hadn't been sexually abused as a child[15] or any of that, thank you very much, but she did have another quality you often found in people who go into her line of work.

Tawny was, she could admit to herself, inherently lazy[16] and easily bored[17].

People always talk about how the girls are damaged[18] or lacked self-esteem[19], and, yeah, that was true, but the big thing was, most girls simply didn't want to hold a real job. Who does? Think about it— what were the alternatives to what she was now doing?

Take Tawny's sister, Beth. Since graduating high school six years ago, Beth worked data entry[20] for the First Trenton Insurance[21]. She sat in a smelly, airless cubicle[22] in front of a computer screen and

1. numéro
« fantasme écolière »

2. avec socquettes et tout

3. beau gosse

4. voilier

5. pull

6. n'était pas d'humeur

7. la lançait douloureusement

8. se sentait faible et abattue

9. nourrir

10. Elle pensait encore à

11. qui disait

12. Un sacré repoussoir, quand on y pense

13. rigolé

14. son détecteur de connards

15. n'avait pas subi d'abus sexuels dans son enfance

16. paresseuse de nature

17. s'ennuyait facilement

18. sont traumatisées

19. manquent d'amour-propre

20. faisait de la saisie de données

21. Assurances

22. un bureau qui sentait le renfermé

plugged in[1] God-knows-what data—hour after hour, day after day, year after year, stuck in a cubicle smaller than a jail cell[2], until, well, what?

Shudder.[3]

Seriously, Tawny thought, Kill me now.

Here were her options when you broke it down[4]: One, type insurance data mindlessly[5] in a tight, stinky[6] cubicle … or two, dance the night away[7] and drink champagne at a party.

Tough choice, right?[8]

But her job at La Crème wasn't shaping up the way she thought it would[9]. Here, she'd heard it was better than Match.com for meeting eligible guys[10], but the closest thing to a real relationship she'd had was with Carlton. And what had he done? He'd broken her finger and threatened[11] Ralphie.

Some girls did indeed find a rich guy, but for the most part, they were the pretty ones, and when she looked hard in the mirror, Tawny knew that she wasn't. Pretty, that is. She had to pile on more and more makeup[12]. The circles[13] under her eyes were getting darker. She needed repair work on the boob job[14] and even though she was only twenty-three, varicose veins[15] were starting to make her legs look like relief maps[16].

The perky[17] young blonde with the turtleneck gave Tawny a little wave[18]. "Miss, can we talk to you for a moment?"

Tawny felt a tinge of envy[19] for this perky blonde with the toothpaste-commercial[20] smile. The cute guy was probably her boyfriend. He probably treated her nice[21], took her to the movies, held her hand at the mall[22]. Lucky. Sure, they were Bible thumpers[23], but they looked happy and healthy[24] and like they'd never known sadness in their whole lives. Tawny would bet her meager life savings[25] that every person that these two had ever known was still alive. Their parents were still happily married and looked healthy, just like them, only a little older, and they played tennis and had barbecues and big family dinners, where the relatives bowed their heads[1] and said a nice prayer.

Soon, they would tell her that they had all the answers to her problems, and, sorry, Tawny just wasn't in the mood. Not today. Her broken finger ached so damn much. A cop had just threatened to throw her in jail. And her sadistic, psycho puppy[2] of a "boyfriend" was missing and maybe, God willing[3], dead.

The smiling cute boy said, "We just need to talk to you for a brief moment."

Tawny was about to tell them to buzz off[4], but something made her pull up[5]. These two were different from the standard-issue[6] Bible thumpers who stood outside the club and harassed[7] the girls with quoted Scripture[8]. They seemed more ... Midwestern maybe? More fresh scrubbed[9] and bright-eyed. A few years ago, Tawny's grandmother, may she rest in peace[10], had really gotten into some hokey televangelist on a crappy cable network[11]. They had something called the *Wholesome Music Hour* with young teens[12] singing gently with guitars and hand claps[13]. That's what these kids looked like. Like they just escaped from some cable-TV church choir[14].

"It won't take long," the perky blonde assured her.

Here they were, on her doorstep, today of all days. Not at the club's back entrance. Not yelling out a bunch of slogans about sin[15]. Maybe, after all the destruction, with her finger aching and her feet hurting and the rest of her feeling too bone tired to take one more step[16], these two kids were here for a reason. Maybe they had indeed been sent, in Tawny's hour of darkest need[17], to rescue her[18]. Like two angels from above.

Could that be?

A stray tear[19] ran down Tawny's cheek. The perky blond girl nodded at her as though she understood exactly what Tawny was going through.

1. avant lesquels toute la famille inclinait la tête

2. jeune cinglé

3. s'il plaisait à Dieu

4. d'aller se faire voir

5. la retint

6. classiques

7. harcelaient

8. des citations de la Bible

9. propres sur eux

10. Dieu ait son âme

11. avait été emballée par un télévangéliste de pacotille sur une chaîne merdique du câble

12. ados

13. en tapant des mains

14. chorale paroissiale

15. Pas en train de scander des slogans contre le péché

16. trop épuisée pour bouger

17. au moment où elle en avait le plus besoin

18. la sauver

19. Une larme

Maybe, Tawny thought, readying her key[1], I do need saving. Maybe these two kids, unlikely as it sounded[2], were her ticket to[3] a better life.

"Okay," Tawny said, choking back a sob[4]. "You can come in. Just for a second, okay?"

They both nodded.

Tawny opened the door. Ralphie sprinted across the room toward them[5], his nails clacking[6] on the linoleum. Tawny felt her heart soar at the sound[7]. Ralphie—the one good, kind, loving thing in her life. She bent down and let Ralphie run her over[8]. She giggled through a sob and scratched Ralphie in that spot behind his ears for a few seconds and then stood back up[9].

Tawny turned to the perky blonde, who still had the smile in place.

"Beautiful dog," the perky blonde said.

"Thank you."

"Can I pet him[10]?"

"Sure."

Tawny turned to the cute guy. He smiled at her too. But the smile was weird[11] now. Off somehow[12] …

The cute guy was still smiling when he cocked his fist back[13]. He was still smiling when he turned his hips and shoulders and punched[14] Tawny straight in the face[15] with everything he had[16].

As Tawny crumbled to the floor[17], blood spurting out of[18] her nose, eyes rolling back, the last sound she heard was Ralphie whimpering[19].

---

1. en sortant sa clé
2. aussi peu probable que cela paraisse
3. pour elle l'assurance d'
4. ravalant un sanglot
5. se précipita vers eux
6. et on entendit le cliquetis de ses griffes
7. Ce bruit réchauffa le cœur de Tawny
8. laissa Ralphie lui bondir dessus
9. se releva
10. le caresser
11. étrange
12. Presque inquiétant
13. referma le poing
14. donna un coup de poing à
15. en pleine figure
16. de toutes ses forces
17. s'écroulait au sol
18. du sang jaillissant de
19. les gémissements de Ralphie

9

BROOME put the phone back in its cradle[1]. He was still trying to process[2] this—to quote[3] all local newscasters[4]—"latest shocking development."

Goldberg asked, "Who was that?"

Broome hadn't realized that Goldberg had been hovering[5]. "Harry Sutton."

"The shyster[6]?"

"Shyster?" Broome frowned. "What is this, 1958? No one calls lawyers shysters anymore."

"Don't be an asshole because it's easy," Goldberg said. "This have something to do with Carlton Flynn?"

Broome stood, his pulse racing[7]. "Could be."

"Well?"

Something to do with Carlton Flynn? Maybe. Something to do with Stewart Green? Definitely.[8]

Broome was still replaying the conversation in his head. After seventeen years of searching, Harry Sutton claimed to have Cassie, the stripper who vanished with Stewart Green, in his office. She was there right

1. sur son support

2. se faire à l'idée de

3. pour reprendre l'expression de

4. journalistes

5. rôdait autour de lui

6. avocat marron

7. le cœur battant

8. Aucun doute là-dessus.

now—just like that—materializing out of thin air[1]. It was almost too much to take in[2].

With most lawyers, Broome would figure they were full of crap[3]. But Harry Sutton, for all his private-life extremes[4]—and, man, he had loads[5]—would not pull something like this[6]. There was no upside for him for[7] lying about it.

"I'll tell you about it later," Broome said.

Goldberg put his hands on his hips, trying hard to look tough. "No, you'll tell me now."

"Harry Sutton may have located a witness[8]."

"What witness?"

"I was sworn to secrecy.[9]"

"You were what?"

Broome didn't bother to reply. He just kept moving, taking the stairs, knowing that Goldberg, a man who found it exhausting[10] to reach for anything other than a sandwich, wouldn't follow. When he got in his car, his cell phone rang. Broome saw that it was Erin.

"Where are you?" she asked.

"Heading to[11] see Harry Sutton."

Erin had been his cop partner[12] for twenty-three years before retiring[13] last year. She was also his ex-wife. He filled her in on[14] the sudden reappearance of Cassie.

"Wow," Erin said.

"Yes."

"The elusive[15] Cassie," Erin said. "You've been looking for her for a long time."

"Seventeen years."

"So you may get some answers."

"We can hope. You call for a reason?[16]"

"The surveillance video from La Crème."

"What about it?[17]"

"I may have found something," Erin said.

"Do you want me to stop by[18] when I'm done[19] with Sutton?"

"Sure, that'll give me time to hammer this out[1]. Plus you can fill me in on your meeting with the elusive Cassie."

Then, because he couldn't resist: "Erin?"

"What?"

"You said 'hammer[2].' Heh-heh-heh."

"Seriously, Broome?" Erin groaned. "How old are you?"

"Lines like that used to work on you.[3]"

"Lots of things used to work on me," she said, and there was maybe a hint of sadness[4] in her voice. "A long time ago."

Truer words[5]. "See you in a while[6], Erin."

Broome pushed thoughts of his ex away and kept his foot on the accelerator. A few minutes later, he wrapped his knuckles[7] on the pebbled glass. From inside, a gravelly[8] voice called, "Enter!"

He opened the door and stepped fully[9] into the room. Harry Sutton looked like a beloved college professor[10] gone seriously to seed[11]. Broome took in[12] the whole room. There was no one here but Harry.

"Nice to see you, Detective."

"Where is Cassie?"

"Have a seat[13]."

Broome did as asked[14]. "Where is Cassie?"

"She's not here at the moment."

"Well, yes, I can see that."

"That's because you're a trained[15] detective."

"I try not to brag[16]," Broome said. "What's going on here, Harry?"

"She's nearby.[17] She wants to talk to you. But before she does, there are a few ground rules[18]."

Broome spread his arms. "I'm listening."

"First of all, this is all off the record[19]."

"Off the record? What, you think I'm a reporter, Harry?"

"No, I think you're a good and somewhat desperate[20] cop. Off the record meaning just that. You don't

---

1. peaufiner

2. [en argot, veut aussi dire « pénis »]

3. Avant, tu riais à ce genre de blagues.

4. une pointe de tristesse

5. Rien de plus vrai

6. À plus

7. toquetoquait

8. râpeuse

9. entra

10. un amour de prof de fac

11. très décati

12. balaya du regard

13. Asseyez-vous

14. obéit

15. expérimenté

16. de ne pas me vanter

17. Elle n'est pas loin.

18. quelques règles de base

19. tout ceci reste entre nous

20. plus ou moins prêt à tout

1. ne versez pas
ça au dossier
2. Officielle-
ment
3. pas la peine
de faire des
effets de scène
4. éclatant
5. pourquoi ne
pas en rajouter
un peu
6. Faites-la
entrer
7. un entretien
unique et pour
vous seul
8. de son mieux
9. me croire sur
parole
10. Imaginez
que
11. coupable
12. Pas de bol
13. elle aura fini
de vous parler
14. qu'ayant
avancé dans
l'enquête
15. je tombe sur
un nouvel indice
16. ne s'engage
pas à vous aider
à l'avenir
17. n'avait
aucun moyen de
pression
18. qui préférait
ne pas lâcher
la proie pour
l'ombre
19. et savait
se contenter
de ce qu'on lui
donnait
20. ne savait
absolument
pas où
21. s'il ne
contrariait ni
Cassie ni Harry

take notes. You don't put this in the file[1]. As far as anyone knows[2], you never talked to her."

Broome considered that. "And if I say no?"

Harry Sutton stood and reached out his hand. "Good to see you again, Detective. Have a nice day."

"Okay, okay, no need for theatrics[3]."

"No need," Harry said with a bright[4] smile, "but why not throw them in[5] if I can?"

"So it's off the record. Bring her in[6]."

"A few more rules first."

Broome waited.

"Today is a one-time exclusive[7]. Cassie will talk to you in my office. She will answer your questions to the best of her ability[8] in my presence. Then she will vanish again. You will let her. You won't try to learn her new name or identity—and more important, you won't try to find her after this meeting."

"And you're going to just trust me on that[9]?"

"Yes."

"I see," Broome said. He shifted in the chair. "Suppose[10] I think she's guilty[11] of a crime."

"You won't."

"But suppose."

"Tough[12]. When she's done talking to you[13], she goes home. You don't see her again."

"And suppose, after I investigate some more[14], I stumble across something new[15] I need to ask her about."

"Same answer: Tough."

"I can't come to you?"

"You can. And if I can help, I will. But she makes no commitment to do so[16]."

Broome could argue, but he had no leverage here[17]. He was also a one-in-the-hand[18], don't-look-a-gift-horse-in-the-mouth[19] kind of guy. Yesterday he didn't have the slightest clue where[20] Cassie was. Now, unless he pissed off her or Harry[21], he could talk to her.

"Okay," Broome said, "I agree to all your rules."

"Marvelous." Harry Sutton picked up[1] his cell phone and said, "Cassie? It's okay. Come on in now."

DEPUTY Chief Goldberg just didn't give a damn anymore[2].

He was a year from retirement with full pension[3], and it wasn't enough. Not even close. Atlantic City might be a cesspool, but it was a costly one. He had alimony payments up the wazoo[4]. His current love interest[5], Melinda, a twenty-eight-year-old porn star (they were always porn "stars," Goldberg noticed, never just "actresses" or, as in Melinda's case, "the lesser girl in the three-way"), was sucking him dry[6] (and he meant that in two ways, snicker). But, man, was she worth it[7].

Yep, slice it any way you want[8], but in the end Goldberg was a cop on the take[9].

Normally he could justify it easily enough. Bad guys are like one of those mythological beasts where you cut off one bad guy, two more just pop up in its place[10]. Or, better the devil you know[11]—the one you can somewhat control and who won't knock off[12] real citizens and who will give you some dough[13]—than the devil you don't. Or, removing the sleaze[14] from this city was like emptying an ocean with a table-spoon[15]. Whatever, Goldberg had a million of them.

But in this circumstance, justification was even easier: The guy slipping him the Ben Franklins[16] seemed, at least on the surface, to be on the same side as the angels.

So why was Goldberg hesitating?

He dialed the number. It was picked up on the third ring.

"Good afternoon, Mr. Goldberg!"

Reason one for his hesitation: The guy's voice gave him the heebie-jeebies[17]. The man—he sounded really young—was unfailingly polite[18] and spoke in exclam-ation points[19], as though he were trying out for an

1. prit

2. se fichait de tout maintenant

3. avec retraite à taux plein

4. de méga pensions alimentaires à verser

5. nana du moment

6. le saignait à blanc

7. elle en valait sacrément la peine

8. il n'y avait pas à tortiller

9. facile à acheter

10. apparaissent à sa place

11. mieux vaut l'ennemi connu

12. ne va pas aller buter

13. du fric

14. la corruption

15. à la petite cuiller

16. qui lui graissait la patte

17. la chair de poule

18. toujours poli

19. sur un ton enjoué

1. passait une audition pour une comédie musicale

2. pas seulement ça

3. des hommes aguerris

4. les durs, les blasés

5. un petit peu

6. ne voulait pas être mêlé à ça

7. la solution la plus sage

8. de se retirer

9. risquait de fâcher

10. à l'autre bout du fil

11. rien de grave

12. une autre piste

13. leur avait déjà refilé toutes les infos qu'il pouvait

14. ils payaient bien

old-time musical[1]. The sound chilled Goldberg. But there was more to it than that[2].

There were the rumors about this guy. There were stories of violence and depravity done by this guy and his partner, the kind of stories that make grown men[3]—big, tough, world-weary, seen-it-all men[4] like Goldberg—stay up at night, pulling the covers just a wee bit[5] higher.

"Yeah," Goldberg said. "Hi."

Even if the rumors were exaggerated, even if a quarter of the whispers were true, Goldberg had gotten in on something he wanted no part of[6]. Still, the best course of action[7] would be to take the money and shut up. In a sense, what choice did he have? If he tried to back out[8] now or return the money, he might anger[9] that voice on the other end of the phone[10].

The voice said, "What can I do for you, Mr. Goldberg?"

In the background, Goldberg heard a noise that was making his blood freeze.

"What the hell is that?" he asked.

"Oh, nothing to worry about[11], Mr. Goldberg. What did you want to tell me?"

"I might have another lead[12]."

"Might?"

"I'm not sure, that's all."

"Mr. Goldberg?"

"Yes?"

What the hell was that sound in the background?

"Please tell me what you know."

He had already leaked them whatever he could[13] on the disappearance of Carlton Flynn. Why not? He and his partner were interested in finding the missing guy too, and the pay was pretty damn sweet[14].

The last thing Goldberg had leaked was what he learned from Broome: Carlton Flynn had a stripper girlfriend who worked at La Crème.

There was whimpering in the background.

"Do you have a dog?" Goldberg asked.

"No, Mr. Goldberg, I don't. Oh, but I had the best dog when I was a kid! Her name was Ginger Snaps[1]. Cute[2], right?"

Goldberg said nothing.

"You seem reluctant[3], Mr. Goldberg."

"It's Deputy Chief Goldberg."

"Would you like to meet in person[4], Deputy Chief Goldberg? We can discuss this issue at your house, if you'd like."

Goldberg's heart stopped beating. "No, that's okay."

"So what can you tell me, Deputy Chief Goldberg?"

The dog was still whimpering. But now Goldberg thought that maybe he heard another sound too, another whimpering maybe, or something worse, underneath the first—a terrible, pain-stricken noise[5] so nonhuman that paradoxically it could only come from another human being.

"Deputy Chief Goldberg?"

He swallowed and dived in[6]. "There's this lawyer named Harry Sutton. ..."

1. [Biscuits au gingembre]
2. C'est mignon
3. avez l'air hésitant
4. qu'on se rencontre
5. bruit déchirant
6. se jeta à l'eau

10

THE door to Harry Sutton's office opened, and Cassie walked in.

She looked pretty much the same[1].

That was the first thought that hit Broome. In those days, Broome had even known her a little, seen her at the club, and so he remembered her. She'd changed her hair color over the years—she'd been more platinum[2] blond, if he recalled correctly[3]—but that was about it[4].

Some might wonder, if she hadn't changed very much, why Broome hadn't been able to find her in the past seventeen years. The truth was, disappearing is not as hard as you might think[5]. Back in those days, Rudy didn't have even her real name. Broome had eventually found it. Maygin Reilly. But that was where it ended[6]. She had gotten a new ID[7], and while she was something of a person of interest[8], it hardly warranted a nationwide APB[9] or its own episode of *Most Wanted*.

1. n'avait quasiment pas changé
2. platine
3. s'il en avait bonne mémoire
4. c'était à peu près tout
5. moins difficile qu'on ne croit
6. s'arrêtait là
7. identité
8. faisait plus ou moins partie des personnes recherchées
9. son cas ne méritait pas un avis de recherche national

The other change was that she looked wealthier[1] and more—for a lack of a better term[2]—normal. You could dress a stripper down, but you could always see the stripper. Same with the gambler[3], the drinker, heck,[4] the cop. Cassie looked like a classic suburban mom[5]. A fun one maybe. The one who gave as good as she got, who flirted when the mood struck[6], who leaned a little too close when she had a few drinks at the block party[7]. But a suburban mom just the same[8].

She sat next to him and turned and met his eye[9].

"Good to see you again, Detective."

"Same, I guess. I've been looking for you[10], Cassie."

"So I gathered[11]."

"Seventeen years."

"Almost like Valjean and Javert," she said.

"Like in *Les Misérables*."

"You've read Hugo?"

"Nah," Broome said, "my ex dragged me to the musical[12]."

"I don't know where Stewart Green is," she said.

Cool, Broome thought. She was skipping the preliminaries[13]. "You realize, of course, that you vanished at the same time he did?"

"Yes."

"When you both vanished, you two were seeing each other, right?"

"No."

Broome spread his arms. "That's what I was told."

She gave him a half-smile[14], and Broome saw the sexy girl from years ago emerge. "How long have you lived in Atlantic City, Detective?"

He nodded, knowing where she was going with this[15]. "Forty years."

"You know the life. I wasn't a prostitute. I was working the clubs, and I had fun doing it. So, yes, for a while Stewart Green was part of that fun. A small part. But he eventually destroyed it[16]."

"The fun?"

1. plus riche
2. faute d'un terme plus approprié
3. joueur
4. et zut, même
5. la classique mère de famille petite-bourgeoise
6. quand elle était d'humeur
7. pendant une soirée entre voisins
8. quand même
9. se tourna pour le regarder
10. Je vous ai cherchée
11. C'est ce que j'ai cru comprendre
12. m'a traîné à la comédie musicale
13. sautait les préliminaires
14. lui fit un sourire en coin
15. sachant très bien où elle voulait en venir
16. il a fini par tout détruire

"Everything," she said. Her mouth tightened[1]. "Stewart Green was a psychopath. He stalked me[2]. He beat me. He threatened to kill me[3]."

"Why?"

"What part of the word 'psychopath' confused you[4]?"

"So you're a psychiatrist now, Cassie?"

She gave him the half-smile again. "You don't need to be a psychiatrist to know a psychopath," she began, "any more than you need to be a cop to know a killer."

"Touché[5]," Broome said. "But if Stewart Green was that crazy[6], well, he managed to fool a lot of people[7]."

"We are all different things to different people."

Broome frowned. "That's a tad trite[8], don't you think?"

"It is." She thought about it. "I once heard this guy give a friend some advice about dating a girl[9] who appeared really normal but, well, underneath it all, she was tightly wound[10]. You know the type?[11]"

"I do."

"So the guy warned his buddy[12], 'You don't want to open that big ol' can of crazy[13].' "

Broome liked that. "And that's what you did with Stewart?"

"Like I said, he seemed pretty cool at first. But he became obsessed. Some men do, I guess. I'd always managed to joke my way out of it[14]. But not with him. Look, I read all the articles after he vanished about what a great family guy he was, the loving wife he nursed through cancer[15], the young kids. And working where I was, I had seen it all. I didn't judge[16] the married men who came in to blow off a little steam[17] or look for … whatever. Three-quarters[18] of the guys in the club were married. I don't even think they're hypocrites—a man can love his wife and still want some side action, can't he?"

Broome shrugged. "I guess he can.[19]"

"But Stewart Green wasn't like that. He was violent. He was crazy. I just didn't know how much[1]."

Broome crossed his legs. What she was telling him about the beating and violence—it sounded a lot like Tawny's description of Carlton Flynn. Another connection maybe?

"So what happened?" he asked.

For the first time, Cassie looked uneasy[2]. She glanced over at[3] Harry Sutton. Harry had his hands resting on his belly, his fingers interlocked[4]. He gave her a nod[5]. She looked down at her hands.

"Do you know the old iron-ore ruins by Wharton?"

Broome did. It was maybe eight, ten miles from Atlantic City—the start of the Pine Barrens.

"I used to go there sometimes. After work or whenever I needed just to unwind[6]."

Unwind, Broome thought, managing to keep his face blank[7]. A lie. Her first? He couldn't be sure. He was about to follow up with the obvious question: Why were you *really* there? But for now he left it alone[8].

"So one night—well, my last night in this town—I was up in the park by the ruins. I was pretty distracted[9], I guess. Stewart was getting out of control[10], and I really didn't know how to handle it[11]. I had tried everything to get him to back off[12]."

Broome asked her the same question he had asked Tawny. "Didn't you have a boyfriend or anything?"

Something crossed her face.[13] "No."

Another lie?

"Someone you could go to for help? How about Rudy or a friend at the club?"

"Look, that wasn't the way we worked. Or I worked. I took care of myself[14]. People might suspect I was in over my head[15], but I was a big girl. I could handle it."

She looked down[16].

"What happened, Cassie?"

"It's odd[17]. Hearing someone call me that. Cassie."

---

1. à quel point

2. mal à l'aise
3. jeta un coup d'œil vers
4. les mains croisées posées sur le ventre
5. fit oui de la tête

6. de souffler un peu
7. parvenant à rester impassible
8. ne releva pas

9. assez affolée
10. devenait incontrôlable
11. comment gérer la situation
12. pour qu'il me laisse tranquille
13. Elle laissa paraître une émotion fugace.
14. me débrouillais très bien toute seule
15. que j'étais dépassée par les événements
16. baissa les yeux
17. bizarre

1. Tenez-vous-en à

2. Vous essayez de gagner du temps

3. reprit le fil

4. un moyen de me débarrasser de

5. j'avais sorti la grosse artillerie

6. menacé de le faire

7. ne serais jamais allée jusqu'au bout

8. ne me laissait pas tranquille

9. tout raconter à sa femme

10. risque de vous revenir en pleine figure

11. cette fois sans gaieté

12. j'ai sous-estimé

13. l'air très inquiet

14. quand elle put parler de nouveau

15. auriez pu venir me voir

16. les filles du métier

17. contre les citoyens respectables

18. C'est injuste comme remarque

"Would you prefer Maygin?"

She smiled. "You found that out, huh? No. Stay with[1] Cassie."

"Okay. You're stalling[2], Cassie."

"I know," she said. She took a deep breath and dived back in[3]. "I'd started to become desperate for a way to get rid of[4] Stewart, so two days earlier, I dropped the big atom bomb on him[5]. Or I threatened to[6]. I mean, I would never go through with it[7]. But just the threat, I figured, would be enough."

Broome had a pretty good idea where she was going with this, but he waited.

"So anyway, yeah, I told Stewart that if he didn't leave me alone[8], I was going to tell his wife[9]. I would never have really done it. I mean, once that bomb is dropped, the radioactivity will blow back in your face[10]. But like I said, the threat is usually enough."

"But not in this case," Broome said.

"No." She smiled again, but there was no playfulness there now[11]. "To paraphrase that guy giving the warning, I underestimated[12] what would happen when I opened that big ol' can of crazy."

Broome looked over at Harry Sutton. Sutton was leaning forward, his face full of concern[13].

"What did happen when you made the threat?" Broome asked.

Tears came to her eyes. She blinked them away. Her voice, when she found it[14], was soft. "It was bad."

Silence.

"You could have come to me[15]," Broome said.

She said nothing.

"You could have. Before you threatened the bomb."

"And what exactly would you have done, Detective?"

He said nothing.

"You cops always defend us working girls[16] against the real citizens[17]."

"That's not fair[18], Cassie. If he hurt you, you could have told me."

She shook her head. "Maybe, maybe not. But you don't get it. He was stone-cold crazy[1]. He said if I breathed a word[2], he'd use a blowtorch[3] on me and make me tell him where my friends lived and then he'd go find them and kill them too. And I believed him. After what I saw in his eyes—after what he did to me—I believed every word."

Broome let it sit a moment. Then he asked, "So what did you do?"

"I decided that maybe I should go away for a while. You know, just disappear for a month or two. He'd get tired of me[4], move on with his life, go back to his wife, whatever. But even that was scary. I didn't know what he'd do if I just left without his permission."

She stopped. Broome gave her a moment. Then he prompted her a bit[5].

"You said you were at the park?"

She nodded.

"Where at the park?"

Broome waited. When she'd first entered the room— heck, when Broome thought back to what she'd been like in her younger days—there was a calmness about her[6], a confidence[7]. It was gone now. She looked down at her hands, wringing them[8] in her lap[9].

"So I was on this path," she said. "It was dark out. I was alone. And then I heard something up ahead[10]. Coming from behind the bush[11]."

She stopped and put her head down[12]. Broome tried to get her back on track[13] with a softball[14]: "What did it sound like?"

"A rustling[15]," she said. "Like maybe there was an animal. But then the sound grew louder[16]. And I heard someone—a person—cry out[17]."

Again she stopped and looked away[18].

"What did you do next?" Broome asked.

"I was unarmed[19]. I was alone. I mean, what could I do?" She looked at him as though she expected an answer. When he didn't give one she said, "At first I just

1. complètement maboul

2. que si j'en soufflais mot

3. un chalumeau

4. Il se lasserait de moi

5. il essaya de la faire parler un peu plus

6. elle dégageait une sorte de sérénité

7. air sûr de soi

8. qu'elle tordait

9. sur ses genoux

10. un bruit devant moi

11. le buisson

12. baissa la tête

13. de lui faire reprendre le fil

14. sans la brusquer

15. bruissement

16. s'intensifia

17. appeler au secours

18. détourna le regard

19. n'avais pas d'arme sur moi

reacted. I started to turn away[1], but something happened that made me pull up[2]."

"What?"

"Everything went quiet.[3] Like someone had flicked a switch[4]. Total silence. I waited for a few seconds. But there was nothing. The only thing I could hear now was my own breathing[5]. I pressed up against this big rock[6] and slowly moved around it—toward where I heard the noises before. I finally turned the corner, and he was there."

"Stewart Green?"

She nodded.

Broome's mouth felt dry[7]. "When you say 'he was there' … ?"

"He was lying on his back. His eyes were closed. I bent down[8] and touched him. He was covered in blood[9]."

"Stewart?"

She nodded.

Broome felt his heart sink[10]. "Was he dead?"

"I thought so."

A hint of impatience sneaked[11] into his voice. "What do you mean, 'thought so'?"

"I'm neither a psychiatrist nor a physician," she snapped back[12]. "I can only tell you what I thought. I thought that he was dead. But I didn't check for a pulse[13] or anything. I already had his blood all over me, and I was completely freaking out[14]. It was so weird. For a moment, everything slowed down[15], and I was almost happy. I know how that sounds, but I hated him. You have no idea how much. And my problem, well, it was taken care of now. Stewart was dead. But then I quickly sobered up[16]. I realized what would happen, and please don't tell me I'm being unfair. I could almost see exactly how it'd go. I'd run back down[17] to a phone booth[18]—I didn't have a cell phone back then[19], did anyone?—and I'd call and report it and you cops would look into it[20] and you'd find out how he was harassing me[1] and worse. Everyone would say what a nice family man he was and how this stripper-whore had taken him for all he was worth[2] and, and, well, you see what I mean. So I ran. I ran, and I never looked back[3]."

"Where did you go?"

Harry Sutton coughed into his fist[4]. "Irrelevant[5], Detective. This is where her story ends for you."

Broome looked at him. "You're kidding[6], right?"

"We had a deal."

Cassie said, "It's the truth, Detective."

He was about to call her on it[7]—tell her, no, it's at best[8] the partial truth—but he didn't want to chase her away[9]. He tried to ask for some details, hoping to learn more or figure out what was what. Mostly[10] he wanted to know how badly injured (or, uh, dead) Stewart Green was, but if there was more to mine[11] here, he wasn't getting it[12].

Finally Harry Sutton said, "I think you've learned all you can here, Detective."

Had he? What had he learned in the end? He felt just as lost as before—maybe more so. Broome thought about the other men, the connections, all those men gone missing. Had they been killed? Had they been injured and, what, run off[13]? Stewart Green had been the first. That much Broome was pretty sure about.[14] Did he recover from this attack and ... ?

And what?

Where the hell was he?[15] And how did this connect to Carlton Flynn and the others?

Cassie rose. His eyes followed her. "Why?" Broome asked.

"Why what?"

"You could have stayed hidden[16], kept your new life safe." He glanced at Harry Sutton and then back to her. "Why come back?"

1. qui révélerait qu'il me harcelait

2. avait profité de lui un maximum

3. sans un regard en arrière

4. toussa dans son poing

5. Peu importe

6. Vous plaisantez

7. sur le point de la contredire

8. au mieux

9. la faire fuir

10. Surtout,

11. s'il y avait plus à découvrir

12. on ne voulait pas le lui donner

13. pris la fuite

14. Broome était au moins à peu près sûr de ça.

15. Où diable était-il ?

16. cachée

1. Vous m'auriez cherchée des années

2. se rencontrer

3. l'heure et le lieu

4. d'attendre que vous débarquiez sur mon palier

5. Je n'y crois pas.

6. Je ne fais pas beaucoup d'efforts pour vous convaincre.

7. votre petite vie bien réglée

8. une façon de vous purifier

9. de renverser les rôles

10. d'en tirer des conclusions

11. Vous essayez de jouer sur les mots

12. avant de répondre

13. un détective privé

14. engagé

15. pour dénicher des ragots sur

16. Ce qui m'intéresse, c'est d'élucider

17. Point final.

18. C'est logique

19. poignée de la porte

"You're Javert, remember?" she said. "You'd hunt me across the years[1]. Eventually Javert and Valjean have to meet up[2]."

"So you decided to control the time and place[3]?"

"Better than you just showing up on my doorstep[4], right?"

Broome shook his head. "I don't buy it.[5]"

She shrugged. "I'm not trying that hard to sell it.[6]"

"So is that it, Cassie? You're done here?"

"I'm not sure I understand."

Oh, but she did. He could see it in her eyes.

"Do you just go back to your regularly scheduled life[7] now?" Broome asked. "Has this been cleansing[8] for you? Did it give you everything you need?"

"I think it has," she said. "Do you mind if I ask you a question?"

Trying to turn the tables[9], Broome thought. Defensive. The question was, why? He gestured for her to go ahead.

"What do you do with this information?" she asked.

"I add it to the other evidence I have and try to draw conclusions[10]."

"Did you ever tell Stewart Green's wife the truth about him?"

"Depends on whose truth."

"You're playing semantics with me[11], Detective."

"Fair enough. Before now, I only heard rumors about Stewart Green. I really didn't know for sure."

"Will you tell his wife now that you know?"

Broome took his time with that one[12]. "If I think it will help find what happened to him, yeah, I'll say something to her. But I'm not a private eye[13] hired[14] to dig up dirt on[15] the man."

"It may make it easier for her to move on."

"Or it may make it harder," he said. "My concern is solving[16] crimes. Period.[17]"

"Makes sense[18]," she said with a nod, reaching for the doorknob[19]. "Good luck with the case."

"Uh, before you go …"

She stopped.

"There's one big thing we've been dancing around[1], what with all our[2] clever Victor Hugo references[3]."

"What's that?"

Broome smiled. "The timing of[4] this little meeting."

"What about it?"

"Why now? Why, after seventeen years, did you choose to return now?"

"You know why."

He shook his head. "I don't, no."

She looked toward Harry for guidance[5]. He shrugged his shoulders. "I know about the other man vanishing."

"I see. How did you learn about him?"

"I saw it on the news," she said.

Another lie.

"And, what, you see a connection between what happened to Stewart Green and what happened to Carlton Flynn?"

"Other than the obvious[6]?" she said. "Not really, no."

"So hearing about it sort of reminded you of the past? Brought it back to you somehow[7]?"

"It's not that simple." She looked down at her hands again. Broome could see it now. There had been a ring on her wedding finger[8]. He could see the tan line[9]. She had taken it off[10], probably for this meeting, and didn't feel comfortable[11] without that. That explained all the hand wringing. "What happened that night … it never really left me. I ran away. I changed my name. I built a new life. But that night followed me everywhere[12]. It still does. I guess I thought that maybe it was time to stop running[13]. I thought that maybe it was time to confront it[14] once and for all[15]."

---

1. un sujet important que nous n'avons pas abordé

2. à force d'

3. allusions à Victor Hugo

4. Le moment choisi pour

5. consulta Harry du regard

6. les aspects évidents

7. À fait resurgir des souvenirs

8. une alliance à son annulaire gauche

9. la marque du bronzage

10. l'avait retirée

11. ne se sentait pas à l'aise

12. m'a suivie partout

13. que j'arrête de courir

14. d'y faire face

15. une fois pour toutes

11

1. extrêmement
branchées
2. cette mission
3. sans problème
4. savait si bien
obtenir des
informations
5. fer à souder
6. une extrémité
plus fine
7. de plus de
500°C
8. le tester
9. la faisait
beaucoup
souffrir
10. était
allongée sur le
dos
11. et se tenait
le nez
12. chaussures
de sport
13. poitrine

EVERYONE called them Ken and Barbie.

So, to be safe—and because secret identities were awfully cool[1]—they started calling themselves that too.

Tawny's broken finger had made this particular assignment[2] ridiculously easy and unchallenging[3]. Barbie had been a little disappointed by that. She was so good at extracting information[4]. Creative. She had a new soldering iron[5] with a finer tip[6], one that reached heat in excess of one thousand degrees Fahrenheit[7], and she really wanted to try it out[8].

But creativity meant improvising. Ken had seen right away that Tawny had a broken finger that was causing her great distress[9]. Why not use it?

After Ken punched Tawny in the face, Barbie had locked the door. Tawny lay on her back[10], holding her nose[11]. Ken put one of his Keds[12] on her chest[13], in the spot between her huge fake breasts, pinning her

102

hard[1] to the floor. He lifted her right hand toward the ceiling[2]. Tawny bucked in pain[3].

"It's okay," he said soothingly[4].

Using his foot as leverage[5], Ken pulled Tawny's arm straight and then wrapped her in an elbow lock[6]. She couldn't move. The hand with the broken finger was exposed and completely vulnerable. He nodded at Barbie.

Barbie smiled and retied[7] her ponytail. Ken loved to watch her, the way she took her own hair in her hand, the way she pulled it back, the way it exposed the softness of her neck[8]. Barbie approached the finger and studied it for a moment.

First, Barbie flicked the broken digit[9] with her own middle finger[10]. Not hard. Just a routine twang[11]. But her eyes lit up[12] when Tawny cried out in pain. Barbie slowly wrapped her four fingers around the broken finger, making her hand into a fist[13]. Tawny moaned[14]. Barbie paused, a small smile on her face. The dog, Ralphie, maybe sensing what was about to happen, scampered to the far corner[15] and whimpered[16]. Barbie looked over at Ken. Ken smiled too. She nodded at him.

"Please," Tawny said through her tears. "Please tell me what you want."

Barbie smiled down at her. Then, without any warning[17], Barbie pulled the broken finger back so far that the finger hit the back of Tawny's wrist[18]. Ken was ready. He moved his foot from Tawny's chest to her mouth, stifling[19] the long, dark[20] scream. Barbie regripped the[21] finger. She started pulling it back and forth as though it were a joystick[22] on one of those horrible video game systems or maybe something stuck in the mud[23] she was trying to break free[24].

Eventually, the jagged edge[25] of the bone broke through, shredding the skin[26] and bandaging.

Then—and only then—did they ask Tawny where Carlton Flynn was.

1. la plaquant
2. plafond
3. s'arc-bouta de douleur
4. d'un ton apaisant
5. pour faire levier
6. le bloqua de son coude à lui
7. resserra
8. la peau douce de son cou
9. appuya sur le doigt cassé
10. majeur
11. une chiquenaude
12. son regard s'éclaira
13. en fermant le poing
14. poussa un cri plaintif
15. fila à l'autre bout de la pièce
16. gémit
17. sans prévenir
18. poignet
19. étouffant
20. sinistre
21. se saisit à nouveau du
22. une manette
23. coincé dans la boue
24. d'extirper
25. le côté fracturé
26. déchirant la peau

1. ayant dû
deux fois lui
faire reprendre
connaissance

2. sans être
consciencieux

3. recueilli

4. avoir
temporairement
perdu la raison

5. dans un délire

6. fulmina
contre

7. du fait qu'il
ne s'était jamais
pointé

8. malheureuse-
ment

9. gisait

10. poupée de
chiffon

11. marmonnait
de façon
incohérente

12. de le
réconforter

13. une tiédeur
l'envahir

14. La liste de
chansons

15. garde
l'esprit ouvert

16. commencer le
spectacle par

17. couler

18. Juste avant
la fin

But now, forty minutes later, reviving her twice from blacking out[1], they knew for sure that Tawny did not know. In truth they knew it earlier but Ken and Barbie did not get where they were today by not being thorough[2].

They had, however, gathered[3] some potentially useful information. After the pain became too much—after her sanity had temporarily fled[4]—Tawny just started talking in a delirious flow[5]. She ranted about[6] her childhood; her sister, Beth; her thinking that they, Ken and Barbie, were angels sent to help her. She told them about a cop named Broome and her boss, Rudy, and other people at the club. She told them about Carlton Flynn, about how he had been the one to break her finger, about how he hadn't showed up[7] on that last night.

But, sadly[8], Tawny didn't know where Carlton Flynn was now.

Tawny lay[9] on the floor like a broken rag doll[10]. She was mumbling incoherently to herself[11]. Barbie was petting Ralphie, the dog, trying to comfort him[12]. She smiled up at Ken, and he felt his entire being go warm[13].

"What are you thinking about?" he asked her.

"The playlist[14]."

He wasn't surprised. Barbie was such a perfectionist. "What about it?"

"Please be open-minded[15]," she said.

"I will."

"Promise?"

"I promise."

Barbie sighed, and again she retied the ponytail. "I think we should open the show with[16] 'Let the River Flow[17]' and then move into 'What Color Is God's Skin?' "

Ken thought about it. "When do we go into 'Freedom Isn't Free'?"

"Right before the closer[18]."

"That's awfully late.[1]"

"I think it will work."

"It will only work," he said, "if we use jazz hands[2] in the choreography."

Barbie frowned[3]. "You know how I feel about jazz hands."

Ken and Barbie were both counselors[4] at Camp SonLit. The T at the end was in the shape of a cross[5]. That was where they met and first … connected[6]. Oh, but not like that. It was all very appropriate[7]. They had both, in fact, taken a chastity pledge[8], something Ken believed gave them discipline and helped them focus their energy.

Ken had been something of a celebrity at the camp, and so Barbie made it a point[9] to meet and befriend him[10]. The year before, Ken had been a featured[11] singer with the ultraexclusive Up with People, performing[12] around the world with the famed[13] "leadership" organization. It wasn't love at first sight[14], but there was an immediate draw[15], something deep inside that drew them to each other. They both felt it. Neither knew what it was—until another counselor named Doug Waites crossed their path[16].

Waites was a senior[17] counselor, in charge of the boys ages ten to twelve. One night, after the campers had been put to bed and night prayers[18] were over, Barbie had come to Ken for help. Waites would not leave her alone, Barbie told him. Waites asked her out[19] repeatedly. He looked down her shirt[20] whenever there was an opportunity[21]. He spoke to her in an inappropriate way and treated her in a manner she found disrespectful[22].

Ken's hands had tightened into fists as he heard all this.

When Barbie finished telling him about Waites's transgressions, Ken made a suggestion. He told her that next time Waites asked her out, she should tell him to meet her in a secluded spot[23] in the woods at

1. C'est vraiment un peu tard.

2. [geste chorégraphique style pom-pom girl : mouvements des mains, doigts écartés]

3. fronça les sourcils

4. animateurs

5. en forme de croix

6. s'étaient rapprochés

7. comme il faut

8. fait vœu de chasteté

9. fit exprès

10. de devenir amie avec lui

11. vedette

12. en tournée

13. célèbre

14. n'avait pas été le coup de foudre

15. attirance

16. n'ait croisé leur chemin

17. chef

18. les prières du soir

19. lui proposait des sorties ensemble

20. son décolleté

21. en toute occasion

22. qu'elle trouvait irrespectueuse

23. endroit isolé

105

1. s'enflamma
2. soi-disant
3. prit les choses en main
4. hypnotisée
5. un voyage avec d'autres adolescents
6. qui représentaient des scènes de l'enfer particulièrement atroces
7. sans manches
8. des tisonniers brûlants
9. leurs parties génitales
10. De façon très visible
11. avaient trouvé cela répugnant
12. lui avait donné des frissons [de plaisir]
13. quand le besoin s'en faisait sentir
14. harcelait
15. apportait de l'alcool en douce dans la colo
16. jeune pervers
17. avait souillé un soutien-gorge
18. mafieux haut placé

an hour of their choosing. Barbie's eyes fired up[1] in a way Ken would grow to love.

Two nights later, after bedtime prayers and all the campers were sound asleep, Doug Waites made his way to that spot deep in the woods for his alleged[2] rendezvous with Barbie. Ken took over from there[3]. Barbie watched, mesmerized[4], fascinated. She had always been drawn to pain. During a teen tour[5] to Florence, Italy, she remembered visiting the famed Duomo cathedral in the center of the city. On the ceiling of the dome were frescos depicting the most gruesome scenes of hell[6]. Here, in a sacred church where you were not allowed to wear shorts or sleeveless[7] dresses, there were naked people—sinners—having hot pokers[8] inserted into their rectums and private parts[9]. Clear as day[10]. Easy for any tourist to see. Most of the teens had been repulsed[11]. But some, like Barbie, couldn't turn away. The agony on the faces of those sinners drew her, captivated her, made her tingle[12].

When Ken finally untied Doug Waites, he left him with a simple warning: "If you ever speak of this, I will come back and it will be worse for you."

For the next two days, Doug Waites did not speak at all. He was taken away on the third day. Neither Ken nor Barbie ever heard from Waites again.

They continued as counselors, occasionally disciplining others when the need arose[13]. There was the nasty boy who mercilessly bullied[14] others. There was another counselor who sneaked alcohol into the camp[15] and gave it to the young campers. Both were taken to that same spot in the woods.

At one point, Ken and Barbie made what some might consider a mistake. They had tortured a filthy young man[16]—he had sneaked into a girl's cabin and defiled someone's brassiere[17]—but they didn't realize that the filthy young man's father was a leading mobster[18] from New York City. When his father learned what happened—tormenting his son until he spilled the beans[1]—he sent his two best soldiers to "take care" of Ken and Barbie. But Ken and Barbie were no slack amateurs anymore[2]. When the two mobsters came for them, Ken and Barbie were ready. They turned the tables on them. Ken killed one of them with his bare hands[3]. The other had been captured and taken into the woods. Barbie took her time with him. She was more thorough than ever. Eventually they had let the other soldier live, though in his case, it probably would have been kinder to have put him down[4].

When word got back to the father-mobster who had put out the original hit[5], he had been duly impressed[6]—and maybe scared[7]. Instead of sending out more soldiers, he offered them both peace and work. Ken and Barbie agreed[8]. These were, they realized, bad guys hurting other bad guys. It felt to them like destiny. When camp ended, they left their respective families, telling their loved ones that they would be traveling missionaries[9], which, in some sense[10], was true.

The cell phone rang. Ken picked it up[11] and said, "Good afternoon, Mr. Goldberg!"

When he finished the call, Barbie moved toward him[12]. "We have another lead[13]?"

"We do."

"Tell me."

"An attorney named Harry Sutton. He represents whores."

Barbie nodded.

They both knelt down[14] next to Tawny. Tawny began to cry.

"You get it now," Ken said to her. "How wrong this life is for you."

Tawny continued to cry.

1. jusqu'à ce qu'il crache le morceau
2. n'étaient plus des amateurs
3. à mains nues
4. de l'avoir achevé
5. avait envoyé ses tueurs
6. favorablement impressionné
7. voire effrayé
8. acceptèrent
9. qu'ils allaient devenir missionnaires itinérants
10. en un sens
11. décrocha
12. s'approcha de lui
13. piste
14. s'agenouillèrent

1. pour quitter la ville
2. de rentrer directement chez elle
3. la décision raisonnable à prendre
4. avait contribué comme elle pouvait
5. de retourner à l'abri dans son cocon
6. Au lieu de ça,
7. se dirigea vers
8. dans le coin sombre au fond de la salle
9. C'est sa vieille copine Lorraine qui tenait le bar.
10. Qu'est-ce que je te sers ?
11. avec des glaçons
12. rondelles de citron vert
13. la marque Truc
14. allongée d'eau
15. versée d'
16. détestait
17. les textos
18. c'était parfois bien utile, la preuve :
19. déceler le mensonge dans sa voix
20. ni lui poser
21. sirotait son verre
22. de temps en temps
23. lui ai fait une passe à l'œil

"We will give you a chance," Barbie said, her smile beatific. She reached into her handbag and pulled something out. "This is a bus ticket out of here[1]."

"You'll use it?" Ken asked.

Tawny nodded vigorously.

"When you first saw us," Barbie said, "you thought we were angels sent to save you."

"Maybe," Ken added, "you were right."

MEGAN had planned to go straight home[2].

That would have been the prudent course to take[3]. She had done her bit[4]—or as much of it as she could—and now it was time to slip back into her safe cocoon[5].

Instead[6] she headed over to[7] La Crème.

She sat now at the bar, the one in the far back dark corner[8]. Her old friend Lorraine was working it.[9] When she first entered, Lorraine had said, "Am I supposed to be surprised?"

"I guess not."

"What can I get you?[10]"

Megan pointed at the bottle behind Lorraine. "Grey Goose on the rocks[11] with four limes[12]."

Lorraine frowned. "Instead of Grey Goose, how about Brand X[13] watered down[14] and poured from[15] a Grey Goose bottle?"

"Even better."

While Megan, like most adults, bemoaned[16] e-mails and texting[17], here was where it came in handy:[18] She'd texted Dave that she'd be home late tonight, knowing, of course, that he wouldn't be able to hear the lie in her tone[19] or follow up with[20] too many questions.

She nursed the drink[21] and told Lorraine about her visit with Broome.

"Do you remember him?" Megan asked.

"Broome? Sure. I still see him on occasion[22]. Good guy. I threw him a one-timer[23], what, nine, ten years ago."

"You're kidding."

"Love me for my generosity of heart." Lorraine cleaned a glass with an old rag[1] and offered up that smile. "Actually I liked him."

"You like everybody."

"Generosity of heart."

"Not to mention body."

Lorraine spread her arms. "Be a shame to let this go to waste.[2]"

"Truer words."

"So," Lorraine said, stretching out the word[3], "did you tell Broome about my maybe seeing Stewart Green?"

"No."

"Why not?"

"I didn't know if you'd want me to."

"Could be important," Lorraine said.

"Could be."

Lorraine kept cleaning the same glass. Then: "It probably wasn't Stewart I saw."

Megan said nothing.

"I mean, it probably just looked like him[4]. Now that I hear your story, I mean, you saw him dead, right?"

"Maybe."

"So if you saw him dead, then I couldn't have seen him alive[5]." Lorraine shook her head. "Man[6], did I just say that? I need a drink. Either way[7], I was probably wrong[8]."

"Hell of a thing to be wrong about[9]," Megan said.

"Yeah, well." Lorraine put the glass down. "But for the sake of argument, let's say[10] I did see Stewart Green."

"Okay."

"Where has he been for the past seventeen years? What's he been doing all that time?"

"And," Megan added, "why come back now?"

"Exactly," Lorraine said.

"Maybe we should tell Broome."

1. vieux torchon

2. Ce serait dommage de gâcher tout ça.

3. avec insistance

4. c'était sans doute juste quelqu'un qui lui ressemblait

5. vivant

6. Bon sang

7. De toute façon

8. je me suis sûrement trompée

9. Impossible de se tromper sur ce genre de choses

10. pour les besoins de la discussion, imaginons

Lorraine thought about it. "Maybe."

"I mean, if he's back …"

"Yeah, tell him," Lorraine said, snapping the rag across the bar[1]. "But don't tell him who you heard it from[2], okay?"

"You will remain uninvolved[3]."

"The way I like it[4]."

"Despite your generosity of heart."

Lorraine was cleaning a glass with too much intensity[5]. "So now what, sweetheart[6]?"

Megan shrugged. "I go home."

"Just like that?"

"If Stewart Green really is back …" The thought made her shudder[7].

"You'd be in serious danger[8]," Lorraine said.

"Right."

Lorraine leaned on the bar. Her perfume smelled of jasmine[9]. "Did Broome ask why you came back?"

"Yep."

"And you gave him all that talk about needing to find[10] the truth."

"Talk?"

"Yeah," Lorraine said, "talk. You've been gone for seventeen years. All of a sudden[11] you need to find the truth?"

"Whoa, what are you talking about? You came to me, remember?"

"That's not what I mean," Lorraine said. Her voice grew gentle[12]. "You were coming down here already, right?"

Megan shifted on the barstool[13]. "One time."

"Fine, one time. Why?"

A patron came over and placed an order[14]. Lorraine served up a drink and a double entendre[15]. The patron laughed and took his drink back to his table.

"Lorraine?"

"What, sugar[16]?"

"What's the secret of happiness?"

1. en faisant claquer le torchon sur le bar
2. qui te l'a dit
3. hors du coup
4. C'est tout ce que je voulais entendre
5. un peu trop énergiquement
6. ma chérie
7. la fit frémir
8. Tu es vraiment en danger
9. sentait le jasmin
10. lui as servi le truc habituel comme quoi il te fallait découvrir
11. Tout d'un coup,
12. se radoucit
13. tabouret de bar
14. passa une commande
15. remarque un peu osée
16. mon cœur

"The little things."

"Like?"

"Change the drapes[1]. You won't believe how far that goes.[2]"

Megan looked doubtful[3].

"Oh, honey, I'm as messed up as the rest[4]. I just learned not to care so much[5]. You know? We fight wars for freedom[6], right, and then what do we do with that freedom? We tie ourselves down[7] with possessions and debt[8] and, well, other people. If I seem happy, it's because I do what I want when I want."

Megan finished the drink and signaled for another[9]. "I'm happy," Megan said. "I'm just feeling antsy.[10]"

"That's normal. I mean, who doesn't? You got good kids, right?"

"The best," Megan said, feeling herself light up[11] despite herself. "I love them so much it hurts."

"See? That's great, but it wouldn't be for me[12]."

Megan eyed the drink, enjoying the warmth of it[13]. "You know what sucks about being a[14] mother?"

"Diapers?[15]"

"Well, yes. But I mean now. Now that they are older and more or less real human beings[16]."

"What?"

"You live for their smile."

Lorraine waited for her to say more. When she didn't, Lorraine said, "Care to elaborate?[17]"

"When something goes well for them—like with Kaylie, if she scores[18] in her soccer game—I mean, when your child smiles, you well up[19]. You are so damned happy, but then, well, see, when they don't …"

"You're unhappy," Lorraine said.

"It's a little more complicated, but yes. That's what I hate: My happiness is totally dependent on their smiles. And I'm not one of those parents who live vicariously[20] through their kids' accomplishments[21]. I just want them happy. But I used to be a functioning

---

1. les rideaux

2. Tu n'imagines pas à quel point ça te fera du bien.

3. parut sceptique

4. aussi à la masse que les autres

5. à ne pas prendre les choses trop à cœur

6. la liberté

7. On s'encombre

8. des dettes

9. fit signe qu'elle en voulait un autre

10. J'ai juste la bougeotte.

11. consciente que son visage s'éclairait

12. ce n'est pas mon truc

13. apaisée par le réconfort qu'il apportait

14. ce qui craint, quand on est

15. Les couches ?

16. de vraies personnes

17. Tu veux développer ?

18. marque un but

19. tu es tout émue

20. par procuration

21. talents

adult with my own emotions. Now, as a mother, my happiness seems solely dependent on[1] their smiles. They know it too[2]."

"Interesting," Lorraine said. "You know what it sounds like?"

"What?"

"An abusive relationship[3]. Like with my ex. You start to live to please them. They manipulate you with their moods."

"That's a little harsh[4]."

"Yeah, probably," Lorraine said, clearly not buying it[5] but not in the mood to argue the point[6]. "So you still haven't told me why you really came back down here. I mean, before my visit."

The simple answer: Megan had missed it. She was about to tell Lorraine that, but Lorraine was staring off to her right[7]. Megan followed her gaze[8]. She frowned when she saw where Lorraine was looking.

"Ray's table," Megan said.

"Yep."

The table was empty now, but that had been *his* table—the corner where Ray used to sit. She had blocked on him[9]. Man oh man, how she had blocked on him. Now, for just a second, she let Ray back in[10]. Over the years, she had turned their relationship into something of a crush[11], a deep, hard summer romance[12] that could never have survived the light of reality[13]. But now, for a brief moment, she let herself remember the intense way Ray used to look at her, the electricity in his kiss, the late nights holding on to him for dear life[14], nearly out of breath[15] with passion.

Lorraine was smiling now.

"Subtle[16]," Megan said to her.

"Yeah."

"Do you know what happened to him[17]?"

The smile fled[18]. "You really want to know?"

"You opened this door.[19]"

"No, sweetheart, you did. I'm just trying to help you close it."

She had a point[1]. "So help me. Is he okay?"

Lorraine again made herself busy with the glass cleaning.

"Lorraine?"

"For a while[2]—I mean, after you ran off—he came in here every night. He sat at that table and drank. During the day he'd hang out at your place[3]. This went on for[4], I don't know, a couple of months, I guess. Maybe a year. He just waited for you to come back."

Megan said nothing.

"It got bad[5]. Eventually he stopped[6] coming in. He left Atlantic City. Moved[7] to California, I think. Drank some more. Came back." She shrugged.

Megan sat there, let it sink in[8]. She had owed him better.[9] She had been young and maybe stupid, but then again what were the alternatives[10]? Lorraine was looking at her now. She wouldn't ask but Megan could see the question in her eyes: *Why didn't you at least call him?* She looked away so her eyes wouldn't give away the answer[11]: *Because I wasn't sure that he wasn't a murderer[12]*.

Only now, of course, reality had shifted[13]. Stewart Green might not be dead at all. And if Stewart Green wasn't dead …

Lorraine had an odd look on her face.

"What?" Megan said.

"Nothing."

"So where is Ray now?" Megan asked.

"He's around[14], I guess."

"You guess? Come on, Lorraine. Tell me what he's doing. Is he still working as a photographer?"

Lorraine winced[15]. "In a manner of speaking[16]."

"What? Oh, wait, he's not into porn[17], is he?"

"No, honey, porn is way classier than[18] what Ray's doing."

"What's that supposed to mean? What's he doing?"

---

1. n'avait pas tort

2. Pendant un certain temps

3. il traînait chez toi

4. Ça a duré

5. Ça a empiré

6. Il a fini par ne plus

7. Est parti vivre

8. essayant d'assimiler tout ça

9. Il n'avait pas mérité ça de sa part.

10. quel autre choix avait-elle

11. pour qu'on ne lise pas la réponse dans ses yeux

12. meurtrier

13. la situation avait changé

14. dans les parages

15. fit la grimace

16. En quelque sorte

17. il ne donne pas dans le porno

18. est bien plus classieux que

1. foutre en
l'air ta vie bien
rangée

2. se dirigea
vers un tiroir

3. en sortit

4. fichier

5. griffonna
quelque chose
au dos

6. étoile

7. [célèbre
trottoir
d'Hollywood, où
certaines stars
ont une étoile et
leur nom]

8. le bar que
Ray fréquente

9. Le type
pour qui Ray
travaille.

10. au bout de
la rue

11. Coureur de
femmes rondes

12. L'avantage
de vieillir

13. c'est que je
plais à tout le
monde

14. les minets
ou amateurs de
femmes mûres

15. J'ai de quoi
satisfaire tous
les goûts.

16. Oui, en
gros.

"Look," Lorraine said, "who am I to judge? You want to screw up your little life[1], fine, here." She headed for the drawer[2] and pulled out[3] a long metal box. Megan almost smiled, remembering. Lorraine's magic business-card file[4] of contacts.

"You still keep that?" Megan asked.

"Of course. I even keep them in preference order. Let me see. … Ah, here it is." She took out a card, turned it over, and scratched something on the back[5]. Megan took the card. The logo was what looked like a star[6] on the Hollywood Walk of Fame[7] with a camera in the middle. It read:

Celeb Experience: Paparazzi for Hire.

Oh man.

She turned the card over. Lorraine had written: *Weak Signal Bar and Grill*.

"Is this where Ray hangs out[8]?" Megan asked.

"No, but Fester does."

"Who?"

"Guy who Ray works for.[9] Fester. Used to be a bouncer back at that old club down the street[10], you don't remember him?"

"Should I?"

"Not really. Anyway, I've known Fester for years. Got him filed under 'Chubby Chaser[11].' The one benefit of age[12]— I got crossover appeal[13] now. I'm fat enough for the chubby chasers. I'm old enough for the cougar chasers or the MILF lovers[14], whatever. I'm like the complete package here.[15]"

Megan stared at the card.

"Do you want my advice?" Lorraine asked.

"Go home and change my drapes?"

"Pretty much, yeah.[16]"

114

12

1. allée

2. une maison
sur deux niveaux

3. revêtement
en briques et en
aluminium

4. gravit
les quelques
marches en
béton

5. bloquant
l'accès à

6. demeure
STRICTEMENT
sans prétention

7. expert-
comptable

8. On aurait pu
penser

9. que ça
le rendrait
terriblement
envieux

10. Oui et non.

11. le
soulagement

12. le sentiment
que ça aurait
très bien pu être
sa vie à lui, ça

13. patrouillant
ensemble

BROOME pulled his car into the driveway[1] of a split-level[2] with brick and aluminum siding[3]. He parked in front of the two-car garage below the bedroom window and started up the concrete steps[4]. A tricycle was on its side, blocking the path to[5] the door. This oh-so-ordinary dwelling[6] was where ACPD Detective Erin Anderson, the only woman Broome would ever love, lived with her husband, a CPA[7] named Sean.

Whenever he visited, Broome couldn't help but think, *It could have been me.* One would have thought[8] that would lead to a strong yearning on his part[9]. It did and it didn't.[10] His most immediate and powerful reaction was relief[11]—a there-but-for-the-grace-of-God, whistling-past-the-graveyard sort of escape from his own destiny[12]. But then, well, he looked at Erin's face and all that fell away.

Years ago, he and Erin had started off as cop partners riding together[13]. They had quickly fallen deeply in love and married. That was the end of their riding together—no married couples in the same squad car[1]—and the beginning of their troubles[2]. The marriage, despite the love, was a disaster. That was how it worked sometimes. Marriage builds bonds[3] in some relationships. It destroys everything in others.

He knocked on the door. Erin's four-year-old, Shamus, answered it, a melted[4] ice pop[5] lining his mouth red[6] and coloring his teeth. The kid looked exactly like his father, and for some reason that pissed Broome off[7]. "Hey, Uncle Broome."

Even kids called him Broome.

"Hey, kid. Where's Mom?"

"I'm in the kitchen," Erin shouted.

After he and Erin divorced, they petitioned[8] to ride again together as partners. It took a while, but permission was finally granted[9]. Balance was restored[10]—at least, their version of it. But they couldn't let each other go. Even as they tentatively[11] began to date[12] other people, Broome and Erin continued to sleep together on the side[13]. This went on for a long time. Too long. They would try to make themselves stop, but when you are in close proximity hour after hour, well, as they say, the flesh is weak[14]. They had hooked up[15] several times during her courtship with Sean, even as Sean and Erin grew serious[16], finally stopping once and for all when the new couple said, "I do."

But even now, even after all these years, the feelings were still there, that undercurrent. Last year, with two kids in tow[17] and twenty-five years on the job[18], Erin had taken early retirement[19]. Well, semiretirement— one day a week for managerial purposes[20]. Broome remained a part of her life. He came to her for advice[21]. He came to her for help on a case[22]. He came to her because even though she had clearly moved on and her new marriage made her happy and he had blown his best chance at true happiness[23], Broome was still in love with her.

The computer's wallpaper[1] was a family photo of Erin, Sean, the two kids, and the dog in front of the Christmas tree. Broome tried not to roll his eyes[2].

"How was your meeting with Cassie?" Erin asked.

"Strange."

"Do tell[3]."

He did. Erin wore a bright green polo shirt and a pink skirt that showed off[4] her legs. She always had great legs. She looked at him the way she always did, and he tried to pretend that it wasn't affecting him[5]. Erin was happy now. She was a mother and in love with Sean. Broome had been relegated to the[6] past, someone she still cared about and loved in a way, but nothing that kept her up at night anymore.

Part of him was glad about that. Most of him was heartbroken.[7]

When he finished Erin said, "So what do you make of it[8]?"

"Don't know."

"Any clue at all?[9]"

Broome thought about it. "She wasn't lying, but I don't think she was telling the entire truth. I need to look into it more." He gestured with his chin toward[10] the laptop and files. "What have you got?"

Her smile said that she found something big[11]. "The surveillance videos from La Crème."

"What about them[12]?"

"I've been going through them."

Erin clicked a button on the keyboard[13]. The Anderson family Christmas picture vanished, thank the Lord[14], and a still frame[15] from the video appeared. Erin hit[16] another key. The video came to life[17]. There were maybe two seconds of silence and then a group of clearly inebriated[18] men stumbled out the club's entrance[19].

"Did you see Carlton Flynn in any of the videos?" Broome asked.

"No."

1. fond d'écran	
2. lever les yeux au ciel	
3. Raconte.	
4. mettait en valeur	
5. ça ne l'émouvait pas	
6. faisait maintenant partie du	
7. D'un autre côté, il en restait inconsolable.	
8. qu'est-ce que tu en conclus	
9. Tu n'as aucune idée ?	
10. montra du menton	
11. quelque chose d'important	
12. Eh bien	
13. clavier	
14. Dieu merci	
15. un arrêt sur image	
16. appuya sur	
17. s'anima	
18. visiblement soûls	
19. sortit de la boîte en titubant	

"Then what?"

"Just watch," Erin said with the small smile on her face. "What do you see on the screen[1]?"

"A bunch[2] of drunk idiots leaving a strip joint."

"Look closer[3]."

He sighed and squinted at the screen[4]. She hit another key on the computer. Yet another group of drunks came stumbling out. She hit the key again. Another group. One more click of the key. This time, a couple came out, also clearly inebriated. The woman stopped suddenly, turned to the man, grabbed the beads[5] around the man's neck, and pulled him in for a hard kiss[6].

Broome frowned at the sight. He was about to ask her what the big deal was[7] when he stopped. Something clicked into place[8].

"Wait, go back one[9]."

Still smiling, Erin clicked the back button. Broome squinted again. The drunken men were wearing beads too. She clicked back again. The same thing. Broome thought back to his own work with the videos. So much drinking. So much partying.

And so many beads.

"Mardi Gras," Broome said softly.

"Bingo[10]," Erin said. "Now guess what day Mardi Gras was this year."

"February eighteenth."

"And for the bonus points[11], guess what day Mardi Gras was seventeen years ago."

"February eighteenth."

"Correct answers. Mardi Gras is a different date every year—the day before Ash Wednesday[12], forty-seven days before Easter[13]. So I checked[14] the other guys you had on your list. For example, when Gregg Wagman vanished three years ago on March fourth ... ?"

"It was Mardi Gras?"

Erin nodded[15]. "It pretty much fits[16] for every missing guy you have. I mean, some of the guys were re-

---

1. à l'écran
2. Un groupe
3. Regarde mieux
4. regarda l'écran en plissant les yeux
5. attrapa le collier de perles
6. le tira vers elle pour l'embrasser goulûment
7. ce qu'il y avait de si important
8. Ça fit tilt tout d'un coup
9. reviens à l'image d'avant
10. Gagné
11. pour quelques points de plus
12. le mercredi des Cendres
13. Pâques
14. j'ai vérifié
15. acquiesça de la tête
16. Ça correspond plus au moins

ported missing later—days or even weeks—but when I go through the file[1], none vanished *before* Mardi Gras. I'm not saying I can prove they all disappeared on that day—or in some cases, past midnight that night—but it all works into that nice little theory of yours[2]."

"So it isn't a particular day or month," Broome said.

"It is not."

"Whatever is going on," Broome said, "and we don't know what that is—it could be murders or runaways or who knows[3], but whatever is going on …"

Erin nodded. "It starts on Mardi Gras."

Broome's cell phone rang. He checked the caller ID and saw it was from the station[4]. "Hello?"

"Detective Broome?"

"Yes?"

"A photograph just arrived at the station. I think you're going to want to see it."

HARRY Sutton's law office offered up the perfect Atlantic City view. In the distance[5]—and by distance he only meant three blocks east—you could see the aging albeit still somewhat grand hotels[6] along the Boardwalk. But between those high-rises[7] and his shabby[8] office building was pretty much a vast wasteland of decay[9]. Whatever wealth[10] or beauty the hotels and casinos gave off[11], they were self-contained[12] and not the least bit contagious. There is no trickle down.[13] If the hotels are flowers, they remain stuck in the middle of the weeds[14].

It wasn't just that Harry liked the sex, gambling, and action of this city, though there was no doubt all of that was intoxicating[15]. It was that these people—the native population[16] if you will[17]—were also powerless. In his white-shoe-lawyer days[18], Harry had helped the most powerful, those who had the game of life ridiculously rigged for their benefit[19] from birth, yet still needed to cheat[20]. The people here were the dir-

1. d'après les dossiers

2. tout ça tend à confirmer ta petite théorie

3. que ce soient des meurtres, des disparitions volontaires, ou que sais-je

4. le commissariat

5. Au loin

6. les hôtels un peu décrépis bien qu'encore grandioses

7. grandes tours

8. miteux

9. une large zone très dégradée

10. richesse

11. arboraient

12. formaient des entités indépendantes

13. Il n'y a pas de retombée positive.

14. mauvaises herbes

15. enivrant

16. les autochtones

17. pour ainsi dire

18. Quand il était un avocat chic

19. à qui la vie souriait

20. de tricher

1. sans aucun avantage
2. s'appelait pas de chance
3. seraient passés à côté d'un coup de veine
4. sauf si ça devenait de la déveine
5. Peu importait s'ils étaient coupables ou innocents.
6. le bien et le mal
7. Quoi qu'il advienne dans leurs existences misérables
8. faisait en sorte qu'ils aient connu cette sensation
9. au moins une fois
10. Arrêtez votre numéro de charme
11. allez droit au but
12. tout de suite
13. Faites ce qu'il faut pour.
14. avait l'habitude de
15. ne l'impressionnait pas beaucoup
16. en quoi ça regarde
17. par courrier
18. sur ce coup

ect opposite. They had been born with nothing going for them[1]. The only luck they knew was bad[2]. They wouldn't know a break[3] unless it involved a bone[4].

What they needed, what they deserved, was to know what it was like—at least once in their lives—to have someone on their side. To be respected. Just once. Nothing more. Forget guilt or innocence[5]. Forget right or wrong[6]. Whatever else happened in their mostly pathetic lives[7], Harry Sutton would make sure that they knew that feeling[8] at least once[9].

That was why Harry Sutton had stayed in Atlantic City.

That and he loved the sex, gambling, and action.

The phone rang. He picked it up himself and said, "Harry Sutton, Attorney at Law."

"I need to see your client again."

It was Broome.

"Stop wearing me down with the charm[10] and get to the point[11]," Harry said.

"I need to see her right away[12]."

Harry didn't like the panic in the cop's voice. "I don't know if that's possible."

"Make it possible[13]."

Sutton was used to[14] cop impatience and intimidation. It didn't faze him much[15], but something odd was happening here. "What's wrong?"

"There have been new developments."

"Such as?"

"There may be other victims."

Silence.

"I don't see how that involves[16] my client."

"I got a photograph in the mail[17]."

"From whom?"

"I don't know. It came in anonymously. Look, just trust me here[18]. I need to know if she recognizes anyone or anything in it."

Sutton hesitated.

"Harry?"

120

"What?"

"You notice I'm not making any threats[1]. I'm not, for example, telling you that I could probably track her down[2] now and go to her house and tell her neighbors[3]. I'm not saying I'm going to get a composite sketch[4] of her in all the papers[5], stuff like that[6]."

"Well, it's reassuring to hear that you're keeping your word[7]."

"I don't have time for games, Harry. We could be dealing with a serial killer here[8]. I'm doing my best[9] to keep her out of it[10]. She came back to do the right thing. Let's let her finish the job."

"I can call and ask her," Harry said.

"A lot of things are breaking[11] so I need to stay close to the precinct[12]. Can you bring her down here?"

"To the precinct? You're joking, right?"

"It'll be fine."

"No, it won't. We'll meet you at the Heritage Diner." It was only a block from the precinct—not perfect but it would be okay.

"I need her here pronto[13]."

"Then let me go so I can call her," Harry said. "If you don't hear back from me[14], let's assume[15] we'll meet at the diner[16] in half an hour."

Harry hung up the phone and dialed[17] Cassie's cell phone. She answered on the third ring. "Hello?"

He heard noises in the background that strongly indicated[18] that she wasn't driving home. "Where are you?"

"At La Crème."

Harry Sutton wasn't surprised. Broome had seen it too. Something other than righting a wrong[19] had called her back here.

"I was about to call you," she said.

"Oh?"

"I want to tell Broome something important."

"Well, this will work out fine[20] then."

"Why? What's up?"

1. que je ne lance aucune menace

2. retrouver sa trace

3. voisins

4. un portrait-robot

5. journaux

6. ou ce genre de choses

7. vous tenez votre promesse

8. Il pourrait bien s'agir d'un tueur en série.

9. Je fais de mon mieux

10. pour ne pas l'impliquer

11. Ça se précipite pas mal,

12. commissariat

13. illico

14. Si je ne vous rappelle pas

15. disons que

16. au café

17. composa

18. laissaient présumer

19. le besoin de réparer un tort

20. ça tombe bien

Harry Sutton explained about Broome's call and his desire to meet at the Heritage Diner. "Is that okay for you?" he asked.

"I guess so," Cassie said. There was a brief pause[1]. "Do you have any idea what's in this photograph?"

"No, but Broome clearly thinks it's important. He said something about a serial killer."

Some men laughed in the background. Harry held on to the[2] phone and waited.

"Cassie?"

"Okay," she said. "I'll meet you at the diner in fifteen minutes."

Harry Sutton hung up the phone. He spun[3] his chair and took another look out the window at the familiar view of his city. There was a knock on the door.[4] He checked his watch.[5] Late. He didn't have time for any more business tonight, but it wasn't his way to send anyone away[6].

"Enter!" he shouted with his customary gusto[7].

A young couple who very much didn't belong[8] opened the door and stepped[9] into the office.

The pretty blond girl said, "Good evening, Mr. Sutton!"

They were both clean-cut[10] and smiling and neatly dressed[11], and for some reason, a reason Harry couldn't put his finger on[12]—a reason that he'd soon learn was primitive and instinctive and absolutely correct—Harry felt more fear than he'd ever felt in his life.

1. un silence

2. resta au

3. fit pivoter

4. On frappa à la porte.

5. Il regarda sa montre.

6. il n'était pas du genre à envoyer balader les gens

7. entrain habituel

8. qui faisaient un peu tache dans le décor

9. entrèrent

10. propres sur eux

11. bien habillés

12. qu'Harry avait du mal à cerner

13

STILL at La Crème, Megan fingered[1] the "Celeb Experience: Paparazzi for Hire" card. She flipped it over[2] and read "Weak Signal Bar and Grill." A text buzzed[3] her phone. She checked it and saw that it was from Dave:

WHERE ARE YOU???

She debated ignoring it[4], but really, how long could she do that? In the long run[5], it would cause more problems. She wondered about what to do here[6], what she should say now[7]—and what she would be forced to[8] tell him in the next few days. That façade she had created all those years ago had become over the years[9] more her than, uh, her[10]. But that didn't mean Dave would understand.

She looked at his simple message again: Where are you???

Façade, Megan knew, was really just a politically correct term for lie[11]. She had lied to Dave the first

1. tripotait

2. la retourna

3. L'arrivée d'un message fit vibrer

4. se demanda si elle allait l'ignorer

5. Au bout du compte

6. quoi faire

7. dès maintenant

8. ce qu'elle serait obligée de

9. avec le temps

10. plus réelle que ... la réalité

11. façon politiquement correcte de dire «mensonge»

1. à peine 4 mois
2. elle avait désespérément besoin d'argent
3. Sans avenir
4. en dévalisant des mecs
5. décontracté
6. étudiante [dans une université mixte]
7. en année de licence
8. prétendait-elle
9. traînait
10. versait un truc dans leur verre
11. leur volait leur fric
12. du centre-ville
13. Les hommes mariés se faisaient rares.
14. déboula dans l'hôtel
15. en criant
16. en beuglant
17. malgré leur air contents d'eux
18. les étudiants
19. avaient rarement du liquide sur eux
20. le destin
21. timide
22. Quelque chose en lui l'attira.
23. pas de coup de foudre
24. finissait ses études à
25. rendez-vous en tête à tête
26. bibliothèque
27. se contenta d'empiler quelques bouquins

time they met, at the hotel bar in Boston, a scant four months[1] after she had run away from Atlantic City. She was alone and scared and badly in need of cash[2]. With no prospects[3] and afraid to even work at one of the local clubs, Megan survived by rolling guys[4]. She'd dress in the casual[5] jeans look of a co-ed[6] ("I'm a senior[7] at Emerson," she'd claim[8]), hang out[9] at hotel bars, get guys (preferably married ones) drunk or sometimes slip something into their drink[10], take them upstairs to their rooms, rob them[11], and disappear into the night.

On that particular night, she decided to try the Loews downtown[12] hotel for the first time. The pickings in the married category had been slim[13]. A group of Harvard boys stumbled their way in[14], whooping[15] and hollering[16]. She tried not to hate them with their smug faces[17] and soft hands.

She figured that this would be easy money, though she knew college kids[18] rarely carried cash[19], and then something surprising happened. Who knew what? Call it fate or destiny[20] or whatever, but she started talking to one of them, a shy[21], sweet guy named Dave Pierce. Something about him simply drew her.[22] He made her feel warm and comfortable. It wasn't like with Ray. There was no immediate thunder crack[23]. That would come later. But there was something else, something deep and strong and real.

So she lied to him. What choice did she have?

They talked all night, and it was wonderful. He was graduating from[24] Harvard. She claimed to be graduating from Emerson. When they got together for their first real date[25] a week later, she even told him to meet her at the Emerson College library[26]. This was in the days before you needed student IDs to get into every building. She simply stacked a bunch of books[27] on a table and waited for him.

The lies just continued.

124

She knew plenty[1] about the campus. She told him that she lived in the Colonial Residence Hall but claimed that he couldn't stop by[2] because she had a difficult roommate[3] who hated company. In terms of family, she told him the truth—she was an only child and her parents had died young. She made up a fake, normal, boring childhood in Muncie, Indiana, and acted as though the memories of losing her parents made talking about it too much to bear[4]. Dave was sympathetic. If there were holes[5] in her story—and there were—Dave never looked too closely at them[6]. He was both[7] a trusting soul[8] and in love. If she chose to keep things from him[9], well, that added to the mystery and maybe even the attraction. In his naïve world, it couldn't be anything major. What difference could a few contradictory life details make anyway?

Plus[10] Maygin-Cassie-Megan was an awfully good liar[11].

But now the façade—read: lies[12]—were in serious jeopardy of crumbling[13]. After all the years, after all the hard work, she had chosen to risk it all. And for what? Righting the past[14]? A little excitement? Or subconsciously[15], did she want to get caught[16]? Was the mask simply too heavy to wear for the rest of her life?

How would Dave react to the truth[17]?

Megan took a deep breath and texted back:

THE PRESIERS ARE DRIVING KAYLIE'S CARPOOL TODAY. JORDAN HAS MATH TEST[18]. MAKE SURE HE STUDIES.

There was a brief pause and then another text from Dave:

WHERE ARE YOU?!?!?

1. en savait beaucoup
2. passer la voir
3. camarade de chambre
4. étaient bien trop pénibles à évoquer
5. des failles
6. n'y fit jamais très attention
7. à la fois
8. confiant par tempérament
9. avait choisi de lui cacher certaines choses
10. Et puis,
11. mentait très bien
12. ou plutôt les mensonges
13. risquait sérieusement de s'écrouler
14. Pour réparer le passé
15. inconsciemment
16. se faire choper
17. en apprenant la vérité
18. un contrôle de maths

Megan stared at the small screen for a moment. Then she typed[1]:

I HAVE SOMETHING I HAVE TO DO. NOT SURE WHEN I'LL BE HOME. LOVE YOU.

Another pause. Megan waited for the phone to ring[2]. It didn't. Instead[3] she received another text from her husband:

I DON'T UNDERSTAND.

She quickly replied.

IT WILL BE OKAY. JUST TRUST ME.

Ha. She meant it and really, when you thought about it, what a joke[4]. Trust me. Talk about irony[5]. She didn't wait for a reply. Time to visit Broome again.

She closed up her phone and started to rise from the barstool. The crowd was picking up[6], and Lorraine was busy. She nodded a good-bye at her old friend, and Lorraine arched an eyebrow in return[7]. She headed to the door, threading through[8] men who openly stared at her. In normal society, men want to stare like this, but we force them to be surreptitious[9]. In here, the cover charge[10] gives them the right to put such pretenses away[11].

She wondered for a brief second whether Dave had ever been to a place like this. If he had, he hadn't told her, but as she knew too well, most married men don't. Had he been to a club like this before? Would he too enjoy openly[12] ogling[13] or having a lap dance or what? Did it matter?

Fifteen minutes later, Megan entered the Heritage Diner. The place was wonderfully old-school[14]. The booths still held those small jukeboxes, though she doubted that they worked. A man with thick clumps

---

1. tapa
2. s'attendait à ce que le téléphone se mette à sonner
3. Au lieu de ça,
4. quelle blague
5. Ça, c'était de l'ironie !
6. Il y avait de plus en plus de monde
7. leva un sourcil en réponse
8. se frayant un chemin parmi
9. n'observer qu'à la dérobée
10. le droit d'entrée
11. laisser les faux-semblants au vestiaire
12. ouvertement
13. se rincer l'œil
14. délicieusement démodé

126

of ear hair[1] worked the cash register[2]. Pastries aged under glass covers.[3] The wall had signed[4] photographs of local news anchors[5]. The waitresses wore uniforms and attitudes[6].

Broome stood[7] when she entered and approached.

"Thanks for agreeing to see me," he said.

"Where's Harry?"

"Not here yet." They slid[8] into the booth. "Would you like something to eat?"

"No, thank you."

Broome pointed to his own cup. "I'm having coffee. Would you like some?"

Megan shook her head, glanced back at the door. "Harry should be here any second."

"Do you mind if we get started?" Broome asked. "I'm a little pressed for time.[9]"

"Without my lawyer?"

"You don't need a lawyer. I don't suspect you of anything[10], and the clock is really ticking[11]. So is it okay?"

When she didn't reply, Broome just dived in.

"Does Mardi Gras mean anything to you?" he asked.

"I thought you were going to show me a picture."

"I will in a second. But I wanted to ask about Mardi Gras first."

"If it means something to me?"

"Yes."

"You know it does."

"Do you mind[12] telling me what?"

"I thought you were in a rush[13]."

"Just bear with me[14], okay?"

Megan sighed. "The night I told you about, when I ran away. It was Mardi Gras."

Broome seemed satisfied. "Anything else?"

"Like?"

"Like anything. Like, do you remember anything odd happening on other Mardi Gras? Do you remem-

Sidenotes:
1. des touffes de poils dans les oreilles
2. était à la caisse
3. Des pâtisseries rassissaient sous des cloches de verre.
4. dédicacées
5. de présentateurs de JT
6. avaient un air revêche
7. se leva
8. se glissèrent
9. Je n'ai pas beaucoup de temps.
10. ne vous soupçonne de rien
11. l'heure tourne
12. Ça vous ennuierait de
13. que vous étiez pressé
14. Un peu de patience

ber any creepy[1] guys hanging around the club on Mardi Gras? Anything."

She thought about it. "No."

Broome had a manila folder[2] in front of him. He tapped it with his index finger. Megan waited for him to open it. The waitress came over with a coffeepot[3]. "Hot top on that[4], hon?" she asked, working a piece of gum[5] the size of a kitchen sponge[6]. Broome shook her off[7].

When she left, Broome stopped the finger tap[8] and flipped open the folder[9]. He slid the photograph across the table to her. Megan figured she had nothing to hide[10]—at least, that was what she had told herself—so she hadn't prepared herself for any kind of deception or, well, façade.

When her eyes landed on[11] the photograph, her entire body jolted[12].

There was no time to cover it up.[13] He saw it. No question.[14] Megan slowly reached out and pulled the photograph closer.

"Do you recognize the picture?" he asked.

Buy time[15], she thought. Get control.[16] "If you're asking if I've seen this picture before, the answer is no."

"But you recognize the location[17], right?"

Megan nodded slowly.

"Do you mind telling me from where?"

She swallowed[18]. "This is the part of the park I told you about earlier[19]. The iron-ore ruins."

"Where you found Stewart Green bleeding[20]?"

"Yes."

Silence.

"Do you recognize the man in the photograph?"

There was a man with blond tips and a tight T-shirt in the upper-left-hand corner[21]. Broome probably surmised[22] that Megan had recognized the man and that was what had thrown her[23]. "I really can't see his face," she said.

"No idea who it is?"

"No, none."

"But this is definitely the spot[1] where you last saw Stewart Green?"

She pretended to[2] look again, even though there was no doubt. "Yes."

Broome put both hands on the table, palms down[3]. "Anything else you can tell me about the picture?"

The fact that Broome had a picture of that path in the Pine Barrens was surprising, yes, but not shocking or stunning[4]. What had stunned her—what was making it hard to move or talk or function—wasn't the locale[5] or the man with the frosted tips.

It was the photograph itself.

"Where did you get this?" she asked.

"Why?"

She had to be careful here. She shrugged with as much nonchalance as she could muster[6] and told yet another lie[7]. "I was just wondering how you got a photograph of the exact spot I told you about."

He studied her face. She tried to meet his eye.

"It was mailed to the precinct anonymously. In fact, someone went through quite a bit of trouble[8] to make sure I didn't know who sent it."

Megan felt the tremor run straight down her spine[9]. "Why?"

"I don't know. You have a thought?"

She did. When Megan had first fallen for[10] Ray Levine, she had known nothing of photography. But he taught her[11]. He taught her about light and angle and aperture[12] and composition and focus[13]. He had taken her to his favorite spots to shoot[14]. He constantly took photographs of the woman—her—he purportedly[15] loved.

Over the years, Megan had Googled[16] Ray's name, hoping to see new photographs by him, but there was only the stuff from before they met, when he was still a big-time photojournalist. Nothing after. But she

1. vous êtes sûre que c'est l'endroit

2. fit mine de

3. les deux mains à plat sur la table

4. sidérant

5. le cadre

6. aussi nonchalamment que possible

7. mentit à nouveau

8. s'est donné beaucoup de mal

9. fut parcourue d'un frisson

10. était tombée amoureuse de

11. il lui avait tout appris

12. l'ouverture

13. la mise au point

14. dans les endroits qu'il aimait photographier

15. prétendument

16. cherché sur Google

1. elle n'avait quasiment aucun doute

2. Elle entendit Broome marmonner

3. était de tout évidence un vieux flic

4. gris paille de fer

5. les pouces dans les passants de son pantalon

6. dévoilant ainsi

7. pris dans les poils touffus de sa poitrine

8. avait sans doute dans les 55 ans

9. ahuri et désorienté

10. choisit

11. le suivit d'un pas traînant

12. s'affaissa dans son siège

13. dont on viendrait de couper les ficelles

14. En vain.

15. plissa les yeux

16. un bref signe de tête

17. glissa les yeux vers

18. à qui ai-je l'honneur

19. en se penchant trop près d'elle

20. lui faisant de l'œil

still remembered his work. She knew what he liked to do with a camera—angles, composition, lighting, aperture, whatever—and so now, even after all these years, there was very little doubt in her mind[1]:

Ray Levine had taken this photograph.

"No," Megan said to Broome. "No thought."

Under his breath, she heard Broome say[2], "Oh, damn, not now."

She turned, figuring to see Harry Sutton, but no, that wasn't the case. Two men had just entered the diner. One had older cop written all over him[3]—steel-wool gray[4] hair, badge hanging from his belt, thumbs hitching up his pants[5] as though the task was somehow grand and full of importance. The other man wore a ridiculously bright Hawaiian shirt. The top three buttons were opened, thereby displaying[6] gold chains and medallions enmeshed in ample chest hair[7]. He was probably mid-fifties[8], maybe older, and looked dazed and disoriented[9]. The older cop grabbed[10] a booth and slid in. Hawaiian Shirt shuffled behind him[11] and collapsed into his seat[12] like a marionette with his strings cut[13].

Broome kept his head low, near his coffee, clearly trying to hide. It was a no-go.[14] Older Cop's eyes narrowed[15]. He rose and said something to Hawaiian Shirt. If Hawaiian heard, his face didn't show it. He just sat there staring at the table as though it held some deep, dark secret.

Older Cop started toward them. Broome quickly put the photograph back into the folder, so his approaching comrade couldn't see it.

"Broome," Older said with a curt nod[16].

"Chief."

There was a tension there. Goldberg let his eyes walk on over to[17] Megan. "And who might this be[18]?"

"This is Jane," Broome said. "An old friend."

"She doesn't look old," Goldberg said, leaning into her personal space[19] and giving her the eye[20].

130

"What a charmer[1]," Megan said in pure monotone[2].

Goldberg didn't like that. "You a cop?" he asked her. Man,[3] Megan thought, she really had changed over the years[4]. "Just a friend."

"Friend, right." Goldberg smirked[5] and turned back to Broome. "What are you doing here?"

"Having a cup of coffee with an old friend."

"You see who I'm with?"

Broome nodded.

"What should I tell him?"

"We're getting closer[6]," he said.

"Anything more specific?"

"Not right now."

Goldberg frowned and turned away. When he left, Megan looked a question at him[7]. Broome said, "The man with him is Del Flynn, Carlton's father."

Megan turned and looked at him. The father's gold chain glistened off his exposed chest[8]. His horrible Hawaiian shirt was so orange, so bright—almost in defiance of what he was going through[9]—another façade, though in this case, a totally pointless[10] one. Even a blind man[11] could see the devastation. It consumed everything around[12] Del Flynn. It made his shoulders slump. His face, badly in need of a shave[13], sagged[14]. There was the dazed look[15], the thousand-yard stare[16].

It is every parent's nightmare[17]—what had happened to this man. Megan thought now of her own kids, her stupidly cavalier comment[18] about hating that she lived[19] for their smile, and then she looked back at Carlton Flynn's father.

"Scary, right?" Broome said.

She said nothing.

"You see what I'm trying to do now?"

She still said nothing.

"Stewart Green had parents too," he went on. "He had a wife and kids. Look at the guy over there. Now imagine his sleepless night[20]. Imagine him waiting

1. Quel charmeur

2. d'une voix monotone

3. Eh ben

4. avait dû vraiment changer avec les années

5. railla

6. Ça progresse

7. le regarda d'un air interrogateur

8. brillait sur son torse

9. comme un défi à ce qu'il était en train de vivre

10. inutile

11. un aveugle

12. Elle imprégnait tout ce qui entourait

13. qui avait bien besoin d'être rasé

14. était tout relâché

15. regard ahuri

16. les yeux fixant le vide

17. le cauchemar de tout parent

18. à sa phrase idiote et désinvolte

19. ne vivait que

20. sa nuit blanche

to find an answer. Imagine that agony stretching out for[1] a few days. Then weeks. Then months and even years. Imagine that torment[2]."

"I got it," Megan said with a snap[3]. "You're the master of the subtle, Broome."

"Just trying to make you understand." He signaled for the check[4]. "Anything else you can tell me about that photograph?"

Ray, she thought, but there was no way she could tell him that. She shook her head. "No, nothing."

"Anything else about anything?"

Broome looked at her hard. She had come here prepared to tell him something important. Now she wasn't so sure if she should. Her head spun.[5] She wanted it to settle[6], give herself a chance to think it through clearly[7].

Broome waited.

"A person who shall remain nameless[8]," Megan began, "maybe—and I stress the word maybe[9]—saw Stewart Green recently."

Now it was Broome's turn to be stunned. "Are you serious?"

"No, I just made it up[10]. Of course, I'm serious. But the source wasn't sure. It could have just been a guy who looked like[11] Stewart. It's been seventeen years, remember?"

"And you won't tell me the source's name?"

"I won't, no."

Broome made a face[12]. "You want me to show you that grieving father[13] again?"

"Only if you want me to get up and leave right now."

"Okay, okay." He put his hands up in mock surrender[14]. "When did your source see Stewart?"

"In the past few weeks."

"Where?"

"In town."

"Where in town?"

"La Crème. And it's dark in there." Megan opened her mouth and almost said the word *she*[1], but she held it back[2] at the last moment. "The source said it was only for a second and it might not have even been him[3]."

"This source," he said. "Is he or she reliable?[4]"

"Yes."

"Do you think he or she saw Stewart Green?"

"I don't know."

"And again I ask, anything else you can tell me?"

Megan shook her head. "That's it[5]."

"Okay, then we're done here." Broome rose. "I got to hurry to the crime scene."

"Wait, hold up[6]."

He looked down at her[7].

"What crime scene?"

"The iron-ore ruins, remember?"

She frowned. "Do you really think, what, there might still be blood or fibers[8] or something after all this time?"

"Blood or fibers?" he repeated with a shake of his head[9]. "You watch too much *CSI*."

"Then what?"

"Sometimes history repeats itself."

"What do you mean?"

"The man in the photograph I showed you."

She waited, but she already knew. His eyes drifted back to[10] the booth in the corner.

"It's Carlton Flynn."

---

1. faillit dire « elle »

2. se retint

3. que ce n'était peut-être même pas lui

4. Est-ce que cette personne est fiable ?

5. C'est tout.

6. pas si vite

7. baissa les yeux vers elle

8. des fibres textiles

9. en secouant la tête

10. Son regard revint vers

14

1. ne pouvait
s'empêcher de
regarder du coin
de l'œil
2. tourné vers le
passé
3. en était la
preuve absolue
4. est-ce que
Ray enverrait
5. à supposer
que ce soit lui
6. Mais
surtout,

7. Quel rôle
8. quel pouvait
bien être le
rapport avec
9. n'en avait pas
la moindre idée

MEGAN stayed where she was for a moment. She kept sneaking glances at[1] Flynn's father, but her mind was firmly in the past[2]. Ray. The photograph proved it beyond a doubt[3].

Ray was back.

But what did that mean? Why would Ray send in[4] that photograph to Broome—assuming he was the one[5] who did? More to the point,[6] why had he taken it in the first place?

She still had so many questions. The truth was, Megan did believe Lorraine. She wouldn't be wrong about something that important. So the question was, how could Stewart Green be back? Where had he been for the past seventeen years? What really happened that night? What part[7] did Ray play—and how could it possibly relate to[8] a young guy named Carlton Flynn seventeen years later?

She had no clue[9].

Part of the reason Megan had never contacted Ray was to protect him—as he had tried to[1] protect her. But now, seventeen years later, with another missing man in the same remote part[2] of the park … it simply didn't add up[3].

She took out the business card again. Fester at the Weak Signal.

Megan could still do the smart thing[4]. Yes, she had opened that closet door, but nothing had really fallen out[5]. She could simply close it again. No real damage done[6]. She had done her part[7]. She could get back in her car and go home and she could make up a new story for Dave, maybe pick up the new Weber grill on the way, tell him that was what she was doing and that she wanted to surprise him with it[8]. She could do that, and it would all be over[9].

She had turned her back on this world[10] seventeen years ago. She would call Harry Sutton, even though he had never showed for this meeting, and tell him she was done. She owed this city nothing[11].

And Ray?

An ex-boyfriend. Nothing more.

But that had always been a problem. By definition you break up[12] with an ex. You may do it poorly[13] or well, but one or both of you lose the feeling[14] and you end it. That hadn't been the case here. She had been crazy about him. He had been crazy about her. They didn't so much break up[15] as get ripped apart[16]. She hated the term but maybe what they had needed, like every couple, was some kind of closure[17].

Ray could be in serious trouble[18].

Ray could *be*[19] serious trouble.

She sneaked another glance at Carlton Flynn's father in the Hawaiian shirt. He was looking toward her. Their eyes met. Not for long. Not for more than a second or two, but she could feel his grief, his confusion, his rage. Could she just walk away from that? Could she just walk away from Ray again too?

1. tout comme lui avait essayé de

2. coin très isolé

3. ça ne collait vraiment pas

4. encore écouter la voix de la raison

5. ne s'en était vraiment échappé

6. Pas de véritables dégâts

7. contribué comme elle avait pu

8. lui faire la surprise

9. ce serait fini

10. avait laissé ce monde derrière elle

11. ne devait rien à cette ville

12. on rompt

13. mal s'y prendre

14. ne ressent plus la même chose

15. n'avaient pas rompu

16. mais plutôt été arrachés l'un à l'autre

17. quelque chose qui leur aurait permis de tourner la page

18. avoir de gros ennuis

19. lui valoir

The selfless part of her[1] knew that she couldn't or at least shouldn't. The selfish part[2], too, didn't want to close that door just yet[3]. Closing the door meant going back to her regular[4] life, one day passing and then the next. She should welcome that[5], but right now, the thought of that, the idea of simply returning forevermore to the status quo,[6] terrified her.

There was no choice really.

She had to find Ray. She had to ask him about that photograph. She had to ask him about what really happened to Stewart Green seventeen years ago.

Avoiding the eyes[7] of Carlton Flynn's father, Megan slid out of the booth and started toward the Weak Signal to find Fester.

THE big break came when Broome arrived at the ruins of the old iron-ore mill.

"Blood," Samantha Bajraktari said.

The spot was remote. No cars or vehicles of any sort. Explaining the history of the eighteenth-century iron-ore mill, a New Jersey park ranger[8] (a phrase that sounded suspiciously like an oxymoron[9]) had marched them up[10] a rather narrow path. The group consisted of Broome, an old-timer[11] named Cowens, two county uniforms[12] Broome didn't know, and two crime unit technicians[13]—one of whom was the aforementioned[14] Samantha Bajraktari. The uniforms and crime technicians led the way[15]. Cowens, a lifetime cigar smoker[16], huffed and puffed[17] until he dropped to the back of the pack.[18]

Broome bent down next to Bajraktari. She had been lead tech[19] for five years now and was without a doubt the best Broome had ever known. "How much blood is that?"

"Don't know yet."

"Enough to cause death?[20]"

Bajraktari did a yes-no tilt with her head[1]. "Not what I'm seeing here, but it's hard to say. It looks like some of it has been buried under the dirt[2]."

"Like with a shovel[3]?"

"Or even a shoe, I don't know. It's just covered up[4]."

"How about a blood type or DNA match on[5] Carlton Flynn?"

Bajraktari frowned. "We've been here five minutes, Broome. Shoo.[6] Give me a little space[7], will you?"

The two uniforms surrounded the area with yellow crime-scene tape[8], which just looked plain silly[9] out in the middle of nowhere. Night was starting to fall. They wouldn't be able to work out here much longer tonight. It was too far to drag the big spotlights out[10]. Broome looked at the remains[11] of what had been a furnace two hundred years ago. He started pacing[12], realized that maybe he was too close to the crime scene and might mess something up[13], headed back down the path.

Cowens, cigar firmly planted in mouth, finally caught up[14]. He bent down, his hands on his knees, trying to suck in[15] oxygen. "Find a body?" he managed to ask.

"Not yet."

"Man, I'd hate to have[16] walked all this way for nothing."

"You're a people person[17], Cowens."

"Plus if they find a body, they'll get some kind of vehicle up here. I don't feel like walking back[18]. My feet are killing me.[19]"

"You didn't have to come. I told you that at that parking lot."

Cowens waved him off and managed to straighten up[20]. He adjusted his pants and patted his hair[21]. Broome said nothing. Then Cowens made his way toward Bajraktari, pulling down the yellow tape as he did.

1. hocha la tête d'un air dubitatif

2. recouvert de terre

3. une pelle

4. recouvert

5. Peut-on comparer avec le groupe sanguin ou l'ADN de

6. Oust !

7. un peu d'air

8. un ruban

9. ridicule

10. faire venir les gros projecteurs jusque-là

11. les vestiges

12. à faire les cent pas

13. risquait de compromettre le relevé des indices

14. les rejoignit

15. d'inspirer

16. j'espère que je n'ai pas

17. Ce qui est bien chez toi, c'est que tu te soucies de ton prochain

18. n'ai pas envie de me taper le retour à pied

19. J'ai très mal aux pieds.

20. se redresser

21. se recoiffa

"Hey, Samantha," Cowens said, offering up a big smile. "You look nice tonight."

Bajraktari looked up at him with blank eyes[1]. "You're contaminating my crime scene, Cowens."

"I was just saying. Even in that crime tech Windbreaker[2], you look really pretty." Cowens smiled a little more, then suddenly dropped it. "Uh, I'm not harassing you[3] or nothing. I'm just saying."

Broome shook his head. Now he got why Cowens had wanted to come along. He was sweet on[4] Samantha Bajraktari. Unbelievable.[5]

"Just get behind the yellow tape," Bajraktari snapped[6].

But suddenly Cowens wasn't listening. He turned his head slowly side to side[7]. A funny look crossed his face.[8]

"What?" Bajraktari said to him.

Cowens narrowed his eyes. "I'm getting a little déjà vu here.[9]"

"The trolling spot for trannies[10] looks a little like this," Bajraktari said.

"Har-har[11]."

Samantha Bajraktari went back to work. Still looking confounded[12], Cowens stumbled back toward the tape. Broome meanwhile had an idea. Holding up the photograph in his right hand, he began to circle[13], trying to figure out exactly where the picture had been taken. He moved up the hill a little, looking back every few steps[14], trying to calculate the spot. The journey took him off the path.[15]

He stepped slowly, keeping his eyes on the ground and then … Bingo.

"Bajraktari," Broome called back.

"What?"

"I got what looks like a shoe print[16] over here. Do you think you can get a mold[17]? In fact, you guys should probably go over[18] the whole area, see if you can find anything."

Marginal glossary notes:

1. impassible
2. [coupe-vent doublé]
3. ne veux pas te harceler
4. avait le béguin pour
5. Incroyable.
6. dit d'un ton sec
7. de droite à gauche
8. Il fit une drôle de grimace.
9. J'ai une impression de déjà-vu.
10. L'endroit où se baladent les travelos
11. Ha Ha !
12. perplexe
13. tourner en rond
14. tous les deux ou trois pas
15. L'exercice lui fit quitter le sentier.
16. une empreinte de chaussure
17. un moulage
18. examiner

"No problem, if all of us don't clop around[1] like a bunch of Clydesdales[2]."

Bajraktari said something to the other tech[3], a guy who looked to be maybe thirteen years old. The tech headed toward where Broome was standing. Broome showed him the shoe print and carefully made his way back to the clearing[4]. He stood next to Cowens and tried to think it through.

Seventeen years ago, on Mardi Gras, Stewart Green had come to this rather remote spot and got—what?—stabbed[5] before disappearing forever. Now Broome had a picture, not date stamped[6] unfortunately[7], showing Carlton Flynn, another man who vanished on Mardi Gras, in this same remote area. Plus they had just found spilled blood, clearly not seventeen years old. And finally, seventeen years after Stewart Green vanished, there were two other new, strange developments. One, the sudden reappearance of the elusive[8] Cassie—why had she come back, and was she telling the truth? And two, the possible sudden reappearance of Stewart Green.

Was his return related to[9] Cassie?

If not, it seemed like a hell of a coincidence[10]. If he was back at all, that is.[11] Cassie could have just been making that up[12] or her "source" could have been wrong.

So add up all the new clues[13] and … Broome didn't have a clue[14].

And right then, mulling it over[15] in the Pine Barrens, the big break came[16] from a most unlikely source[17].

"I remember now," Cowens said.

"What?"

"That déjà vu I was talking about before. I remember what it was from." Cowens took the cigar out of his mouth. "That big murder case."

That caught[18] Broome's attention. "What big murder case?"

1. si on ne vient pas tous piétiner

2. comme un troupeau de percherons

3. agent de la police scientifique

4. regagna la clairière

5. poignardé

6. sans date imprimée

7. malheureusement

8. insaisissable

9. Est-ce que son retour avait un rapport avec

10. une coincidence vraiment extraordinaire

11. À supposer qu'il soit vraiment de retour, bien sûr.

12. inventer ça de toutes pièces

13. indices

14. n'était pas plus avancé

15. alors qu'il cogitait

16. l'enquête progressa d'un coup

17. grâce à une intervention des plus inattendues

18. La remarque éveilla

"You remember. What the hell was the guy's name? Gunner, Gunther, something like that."

Broome tried to remember, feeling his pulse pick up pace[1]. "He was stabbed, right?"

"Right. Some hikers[2] found him up here, what, gotta be twenty years ago? Multiple stab wounds[3]."

"And you're sure this is the spot?"

"Yeah, pretty[4] sure, with the old furnace and that rock. Yeah, this is the place."

"Do you remember when this was?"

"Like I said, twenty years ago."

"I mean the date."

"You're kidding, right?"

"How about time of the year?"

Cowens thought about it. "It was cold."

"Like now?"

"I don't know. I guess."

Broome could look that up[5] when he got back to the station. "Were you the lead?[6]"

"Nah, I was still in uniform. Morris caught it, I think, but I was there on the bust[7]. Well, not really there. I was backup to the backup[8]. Barely got out[9] of the squad car. The perp[10] surrendered[11] easily."

"The case was cleared[12], right?"

"Yeah, it was pretty much a slam dunk[13]. A love triangle[14] or something, I don't remember. I remember the perp was all crying, said he didn't even know the guy, that his girl would never cheat on him[15], the usual."

"They get a confession[16]?"

"Nope. Guy swore he was innocent. Still does, I think. But he got life[17]. I think he's serving it[18] in Rahway."

1. pris de palpitations
2. promeneurs
3. Plusieurs coups de couteau
4. presque
5. pourrait vérifier ça
6. C'est toi qui menais l'enquête ?
7. pour l'arrestation
8. renfort pour les renforts
9. Quasiment pas sorti
10. Le suspect
11. s'est rendu
12. a été résolue
13. sans surprises
14. triangle amoureux
15. ne l'aurait jamais trompé
16. des aveux
17. a pris perpète
18. qu'il purge sa peine

15

ARTERIES hardened[1] and lungs blackened[2] just by opening the door of the Weak Signal Bar and Grill. The seedy crowd brought plenty of colorful terminology to mind[3], but "health conscious[4]" and "long life span[5]" were not among them[6]. The television behind the bar played *SportsCenter*. There was a neon sign for Michelob in the window. According to the chalkboard[7], tonight was "Ladies Night" featuring "Dollar Drafts[8] for Chicks[9]," a marketing ploy[10] that drew in[11], it appeared, a certain female clientele. For example, one straw-haired[12] woman, who was cackle-laughing[13] in a "notice me" manner[14], wore a yellow T-shirt that read "Sloppy Seconds[15]," which, alas, seemed all too apropos.

Megan felt as though she had to wave away the smoke[16], even though no one was smoking. It was that kind of place. The décor was dartboards[17], shamrocks[18], and sponsored sport team photographs. She was decked out in suburban-mom wear[19], a camel

1. Les artères se durcissaient
2. les poumons noircissaient
3. Des expressions pittoresques venaient à l'esprit devant la clientèle minable
4. soucieux de leur santé
5. longévité
6. n'en faisaient pas partie
7. l'ardoise
8. Un dollar la bière
9. les filles
10. ruse
11. attirait
12. aux cheveux couleur paille
13. gloussait
14. pour se faire remarquer
15. Toujours dispo
16. écarter la fumée
17. cibles de jeu de fléchettes
18. trèfles
19. habillée en mère de famille bourgeoise

141

hair coat with a Coach bag, and while that look definitely stood out in here[1], no one really stared. This was a bar where plenty of people came because you did *not* know their name. She probably wasn't the first seemingly content wife who'd wandered in here from the convention[2] center looking for anonymity.

Lorraine had described Fester thusly[3]: "Cue ball bald[4] and slightly larger[5] than a planet." Strangely, there were at least three men in here that fit[6] that description, but this was hardly the time to[7] worry about shyness or niceties[8]. She took a quick glance around, hoping that maybe Ray was here too. That would make it easier, wouldn't it? Eliminate the middleman[9]. Her heart did a little two-step[10] at the thought.

Was she really prepared to see Ray? And when she did, what would she say to him?

No matter. Ray wasn't here. One of the possible Festers was giving her the eye. She approached him and said, "Are you Fester?"

"Honey, I can be anyone you want me to be."

"If I had more time, I'd probably swoon[11] and demand that you take me. But I'm pressed for time. Which one of you guys is Fester?"

The man scowled[12] and pointed toward another guy—the biggest of the possible Festers—with his thumb. Megan thanked him and approached.

"Are you Fester?"

The man had forearms[13] like marble columns at[14] the Acropolis. The beer mug[15] looked like a shot glass[16] in his enormous hand. "Who wants to know?"

"Who do you think?[17] Me."

"And you are?"

"My name isn't important."

"Are you a process server[18]?"

Megan frowned. "Do I look like a process server?"

He looked her over[19]. "Kinda, yeah[20]."

Man, Megan thought for the second time today, she really had changed.

Sidenotes:
1. tranchait sur les autres
2. des congrès
3. de la façon suivante
4. Chauve comme une boule de billard
5. plus gros
6. correspondant à
7. ce n'était pas le moment de
8. des bonnes manières
9. l'intermédiaire
10. bondit
11. je me pâmerais sans doute
12. se renfrogna
13. les avant-bras
14. [gros] comme les colonnes de marbre de
15. Sa chope à bière
16. un verre à liqueur
17. À votre avis ?
18. un huissier
19. l'examina
20. Plutôt, ouais

"I'm looking for an employee of yours."

"To serve him a subpoena[1]?"

"No. I'm not a process server."

"Who are you looking for?"

"Ray Levine."

If Fester knew the name, he didn't show it. He lifted his beer and took a deep swig[2]. "Why would you be looking for Ray?"

Good question. She wondered what to say here and went with the truth[3]. "He's an old friend."

Fester studied her a little more. "What do you want with him?[4]"

"No offense[5], but are you his employer or his mother?"

He smiled at that. "Let me buy you a drink."

"You're kidding, right?"

"It's okay. I'm harmless[6]. What's your poison?[7]"

Megan sighed, took a deep breath. Her phone kept buzzing. She reached into her purse and put it on silent[8]. Slow down[9], she thought. Don't press it[10] and maybe you'll get what you want. "Fine, whatever you're having[11]."

He ordered her some kind of light beer with a fruit in it. She hated light beer, especially with fruit, but it was too late. She took a sip[12].

"What's your name?" Fester asked.

"Cassie."

Fester nodded slowly. "You're the one, right?[13]"

"The one what?"

"The one who broke Ray's heart[14]. The one who crushed his soul[15] and left him the wreck of a man[16] he is today."

Megan felt something in her chest give way[17]. "He told you that?"

"No, but it's obvious. How do you know he wants to see you?"

"I don't."

143

1. Pour l'assigner en justice

2. en avala une grande lampée

3. opta pour la vérité

4. Qu'est-ce que vous lui voulez ?

5. Je ne voudrais pas vous vexer

6. Je ne suis pas dangereux.

7. Vous marchez à quoi ?

8. en mode silencieux

9. Moins vite

10. Prends ton temps

11. la même chose que vous

12. but une gorgée

13. C'est vous, hein ?

14. Celle qui a brisé le cœur de Ray

15. qui a écrabouillé son âme

16. a fait de lui l'épave qu'

17. quelque chose en elle se briser

"He's working a job right now anyway," Fester said, his eyes narrowing. "Wait, don't I know you? You used to work down here, right?"

This wasn't good.

"I was a bouncer," Fester said. "Back in the day. Who are you again? I know I've seen your face[1]."

"I'm just looking for Ray," she said.

Fester kept studying her face. She didn't like that. She was about to leave when, without warning[2], Fester took out his phone and snapped a picture of her.

"What the hell did you do that for?"

"My porn collection." Fester's huge fingers were working the keyboard[3]. "Actually, I'm sending this pic[4] to Ray. If he wants to see you, he'll let me know and then I can let you know. You want to give me your cell phone number?"

"No."

"Then how about another drink?"

KEN and Barbie began to clean up[5].

Barbie lovingly packed away[6] her favorite new tool—the soldering iron with a sharp needle tip[7]. It still reeked of[8] scorched flesh[9]. Through trial and error[10], Barbie had figured out the most sensitive spots[11], the nerve endings[12] that when merely touched[13], not to mention penetrated with scorching heat[14], caused the most searing pain[15], and applied those lessons to the lawyer named Harry Sutton.

Barbie took off her hospital scrubs[16], her surgical hair cap[17], her latex gloves[18], and packed them away. Ken would do the same but not right away. He knew that no matter how careful you were, DNA got left behind[19]. There was just no way to prevent that completely. Laboratories could do amazing things nowadays, and the best way to handle that[20] was to recognize and respect it.

So what to do?

---

1. Je reconnais votre visage.
2. sans prévenir
3. martelaient le clavier
4. photo
5. tout remettre en ordre
6. rangea avec soin
7. à l'embout très fin
8. empestait
9. la chair brûlée
10. Avec l'expérience
11. découvert les endroits les plus sensibles
12. les terminaisons nerveuses
13. à peine effleurées
14. ou pire encore si on les soumettait à une chaleur extrême
15. la douleur la plus intense
16. quitta sa blouse d'infirmière
17. calotte de chirurgien
18. gants en latex
19. on laissait de l'ADN derrière soi
20. la meilleure approche

Ken used obfuscation[1]. He kept random people's DNA samples[2]—hair, spare tissue[3], saliva, whatever— in Tupperware containers. Sometimes he found the samples in public restrooms[4], disgusting as that might sound[5]. One very good spot was at summer camp. Many of the counselors used the disposable razors[6], which he could easily swipe[7]. Urinals[8] provided pubic hair[9]. Showers gave you more.

With his gloves still on, Ken opened a container and, using tweezers[10], plucked out[11] some hair and tissue and placed the sample near—and even on— Harry Sutton. It would be enough. He closed the Tupperware and put it back into his bag. He was doing the same with his scrubs when Harry Sutton's cell phone rang.

Barbie looked at the caller ID. "It's Cassie."

Cassie. Harry Sutton had proved to be much stronger than one could imagine or endure—or maybe he didn't know the truth about her. After much persuasion involving the soldering iron and his urethra[12], he had told them that the witness[13] Deputy Chief Goldberg had told Ken about was an ex-exotic dancer named Cassie. Harry Sutton gave up[14] nothing else on her, but they found her phone number on his cell phone.

Barbie answered the call and put on her sweetest voice[15]. "Harry Sutton's office."

"Hi, is Harry there?"

"May I say who's calling?"

"Cassie."

"Oh, I'm sorry. Mr. Sutton is not available right now." Barbie looked at Ken. He gave her a thumbs-up[16]. "May I have your full name and address so I can give him a thorough[17] message?"

"Wait, isn't this Harry's cell?"

"Mr. Sutton's phone automatically rings to me when he's indisposed[18]. I'm sorry, Cassie. I didn't catch your last name[19]."

1. pratiquait le brouillage

2. des échantillons

3. des bribes de mouchoir en papier

4. les toilettes

5. aussi dégoûtant que cela puisse paraître

6. des rasoirs jetables

7. frotter

8. Les urinoirs

9. des poils pubiens

10. une pince à épiler

11. arracha

12. urètre

13. le témoin

14. ne révéla

15. prit sa voix la plus suave

16. lui fit signe que c'était parfait

17. plus complet

18. souffrant

19. n'ai pas saisi votre nom de famille

1. La communication fut coupée.

2. en faisant la moue

3. ne s'est pas confiée à moi

4. fait très attention

5. pour notre mission

6. Sans aucun doute

7. Ce ne sera pas difficile de trouver

The phone call disconnected.[1]

"She hung up," Barbie said with a pout[2].

Ken walked over and put his arm around her. "Don't worry about it."

"I really thought I sounded like a secretary."

"You did."

"But she didn't open up to me[3]."

"Which tells us something," Ken said.

"What?"

"She is being very careful[4]."

Barbie, feeling better, started nodding. "Which means she's very important to our assignment[5]."

"Most definitely[6]."

"So what next?"

"We have her cell phone number," Ken said. "It will be no trouble finding out[7] where she lives."

16

UNDER the strobe of Ray's flash, the woman looked like the proverbial deer[1] in the headlights[2].

"Who's the lucky girl, George?" Ray called out.

George Queller, perhaps Fester's most frequent client, put a protective arm around his date. "This is Alexandra Saperstein."

Flash, snap, flash, snap. "How did you two meet?"

"On JDate.com. It's a Web site for Jewish singles[3]."

"Sounds like destiny."

Ray didn't point out the obvious[4]—George was not Jewish. This was a job. His mind couldn't be further away[5], but really who wanted to be present when you did work like this?

Alexandra Saperstein seemed to shrink under the attention[6]. She was pretty enough[7] in a mousy sort of way[8], but she had that cower 'n' blink[9] that Ray often associated with past abuse[10]. The flashbulbs weren't helping[11]. Ray turned it off, kept snapping, took a step

1. *aussi apeurée qu'une biche*

2. *surprise par les phares d'une voiture*

3. *célibataires*

4. *ne souligna pas l'évidence*

5. *Il avait l'esprit totalement ailleurs*

6. *se faire de plus en plus petite, intimidée par tant d'attention*

7. *plutôt jolie*

8. *dans le genre timide*

9. *une façon de se recroqueviller*

10. *aux victimes de maltraitance*

11. *n'arran-geaient rien*

1. un peu d'air

2. le regarda bizarrement

3. arrivaient devant

4. maître d'hôtel

5. à l'accent français très prononcé

6. de son vrai nom

7. prononce sa réplique

8. cacher sa honte

9. Est-ce que vous allez révéler

10. Quelque chose en Ray s'était éteint.

11. d'un ton hautain

12. le jeter dehors

13. lui tendit

14. à travers la vitre

15. s'installa

16. Ça n'allait pas durer.

17. quand on ralentit

18. enregistrer

19. terreur naissante

20. réglant la mise au point

21. un air perplexe se peignit sur

22. qu'elle avait bien lu

23. poussé la folie un peu plus loin

back to give the terrified young lady space[1]. George noticed and gave him a funny look[2].

As they neared[3] the restaurant, Maurice, the maître d'[4] with the heavy French accent[5]—real name[6]: Manny Schwartz, who probably should be on JDate—came to the bistro door, opened his arms wide, and cried, "Monsieur George, welcome. I have your favorite table all ready for you!"

George glanced over at Ray, waiting for Ray to deliver the line[7]. Keeping his face behind the camera worked here because Ray could hide his shame[8] as he shouted it, "Will you two be releasing[9] what you ate to the press?"

A little piece of Ray died.[10] We'll see," George said in a haughty tone[11].

The new couple entered. Ray pretended to want to follow them, and Maurice pretended to push him out[12]. A waiter came up to Alexandra and handed her[13] red roses. Ray snapped pictures through the window[14]. George pulled out the chair for Alexandra. She sat, settled in[15], finally looking comfortable for the first time.

It wouldn't last.[16]

Ray had the camera on her face. He couldn't help it. Part of him knew that he should look away—like slowing down[17] to view a car accident—but the artist part of him wanted to record[18] the moment of dawning horror[19]. As Alexandra looked down at the menu, Ray felt his cell phone buzz. He ignored it, adjusting the focus[20]. He waited. First, a look of confusion crossed[21] Alexandra Saperstein's face. She squinted to make sure she read it right[22]. Ray knew that George had upped his crazy ante[23]—that the headline on top of the menu now read:

George and Alexandra's First Date
Tasting Menu
Let's Save This to Show Our Grandkids!

The realization dawned on Alexandra now[1]. Her eyes opened wider, but the rest of her face fell. She put her hands to her cheeks. Ray snapped away. This could very well be his own version of Munch's *The Scream*[2].

Champagne was poured. The new script called for[3] Ray to barge in[4] and take a table photograph of the toast. He started toward the door. The phone buzzed again. Ray took a quick glance and saw it was a photograph from Fester. Bizarre. Why the hell would Fester be sending him a photograph?

Still moving inside the bistro, Ray scrolled down[5] and hit the open attachment feature[6]. He lifted his camera as George lifted his glass. Alexandra looked to Ray for rescue[7]. Ray took a quick peek[8] at the incoming[9] photograph and felt his heart stop.

The camera dropped to his side.[10]

George said, "Ray?"

Ray stared down at his cell phone. Tears started brimming in his eyes.[11] He started shaking his head. It couldn't be. So many emotions ricocheted through him[12], threatened to overwhelm him[13].

Cassie.

It was a mind game[14], someone who looked like her, but, no, there was no doubt in his mind. She had changed in seventeen years, but there was no way he'd forget[15] anything about that face.

Why? How? After all the years, how …

He reached out and tentatively[16] caressed the image with his finger.

"Ray?"

Ray kept his eyes on the photograph. "Alexandra?"

He heard her shift in her chair.

"It's okay. You can go."

He didn't have to tell her twice. She was up and out the door[17]. George stood and followed her. Ray got in his way[18]. "Don't."

"I don't understand, Ray."

1. Alexandra réalisa enfin.

2. le Cri, de Munch

3. D'après le nouveau scénario,

4. devait faire irruption

5. fit défiler le mail

6. ouvrit la pièce jointe

7. pour qu'il vienne à sa rescousse

8. jeta un coup d'œil

9. qui venait d'arriver

10. Il en lâcha son appareil photo.

11. Il sentit les larmes lui monter aux yeux.

12. Il fut assailli par une myriade de sentiments

13. qui le bouleversaient

14. On cherchait à lui faire peur

15. impossible pour lui d'oublier

16. timidement

17. se leva et fila

18. lui barra le chemin

149

1. Ray repensa à la célèbre réplique de Bogart sur tous les bars de toutes les villes du monde

2. impossible que ce soit

3. appuya sur le numéro de Fester dans le répertoire

4. comme de la merde

5. ne l'emmenait jamais au restaurant

6. je me plie en quatre

7. elle panique et elle se casse

8. lui fit signe de patienter une seconde

9. le répondeur

10. se déclencha

11. se dirigea vers la porte

12. du romantique

13. Tout d'abord

14. il y a une différence subtile entre l'eau de rose

15. et la contrainte

16. c'est des conneries

17. l'expérience prouve le contraire

18. les traitent comme des chiens

Alexandra fled. George collapsed back into his chair. Ray stared at the photograph. Why had Fester taken it? He tried to calm down enough to gather clues. They were at a bar. Probably the Weak Signal. The old Bogie line about of all the gin joints in all the world came to him[1], but of course, she hadn't walked into his. She had walked into Fester's. And there was no way this was[2] a coincidence.

"Why, Ray?"

"One second," he told George.

He pressed Fester's speed dial[3]—pathetically, Ray thought, Fester, his boss, was the only person he had on speed dial—and heard it ring.

"I don't get it, Ray," George said. "This girl, Alexandra? Online she's telling me that her last boyfriend treated her like crap[4] and ignored her and never took her out[5]. Here I am, going the extra mile[6], and she freaks out on me[7]. Why?"

Ray held up a one-second finger[8]. Fester's voice mail[9] kicked in[10]. His message said, "Fester. Beep."

Ray said, "What the hell is going on with that picture? Call me now."

He hung up and started heading out[11].

"Ray?"

It was George again.

"I don't get it. I'm just trying to make the night special for them. Don't they see that? Online they all say they want romance[12]."

"First off[13]," Ray said, "there's a fine line between romance[14] and restraining order[15]. You got that?"

George nodded slowly. "I guess so. But they all say—"

"Second, what women say is crap[16]. They say they want romance and to be treated like a princess, but all empirical evidence says otherwise[17]. They always choose the guy who treats them like dirt[18]."

"So what should I do?" George asked, clearly confused. "Should I treat them like dirt too?"

Ray thought about it. He was about to launch into a long spiel of advice[1] but now, looking at George's face, he said, "Don't change a thing[2]."

"What?"

"I'd hate to live in a world without guys like you. So don't change. You be the romantic instead of the asshole[3]."

"You really think so?"

"Well, not if you want to score[4]. If you want to score, you're hopeless[5]."

George gave a half-smile at that[6]. "I don't just want to score. I want to find a true companion."

"Good answer. Then don't change. Stick to your guns[7]." Ray took another step, stopped, turned back. "Well, maybe back off a little[8]. The personalized menus are way over the top[9]."

"Really? You think? Maybe it's just the font[10]."

Ray's cell phone rang. It was Fester. He quickly picked it up.

"Fester?"

"So you know the girl in the picture, I assume," Fester said.

"Yes, what does she want?"

"What do you think she wants? She wants to talk to you."

Ray could actually feel his heart beating in his chest. "Is she still at the Weak Signal? I'm on my way."

"She just left."

"Damn."

"But she left a message."

"What?"

"She said to meet her at Lucy at eleven."

17

1. lui raconta les traces de sang qu'ils avaient trouvées

2. les souvenirs de Cowens

3. et non à son ancien bureau à elle,

4. juste en face de celui de Broome

5. beau gosse aux cheveux gominés

6. ne se souvenait jamais de son nom

7. un jour, très inspiré,

8. s'était mis à l'appeler

9. ridiculement bien rangé

10. l'eau de Cologne

11. que ça m'ait échappé

BROOME called his ex, Erin, from the scene and filled her in on the found blood[1] and Cowens's recollection[2].

"I'll get over to the precinct and start the research," she said.

When Broome arrived, Erin was sitting at his desk rather than her former one[3] directly across from his[4]. That desk, where she sat for more than a decade, was now used by some slick-haired pretty boy[5] who dressed in Armani suits. Broome kept forgetting his name[6] and in a fit of originality[7] had taken to calling him[8] "Armani." Armani wasn't here so Broome slipped into his seat. The desk was ridiculously neat[9] and smelled of cologne[10].

"I can't believe I missed it[11]," Erin said.

"We were searching for missing men, not dead ones. So what you got?"

"The victim's name was Ross Gunther, age twenty-eight."

Erin handed him the photograph, the body splayed on its back[1]. The blood was thick[2] around his neck, like he was wearing a crimson scarf[3].

"Gunther was born in Camden, dropped out[4] of Camden High, lived in Atlantic City," Erin said. "A true nowhere man[5] headed for a life of nothing[6]. He was single, fairly long sheet of loser stuff[7]—assault, battery[8], criminal mischief[9]. He also did a little enforcing[10] for a loan shark[11]."

"How was he killed?"

"His throat was slit[12]—aggressively."

"Aggressively?" Broome took another look at the photograph. "Looks like he was almost decapitated."

"Ergo, my use[13] of the term aggressively. As you know already, Morris handled the case[14]. If you want to talk to him, he's down in Florida."

"How old is he now?"

"Morris?" She shrugged. "Got to be eighty, eighty-five."

"He was already senile when I joined the force[15]."

"I don't think you'll need to talk to him anyway."

"He got his man, right?"

Erin nodded. "Gunther had recently started seeing a girl named Stacy Paris. Problem was, Paris was engaged[16] to a hothead[17] named Ricky Mannion. Both men were the very possessive type, if you know what I mean."

Broome knew all too well[18] what she meant. He'd seen the possessive type too many times in his career—overly jealous short fuse[19], mistakes control for[20] love, always holds the girl's hand in public like a dog marking territory, chockful of raging insecurity[21] that he's trying to mask in the macho[22]. It never ends well.

"So Morris got a warrant[23] for Mannion's house," Erin said. "They found enough evidence to put him away[24]."

"Like what kind of evidence?"

1. gisant sur le dos
2. abondant
3. une écharpe cramoisie
4. a décroché
5. Un véritable paumé
6. bien parti pour une vie nase
7. avec une longue liste de délits minables à son actif
8. coups et blessures
9. vandalisme
10. a aussi été recouvreur de dettes
11. un usurier
12. On lui a tranché la gorge
13. D'où mon choix
14. était chargé de l'affaire
15. je suis rentré dans la police
16. fiancée
17. tête brûlée
18. ne voyait que trop
19. soupe au lait
20. confond domination et
21. habité par un sentiment d'insécurité refoulé
22. de cacher sous des allures de macho
23. a obtenu un mandat de perquisition
24. l'envoyer sous les verrous

1. l'arme du crime
2. cranté
3. l'avait essuyée
4. des traces
5. correspondaient à celui de
6. qu'il avait laissé à côté de la machine à laver
7. Waouh
8. Je te donne en mille
9. ce qu'il a prétendu
10. victime d'un coup monté
11. Ne te laisse pas impressionner.
12. a été vite réglée
13. 25 ans incompressibles
14. il y a à peine une heure ?!
15. a eu lieu
16. le lendemain matin
17. théoriquement, ce n'était plus
18. c'est le cas pour

"Like the murder weapon[1]." She showed him the photograph of a long knife with a serrated edge[2]. "Mannion had wiped it off[3], but there were still remnants[4] of blood. They positively tied it to[5] the victim. The early days of DNA. And if that wasn't enough, they also found Gunther's blood in Mannion's car and on a shirt he left by the washing machine[6]."

"Yowza[7]," Broome said.

"Yeah, a real Einstein, this Mannion. You'll never, ever, guess[8] what he claimed[9]."

"Wait, let me think. Hmm. He was—don't tell me—framed[10]?"

"Wow, you're good."

"Don't be intimidated[11]. I'm a trained detective."

"So you probably know how this all ended. The case was open and shut[12]. Mannion got twenty-five to life[13] in Rahway."

"What happened to this girl? This Stacy Paris?"

"You just found the body, what, an hour ago?[14] I'm still working on it."

"And the big question," Broome said.

Erin smiled. "You want to know when this murder occurred[15]?"

"And I thought I was the trained detective."

"March eleventh, eighteen years ago. And, yes, it was Mardi Gras. Or I should say it was the morning after[16]. See, that's the thing. Mardi Gras was actually March tenth that year, but our boy Gunther's body was found after midnight."

"So technically speaking it was not[17] Mardi Gras."

"Exactly. And that happens with[18] a few of the missing people cases too. It makes it harder to see the pattern."

"So we need to look at murders or missing people on or around that date—and we need to look for people murdered or missing at or around that park. That area was pretty remote. A body could be there for days or even weeks."

"I'm on it[1]," Erin said.

Broome stared, chewing on a hangnail[2].

"That's disgusting," Erin said.

He kept at it.[3] "This Mannion guy."

"What about him?"

"If we're right about this pattern, about there being some—I don't know—Mardi Gras killer or whatever the hell he is …" Broome stopped. "Mannion's been serving, what, eighteen years for a crime he didn't commit."

"Let's not jump the gun[4], Broome."

"Detective?"

Broome started at the[5] voice. He turned to see Del Flynn and his loud[6] Hawaiian shirt. There had to be at least ten gold chains around his neck. Broome spotted[7] a gold Saint Anthony medal, a gold ship anchor[8], and a gold mud flap-like[9] silhouette of a curvy girl[10]. Variety pack.[11]

"Mr. Flynn?"

Goldberg was standing a few feet back behind him. Del Flynn, Broome had already been reminded several times, possessed beaucoup bucks[12]. The mayor[13] and several other muckety-mucks[14] had called, as though the Atlantic City Police Department had a VIP line[15] for missing people. Then again, maybe it did, who knew[16]? Broome didn't hold it against the man[17]. If your son vanishes, you go all out[18]. You don't hold back.[19] Broome got that.

Broome introduced Flynn to Erin. Erin nodded and then put her head back down. Erin had never been good with the families of victims. "They're broken," Erin had told him before. Broome looked now into Flynn's eyes and thought "shattered[20]" was more accurate[21]. "Broken" suggested something clean and all the way through[22] and fixable[23]. But what happened to them was messier[24], more abstract, filled with shards[25] and no hope of recovery[26].

"Did you find something new?" Del Flynn asked.

1. Je suis dessus

2. en se mâchouillant un ongle

3. Il ne s'arrêta pas pour autant.

4. Pas de conclusions hâtives

5. sursauta, à cette

6. voyante

7. distingua

8. ancre de marine

9. bien carrossée

10. de pin-up

11. Un bel assortiment.

12. était bourré de fric

13. maire

14. gros bonnets

15. une ligne directe spéciale « personnages de marque »

16. allez savoir

17. n'en voulait pas à ce type

18. tous les moyens sont bons

19. On ne lésine pas.

20. brisé

21. précis

22. de cassure nette

23. de réparable

24. plus en vrac

25. petits éclats

26. sans espoir de s'en remettre

"It's too early to tell, Mr. Flynn."

"But something?"

The desperation in his voice was more than just audible.[1] It was a living, breathing horrible thing. It filled the room. It suffocated all around it[2]. Broome looked for Goldberg to step in[3]. Goldberg looked right through him[4].

Flynn reached out and grabbed Broome's arm with a little too much force. "Do you have any children, Detective?"

Broome had been asked this more than once during his years in law enforcement[5]. He always found it borderline patronizing[6]—really, it made no difference—but again, seeing that shatter[7], he got it. "No, sir, I don't. Detective Anderson here does though[8]."

Yep[9], Broome had tossed his lovely ex under the bus[10]. Flynn's eyes moved toward Erin. Erin kept her head down. After a few uncomfortable seconds, Broome mercifully moved between them[11].

"Mr. Flynn," Broome said, "I assure you that we're doing all we can to find your son. But if we have to stop to provide you progress reports[12] when we're trying to work, that's going to slow us down[13]. You see that, right? I could spend time investigating clues and searching for your son. Or I could spend it filling you in on[14] every development. Do you understand what I mean?"

"I want to help."

"Then let us be[15], okay?"

Flynn's shattered eyes flared at that[16]—a brief flash of anger[17] before the destruction flooded back in[18]. Goldberg stepped in[19] now. "I think, Detective Broome, that what Mr. Flynn is asking—"

Del Flynn put his hand on Goldberg's arm, stopping him. "Later," Flynn said. He started down the corridor. Goldberg threw one final glare[20] at Broome and turned to follow him.

---

1. Le désespoir était palpable dans sa voix.

2. étouffait tout ce qui l'entourait

3. regarda Goldberg, pensant qu'il allait intervenir

4. l'ignora

5. dans la police

6. limite condescendant

7. cette déchirure

8. par contre

9. Eh oui

10. mis son adorable ex sur la sellette

11. s'intercala entre eux pour faire diversion

12. des rapports sur la progression de l'affaire

13. nous ralentir

14. vous mettre au courant de

15. laissez-nous tranquilles

16. s'embrasa en entendant cela

17. accès de colère

18. ne reprenne le dessus

19. intervint

20. regard torve

"I thought Goldberg was going to perform a sex act on that guy," Erin said. "Flynn must have serious juice[1]."

"Don't care[2]," Broome said. "Can you get me the number to Rahway Prison?"

She typed into the computer. It was late, but it wasn't like[3] federal penitentiaries had business hours[4]. Broome called the number, told the dispatcher[5] he was calling about a prisoner named Ricky Mannion. He was told to hold.[6]

"This is Corrections Officer Dean Vanech."

"My name is Broome. I'm a homicide detective with ACPD."

"Okay."

"I'm calling about one of your prisoners, guy named Ricky Mannion."

"What about him?"

"Do you know him?"

"I do."

"Does he still claim he's innocent?"

"Every day. But you know what? Almost every guy in here is innocent. It's amazing, really. Either we are all totally incompetent or—gasp oh gasp[7]—our house guests[8] are full of crap[9]."

"What's your take on him?[10]"

"Meaning?"

"Is Mannion more persuasive[11] than most?"

"About being innocent? Who the hell knows? I've seen guys in here who could put De Niro to shame[12]."

Talking to this Vanech guy, Broome could see, was going to be a waste of time[13].

"I'd like to come up and visit Mannion first thing in the morning[14]," Broome said. "That okay?"

"Well, let me check his social calendar[15]. My, my[16], the First Lady was forced to cancel[17], so Mannion is free. Shall I pencil you in[18] for seven-ish[19]?"

Everyone was a wiseass.[20]

---

1. vraiment
avoir du pognon

2. M'en fous

3. comme si

4. des horaires
de bureau

5. standardiste

6. On lui dit de
rester en ligne.

7. incroyable
mais vrai

8. nos hôtes

9. ne racontent
que des
conneries

10. Que
pensez-vous de
lui ?

11. convaincant

12. De Niro
fait débutant, à
côté d'eux

13. une perte de
temps

14. à la première
heure demain
matin

15. son agenda

16. Ouh là

17. contrainte
d'annuler

18. Je vous
inscris

19. vers 7 h.

20. Encore un
petit malin.

1. confirma le rendez-vous

2. attira son attention

3. débouler dans le commissariat

4. loué

5. une suite à deux chambres

6. très chic

7. situé dans un gratte-ciel

8. et il présentait l'avantage supplémentaire

9. des drogués

10. fêtards du carnaval

11. de la racaille

12. à dire vrai

13. grandi dans un environnement très protégé

14. Le péché avait quelque chose d'attirant

15. un attrait

16. sinon il n'y aurait aucune raison de pester contre

17. de trouver un exutoire salutaire

18. des minables

19. tous étaient impurs et méritaient d'être punis

20. le repaire du diable

Broome made the appointment[1]. He was hanging up the phone when something caught his eye[2]. He turned his head and saw Cassie rush into the station[3]. She spotted Broome and rushed toward him.

"There's a problem," Cassie said.

"GOT it."

As Ken promised, the cell phone number quickly told all.

Because they were unsure how many days this particular job would take, Ken and Barbie had rented[4] a two-bedroom suite[5] at the sleek[6] skyscraper[7] hotel called the Borgata. The Borgata was supposedly the nicest hotel in Atlantic City, plus it had the added advantage[8] of being away from the Boardwalk, the cesspool strip of gamblers, drug addicts[9], sinners, carnival barkers[10], and overall filth[11].

Still, Barbie thought, the Borgata had a filth all its own. You could not escape it in Atlantic City, and truth be told[12], she didn't really want to. She was disgusted and exhilarated in equal measure. She wanted to dive into the filth and take a bath at the same time.

Barbie had grown up protected[13] but she was not naive. She understood that human beings were complex. There was a draw to sin[14], an allure[15], or there wouldn't be a need to rail against it[16]. The key was to have some sort of healthy outlet[17]. She felt now that she and Ken had that. Their victims—if that was the right word—were scum[18]. Ken and Barbie hurt them, yes, but none were pure or undeserving[19]. Sometimes, the pain even opened the victim's eyes, brought on a form of redemption. Tawny, for example. Barbie felt good about that. She had experienced momentary pain that could, in the end, save the rest of her life.

Staying here at the Borgata—living for a short while in the devil's lair[20], in the very heart of temptation—worked for her. It educated her. It was like sneaking into enemy camp and learning their secrets. When

Barbie walked through the casino, she could see the looks of lust[1] on the men's faces, but she also half expected someone to point at her and shout, "She doesn't belong!"

"How did you trace back the number[2]?" Barbie asked.

She sat on the love seat[3] facing the window. In the distance she could see the lights of the Boardwalk.

"Online," Ken said.

"You were able to trace a cell phone on the computer?"

"Yes."

"How?"

"I Googled 'trace cell phone.' "

She shook her head. "That's it?"

"Well, they did charge me[4] ten dollars."

Ken looked over the keyboard and smiled at her. Barbie felt it in her toes[5]. A pink shirt collar popped over[6] his lime-green[7] sweater. His khakis were pleated[8]. He looked, she thought, very handsome. They always held hands[9] as they walked through the hotel. She loved that, the feel of his hand in hers, but sometimes, when a man's gaze[10] would linger too long[11], she could feel his grip tighten against her[12]. She could feel the heat then, the rush, the tingle[13].

"So whose phone is it?" she asked.

"A man named David Pierce."

"And who is he?"

"I'm not sure. He's a labor attorney[14] in Jersey City. I don't see any connection to our work here. He seems to be a citizen. Married, two kids."

"A woman called Harry Sutton's cell phone," Barbie said.

Ken nodded. "There are four T-Mobile cell phone lines under this account[15]. I assume one for him, one for his wife, one for each of his two children. The number we traced was not the main number—the one usually used by the billing name[16]."

1. les regards concupiscents

2. es-tu remonté au détenteur du numéro

3. la causeuse

4. ça m'a tout de même coûté

5. en fut émoustillée jusqu'au bout des ongles

6. dépassait de

7. vert citron

8. Il portait un pantalon à pinces.

9. se tenaient toujours la main

10. le regard d'un homme

11. s'attardait trop longtemps sur elle

12. qu'il la serrait un peu plus fort

13. une tiédeur l'envahir, une euphorie, comme un picotement

14. avocat spécialisé en droit du travail

15. sur ce compte

16. le nom sur la facture

"How old is the daughter?"

"Fifteen. Her name is Kaylie."

"The woman I spoke with was, well, a woman."

"It has to be the wife then. Her name is Megan."

"How does she fit in?[1]"

Ken shrugged. "I don't know yet. I just plugged in[2] their address in Kasselton into MapQuest. The drive shouldn't take us more than[3] two hours." He turned toward her, and she could see the glint in his eye[4]. "We could go up there right now and get the answers. The kids might not even be in bed yet."

Barbie bit her fingernail[5]. "A suburban mother with two children?"

Ken said nothing.

"We normally hurt those who deserve it," she went on. "It is why we work in this particular world."

Ken rubbed his chin[6], considered her point[7]. "If this Megan Pierce is involved with Harry Sutton, then she is far from an innocent[8]."

"Are you sure about that?"

He held up his car keys and gave them a little jangle[9]. "Only one way to find out for sure."

Barbie shook her head. "This is really big. We should check in with our employer first."

"And if he gives us the okay?"

"Like you said." Barbie gave a shrug. "They're less than two hours away."

1. Qu'est-ce qu'elle vient faire dans tout ça ?
2. viens de saisir
3. En voiture, on met au maximum
4. lueur dans son regard
5. se mordit un ongle
6. se frotta le menton
7. réfléchissant à ce qu'elle venait de dire
8. loin d'être innocente
9. les fit cliqueter

18

HALF an hour earlier, Megan had heard the sickly sweet[1] voice on Harry Sutton's phone say, "Mr. Sutton's phone automatically rings to me when he's indisposed. I'm sorry, Cassie. I didn't catch your last name."

Megan disconnected the call[2].

Fester was standing next to her at the bar. "Something wrong?"

Megan stared at her phone. She tried to conjure up Harry's office in her head[3]. There was one desk, one window, a file cabinet[4], a worn couch[5].....

But there was no place for a receptionist.

So who had just answered[6] his phone?

A very bad feeling[7] started gnawing in the pit of her stomach[8].

Fester said, "Hello? You still here?"

"I have to go."

"Whoa, I thought you were looking for Ray. Why don't we wait till he replies?"

1. doucereuse

2. avait raccroché

3. de visualiser le bureau d'Harry dans son esprit

4. classeur à tiroirs

5. vieux canapé

6. qui venait de répondre sur

7. Un mauvais pressentiment

8. à lui ronger les tripes

"Tell him I'll meet him at Lucy."

"Huh?"

"Just tell him that. Lucy at eleven o'clock. If I can't make it[1], I'll call you at this bar."

"Wait a second," Fester said.

But she didn't. She hurried out of the[2] Weak Signal, wading her way through the crowd[3], desperation coming off them in waves[4]. When she reached the street, she had to stop for a moment and suck in oxygen. She hurried over to Harry Sutton's office, passing a young couple in the hallway[5], but the lights were out and the door was locked.

That was when she decided to find Broome.

At the station, after Broome's partner, a woman who introduced herself as[6] Detective Erin Anderson, left the room, Megan filled Broome in[7]. He listened without interrupting. She finished up by saying, "I'm worried about Harry."

"Oh, I wouldn't be[8]," Broome said. "I mean, not based on this. You know Harry. He's a player from the word 'go'.[9] I know he loves the girls, but he also *loves* the girls, if you know what I mean. One of them probably answered his phone."

"And pretended to be[10] his receptionist?"

"Sure, why not? She was probably just trying to be funny."

"Yeah," Megan said with a frown. "Hilarious."

"You think Harry chooses them for their witty repartee[11]?"

Megan shook her head. "I got a bad feeling about this."

"We can call him again."

"I tried. No answer."

"I'd send a squad car by his house, but what's the point[12]? He goes out every night. Did you tell anyone you were going to see him?"

"No."

1. j'ai un empêchement

2. se rua hors du

3. se frayant un chemin parmi les clients

4. manifestement plus désespérés les uns que les autres

5. le couloir

6. se présenta comme étant

7. mit Broome au courant

8. je ne vois pas pourquoi

9. C'est un séducteur comme pas deux.

10. s'est fait passer pour

11. parce qu'elles ont de l'esprit

12. à quoi bon

"So I'm not sure I follow. What makes you think he's in danger?"

"Nothing, I guess. The woman's voice. I don't know. It sounded so sickly sweet."

"Oh," Broome said, "well, why didn't you say so in the first place[1]?"

Megan frowned. "Could you be, I don't know, a little more patronizing?"

" 'Sickly sweet'?"

"Okay, I get it."

"No, Cassie or whatever your name is, I don't think you do." Broome moved a little closer[2]. "May I be blunt[3]?"

"Because so far you've been circumspect[4]? Sure."

"You look good[5]. Really, really good."

"Uh, thanks."

"Not that way[6]. I mean you look like the years have been a friend to you[7]. You look healthy and happy and, most important of all, you look like you have[8] someplace to go. Do you know what I mean?"

She said nothing.

"That's the definition of happiness, you know. Most of the girls down here, they'll never have that. A place to go."

"Detective Broome?" she said.

"Yes?"

"You're deep.[9]"

Broome smiled at that one. "Yeah, philosopher detective. Do yourself a favor anyway[10]. Go to that place."

"The, uh, place to go?"

"Yeah, home or whatever. The place where you have people waiting for you."

"You're not listening to me, Detective."

"No, I am. Now you need to listen to me. What are you still doing down here?"

---

1. tout de suite

2. se rapprocha un peu

3. vous parler franchement

4. vous avez pris des gants

5. êtes toute belle

6. Ce n'est pas ce que je veux dire

7. les années vous ont épargnée

8. vous donnez l'impression d'avoir

9. C'est profond, comme remarque.

10. Ne faites pas l'imbécile

She stayed quiet for a moment[1]. He waited, watched her. The truth was, despite her sarcasm[2], Broome was scoring points[3].

What was she still doing here?

She thought now about her home, her "place to go"—about Kaylie and Jordan, about poor Dave, probably pacing and running his hand through his hair[4] the way he did when he was anxious[5], wondering what had suddenly happened to the woman he'd slept beside for the past sixteen years.

With a weak voice[6], Megan said, "I thought you wanted me to stick around[7] in case something new developed[8]."

"I got what I need for now[9]. If I need more, I'll call Harry. I made you a promise about anonymity. I plan on keeping it.[10]"

"Thank you," she said.

"You're welcome.[11] Now get out of here before the chief sees you and starts asking questions."

She wanted to protest. This felt somehow wrong, but either way[12] there was nothing to gain[13] staying here. Without uttering another word[14], Megan headed back outside[15]. She had parked around the corner. She slipped into the front seat and thought about what to do. The answer was obvious.

Broome was right. But for some reason, as she sat in the car, tears started brimming in her eyes. What the hell was wrong with her? She started up the car[16] and prepared to go straight home[17]. Forget all this. Forget La Crème and Lorraine and Rudy and Stewart Green and Harry Sutton. They had been something she'd caught a glimpse of[18] in her rearview mirror[19], that's all.

But what about Ray?

She checked the car clock. Why had she suggested that they meet at Lucy of all places[20]? Her keys hung from the ignition slot[21]. In all the years she'd known him Dave had never asked about that bronze, slightly rusted[1] key. She'd always kept it with her. She doubted it would still open the door—it was close to twenty years old now—but that key was the only souvenir, the only remembrance, she had allowed herself to keep from her old life.

One key.

She touched it now and thought about the last time she'd used it. She wanted to see Ray. She didn't want to see him.

It was one thing to play with fire—it was another thing to leap directly[2] into the flames.

Go home, Cassie or Megan or whoever I really am. We appreciate this breaking bulletin[3] to solve an old disappearance, but it is now time to return to our regularly scheduled life.

On the one hand, this whole crazy day still felt like a no-harm-no-foul situation[4]. She could leave here unscathed[5]. On the other, she kept looking over her shoulder[6], as though she were being followed. She felt that the world was closing in on her[7] now, that Stewart Green was still there, smiling that horrible, awful smile, readying to pounce[8]. Yes, her best chance, the smart move[9], was to go home, but now she wondered if even that would do any good, or if it was already too late.

Lucy. At eleven P.M.

Lucy was in Margate, five miles from where Megan now was. No matter how much she tried to convince herself otherwise, no matter how dangerous or volatile[10], she knew that there would be no peace or closure until she saw Ray. Besides, forgetting everything else, how could she come down all this way and not see Lucy?

She drove south on Atlantic Avenue until, up ahead[11], she saw Lucy, hovering in the dark[12], silhouetted by the moon[13]. As always, no matter how many times she had seen her, Megan stared up at Lucy in childlike awe[14].

1. légèrement rouillée

2. se jeter

3. cette interruption momentanée des programmes

4. semblait pour l'instant n'avoir pas porté à conséquence

5. indemne

6. était toujours à regarder derrière elle

7. une menace planait

8. prêt à bondir

9. ce qu'elle avait de plus malin à faire

10. explosif

11. droit devant

12. flottant dans le noir

13. se détachant à la lumière de la lune

14. avec le regard admiratif d'un enfant

Lucy was a massive[1] elephant—"massive" meaning six stories tall[2].

Built in 1882, Lucy the Elephant was one of the country's greatest and oldest roadside[3] attractions and an architectural wonder[4]—a sixty-five-foot[5] elephant-shaped structure that originally housed, of all things, a real-estate office[6]. During her 130-year reign on the New Jersey shore, Lucy had also been a restaurant, a tavern (closed during Prohibition), a private beach cottage, and now a place for tourists to visit for four dollars a pop[7]. The ninety-ton[8] pachyderm was made up of a million pieces of wood with an outer sheath[9] of hammered tin[10]. You entered Lucy through either of her thick hind legs[11], climbed the spiral staircase[12] into a main room of curving plaster[13] the color of Pepto-Bismol[14] or, so they say, of an elephant's stomach. You could walk over to Lucy's head and check out the ocean from her windows/eyes. There was another window in the ass area[15], known to those who take care of her as her "pane in the butt[16]." There were photographs and a video show and even a bathtub[17]. Climb another set of stairs and you could step outside on the top of Lucy's back for one of the great views of the Atlantic Ocean. On a clear day, boats out there could see Lucy from eight miles out.

Megan had always loved Lucy. She couldn't say exactly why. Twenty years ago, she had taken to[18] visiting on her day off, grabbing a burger and fries at Lucy's outdoor café, sitting on the same bench[19] not far from the old girl's trunk[20]. It was there she met and started seeing one of Lucy's caretakers and tour guides, a sweet, though overly needy[21], guy named Bob Malins. The relationship didn't last long, but before she broke up with him, Megan surreptitiously pocketed[22] his key to Lucy, brought it to a local hardware store[23], and made a copy of it.

That was the key she still kept on her chain.

Bob never knew[1], of course, but late at night, when Megan needed to get away from the club and the apartment she shared with four other girls, she would use the key and unroll a blanket and disappear inside Lucy. When she fell for[2] Ray, this was the place they would meet up. She brought no other man here, not ever. Only Ray. They would use the key and climb that spiral staircase and make the sweetest, gentlest love.

She parked the car and slipped out. She closed her eyes and breathed in the salty ocean air. It all started coming back to her. Her eyes opened. She looked up at Lucy and shivered at the rush of memories[3].

From behind her, a voice—*the* voice, really—said, "Cassie?"

She couldn't move.

"Oh my God," he said with an ache[4] that tore a hole in her heart[5]. "Cassie."

DAVE Pierce felt as though a giant hand had picked up his life and started shaking it like a cheap snow globe[6].

He sat now in front of the computer in the spare[7] bedroom Megan had converted last year into a home office. His stomach hurt. He hated turmoil[8]. He didn't handle pressure well[9]. When he was feeling this way, when the walls seemed to be closing in on him[10], Megan was always there. She would rub his temples[11] or massage his shoulders or whisper soft, soothing[12] words in his ear.

Without her, he felt adrift[13] and scared. Megan had never done anything like this before. She had never been out of touch[14] for more than an hour or two. Her sudden erratic behavior[15] should have surprised him, shocked him even, but the worst part was, it hadn't. Maybe that was the most troubling part—how easily every given perception[16], everything he had taken for granted[17], could shift[18].

1. ne l'avait jamais su

2. tomba amoureuse de

3. trembla alors que les souvenirs l'assaillaient

4. d'un ton si empreint de douleur

5. qu'il déchira le cœur de Megan

6. une boule à neige bon marché

7. d'amis

8. le chaos

9. supportait mal la pression

10. il se sentait oppressé

11. était là pour lui masser les tempes

12. rassurants

13. se sentait abandonné

14. injoignable

15. Son comportement tout à coup déconcertant

16. toutes ses façons de voir

17. tout ce qui lui avait semblé aller de soi

18. basculer

1. Il avait le doigt sur

2. bouton de la souris

3. ce qui le fit sursauter

4. Mais bon sang

5. tu ne peux pas frapper

6. gamin sensible

7. changea de ton

8. vieux

9. la grosse blague dans la famille

10. C'est juste !

11. Cela dit, va te coucher.

12. un baiser avant d'aller se coucher

13. vint se blottir dans ses bras

14. au bord des larmes

15. s'écartèrent l'un de l'autre

16. fut naturellement attiré par

17. l'écran de l'ordinateur

His finger hovered over[1] the mouse button[2]. Dave looked at the screen. He didn't want to make the final click, but really, what choice did he have anymore?

Jordan threw open the door, startling him[3]. "Dad?"

"For crying out loud[4], what did I tell you about knocking[5]?"

"I'm sorry—"

"I've told you a hundred times," he said, louder than he intended. "Knock first. Is that so hard to remember?"

"I didn't mean to …"

Jordan's eyes filled with tears. He was a sensitive kid[6]. Dave had been like that when he was little too. He quickly backed off[7].

"I'm sorry, sport[8]. I just got a lot going on, that's all."

Jordan nodded, trying to keep the tears back.

"What's up, pal?"

"Where's Mom?"

Good question. He stared at the screen. One more click and he'd know the answer. To his son he said, "She's doing something for Grandma. Shouldn't you be in bed?"

"Mom said she'd help me with math."

"Why didn't you ask me?"

Jordan frowned. "With math?"

It was a big family joke[9], how bad Dave was in math. "Point taken.[10] Get in bed though.[11] It's late."

"I didn't finish my homework."

"I'll write your teacher a note. Get some sleep, okay?"

He came closer to his father. The boy still liked a good-night kiss[12]. His sister had stopped participating in that ritual years ago. When Jordan hugged him[13] now, Dave felt the tears push into his eyes[14]. He held on to his son for a second longer than usual. When they released each other[15], Jordan's eyes naturally gravitated toward[16] the computer monitor[17]. Dave quickly minimized the screen, turning it into a tiny icon in the bottom corner.

"Good night, pal[1]."

"Good night, Dad."

"Close the door, okay?"

He nodded, doing as he was asked. Dave wiped his eyes and hit the icon. The screen came back on. He moved the arrow back over the link[2]. One more click would tell him exactly where his wife was.

When he had first gotten the cell phones and signed a contract that would have made his mortgage broker feel inadequate[3], the salesman[4] had offered a bunch of mind-numbing[5] smart-phone options, most of which Dave had ignored. But when the salesman raised the idea of activating the GPSs on the phones for only five dollars per month, Dave had accepted. At the time he had pretended to himself that it was for peace of mind[6]—in case of an emergency[7]. Suppose Jordan went missing? Suppose Kaylie didn't call in for hours? Suppose Megan got carjacked[8]?

But the truth was, a truth that Dave had never even whispered to himself[9], he had never fully trusted the woman he loved and fully trusted. Yes, that made no sense. She had a past. He knew that. So did he. Everyone did, he supposed. You come to a new relationship shedding the skin of the old ones[10]. That was a good and healthy thing.

But with Megan, there was something more. Much of what she told him about her past didn't really add up[11]. He didn't exactly ignore it, but he let it go. Part of him didn't want to threaten the good karma[12]. Even now, after all these years, he still couldn't believe that Megan had chosen him. She was so beautiful and smart and when she looked at him, when she smiled at him, even now, even after all these years, he still felt the pow[13]. When you are lucky enough to experience that, when you get to have that pow as part

---

1. fiston

2. remit la flèche sur le lien

3. bien plus compliqué que celui de son crédit immobilier

4. vendeur

5. un nombre invraisemblable d'options

6. sa tranquillité d'esprit

7. d'urgence

8. ne se fasse voler sa voiture

9. n'avait même jamais osé s'avouer

10. en faisant peau neuve

11. ne collaient pas vraiment

12. tenter le diable

13. en était encore tout remué

of your daily life, you don't look too hard at the whys and hows[1].

Dave had been happily passive, struck dumb[2] by what he considered his blind luck[3], but today had shattered the calm[4]. That giant hand kept shaking and shaking his world, and when it was put back on the shelf[5], it would never be the same. That was the part they tell you but you can't ever really believe—how fragile it all is.

Night had long since[6] fallen. The house was quiet. He wondered whether he had ever felt alone, and he guessed that the answer was no. So without thinking about it any longer[7], Dave clicked the icon.

A map came up[8]. Then Dave Pierce hit the zoom button[9] once, twice, three times, closing in slowly on[10] exactly where his wife now was.

19

1. toujours
séduisant

2. mais teinté
d'angoisse et de
perplexité

3. d'y voir clair

4. la submerger

5. la porter

6. Un ancien
amant

7. incarne le
parfait « Et
si... »

8. le chemin
qu'on a choisi de
ne pas suivre

9. se détache de
l'autre, avec le
temps

10. n'a plus les
mêmes buts
ni les mêmes
besoins

11. Mais eux
avaient été
arrachés l'un à
l'autre

12. comme s'ils
avaient été
victimes d'une
catastrophe
naturelle

MEGAN and Ray faced each other, maybe ten yards apart.

For the first time since that horrible night seventeen years ago, Megan was looking at the man she had loved and abandoned. Ray stared back, seemingly frozen, his still-handsome[1] face a mask of anguish and confusion[2].

Emotions ricocheted through her. She didn't move, didn't think, didn't try to sort through them[3]. Not yet. She just let them overwhelm her[4], take her down, bring her up[5]. Former lovers[6] are always the ultimate what-if,[7] the supreme road-not-taken[8], but with Ray, it was even deeper. Most couples move on for a variety of reasons. One outgrows the other[9], one or the other loses interest, loses that feeling, has different goals and wants[10], finds someone new.

None of that happened with Ray. They were instead torn asunder[11] as if by a natural disaster[12], and when that happened, her feelings for him—yes, it was

171

love—had been as intense as ever. He, she was sure, had felt the same. There was no gentle distancing[1], no harsh words[2], no hardening of the heart[3]. One moment they were together, connected[4], in love. The next it was all gone in a pool of blood[5].

Without warning[6], Ray broke into a sprint[7]. She did the same as though suddenly released from some unseen gate[8]. They ran into each other[9] hard, the impact sending them reeling[10]. They held on tight, neither speaking, her cheek against his chest. She could feel the muscles under his shirt. Supposedly[11], once a moment passes, it is gone forever, but the truth was, it startled her how fast the years could fall away[12], how quickly we can go back and find the old us, the true us, the us that never really leaves.

A friend once told Megan that we are always seventeen years old, waiting for our lives to begin. More than ever, clutching to[13] this man, Megan understood that.

They didn't let go. For nearly a minute they just stayed there, holding each other under Lucy's watchful[14] eye. Finally Ray said, "I have so much I want to ask you."

"I know."

"Where have you been all these years?"

"Does it matter?" she said.

"I guess not."

The grip loosened a bit.[15] She pulled back and looked up into the face. He had two, maybe three days of stubble[16]. His hair was still tousled[17] albeit with a bit of gray now at the temples[18]. When she looked into those dark blue eyes of his, the jolt sent her into a free fall[19]. She felt her knees buckle[20].

"I don't understand," Ray said. "Why are you back?"

She cleared her throat[21]. "Another man is missing."

She wanted to gauge his reaction[22], but all she saw was pain and confusion.

"It happened on February eighteenth," she said. "The same day as Stewart Green disappeared."

"Disappeared?" he repeated.

"Yes."

Ray opened his mouth, closed it again. Behind him Ventura's Greenhouse, a popular restaurant and what they called "beer garden," was in full swing[1]. People were watching them. Megan took his hand and walked to the far side[2] of Lucy, near the old gift shop[3], where they'd be out of sight[4].

"So," Ray said, something odd in his voice, "after seventeen years, you come back and now another man is, I don't know, gone."

Megan turned to him. "No, I came down after."

"Why?"

"To help."

"Help with what?"

"To help figure out what happened. I tried to run away from it, but now he's back."

Ray shook his head, looking even more confused[5]. "Who's back?"

"Stewart Green."

His voice had a snap in it now[6]. "How can you say that?"

"Someone saw him."

"Who?"

She shook her head. "It doesn't matter."

Ray looked dazed[7]. "I don't understand any of this."

"Yes, Ray, you do."

"What are you talking about?"

"I saw the photograph you sent the cops."

Again he opened his mouth. Again nothing came out[8]. Megan turned toward the fence[9] that surrounded[10] Lucy. She put one foot on the wall of the gift shop and hoisted herself up and over it[11]. She took out the old key and showed it to him. "Come on."

"You think that still works?"

"Doubt it.[12]"

1. plein à craquer
2. à l'autre bout
3. boutique de souvenirs
4. hors de vue
5. l'air encore plus perplexe
6. Son ton devint cassant
7. abasourdi
8. aucun son n'en sortit
9. la grille
10. entourait
11. se hissa et sauta par-dessus
12. M'étonnerait.

Ray didn't hesitate. He hopped the fence too[1]. They moved under Lucy's belly[2], the one that housed[3] the structure's largest room, toward her rear leg[4]. As she put the key in the lock, Ray came up close to her. She could feel the heat from him[5].

He tried to keep the pain from his voice[6], but he couldn't do it. "Why did you run away that night?"

"You know why, Ray."

"Did you kill him?"

That made her stop. "What?"

"Did you kill Stewart Green?"

"No," she said. She moved closer to him, looked into his eyes again[7]. "I never told you how abusive he was[8]. How he hurt me."

He frowned. "You think I didn't know?"

"I guess you did.[9]"

The key didn't work.

"Just tell me why you ran[10]," Ray said. "Tell me what happened that night."

"I took that path up to the[11] ruins. I heard a noise and ran over to that big rock on the right. You know the one[12]."

He didn't need to nod.

"I saw Stewart lying there in a pool of blood." She stopped.

"So you ran?"

"Yes."

"Because you thought the police would blame you[13]?"

A tear ran down her cheek[14]. "In part[15]."

Megan waited, hoping that she wouldn't have to say the other part[16], that he would see it[17]. It took a second or two, but his eyes began to widen[18].

"Oh my God," Ray said. "You thought it was me."

She said nothing.

"You ran," he said slowly, "because you thought I killed Stewart Green."

"Yes."

---

1. sauta lui aussi par-dessus la grille
2. ventre
3. abritait
4. patte arrière
5. la chaleur de son corps
6. de masquer sa douleur quand il reprit la parole
7. le regarda à nouveau droit dans les yeux
8. à quel point il était brutal
9. Je suppose que si.
10. t'es enfuie
11. le sentier qui mène aux
12. vois lequel
13. te croirait responsable
14. coula sur sa joue
15. En partie
16. formuler l'autre raison
17. qu'il comprendrait tout seul
18. s'écarquillèrent

"Were you scared of me?[1] Or were you trying to protect me?"

She thought about it. "I could never be afraid of you, Ray. You always made me feel safe.[2]"

Ray shook his head. "It explains so much. Why you never came back. Why you never reached out[3]."

"They'd either think I did it. Or you.[4] There was no other way.[5]"

Ray took the key from her hand and tried the lock again[6]. It didn't open. He looked lost, devastated[7].

"I must have arrived right after[8] you ran," he said.

"Was Stewart still lying there?"

Ray nodded. "He was bleeding[9]. I figured that he was dead." He closed his eyes and turned away. "I ran down the hill. I went to your place[10], afraid, I don't know. I just didn't know. But you were gone. I came here, to Lucy. I thought maybe you'd be hiding inside or something. I waited. But you never showed[11], of course. I searched for you. For years. I didn't know if you were dead or alive. I saw your face on every street, in every bar." He stopped then, blinked it away[12], found her eyes again. "Eventually I moved across the country.[13] To Los Angeles, as far away from this place as I could get."

"But you returned."

"Yes."

"Why?"

Ray shrugged. "You know I hate all that mystical crap[14], right?"

Megan nodded.

"But something drew me back here[15]. I don't know what. I couldn't help it[16]."

She swallowed. The realization was reaching her[17], sinking in even as she spoke[18]. "And when you returned to Atlantic City, you went back to that spot in the park."

He nodded. "Every February eighteenth."

---

1. Tu avais peur de moi ?

2. Je me suis toujours sentie à l'abri avec toi.

3. n'as jamais fait signe

4. On aurait pensé que que le coupable était toi ou moi.

5. Il n'y avait pas d'autre solution.

6. de la glisser à nouveau dans la serrure

7. perdu, accablé

8. juste après que

9. couvert de sang

10. chez toi

11. n'es jamais venue

12. chassa l'image

13. J'ai fini par déménager très loin.

14. toutes ces conneries genre sciences occultes

15. m'a poussé à revenir

16. Je n'ai pas pu résister.

17. Elle commençait à comprendre

18. formulant sa pensée au fur et à mesure

"You took pictures," she went on. "Because that's what you do, Ray. You see the world through that lens. You process things that way[1]. And you took that picture—the one of Carlton Flynn the night he vanished."

"How did you know it was me?"

"Come on, Ray. I still know[2] your work."

"So what did you think when you saw it?" Ray asked, a slight edge in his tone[3]. "That I did it, right? I killed Stewart and seventeen years later, on the anniversary of[4] that horrible night, I, what, killed this Flynn guy?"

"No."

"Why not?"

"Because you sent that picture to the police," she said. "You didn't have to take that risk. You're doing the same thing I am. You're trying to help them. You're trying to figure out what really happened that night."

When Ray looked away now, her heart broke anew[5]. Tears came to her eyes. "I was wrong," she said. "All this time[6] I thought ... I'm so sorry, Ray."

He couldn't look at her.

"Ray, please?"

"Please what?"

"Talk to me."

He took a few deep breaths[7], putting himself together a piece at a time[8]. "I still go to the ruins on the anniversary. I sit there, and I think about you. I think about all we lost that night."

She moved closer to him. "And you take pictures?"

"Yes. It helps. It doesn't help. You know what I mean."

She did. "So that picture you sent to the police ..."

"It was stolen[9]. Or at least, someone tried to steal it[10]."

"What?"

"I worked this stupid job for[11] Fester—paparazzi at some over-the-top[12] bar mitzvah. Someone

176

jumped me[1] on the street and stole my camera. At first I figured that it was a routine robbery[2]. But then I saw Carlton Flynn on television and I remembered the photograph I took[3]. I had a copy on my computer too."

She said, "So you think whoever[4] jumped you—"

"Killed Stewart Green and Carlton Flynn. Yes."

"You say 'killed.' But we don't know that. They're missing."

"We both saw Stewart Green that night. You think he survived?"

"I think it's possible. You don't?"

Ray said nothing. He looked down and shook his head. She moved closer to him. She reached up and pushed the hair off his forehead[5]. He was still so damn handsome. She moved her hand to his cheek. Her touch made his eyes close[6].

"All these years," Ray said, his eyes finding hers[7], "I still look for[8] your face. Every day. I've imagined this moment a thousand times."

"Was it like this?" she asked softly.

He pointed to[9] the hand resting on his cheek[10]. "You weren't wearing a wedding ring[11]."

She took her hand away slowly. "Why are you still in this town, Ray, working for Fester? Why aren't you doing what you love?"

"It's not your problem, Cassie."

"I can still care.[12]"

"Do you have kids now?" he asked.

"Two."

"Boys, girls?"

"One girl, one boy."

"Nice." Ray chuckled to himself[13] and shook his head. "You thought I killed Stewart?"

"Yes."

"That helped, I bet.[14]"

"What do you mean?"

1. m'a agressé
2. une agression toute bête
3. que j'avais prise
4. la personne qui
5. dégagea les cheveux de son front
6. Il ferma les yeux à son contact.
7. en la regardant dans les yeux
8. cherche encore
9. désigna
10. posée sur sa joue
11. ne portais pas d'alliance
12. J'ai encore le droit de me soucier de toi.
13. rit dans sa barbe
14. Je parie que ça t'a aidée.

"To move on.[1] Thinking your boyfriend was a murderer."

She wondered whether that was true.

Ray studied her wedding ring. "Do you love him?" he asked.

"Yes."

"But you still feel something for me[2]."

"Of course."

Ray nodded. "This isn't a line you want to cross.[3]"

"Not now, no."

"So the fact that you still feel for me," he said. "That will have to be enough.[4]"

"It's a lot."

"It is." Ray took her face in his hands. He had big hands, wonderful hands, and again she felt her knees start to give way[5]. He tried a rakish grin[6]. "If you ever do want to cross that line—[7]"

"I'll call you."

His hand slipped away then[8]. Ray took a step back[9]. She did too. She turned, hopped the fence, and walked back to her car.

She started to drive. For a little while she could still see Lucy in her rearview mirror, but that didn't last[10]. She took the expressway[11] to the Garden State Parkway[12] and drove all the way home[13]—all the way back to her family[14]—without stopping.

20

DEL Flynn's mansion didn't have a sign reading "Tacky[1]" on it because, really, it would have been redundant[2]. The theme was white. Blindingly white.[3] Interior and exterior. There were faux marble columns of white, nude statues in white, white brick, a white swimming pool, white couches[4] against white carpets[5] and white walls. The only splash[6] of color was the orange in Del's shirt.

"Del, honey, you coming to bed?"

His wife, Darya—Mrs. Del Flynn Number Three—was twenty years his junior[7]. She wore tourniquet-tight white[8] and had the biggest chest, ass[9], and lips money could buy. Yes, she didn't look real, but that was how Del liked his women now—like curvy cartoons[10] with exaggerated features and figures[11]. To some it was freakish.[12] To Del it was sexy as all get-out[13].

"Not yet."

"You sure?"

1. Vulgaire
2. superflu
3. D'un blanc aveuglant.
4. des sofas
5. sur de la moquette blanche
6. seule touche
7. avait 20 ans de moins que lui
8. était toujours sanglée de blanc
9. la plus grosse poitrine, le plus gros cul
10. des filles bien faites de dessin animé
11. silhouettes
12. Certains trouvaient ça dérangeant.
13. incroyablement sexy

Darya was wearing a white silk robe[1], and nothing else. His favorite[2]. Del wished that the old stirring[3]—his constant life companion, his curse[4], if you will, that had cost him his beloved[5] Maria, Carlton's mother, the only woman he ever loved[6]—would return without the aid of a certain blue pill. But for the first time in his life, there was no need or desire.

"Go to bed, Darya."

She disappeared—probably, he figured, relieved that she could just watch TV and pass out[7] from whatever combo[8] of wine and pills got her through the night[9]. In the end all women were the same. Except for his Maria. Del sat back in the white leather chair. The white decor was Darya's doing. She said it signified purity or harmony or a young aura—some New Age bullshit like that[10]. When they first met, Darya had been wearing a white bikini and all he wanted to do was defile that[11], but he was really growing tired of the white. He missed color. He missed leaving his shoes on[12] when he walked in the house. He missed the old dark green couch in the corner. An all-white house is impossible to maintain[13]. An all-white house sets you up for failure.[14]

Del stared out the window. He was not much of a drinker. His father, a first-generation Irish immigrant, had owned a small pub in Ventnor Heights. Del was practically raised[15] in that place. When you see it up close[16] every day, the destruction booze can cause,[17] you got no taste for it[18].

But right now he sat with a bottle of his favorite, Macallan Single Malt, because he needed to be numb[19]. Del had made a lot of money. He learned the restaurant business, the ins and outs[20], and realized that it was a pretty lousy way of[21] making a dollar[22]. So he went into restaurant supply[23]—linens[24], plates, silverware[25], glasses, you name it[26]. He had started small, but eventually he was the biggest supplier in southern New Jersey. He took that money and bought up property, mostly those private storage units[1] on the outskirts of town[2], and made a mint[3].

It all meant nothing.

Sure, that was a cliché, but right now, all Del saw was Carlton. His boy. The disappearance sat on[4] Del, consumed him[5], made it impossible to breathe. He looked out the window. The pool was covered for the winter, but he could see his son out there, swimming with his buddies[6], swearing too casually[7], flirting with whatever honey[8] happened to look his way. True, his son—his only son—was soft. He spent too much time primping[9], too much time in the gym and waxing his body[10] and plucking his eyebrows[11], as if that crap was manly[12]. But when his son smiled at him, when his son hugged Del and kissed his cheek because that was what Carlton always did when he left for whatever club at night, Del's chest filled with something so real, so wonderful and life affirming[13], that he knew, just knew, that he had been put on this planet to feel just that way.

And now, poof, his son, the only thing in his life that truly mattered, that was truly irreplaceable, was gone.

What was Del supposed to do? Sit back and wait[14]? Trust the police to take care of his own offspring[15]? Stick to the rules[16] in a city that never played fair[17]?

What kind of father does that?

You take care of your own. You protect your son, no matter what the cost.

It was midnight. Del fiddled with the gold chain around his neck, the Saint Anthony medal Maria had given him on their tenth wedding anniversary. Saint Anthony, she explained, was the patron saint of lost things. "Don't ever lose us, okay?" she said, as she put it around his neck. Then she put one around Carlton's neck too. "Don't ever lose Carlton and me."

Prophetic.

1. box de stockage pour particuliers

2. en banlieue proche

3. avait fait fortune

4. oppressait

5. le consumait

6. potes

7. parlant vulgairement

8. toute nana qui

9. à se faire beau

10. à s'épiler le corps à la cire

11. les sourcils à la pince à épiler

12. était viril

13. régénérant

14. Attendre en se tournant les pouces

15. son propre rejeton

16. Respecter les règles du jeu

17. qui trichait toujours

From the bedroom he could hear the television. Darya was watching on their new fifty-three-inch, 3-D screen with the surround sound. Here Del was—in this white home, sitting here in the lap of luxury[1]— and he was powerless[2]. He felt helpless and impotent[3] and fat and comfortable while his boy was out in the cold and dark somewhere. Carlton could be alone somewhere. He could be trapped[4] or crying or in tremendous pain[5]. He could be bleeding or calling out to his father to save him.

When Carlton was four, he had been scared to go on the "big boy" slide[6] at the playground[7]. Del got on him about that[8], even going so far as to call him a[9] baby. Nice, right? Carlton started to cry. That just pissed Del off even more. Finally, merely to please[10] (or shut up) his old man[11], Carlton started climbing up the ladder[12]. The ladder was too crowded, the kids jostling one another[13] as they made their way up. Carlton, the smallest kid on the ladder, lost his balance[14]. Del could still remember that moment, standing at a distance, his arms crossed as he watched his only son topple backward[15], knowing, even as he started to run toward him, that there was no way he was going to get there in time, that he, the boy's father, had not only shamed[16] his son and caused the fall[17] but also that he was powerless to do anything to save him.

Little Carlton landed wrong[18], his arm snapping back like a bird's wing[19]. He screamed in pain. Del had never forgotten that moment. He had never forgotten that feeling of powerlessness or that horrible scream. Now that scream was back, haunting his every waking moment, shredding his insides like hot shrapnel[20].

Del took another sip of the Macallan. Behind him, someone cleared his throat. Normally Del was on the jumpy side[21], the kind of guy who leapt at the smallest sound[22]. Maria used to comment about that. He was a light sleeper[23], his nights filled with bad dreams. Maria understood that. She would wrap her arms around him[1] and whisper in his ear and calm him. No one did that now. Darya could sleep through a rock concert. Del just had to deal with his terrors alone now.

God, he had loved Maria.

He'd been so happy back then, living in that dilapidated[2] house on Drexel Avenue, but the demons had called to him[3] and Maria couldn't understand it. When you stepped back and thought about it, the whole thing made no sense. You could be addicted to booze[4] or drugs or gambling[5]. You could lose your house, your health, your money. You could be belligerent[6] and even abusive—but if the cause was, say, booze or pills or the ponies[7], the world understood your pain. Your true love[8] stayed with you and got you help. But if your demon was sex, if you needed what Del needed, what[9] every normal friggin' man[10] in the history of mankind[11] eventually gave in to[12], if you do something that was built into[13] man's DNA, something that really harmed nobody in the way drinking or pills did[14], except through jealousy—then no one understands and you lose everything.

It was her fault, really. Maria's. Raising[15] that kid with no father figure[16] in the house. Not being able to forgive or to understand what a man was like. He had loved her. How did she not get that?

"Good evening, Mr. Flynn."

The voice chilled the room[17]. Del Flynn slowly turned around. When Ken and Barbie smiled at him, the temperature dropped another[18] ten degrees.

"Did you find my son?"

"Not yet, Mr. Flynn."

They both just stood there, looking as though they'd just finished a song on the old *Lawrence Welk Show* or … what was that dumb holiday show[19] his parents used to watch every year? The King family. What the hell ever happened to them?[20] And why did see-

1. le prenait dans ses bras

2. délabrée

3. il n'avait pas su résister au démon de midi

4. porté sur la bouteille

5. le jeu

6. agressif

7. le hasch

8. grand amour

9. ce à quoi

10. tout homme normalement constitué

11. l'humanité

12. finissait par céder

13. inscrit dans

14. de bien moins nocif que l'alcool ou la drogue

15. Avoir élevé

16. sans figure paternelle

17. était glaçante

18. baissa encore de

19. stupide émission à Noël

20. Qu'étaient-ils donc tous devenus ?

ing these two always make him think of the weirdest crap[1]?

"So what do you want?"

"We have a dilemma, Mr. Flynn," Ken said.

"A moral dilemma," Barbie added.

Del knew people. You don't live around here and work with restaurants[2] and trucking[3] and not meet people. One of his best friends growing up[4] was Roily Lember, who was now head of organized crime[5] in the Camden area. Del had gone to him for help with[6] finding his son. He knew that he was making a deal with the devil[7]. He didn't much care. Lember had told him that he'd have his people on the lookout[8], but Del would be better off[9] hiring two expert freelancers—the best in the business[10]. He warned him not to be too shocked by their appearances. Del also reached out to[11] Goldberg, a cop well-known for providing inside[12] information for a fee[13].

No, he was not about to leave this to the cops alone[14].

Del knew that earlier in the day[15] Ken and Barbie had traced down[16] a stripper Carlton had been banging[17]. Her name was Tonya or Tawny or something like that. Earlier, the police had questioned the girl, but she gave them almost nothing[18]. Ken and Barbie had been able to extract more information.

"Are you familiar with[19] a town called Kasselton?" Ken asked.

Del thought about that. "It's up north, right?"

"Yes."

"I don't think I've ever been there."

"How about anybody with the last name Pierce? David or Megan Pierce?"

"No. Do they have something to do with my son?"

Ken and Barbie updated Del[20] on their day[21]. They didn't go into details about[22] how they went about gathering[23] information, and Del didn't ask. He just listened, feeling his heart break and harden at the same time.

Mostly harden.

"Do you think there'll be some blowback[1]?" Del asked.

Ken looked at Barbie, then to Del. "From Tawny? No. From Harry Sutton? Yes. But they won't be able to trace it back to us[2]."

"Or you," Barbie added.

Again Del didn't ask for details. "So now what?"

"We normally follow the evidence[3]," Barbie said, in a voice that sounded almost rehearsed[4], as if she were suddenly playing someone[5] much older. "In this case, that would mean questioning[6] Mr. and Mrs. Pierce."

Del said nothing.

"And," Ken said, "that would mean leaving Atlantic City for Kasselton, thereby widening the circle[7]."

"And adding to the collateral damage[8]," Barbie added.

Del kept his eyes on the window. "So you're here to get my approval[9]?"

"Yes."

"Do you think the Pierces know something?"

"I think the wife does, yes," Ken said. "We know that Detective Broome met with her today. She chose to have a lawyer with her[10]—that lawyer being Harry Sutton."

"That means she had something to hide," Barbie added.

Del thought about that, about his visit to the precinct. "Whatever this Megan Pierce told him—Broome acted on it[11]. He had the crime techs at a park tonight. They found blood."

Silence.

"Do the Pierces have children?" Del asked.

"Two."

"Try to keep them out of it[12]."

1. des retombées

2. remonter jusqu'à nous

3. suivons toutes les pistes

4. artificielle

5. jouait quelqu'un de

6. voudrait dire interroger

7. élargissant ainsi le cercle

8. augmentant les dommages collatéraux

9. pour avoir mon accord

10. d'être accompagnée par un avocat

11. a suivi ses indications

12. les laisser en dehors de tout ça.

It was, Del knew from personal experience, the most merciful thing he could do[1].

MEGAN'S drive home took two hours.

Dave had recently put satellite radio in the car, so she tried to listen to Howard Stern for a while. One time, when she and Dave were alone in the car and listening, Howard had chatted up[2] a stripper named Triple Es, and Megan nearly jumped out of her skin[3] because she immediately recognized the voice as belonging to Susan Schwartz, a girl who worked La Crème back in the day. They had even been roommates[4] for a time.

Oddly enough[5], Megan found Howard Stern to be his least[6] interesting when the show was its most provocative[7]. While far from a prude[8], Megan had found the more graphic bits[9]—the dirty sex, the bodily functions, the freaks—tame[10] but got totally immersed[11] when Howard conducted celebrity interviews or commented on the news with Robin. Megan was always surprised at how often she agreed with him, how much sense he made—Howard could be a wonderful distraction/companion[12] on long, lonely car rides[13]—but tonight, after a few futile minutes, she flicked off[14] the radio and let herself be alone with her thoughts[15].

What[16] now?

It was nearly one A.M. when she reached her driveway. The house was entirely dark, except for the lamp on a timer[17] in the living room. She hadn't called Dave to say she was coming home. She wasn't sure why. She just didn't know what to say to him, how she would answer his obvious questions. She had hoped the two hours in the car would clarify that for her[18]. But it hadn't. She had considered everything from a total fabrication[19] ("A friend—I can't tell you who— had a personal problem") to total truth[20] ("You better sit down for this one") to something in the middle[21] ("I went to Atlantic City, but it's no big deal[22]").

So as Megan parked in her driveway, as she dropped her keys in her purse[1] and opened the car door and closed it quietly, because it was so late and she didn't want to wake anyone[2], she still had no idea what she would say to the man she'd been married to for the past sixteen years.

The house was quiet—almost too quiet[3], as they say[4]—as if the shiny new brick and stonework were somehow holding its collective breath[5]. The stillness[6] surprised her. Despite the late hour[7] Megan figured that Dave would be up[8], waiting for her to return, maybe sitting in the dark, maybe pacing. But there was no sign of any life at all. She tiptoed up the stairs[9] and turned right. Jordan's door was open. She could hear him breathing. Like most eleven-year-olds, when Jordan finally fell asleep, he fell hard and deep and it would take an act of God to wake him up[10].

Jordan always kept his door open and still, at the age of eleven, used a night-light[11]. Megan could see the mounted shark[12] above his head. For some strange reason, Jordan loved fishing more than anything. Neither she nor Dave had ever fished—or remotely enjoyed fishing—but Dave's brother-in-law had taken Jordan when he was four, and the kid just got the bug[13]. For a little while, that brother-in-law took Dave on his local fishing excursions, but when he divorced Dave's sister, that ended. So now at least twice a year, Dave arranged a boys' fishing weekend (some might coin this[14] "sexist," since the females[15] weren't invited, but Megan and Kaylie preferred the word "grateful"), everything from fly-fishing[16] in Wyoming to bass[17] fishing in Alabama and last year, shark fishing off the coast of northern Georgia. That was where Jordan got that particular trophy mount[18].

As always, Kaylie's bedroom door was shut. She had no fear of the dark[19], only invasion of privacy[20]. Kaylie had recently been campaigning[21]—there was no other word for it—to turn the finished basement

1. sac à main
2. réveiller personne
3. presque trop silencieuse
4. comme on dit souvent
5. retenait en quelque sorte son souffle
6. Un tel calme
7. Malgré l'heure tardive,
8. ne serait pas couché
9. monta l'escalier sur la pointe des pieds
10. il aurait fallu un tremblement de terre pour le réveiller
11. une veilleuse
12. le requin empaillé sur le mur
13. était devenu un mordu de la pêche
14. certains trouveraient ça
15. femmes
16. de la pêche à la mouche
17. à la perche
18. ce trophée à accrocher au mur
19. n'avait pas peur du noir
20. seulement qu'on empiète sur son territoire
21. milité

into her new bedroom, ergo,[1] placing her person as far away from the rest of the family as possible, and while Megan was holding firm on the no[2], Dave was caving[3]. His usual justification for giving in sounded like a plea[4]: "She's going to be leaving us soon … we need to let go of the little things[5]… with such little time left, do we really want so much strife[6]?"

Megan risked turning her daughter's knob and opened the door. Kaylie was in her usual sleep position, on her side with her stuffed penguin[7], cleverly named "Penguin," snuggled in close[8]. Kaylie had slept with Penguin since she was eight. It always made Megan smile. Teens[9] may look like adults, may crave[10] adult independence from Mom and Dad, but good ol'[11] Penguin was a constant reminder that there was plenty of parental work yet to be done.

It felt good to be home.

In the end, Megan had done nothing wrong. She gave Broome the important information he needed and returned to where she belonged, unscathed. As she padded through her home[12], Atlantic City was getting smaller and smaller in the rearview mirror. The only thing that had thrown her slightly off her game[13] was seeing Ray, with Lucy looming behind them[14]. She had felt the ache all the way back—the same one she'd always had with Ray—but there were things you can do and things you can't. The idea of "having it all" is indeed nonsense. Still, that desire, that electricity as though your whole being were suddenly revved up to the tenth power[15], that feeling that she wanted to be close to Ray and then even closer and then that's not close enough … it, of course, still haunted her. Sure, she could try to deny it[16]. She had and would again. But if you have that feeling, what do you do about it? It is there. Do you lie to yourself? Do you control it and forget it and move on? And was it a betrayal[17] to admit that she didn't feel that way with

Dave—or was that normal with a man you've known so well? To be expected[1], perhaps even good[2]?

She felt something deeper and richer with[3] Dave, something driven by[4] years and commitment[5], but maybe that was just fancy talk[6]. That sort of electricity—had she ever felt it with her husband? Was it fair to even compare or think such things?

Were such thoughts alone[7] a betrayal?

You don't get to have it all. No one does.

She loved Dave. She wanted to spend her life with him. She would lay down[8] her life for him and the kids without a moment of hesitation. Wasn't that, in the end, the pure definition of true love? And when you took a step back[9], wasn't she really just glamorizing her days[10] in Atlantic City and her time with Ray? We all do that, don't we? We either glamorize or demonize[11] the past.

She approached her and Dave's bedroom door. The lights were off[12]. She wondered now whether Dave would be in there—or had he gone out? She hadn't considered[13] that before. He'd be upset[14]. He had every right to be.[15] Maybe he had run off. Maybe he'd gone out to a bar and drowned his sorrows[16].

But as she started inside, she knew that wouldn't be the case. Dave wouldn't leave his children alone, especially during a time of crisis. A fresh wave of guilt washed over her[17]. She saw now the silhouette of her husband in the bed. His back was to her.[18] Looking at his still form[19], she felt scared about his reaction, but there was relief too. She suddenly felt that it was truly over[20].

Seventeen years ago, Stewart Green had threatened to kill her. That was what had drawn her back to[21] the past as much as old yearnings[22]—the fear that Stewart had somehow survived, that he was back—but Lorraine had probably been wrong on that one[23]. Either way she had done what she could. She had done the right thing. Megan was home now. She was safe.

1. Somme toute prévisible

2. voire une bonne chose

3. de plus intense pour

4. nourri par

5. leur engagement mutuel

6. ce n'étaient que de belles paroles

7. déjà

8. aurait donné

9. avec un peu de recul

10. est-ce qu'elle n'idéalisait pas sa vie

11. on diabolise

12. éteintes

13. envisagé

14. était sûrement fâché

15. Non sans raisons.

16. pour noyer son chagrin

17. La culpabilité l'envahit à nouveau

18. Il lui tournait le dos.

19. cette forme immobile

20. là, c'était vraiment fini

21. Voilà ce qui avait réveillé son intérêt pour

22. tout autant que la nostalgie

23. tout faux

It was over. Or it was about to be.

The decision that had been tormenting her for the entire car ride home[1]—the last sixteen years really—was suddenly clear. She couldn't, pardon the pun[2], dance around her past anymore[3]. She had to come clean[4]. She had to tell Dave everything. She would have to hope, after all the years, that love would conquer all[5].

Or was that just another comforting[6] lie?

Either way, Dave was owed the truth[7].

"Dave?"

"You're okay?"

He hadn't been sleeping. She swallowed, felt the tears sting her eyes. "I'm fine."

Still with his back to her, he said, "You sure?"

"Yes."

She sat on the edge[8] of the bed. She was afraid to move any closer. Dave kept his back to her. He adjusted the pillow[9], settled back in[10].

"Dave?"

He didn't reply.

When she touched his shoulder, he recoiled[11].

"You want to know where I was," she said.

He still wouldn't look at her, still wouldn't say a word.

"Don't shut me out.[12] Please."

"Megan?"

"What?"

"You don't get to tell me what not to do.[13]"

Finally Dave turned toward her, and she saw it in his eyes—the immense and unfathomable[14] pain. It sent her reeling.[15] Lies, she could see, wouldn't work. Neither would any words. So she did the only thing she could. She kissed him. He pulled back for a second, but then he grabbed her behind the head[16] and kissed her back. He kissed her hard and pulled her down toward him[17].

---

1. pendant tout le trajet de retour

2. désolée pour le jeu de mots

3. danser autour du pot

4. lâcher le morceau

5. serait le plus fort

6. rassurant

7. elle devait la vérité à Dave

8. bord

9. remit bien l'oreiller

10. se réinstalla

11. eut un mouvement de recul

12. Arrête de m'ignorer.

13. Tu n'as pas à m'interdire quoi que ce soit.

14. insondable

15. Ça la bouleversa.

16. mit sa main derrière sa tête

17. l'attira vers lui

They made love. They made love for a long time without saying a word. When they were done[1], both completely spent[2], Megan fell asleep. She thought that Dave did too, but she couldn't be sure. It was as if they were in different worlds.

1. Après
2. vannés tous les deux

21

IN 1988, Rahway State Prison officially changed its name to East Jersey State Prison at the request of the residents[1] of Rahway. This request was more than understandable. The residents felt as though being identified by the notorious[2] prison unfairly stigmatized[3] their city and, worse[4], lowered property values[5]. It probably did. Still[6], absolutely nobody other than[7] the residents of Rahway called it East Jersey State Prison. It was a little like the state of New Jersey itself. It might be officially known as the Garden State, but come on[8]—who called it that?

Heading up[9] Route 1-9, Broome could see the prison's huge dome[10], a sight that never failed to remind him of[11] some great basilica in Italy. The maximum-security prison (by whatever name) kept around two thousand inmates[12] locked up, all male[13]. The prison had housed boxers James Scott and, notably[14], Rubin "Hurricane" Carter—the man featured in[15] the Bob Dylan song and Denzel Washington movie. The

Scared Straight! documentaries, in which juvenile delinquents were purportedly[1] rehabilitated by being berated by Rahway lifers[2], were also shot[3] here.

After going through the usual security rigmarole[4], Broome found himself seated across from[5] Ricky Mannion. They say prison shrinks a man[6]. If that were the case here, Broome would hate to have seen[7] Mannion before his arrest. Mannion had to be six-six[8] and weigh over three hundred pounds[9]. He was black with a cleanly shaven head[10] and arms that could double as oak trees[11].

Broome expected the standard prison machismo, but Mannion was giving him pretty much just the opposite. Mannion's eyes flooded with tears[12] when he looked at the badge[13].

"Are you here to help me?" Mannion asked Broome.

"I'm here to ask some questions."

"But this is about my case, right?"

Mannion wasn't behind a glass partition[14]—they sat across a table from each other, his arms and feet cuffed[15]—but he still looked like the proverbial kid pushing his nose against the glass[16].

"It's about the murder of Ross Gunther," Broome said.

"What did you find? Please tell me."

"Mr. Mannion—"

"I was thirty-one when they arrested me. I'm almost fifty now. Can you imagine that? In here all that time for a crime I didn't commit. And you know I'm innocent, right?"

"I didn't say that."

Mannion smiled then. "Think about losing all those years, Detective. Your thirties, your forties, all rotting in this sewer[17], trying to tell anybody, everybody, that you didn't do it."

"Must be tough[18]," Broome said. Mr. Understatement.[19]

"That's what I do. Every day. Talk about my innocence. Still. But people stopped listening a long time

1. prétendument
2. après avoir été réprimandés par des condamnés à perpète de Rahway
3. avaient aussi été tournés
4. s'être soumis au cirque habituel des contrôles de sécurité
5. assis en face de
6. vous ratatine
7. n'aurait pas voulu voir
8. devait faire 2 m
9. peser au moins 140 kg
10. et avait le crâne rasé
11. des bras gros comme des chênes
12. s'emplirent de larmes
13. son insigne
14. une cloison en verre
15. menottes aux mains et aux pieds
16. on aurait quand même dit un de ces gamins le nez collé à une vitrine
17. passés à pourrir dans ce trou à rats
18. Ça doit être dur
19. Le roi de l'euphémisme.

ago. Nobody believed me then. Not even my own mother. And nobody believes me now. I scream and I protest and[1] I always see that same look on every face. Even if they ain't rolling their eyes[2], they're rolling their eyes, if you know what I mean."

"I know what you mean. I still don't see the point."

Mannion lowered his voice to a whisper[3]. "You're not rolling your eyes, Detective."

Broome said nothing.

"For the first time in twenty years, I have someone sitting across from me[4] who knows I'm telling the truth. You can't hide that from me."

"Wow." Broome sat back[5] and frowned. "How many times have you given someone that line of bull[6]?"

But Mannion just smiled at him. "You want to play it that way?[7] Fine. Ask me whatever you want. I'll tell you the truth."

Broome dived in[8]. "When you were first questioned by the police, you said that you'd never met Ross Gunther. Was that true?"

"No."

"So you opened with a lie[9]?"

"Yes."

"Why?"

"You're joking, right? I didn't want to give them a motive[10]."

"So you told a lie?"

"Yes."

"You told the police you didn't know Gunther, even though[11] at least five people saw you attack him at a bar three days before his murder[12]?"

The chains rattled[13] as Mannion shrugged his massive shoulders. "I was young. And stupid. But I didn't kill him. You have to believe that."

"Mr. Mannion, this will go faster—and better for you—if you dispense with the protestations of[14] innocence and just answer my questions, okay?"

"Yeah, sorry. Just a reflex, you know?"

1. J'ai beau crier et protester,

2. ne sont pas là à lever les yeux au ciel

3. se mit à murmurer

4. assis en face de moi

5. se radossa sur sa chaise

6. sorti ce genre de conneries

7. la jouer comme ça ?

8. rentra dans le vif du sujet

9. avez commencé par mentir

10. un mobile

11. alors qu'

12. avant qu'il soit tué

13. Les entraves firent un bruit de ferraille

14. si vous arrêtez de clamer votre

"You've had a lot of time to think about this crime, right? Let's say I believe you[1]. How did the victim's blood get into your house and car?"

"Simple. It was planted.[2]"

"So someone broke into[3] your car?"

"I don't lock my car in my own driveway[4]."

"And the house?"

"The blood wasn't found in the house. It was found by the washing machine in the garage. I left the garage door open. Lots of folks do[5]."

"Do you have any proof that[6] the blood was planted?"

Mannion smiled again. "I didn't at trial[7]."

"But you do now?"

"That's what I was trying to tell everyone. That I had proof. But they said it was too late. They said it wasn't enough."

"What proof, Mr. Mannion?"

"My pants[8]."

"What about them?"

"The police found Gunther's blood in my car, right?"

"Yes."

"And they found a ton of blood[9] on my shirt. I've seen the crime scene pics[10]. They showed them at the trial. The killer practically sawed Gunther's head off[11]. There was a lot of blood."

"Right, so?"

Mannion spread his hands. "So how come they didn't find any blood anywhere on my pants?"

Broome considered that for a moment. "Maybe you hid them."

"So, just so I got this straight[12], I somehow hid[13] my pants—and underpants[14] and socks and, hell, since it was cold out that night, my parka—but I left my shirt behind[15] for the police to find[16]? Oh, and since it was about thirty degrees out[17] that night, why would I have just been wearing a short-sleeve[18] T-shirt anyway? Why would the blood be on that and not on a coat[1] or a sweater[2] or a sweatshirt?"

---

1. Admettons que je vous croie.

2. Quelqu'un l'y a mis exprès.

3. a forcé

4. ma propre allée

5. Il y a plein de gens qui font ça.

6. une preuve que

7. au moment du procès

8. pantalon

9. plein de sang

10. photos

11. avait pratiquement décapité Gunther

12. récapitulons, que je sois sûr d'avoir pigé

13. j'aurais réussi à planquer

14. mon slip

15. j'aurais laissé traîner ma chemise

16. pour que les flics la trouvent

17. env. 0°C dehors

18. à manches courtes

1. un manteau
2. un pull
3. Bonnes questions.
4. casser le jugement
5. pour ce qui concernait Broome
6. tant d'espoir
7. aussi cruel que ça puisse paraître
8. ne laissa rien transparaître
9. accusa le coup
10. Je suis prêt s'il le faut à passer au détecteur de mensonges
11. peut vous en vouloir à ce point-là
12. derrière les barreaux
13. fit la grimace
14. vous trompait
15. croisa les bras
16. un arrangement
17. le type de milieu
18. lever
19. les entraves
20. Il n'y avait personne d'autre dans notre vie.

Good points.[3] Certainly not enough to overturn a conviction[4], but for Broome's purposes[5], it made a lot of sense. Mannion looked at him now with such hope[6]. Broome, cruel as it might seem[7], gave him nothing back[8]. "What else?"

Mannion blinked[9]. "What do you mean, what else?"

"That's all the new proof you have?"

The big man blinked harder. He looked like a little boy about to cry. "I thought you were innocent until proven guilty."

"But you were already proven guilty."

"I didn't do it. I'll take a lie detector test[10], whatever."

"Again let's say you're telling the truth. Who would have it in for you like that[11]?"

"What?"

"You're claiming you were framed, right? So who would want to see you behind bars[12]?"

"I don't know."

"How about Stacy Paris?"

"Stacy?" Mannion made a face[13]. "She loved me. She was my girlfriend."

"And she was stepping out on you[14] with Ross Gunther."

"So he said." He folded his arms[15]. "It wasn't true."

Broome sighed and started to rise.

"Wait. Okay, it wasn't like that."

"What was it like?"

"Me and Stacy. We had an understanding[16]."

"What kind of understanding?"

"It was that world[17], you know?"

"I don't know, Mr. Mannion. Why don't you tell me?"

Mannion tried to raise[18] his hands, but the shackles[19] stopped him. "We were exclusive in our personal lives.[20] But professionally, well, that was okay, if you know what I mean."

"Are you saying Stacy Paris was a prostitute and you were her pimp[1]?"

"It wasn't like that. I cared about her. A lot."

"But you pimped her out[2]."

"Not me. It was just, you know, what she did sometimes. To make ends meet[3]. I mean, it was part of what she did."

"What was the other part?"

"She danced."

"Danced," Broome repeated. "Like what, ballet[4] at Lincoln Center[5]?"

Mannion frowned again. "On a pole[6]."

"Where?"

"Place called Homewreckers[7]."

Broome remembered the place. The sign out front read[8]: "Homewreckers Strip Joint—This Ain't No Gentlemen's Lounge[9]." They also advertised a[10] "You-Ain't-Here-for-the-Food Buffet[11]." The club closed down[12] ten, fifteen years ago. "Did she dance anywhere else?"

"No."

"How about La Crème?"

"No."

Dead end.[13] Or not. "It must have pissed you off.[14]"

"What?"

"The way she, uh, made ends meet?"

He shrugged. "It did, it didn't. Wasn't like I wasn't playing the field too.[15]"

"You didn't have a problem with it?"

"Not really."

"So Ross Gunther was just one of the ways she, uh, made ends meet."

"Right. Exactly."

"And you didn't care about what she did[16]. You weren't a jealous boyfriend."

"You got it.[17]"

Broome spread his hands. "So why did you get into an altercation with him?"

"Because," Mannion said, "Gunther roughed Stacy up[1]."

Broome felt his pulse starting to race[2]. He thought about what Cassie said, about Stewart Green abusing

---

1. son mac

2. lui faisiez faire le tapin

3. Pour arrondir ses fins de mois

4. de la danse classique

5. [célèbre théâtre new-yorkais]

6. De la danse érotique

7. [les Briseuses de ménage]

8. L'enseigne disait

9. C'est pas un club pour gentlemen

10. avaient aussi un slogan :

11. Vous êtes pas ici pour la gastronomie

12. avait fermé définitivement

13. L'impasse.

14. Ça ne devait pas vous plaire.

15. J'étais pas très fidèle non plus.

16. ça vous était égal, ce qu'elle faisait

17. C'est ça.

1. la tabassait
2. sentit son cœur accélérer
3. Ça vous arrivait de frapper
4. je me casse
5. fit la grimace
6. De temps en temps.
7. Rien de très sérieux.
8. Encore un mec bien
9. Comment voulez-vous que je le sache ?
10. M'étonnerait.
11. Vous avez la moindre idée de là où elle pourrait être ?
12. Plus au sud
13. sur le point de se faire piquer
14. à la fourrière

her. He thought about what Tawny said, about Carlton Flynn abusing her. And now he had Stacy Paris and Ross Gunther.

A pattern.

Except that Ross Gunther was dead. Of course, Stewart Green and Carlton Flynn could be dead, probably were. And then there were all the other men who'd gone missing. Where the hell had they gone?

"How about you, Mannion? You ever rough her up?"

"What do you mean?"

"Did you ever hit[3] Stacy? And if you lie to me even once, I'm gone[4]."

Mannion looked away, made a face[5]. "Once in a while.[6] No big thing.[7]"

"No, I'm sure it wasn't." Another prince[8], Broome thought. "After your trial, what happened to Stacy Paris?"

"How would I know?[9]" Mannion said. "You think, what, she writes me or something?"

"Is that her real name? Stacy Paris?"

"Doubt it.[10] Why?"

"I need to find her. Do you have any clue at all where she might be?[11]"

"No. She was from Georgia. Not Atlanta. That other city. Begins with an *S*. More south[12], she said, but she had the sexiest accent."

"Savannah?"

"Yeah, that's it."

"Okay, thanks for your help."

Broome started to rise. Mannion looked at him with the eyes of a dog about to be put down[13] in the pound[14]. Broome stopped. This man had been locked up for eighteen years for a crime he probably didn't commit. True, Mannion had been no saint. He had a fairly long rap sheet[1], including domestic abuse[2], and chances were[3], if he hadn't been caught up in this mess[4], he'd probably be in prison on some other charge[5]. Mannion wouldn't be out doing good, working for the poor or making the world a better place for his fellow man[6].

"Mr. Mannion?"

Mannion waited.

"For what it's worth[7], I think you're innocent. I don't have enough to prove it yet. I probably don't have enough yet to get you a new trial. But I'm going to keep working on it, okay?"

Tears ran freely down Mannion's face[8]. He didn't try to wipe them away[9]. He didn't make a sound.

"I'll be back," Broome said, heading for the door.

The walk out seemed longer than the walk in[10], the corridor longer and more narrow[11]. The guard who accompanied him said, "Did he give you a hard time?[12]"

"No, not at all. He was very cooperative."

At the security checkpoint[13], Broome collected[14] his keys and cell phone. When he turned the phone back on, the thing started buzzing like crazy[15]. Broome could see that there were at least a dozen phone messages, including one from Erin.

Oh, this couldn't be good.

He called Erin first. She picked up on the first ring. "Broome?"

"How bad?" he asked.

"Very."

1. un casier judiciaire bien rempli

2. [pour] violences domestiques

3. il y avait de fortes chances

4. impliqué dans toute cette histoire

5. pour un autre crime

6. son prochain

7. Si ça peut vous consoler

8. Les larmes coulaient à flots sur les joues de Mannion

9. les essuyer

10. qu'à l'aller

11. étroit

12. Il n'a pas été trop pénible ?

13. Au contrôle de sécurité

14. récupéra

15. sans arrêt

22

"Take the next exit[1]," Barbie said.

They were on their way to the home of Dave and Megan Pierce in Kasselton. When they rented[2] the car, the girl behind the counter[3] had been overly flirtatious with[4] Ken, angering Barbie[5]. Ken had pretended to be upset about it[6], but he loved when Barbie got possessive. To soothe her hurt feelings[7] he let Barbie pick out[8] the car—a white Mazda Miata.

"The first exit or the second?" Ken asked.

"The second. Then take your third right."

Ken frowned. "I don't understand why we can't use a GPS."

"I read a study[9]," she said.

"Oh?"

"The study stated[10] that global positioning[11] systems—that's what GPS stands for[12]—"

"I know that," Ken said.

"Well, GPSs harm our sense of direction[13] and thus[14] our brains[15]," Barbie said.

"How?"

"This particular study found that an overreliance on[1] such technologies will result in our using our spatial capabilities[2] in the hippocampus[3]—that's a part of our brain—"

"I know that too."

"Well, we use the hippocampus less when we rely on[4] GPSs, and that makes it shrink[5]. The hippocampus is needed for things like memory and navigation[6]. Atrophy could cause[7] dementia[8] or early[9] Alzheimer's."

"And you believe all that?" Ken asked.

"I do," Barbie said. "When it comes to the brain, I believe in the old adage: Use it or lose it."

"Interesting," Ken said, "though I don't see how your reading directions[10] works my hippocampus any harder[11] than looking at a GPS."

"It does. I'll show you the article later."

"Okay, good. I'd like that. What direction now?"

"No direction," Barbie said. She pointed up ahead[12]. "That's their house."

MEGAN's first thought when she awoke: Pain. A jack-hammer ripped through her skull.[13] Her mouth felt dry. She had slept the sleep of the dead[14] and now arose[15] with what felt a lot like a hangover[16]. It wasn't, of course. She hadn't woken up with a big-time[17] hangover since, well, it had been a long time. Pressure and stress, she figured.

Last night, she and Dave had fallen asleep—collapsed was more like it[18]—in spoon position[19], his arm under her waist. They slept like that a lot. At some point in the night, of course, Dave's arm always went numb[20], stuck in that waist nook[21], and he gently extracted it[22]. She reached now for her husband, needing on some primitive level[23] to feel him, but he wasn't there. She looked past where he slept to the new digital clock with the double iPod dock.

The time was 8:17 A.M.

201

1. si on se repose trop sur
2. facultés visuo-spatiales
3. hippocampe
4. on compte sur
5. ça le fait diminuer de volume
6. l'orientation
7. entraîner
8. une démence sénile
9. précoce
10. le fait que tu lises l'itinéraire [sur une carte]
11. fait plus travailler mon hippocampe
12. désigna un point au loin
13. Elle avait l'impression d'avoir un marteau-piqueur dans la tête.
14. comme une souche
15. se levait
16. comme une bonne gueule de bois
17. sérieuse
18. plus juste
19. en chien de fusil
20. s'ankylosait
21. étant coincé dans le creux de sa taille
22. le retirait délicatement
23. instinctivement

Megan's eyes widened. She swung her legs around[1], her feet hitting the floor[2]. She wondered when the last time she'd slept in past eight on a school day was, but this already seemed to be a day full of comparisons to her distant past. She threw water[3] on her face and a bathrobe on her body[4]. When she reached the bottom of the stairs, her daughter, Kaylie, gave her a knowing[5], teenage smirk[6].

"Late night with the girls[7], Mom?"

She glanced toward the kitchen. Dave was busying himself making pancakes[8]. Made sense though. The kids would have wanted to know where their mother was. Dave probably told them that she was having a rare[9] "girls' night out[10]."

"Yeah, I guess so," Megan said.

Kaylie made a *tsk-tsk* sound. "You girls have to know when to say when[11]."

Megan managed a smile. "Don't be a smart aleck.[12]"

Dave was in his new dark blue business suit with the bright orange tie. He dumped a pile of pancakes on Jordan's plate. Jordan rubbed his hands together[13] and then poured on enough syrup to coat a Toyota[14].

"Whoa, slow down[15]," she told him far too late.

Megan looked up and smiled at Dave. He gave a quick one back and turned away. Suddenly, the good feelings of last night seemed far away. It was odd how fast life could snap back[16] from the most dramatic and jarring[17]. In so many ways, nothing ever changes. She had been so close[18] last night to telling Dave everything, about the lies, the deception[19], her past as Cassie—all of it. She had been willing to do that because last night, she believed with all her heart that it wouldn't change anything. She still loved him. He still loved her.

How naïve that seemed in the light of the day[20].

Now, standing in this remodeled kitchen with Dave, Kaylie, and Jordan, she couldn't believe how close she had come to destroying everything. Dave would never be able to comprehend the truth. How could he? And why should she tell anyway? What was the point in that? It would only hurt him. The crisis had passed. Yes, he would eventually[1] want an explanation for where she had been, and so she'd offer up[2] something vague. But the sort of revelation and catharsis that had seemed so logical last night now seemed pretty close[3] to suicidal insanity[4].

Dave cleared his throat and made a production of looking at his watch[5]. "I better head out.[6]"

"Will you be home for dinner?" Megan asked.

"I'm not sure." Dave avoided her gaze[7]. She didn't like that. "We got a ton to do to prep[8] for this case."

"Okay."

Dave grabbed his work backpack[9], the expensive one she'd bought him for his birthday last year, with the separate laptop compartment[10] and zippered pocket[11] for his cell phone. Megan walked him out[12], leaving the kids in the kitchen. When Dave opened the front door and stepped onto the stoop[13] without kissing her, she put her hand on his forearm[14].

"I'm sorry," she said.

He looked at her, waiting. The sun was shining brilliantly[15] on their little suburban enclave. Down the street she could see the Reale kids hustling into[16] their mom's new SUV[17]. Most driveways had newspapers at the end, either the blue plastic of the *New York Times* or the green plastic of the local paper. There was a white Mazda Miata parked down in front of the Crowleys' house, probably a friend of their son Bradley's on pickup duty[18], and farther down the street, Sondra Rinsky power-walked her two toy dogs[19]. Sondra and Mike Rinsky had been the first to move into this development[20] years ago. They had five kids, but the youngest had started college[21] last year.

Dave still waited.

1. un jour	
2. elle inventerait	
3. avait maintenant des allures	
4. de folie suicidaire	
5. regarda ostensiblement sa montre	
6. Faut que j'y aille.	
7. évitait son regard	
8. un max de prépa	
9. sac à dos	
10. avec une poche pour l'ordinateur portable	
11. une petite avec fermeture Éclair	
12. l'accompagna dehors	
13. sortit sur la véranda	
14. avant-bras	
15. brillait de tous ses feux	
16. se bagarrer pour monter dans	
17. 4X4	
18. qui venait le chercher	
19. promenait ses deux toutous d'un pas sportif	
20. ce nouveau quartier résidentiel	
21. la fac	

1. son mensonge déjà prêt

2. de l'agressivité

3. notre choix de musiques
4. pour un rappel
5. méga cool
6. quand tu parles comme la racaille
7. Non mais, sans déconner.
8. quand même
9. au milieu
10. tout régler
11. Une place pour chaque chose
12. chaque chose à sa place
13. fit un grand sourire
14. Ça doit être ton hippocampe surdéveloppé !
15. on commence par
16. Il était un peu dégarni.
17. le dos voûté
18. de là où ils étaient
19. furieux contre elle

"It was no big deal," Megan said, the lie at the ready[1]. "I was just helping a friend with a personal problem. I had to be there for her, that's all."

"What friend?"

There was an edge[2] in his tone now. "Is it okay if I don't say? She asked me to keep it confidential."

"Even from me?"

She tried a smile and a shrug.

"Does this friend live nearby?" Dave asked.

It was, she thought, a weird question. "Not far."

"A woman from town?"

"Yes."

"So why were you in Atlantic City?"

KEN and Barbie watched the Pierces' house.

"I'm still not sure about the set list[3]," Barbie said. "I mean, I love the rap version of 'O Jerusalem,' but as an encore[4]?"

"It's pretty dope[5]," Ken said.

She smiled. "I love when you talk all gangsta[6]."

"Word.[7]"

"But still[8]. As an encore? I think it should be mid-set[9], don't you?"

"We have four months until camp starts, and you want to figure this out[10] now?"

"I like being organized. A place for everything[11] and everything in its place[12]."

Ken grinned[13]. "Must be that overdeveloped hippo-campus of yours.[14]"

"Ha-ha. But seriously, if we open with[15]—"

Barbie stopped when she saw the Pierces' front door open. A man came out. He wore a dark business suit and carried a backpack in one hand. His hair was thinning.[16] He looked tired, his shoulders slumped[17]. There was someone—a woman—at the door behind him. It might be his wife—hard to tell from this angle[18].

"He's mad at her[19]," Ken said.

"How can you tell?"

"The body language.[1]"

"You're exaggerating."

But just then the woman reached out for the man's arm. The man pulled away, spun[2], and started down the path[3].

The woman shouted, "Wait, hold up[4] a second."

He ignored her. The woman stepped outside[5], into full view, so that Ken and Barbie could see her clearly now. That was when Barbie squeezed[6] Ken's hand and heard herself gasp out loud[7].

"Isn't she … ?"

Ken nodded. "Yes."

"From last night at that law office?"

"Yes, I know."

Silence. The man got into his car and tore down the street[8]. The woman disappeared back into the house.

"She's seen us," Barbie said. "She could identify us."

"I know."

"We're supposed to keep this contained[9]."

"We have no choice now," Ken said.

"So how do you want to handle it[10]?"

Ken thought about it a moment. "The husband," he said.

"What about him?"

"They just had a fight[11]. A neighbor probably witnessed it. Maybe we can pin what happens to her on him[12]."

Barbie nodded. It made sense.

A few minutes later, a teenage girl headed out the front door and got onto[13] a school bus. A few minutes after that, a woman with two kids came up the walkway[14]. The Pierces' front door opened again. A boy who looked about ten or twelve kissed his mother good-bye[15] and left.

Ken and Barbie waited until the street was clear.

"She's alone now," Barbie said.

1. Son langage corporel.
2. tourna casaque
3. avança dans l'allée
4. attends
5. sortit de la maison
6. serra
7. laissa échapper un petit cri
8. partit à toute allure
9. limiter la casse
10. tu veux t'y prendre comment
11. viennent de se disputer
12. mettre sur le dos du type ce qui va arriver à sa femme
13. monta dans
14. arrivèrent devant la maison
15. pour lui dire au revoir

Ken nodded, opening the car door. "Let's get in position."

"SO why were you in Atlantic City?"

Dave's words landed like a body blow.[1] Megan stood there, stunned. Dave didn't wait for an answer. He turned away. She snapped out of it[2] and reached for his arm. "Dave?"

He pulled away and hurried down the path.

"Wait, hold up a second."

He didn't. She debated giving chase[3], but from behind her she heard Kaylie call, "Mom? Can I have lunch money?"

Dave was all the way down the path now. When he slipped into his car, Megan could feel her heart sink[4].

"Mom?"

Kaylie again. "Take a ten from my wallet[5]. I want change[6]."

The car pulled out[7] quickly and sped down[8] the street with a tire squeal[9]. The sound startled[10] the Reale kids. Barbara and Anthony Reale both turned at the exact same moment and watched Dave shoot down the street[11] with disapproving glares[12]. So did Sondra Rinsky and her dogs.

"I only see a twenty[13]," Kaylie said. "Mom? Can I take that?"

Still reeling, Megan stepped back inside and closed the door.

"Mom?"

"Yes," she said, her voice sounding far off in her own ears, "take the twenty. That should cover you[14] for the rest of the week." She headed back into the kitchen. Kaylie rushed out to catch the bus, leaving her dishes[15] in the sink[16]—as always. Megan wondered how many collective man-hours[17] parents had wasted[18] asking their children not to leave their dishes in the sink, to simply put them in the dishwasher, and

1. Elle prit la remarque de Dave en pleine figure.
2. se ressaisit
3. hésita à le suivre
4. eut un pincement au cœur
5. un billet de 10 $ dans mon portefeuille
6. récupérer la monnaie
7. atteignit la route
8. fila dans
9. en faisant crisser les pneus
10. fit sursauter
11. passer en trombe
12. d'un air réprobateur
13. billet de 20
14. te suffire
15. laissant sa vaisselle sale
16. l'évier
17. quel serait le nombre total d'heures
18. passées en vain par les parents à

wondered what sort of nation could have been built with said hours[1].

Jordan walked to school every morning with two friends, the parents rotating who made the walk with them[2]. It was the Colins' week. This arrangement had always driven Dave nuts[3]. In his day[4], Dave would whine[5], you just walked to school with your friends— no helicopter parents necessary. "It's three blocks away[6]!" Dave often cried. "Let them have some independence." But you just don't do that anymore. Kids were under constant surveillance. It was easy to bemoan and criticize[7], but Megan still did it because the alternative[8] was too horrible to contemplate[9].

How had Dave known about her being in Atlantic City?

She hadn't used the E-ZPass[10]. She hadn't even used her credit card. So how did he know? And if he knew where she was, what else did he know?

Dread filled her chest.[11] Once Jordan was out of the house[12], she called Dave's cell phone. No answer. She called again. Still no reply. She knew that he was just ignoring her. His car had Bluetooth, and she had called it enough times to know that the cell service was fine for his entire drive. She called one more time. This time she waited until she got his voice mail.

"Call me," she said. "Don't be like this."

She hung up. On one level, Megan realized that she just had to give him space[13], let him blow off steam[14], whatever. But another part of her didn't like this at all. Dave knew that his wife hated the silent treatment[15]. She tried his phone one more time. Nope, no answer. Terrific. So that was how he was going to play it. Anger started creeping in.[16] Figured.[17] He was all Mr. Understanding[18] last night. He probably just wanted some[19]. Men. In a sleazy nightclub[20] or the comfort of a suburban mini-mansion, it didn't really matter— men are the same. People are shocked when politicians or celebrities blow themselves up[21], but regular

---

1. les heures en question

2. les accompagnant à tour de rôle

3. mis Dave hors de lui

4. De son temps

5. rouspétait Dave

6. à trois rues d'ici

7. râler

8. l'autre possibilité

9. à envisager

10. carte d'abonnement [pour auto-routes]

11. L'appréhension l'envahit.

12. Une fois Jordan parti

13. lui laisser un peu de temps

14. attendre que sa colère s'émousse

15. détestait qu'il refuse de lui parler

16. La colère la prit.

17. Pas étonnant.

18. super compréhensif

19. voulait sans doute juste la bagatelle

20. une boîte de nuit minable

21. foutent leur vie en l'air

men do it too. It is a constant, and so maybe Dave was being nice to her because …

No, she wasn't being fair.

She was the one who had vanished. She was the liar, after all.

So now what?

Megan started to clean up[1] the kitchen—Dave might cook on occasion, but the job of cleaning[2] always seemed to fall on her[3]. She had her tennis group in an hour—doubles at the indoor Kasselton Tennis Club. She wanted more than anything to skip it[4], but you can't play doubles with only three, and it was too late now to find a replacement. How bizarre. From the club called La Crème to the club called Kasselton Tennis—quite the leap[5].

She started up the stairs to change into her tennis whites[6]. The club was old-world with a strict dress code[7]—all players had to wear only white. Ridiculous, really. She thought about her mother-in-law, Agnes. Maybe after tennis she'd go over and see how she was doing[8]. Agnes had been so agitated during Megan's visit yesterday. Wow, was it only yesterday? It felt as though she hadn't seen Agnes in a month.

She let herself think of[9] Ray. The warmth started so she pushed it away with the important logistics[10]: If Ray hadn't killed Stewart Green, then what had happened that night?

Forget it, it didn't matter anymore. It wasn't her concern[11]. She had to put it behind her[12]. She took another step, as if to signify[13] the distance that she was putting between herself and that horrible night, when the doorbell rang[14].

She stopped. No one just came to the door nowadays. People called or texted or e-mailed. No one just stopped by except maybe the FedEx and UPS guys[15] but it was too early for them.

The doorbell sounded again[16], and Megan knew, just knew, that whoever was ringing that bell was

---

1. débarrasser et ranger dans
2. nettoyer ensuite
3. retombait toujours sur elle
4. aurait largement préféré annuler
5. d'un extrême à l'autre
6. mettre sa tenue de tennis blanche
7. resté attaché aux traditions vestimentaires
8. allait
9. s'autorisa à penser à
10. chassa l'émotion en se fixant sur un détail d'importance
11. son problème
12. oublier tout ça
13. comme pour marquer
14. on sonna à la porte
15. livreurs de courrier express
16. La sonnette retentit à nouveau

going to tell her something horrible, that all her attempts at self-comfort[1] were nonsense, that now that the past had found her again, it would not be so easy to shake[2].

The doorbell rang a third time. Whoever it was, he or she had no interest in patience or waiting[3].

Megan headed back down the stairs and reached for[4] the doorknob.

1. *efforts pour se rassurer*

2. *de s'en débarrasser*

3. *n'était vraiment pas très patiente*

4. *tendit la main vers*

23

1. regarda par
la fenêtre à
côté de

2. avant de
répondre

3. la liste
des appels
téléphoniques

4. aviez promis

5. c'est que vous
n'essaieriez pas
de me retrouver

6. passer par

7. C'est ce que je
comptais faire

8. mais Harry
est mort

9. recula en
chancelant

10. qu'elle l'y
invite

THE doorbell rang a fourth time. Megan looked out the window by[1] the door, frowned, and opened it.

"How did you find me?" she asked.

He took his time replying[2]. "Harry Sutton's phone records[3]," Broome said. "Can I come in?"

"You promised[4]."

"I know."

"The last thing you said to me was that you wouldn't track me down[5]."

"I know."

"You should have gone through[6] Harry."

"I would have[7]," Broome said, "except Harry's dead[8]."

Another body blow. Megan actually stumbled backward[9]. Broome didn't wait for an invitation[10]. He stepped into the house and closed the door behind him.

Megan managed to say, "How?"

"We don't have an official cause yet, but it looks like heart failure[1]."

"So he wasn't … ?"

"Murdered. He was.[2] I mean, it may technically be manslaughter[3], but there's no doubt someone is responsible."

"I don't understand."

"Harry was tortured."

Megan's stomach fell anew[4]. "How?"

"You don't want to know. Nothing lethal[5], but …" Broome shook his head. "The strain was too much[6]. His heart gave out[7]."

It was odd how the mind worked. For years she had believed that Ray had killed Stewart Green in an effort to[8] protect her. Now she knew (or at least, strongly believed—wasn't there still a little doubt?) that it wasn't true. But still, despite that[9], the first thought when she heard about Harry Sutton was a simple, horrible one:

Dave had known that she was in Atlantic City.

She dismissed the[10] thought immediately. It was one of those outrageous[11] thoughts that just jump out[12], and you know right away the thought is ridiculous and unworthy of further consideration[13].

The second thought—the more dominant thought—was, well, Harry. She thought about that sweet, comforting[14] smile, his simple honesty—and then she thought about him being tortured to death.

Third thought—one she couldn't shake[15]—was the simplest of all: It was her fault.

She cleared her throat. "Where did you find him?"

Broome took a second on this one[16]. "In his office. He was found first thing this morning."

"So wait, when I stopped by his office and the door was locked …"

"We can't say for certain[17], but he was probably already dead."

1. c'est sans doute un arrêt du cœur

2. Si.

3. ce sera peut-être légalement parlant un « homicide involontaire »

4. eut à nouveau un coup au ventre

5. Aucun coup mortel

6. C'était plus qu'il n'en pouvait supporter

7. a lâché

8. dans l'idée de

9. malgré cela

10. chassa cette

11. monstrueuses

12. vous traversent l'esprit

13. ne mérite pas qu'on s'y attarde

14. réconfortant

15. dont elle ne parvenait pas à se défaire

16. prit son temps avant de répondre

17. avec certitude

Megan met his eye. Broome turned away. Her fault, yes, but now she could see that Broome felt guilty too[1]. Megan had come to him last night. She had warned him that Harry Sutton might be in trouble[2]. He hadn't really listened.

"Interesting," Broome said.

"What is?"

"How you knew something was wrong.[3]"

Whoa. So much for the guilt theory.[4] Megan took a step back. "Hold up a second. You don't think—"

"No," he said quickly, but she wasn't sure whether she believed him or not. "That's not what I'm getting at[5]. I'm just wondering what made you so suspicious[6]?"

"He didn't show up at the diner, for one.[7]"

"Yeah, okay, but that wasn't the only thing, was it? You said something about the receptionist answering the phone?"

"Right," Megan said. "You know Harry's operation[8]."

"Threadbare.[9]"

"Right. He didn't have a receptionist, especially one who'd answer his cell phone. And her voice, that cheery tone[10]—it just gave me the creeps[11]."

"So somehow a woman is involved in this[12]."

"I guess."

"Okay," Broome said, "so let's go through this[13] step by step[14]. We know that Harry spoke to you on the phone."

"Right. He said you wanted to show me that photograph."

"Okay, then he was supposed to meet us. He never showed and never called to cancel[15]. So for the moment we can assume[16] that sometime between the time you called Harry and the time he was supposed to leave for the diner, someone grabbed him[17]."

"You said he was found in his office," Megan said.

"Yes."

"So whoever did this probably grabbed Harry there."

212

Broome nodded. "Makes sense. So go back a second[1]. When Harry called you, where were you?"

"What difference does that make?[2]"

"Humor me.[3]"

She didn't like it, but if it could help find Harry's killer, she was willing to play along[4]. "At La Crème."

"Why?"

"I was visiting[5] old friends."

Broome frowned. "Who?"

She shook her head. "It's not important."

"Like hell it's not.[6]"

Megan wouldn't tell him about[7] Ray, but then again he hadn't been at La Crème anyway[8]. "You know Lorraine."

"Right. Who else?"

"That's it."

He looked doubtful[9]. "Okay, so you were at La Crème. Did you learn anything?"

"No."

"And how about after the diner? Where did you go then?"

"I went to a bar called the Weak Signal."

"Why?"

She hated to lie, but she knew that this was not the way to go[10]. "It was an old haunt of mine[11], okay? I was just taking a tour of[12] my past. What's the difference?"

"And you were there when you called Harry and that receptionist answered?"

"Yes."

Broome rubbed his chin. "Tell me again about the receptionist. Leave nothing out.[13]"

Megan recounted the phone conversation again[14]. She explained how the woman on the phone sounded young[15], how she tried to get Megan to give[16] her real name and address. Broome raised his eyebrow at that[17].

"What?"

"I don't know if I want to scare you," Broome said.

1. revenons un peu en arrière

2. Qu'est-ce que ça change ?

3. Soyez sympa, répondez.

4. prête à coopérer

5. J'allais voir

6. Oh que si.

7. ne voulait pas lui parler de

8. de toute façon

9. n'avait pas l'air convaincu

10. mieux valait ne pas trop en dire

11. C'est un bar où j'aimais traîner

12. Je me replongeais un peu dans

13. N'omettez aucun détail.

14. rapporta de nouveau sa conversation téléphonique

15. avait une voix jeune

16. soutirer à Megan

17. tiqua

213

1. Ce sont les mensonges qui me font peur

2. pour s'amuser

3. ce qui est plus probable

4. c'était dans un but précis

5. Quoi par exemple ?

6. pour en apprendre sur vous

7. eut une nouvelle bouffée d'angoisse

8. Peut-être bien.

9. que ça donne à réfléchir

10. ces tortionnaires

11. le journal d'appels

12. faire un saut à

13. de votre attention

14. comme un automate

"Lying scares me[1]," she said, which was both true and ironic. "What?"

"Well, think about it. Harry was tortured. Maybe someone did that for kicks[2], but more likely[3], there was a purpose to it[4]."

"Like what?[5]"

"Like trying to get information from him. Maybe they got the information before he died, I don't know. But they took his phone, right?"

"I guess."

"And then you call and what does this woman do? She pretends to be a receptionist to solicit information about you[6]. She wants to know your name and where you live."

Megan felt a fresh spike of fear[7]. "You think, what, they're after me?"

"Could be.[8]"

"Why?"

"I don't know, but think about it. After seventeen years, you show up in town. On that same day, Harry gets tortured, and then this woman who stole his phone tries to get you to give her your name." Broome shrugged. "I think it's worth considering[9]."

"And if these torturers[10] have his phone, they have my number in the call log[11]."

"Yes."

"How hard will it be for them to track me down?"

"You know the answer to that."

She did. Everyone did. It would be ridiculously easy. Megan shook her head. She had thought that she could simply pop down to[12] Atlantic City and escape it again.

"My God," she said. "What have I done?"

"I need you to focus with me[13] for a few more minutes, okay?"

She nodded numbly[14].

"After the phone call, you went to Harry's office, right? Before you came to see me."

214

"Yes."

"I don't want to creep you out any more than I already have, but[1] think about the timeline[2] for a second."

"Are you saying they could have been torturing Harry while I knocked[3] on the door?"

"It's possible."

She shivered anew[4].

"But what I need you to do right now is tell me everything about the visit to Harry's office. Leave nothing out. It was late by then. Most of the offices were closed down for the night[5]. So the most important question is who did you see?"

She closed her eyes and tried to think. "There was a janitor[6] by the stairwell[7]."

"What did he look like?"

"Tall, skinny[8], long hair."

Broome nodded. "Okay, that's the regular[9] janitor. Anyone else?"

Megan thought about it. "There was a young couple."

"In the corridor? Near Harry's door? Where?"

"No, they were coming out[10] as I was coming in. The man held the door for me[11]."

"What did they look like?"

"Young, good-looking, preppy[12]. She had blond hair. He looked like he just stepped off a[13] squash court."

"For real?[14]"

"Yes," she said. "They didn't look like torturers."

"What do torturers look like?"

"Good point."

Broome mulled it over[15] for a few moments. "You said a young woman answered his phone."

"Right."

"Could she be the same age as this blonde?"

"I guess." Something crossed Megan's face.[16]

"What?" Broome asked.

---

1. Sans vouloir vous effrayer davantage,

2. à l'enchaînement des événements

3. je toquais

4. frissonna à nouveau

5. étaient fermés pour la nuit

6. un gardien

7. à côté de la cage d'escalier

8. maigre

9. habituel

10. sortaient

11. m'a tenu la porte

12. BCBG

13. avait l'air de sortir tout droit d'un

14. Vraiment ?

15. cogita

16. Megan tiqua.

1. maintenant
que vous le dites

2. ne collaient
pas avec le reste

3. taudis

4. inspirations
profondes

5. releva la tête

6. l'agence
de caution
judiciaire

7. l'expert-
comptable

8. Ce qui amène
à se poser
une question
évidente

9. se turent

10. remarquant

11. plafonds à
caissons

12. tapis

13. peintures à
l'huile

14. si éloignés

15. n'était pas
d'humeur à
expliquer

16. les nantis et
les autres

17. La chance

18. le privilège
de la naissance

"Well, now that you mention it[1], they didn't fit[2]. You know? I mean, you know Harry's office."

"A dump[3]."

"Right," she said.

"So what was a good-looking, preppy couple doing there?" Broome asked.

"You could ask the same about me."

"You're not what you appear to be either," he said.

"No. So maybe they have secrets too."

"Maybe." Broome looked down at his feet. He took a few deep breaths[4].

"Detective?"

Broome looked up again[5]. "We already questioned everyone in Harry's building."

He stopped.

"So?"

"So the only offices that were still open at that time of night were the bail bondsmen[6] on the third floor and the CPA[7] on the second." Broome met her eye. "Neither one of them had clients like you just described."

"You're sure?"

"Yes. Which begs the obvious question[8]: What was that couple doing in that building at that time of night?"

They both fell silent[9]. Broome glanced around now, taking in[10] the vaulted ceilings[11], the Oriental carpets[12], the oil paintings[13].

"Nice house," he said.

She didn't reply.

"How did you do it, Megan?"

She knew what he really meant—how did she escape? "You think these worlds are really that far apart[14]?"

"I do, yes."

They weren't, but she didn't feel like explaining[15]. She had learned the biggest difference between the haves and the have-nots[16]. Luck[17] and birthright[18]. And the luckier you are and the more doors open to you because of your birthright, the more you need to

216

convince others that you made it[1] because of intelligence or hard work. The world is, in the end[2], all about bad self-esteem issues[3].

"So what now?" she asked.

"For one, I need to take you back with me so you can talk to a sketch artist[4]. We need to make an ID on[5] that young couple you saw. You also have to be honest with me."

"I am being honest with you."

"No, you're not. This all comes back to[6] the same person. We both know that."

She said nothing.

"Everything circles back to[7] Stewart Green. You said someone saw him recently."

"I said, someone *maybe* saw him."

"Whatever.[8] I need to know who."

"I promised I wouldn't say."

"And I promised I wouldn't bug you[9]. But Harry is dead. And Carlton Flynn is missing. You come back to town. Someone spots[10] Stewart Green. Whatever it is, whatever is happening to these men, it is all coming to a head now[11]. You can't run away anymore. You can't hide in this big fancy[12] house. Like you just said, Megan, the worlds aren't that far apart."

Megan tried to slow it down[13], tried to think it through[14]. She didn't want to make a mistake here, but she got it. Stewart Green was a suspect here. Broome had to do all he could to find him.

"Megan?"

She looked at him.

"There are others."

A fresh cold shiver crossed her heart.[15] "What do you mean?"

"Every year on Mardi Gras someone vanishes. Or dies."

"I don't understand."

"We can talk about it in the car. And you can tell me who saw Stewart Green."

---

1. avez réussi
2. en fin de compte
3. une question d'amour-propre à préserver
4. un dessinateur
5. Il nous faut identifier
6. On en revient toujours à
7. Tout tourne autour de
8. N'importe.
9. que je n'irais pas vous enquiquiner
10. repère
11. ça se précipite, là
12. chic
13. lever le pied
14. de réfléchir posément
15. Elle fut à nouveau parcourue d'un frisson glacé.

24

1. se repassait
en boucle les
événements de
ces dernières
heures

2. les nuages
noirs amoncelés
au-dessus de

3. sans une
plainte

4. resta là, le
regard rivé sur

5. pendant
encore une
minute

6. reviendrait
à de meilleurs
sentiments

7. vigilant

8. la prendrait
avec passion

9. la serrerait
très fort

10. Envoyez la
pluie artificielle

11. et la chanson
d'amour

12. a déjà
touché le fond

13. réussit à
tomber encore
plus bas

SITTING in the Weak Signal, Ray Levine went over and over the last few hours in his head[1]. Under the dark skies over[2] Lucy, Ray had watched the only woman he ever loved get into her car and drive away. He didn't move. He didn't call after her. He just let her leave his life without a word or a whimper[3]. Again.

When her car was out of sight, he stared down[4] that same street for another full minute[5]. Part of him thought that Cassie would come to her senses[6], turn around, drive back, throw the car door open, run toward him. There, under the watchful[7] eye of Lucy the Elephant, Ray would sweep her[8] in his arms and hold her tight[9] and start to cry and never let her go.

Cue the rain machine[10] and love ballad[11], right?

That didn't happen, of course. The love of his life was gone—again—and when that happens, when a man who is at the bottom[12] manages to drop down even further[13], there is only one thing that a man can do.

Drink heavily.[1]

Fester eyed Ray warily[2] when he first stepped into the Weak Signal. The big man who feared[3] nothing approached Ray tentatively[4].

"Hey, you okay?" Fester asked him.

"Do I have a drink in my hand?"

"No."

"Then that's the answer until I do."

Fester looked confused. "Huh?[5]"

"No, I'm not okay. But I will be once you get your fat ass out of my way[6] so I can get a drink."

"Oh," Fester said, sliding to the right[7], "got it[8]."

Ray grabbed a stool, his body language telling the bartender to make it quick[9]. Fester took the stool next to him. For several minutes, Fester said nothing, giving Ray his space[10]. Odd, but somewhere along the way, Fester had become his best friend—maybe his only friend—but that was more or less irrelevant[11] right now[12]. Right now there was an image of a beautiful woman in his head, the contours of her face, the way she felt when he held her, the smell of lilacs[13] and love, that pow-pow-pow in his belly[14] when her eyes met his—and the only way to get rid of that image was to drown it[15] in booze[16].

Ray longed for one of his blackouts[17].

The bartender poured once, then twice, then with a shrug, he just left the bottle. Ray gulped it[18], feeling it burn his throat[19]. Fester joined him[20]. It took some time, but Ray started feeling the numbness. He welcomed it, encouraged it, tried to ease his path toward oblivion[21].

"I remember her," Fester said.

Ray turned a lazy eye toward[22] his friend.

"I mean, when she came in here, she looked familiar. She danced at La Crème, right?"

Ray didn't reply. Back in those days, Fester had bounced at[23] a few clubs. He and Ray had been acquaintances[24], if not[25] friends, but Fester had a repu-

1. Boire comme un trou.
2. regarda Ray avec circonspection
3. n'avait peur de
4. s'approcha de Ray avec précaution
5. Hein ?
6. quand t'auras giclé,
7. en s'écartant vers la droite
8. pigé
9. de faire vite
10. ne voulant pas le bousculer
11. peu importait
12. là tout de suite
13. le parfum des lilas
14. les pom-pom-pom dans son ventre
15. la noyer
16. dans l'alcool
17. n'avait qu'une envie, sombrer dans l'inconscience
18. avalait d'un trait
19. la boisson lui brûler la gorge
20. but avec lui
21. d'atteindre l'oubli le plus vite possible
22. jeta un œil vague à
23. bossé comme videur dans
24. se connaissaient
25. sans être

1. intervenir
2. garder le contrôle de soi-même
3. Ça craint
4. rasade
5. Ouais.
6. [célèbre psychologue américain qui a sa propre émission de télé]
7. Bien sûr que non.
8. Ferme-la
9. brouillard sinistre et pathétique
10. plus pénible encore
11. qui tourne
12. une bétonnière
13. vomi
14. rendu tripes et boyaux
15. Son estomac gargouillait et criait famine
16. ivre mort
17. en sursaut
18. crâne
19. comme pour l'empêcher d'éclater
20. [benne à ordures]
21. clients
22. plus soûls encore

tation as one of the best. He knew when to strike[1] and more important, he knew how to show restraint[2]. The girls felt safe around him. Hell, Ray felt safe.

"Sucks[3], I know," Fester said.

Ray took another deep sip[4]. "Yep.[5]"

"So what did she want?"

"We aren't going to talk about this, are we, Fester?"

"It will help."

Everyone thinks they're Dr. Phil[6] nowadays. "The hell it will.[7] Just shut up[8] and drink."

Ray poured himself another. Fester said nothing. Or if he did, Ray didn't hear it. The rest of the night passed in an eerie, pathetic haze[9]. He thought about her face. He thought about her body. He thought about the way she looked at him with those eyes. He thought about all he had lost and more painfully[10], he thought about all that could have been. And of course, he thought about the blood. It always came back to that—all that damn blood.

Then he mercifully blacked out.

At some point, Ray opened his eyes and right away knew that he was home in bed, that it was morning. He felt like something twirled[11] in a cement truck[12]. It all felt so familiar. He wondered whether he had gotten sick[13] last night, whether he had prayed to the porcelain god[14] at some point during the blackout. The growl in his stomach was craving food[15], so he thought, probably.

Fester was asleep—more likely passed out[16]—on the couch. Ray got up and shook him hard. Fester woke with a start[17], then groaned and put his hands on either side of his enormous skull[18] as though trying to keep it from cracking open[19]. Both men were still in their clothes from last night. Both smelled like a Dumpster[20], but neither cared.

They stumbled out the door and to the diner down the street. Most of the patrons[21] looked even more hungover[22] than they did. The waitress, a seen-too-

220

much big-hair[1], brought them an urn[2] of coffee before they even asked. She was on the plump side[3], just the way Fester liked them. He gave her a smile and said, "Hi, sugar."

She put down the urn, rolled her eyes, walked away.

"Rough night[4]," Fester said to Ray.

"We've had rougher.[5]"

"Nah, not really. You remember much of it?[6]"

Ray said nothing.

"Another blackout?" Fester asked.

Again Ray didn't reply, pouring the coffee instead[7]. They both took it black[8]—at least, they did right now.

"I know what you're going through," Fester said.

Fester didn't have a clue, not really, but Ray said nothing.

"What, you think you're the only guy who's had his heart crushed[9]?"

"Fester?"

"Yeah?"

Ray put his index finger to his lips. "Shh.[10]"

Fester smiled. "You don't need to talk it out[11]?"

"I don't need to talk it out."

"Maybe I do. I mean, what happened last night. It brought it back for me[12] too."

"Your heartbreak?[13]"

"Yep. Do you remember Jennifer?"

"No."

"Jennifer Goodman Linn. That's her name now. She was the one[14]. You know what I mean?"

"I do."

"Some girls, you just lust after[15]. Some girls, you just really want or you like or you figure will be fun[16]. And then some girls—well, maybe only one girl—she makes you think about forever[17]." Fester leaned forward[18]. "Was Cassie that for you?"

"If I say yes, will you leave me alone[19]?"

"So you get what I mean then."

---

1. une fille blasée à gros brushing
2. fontaine
3. plutôt ronde
4. La nuit a été rude
5. On a connu pire.
6. Tu te souviens de grand chose ?
7. se contentant de servir le café
8. sans lait
9. a le cœur brisé
10. Chut.
11. d'en parler
12. Ça m'a rappelé des trucs
13. Une peine de cœur ?
14. la seule, l'unique
15. tu te contentes de les désirer
16. tu imagines qu'elles te feront passer un bon moment
17. tu te dis que ce sera peut-être l'amour éternel
18. se pencha
19. tu me laisseras tranquille

"Sure," Ray said. Fester was a huge man, but like all men, when you talk about heartache, they get smaller[1] and more pathetic. Ray took a breath and said, "So what happened to you and Jennifer?"

The big-haired waitress[2] returned. She asked what they were having. Ray ordered[3] pancakes, nothing else. Fester ordered a breakfast that included every food group on every chart ever made[4]. It took nearly two full minutes to say it all[5]. Ray wondered if the order came with a side of Lipitor[6].

When the waitress left, Ray went back to his coffee. So did Fester. Ray thought that maybe the moment had passed, that he would now be able to sit and sulk[7] in peace, but it was not to be[8].

"Some asswipe[9] stole her away from me," Fester said.

"Sorry."

"She's married now—to a plumbing contractor[10] in Cincinnati. They got two sons. I saw all these pictures of them on Facebook. They did some Carnival cruise[11] last year. They go to Reds games. She looks really happy."

"Everyone looks happy on Facebook."

"I know, right? What's up with that?[12]" Fester tried to smile, but it couldn't make it through the ache[13]. "I wasn't good enough for her anyway, you know what I mean? I was just a lowly[14] bouncer. Maybe now, with this new business and all, I probably make as much coin as[15] the plumber does. Maybe more. But it's too late, right?"

"Right."

"You're not going to encourage me to go after her?"

Ray said nothing.

"You should see her photos. On Facebook, I mean. She's still just as beautiful as the day she dumped me[16]. Maybe more so."

Ray stared down at the coffee a moment. "You know what beer goggles are[17]?"

"Sure," Fester said. "The more you drink, the better the girl looks.[1]"

"You're looking at those Facebook pictures through heartache goggles[2]."

"You think?"

"I do."

Fester considered that. "Yeah, maybe I am. Or maybe those aren't heartbreak goggles. Maybe those are true-love[3] goggles."

They fell into silence for a moment. The coffee was God's nectar[4]. The headache[5] had become a dull, steady thud[6].

"The plumber is probably making her happy," Fester said. "I should leave it alone[7]."

"Good idea."

"But," Fester said, holding up[8] a finger, "if she walked through that door right now—or, for example"—he shrugged theatrically[9]—"if she, let's say, walked into the Weak Signal looking for me after all these years, I don't know what I'd do."

"Subtle, Fester."

He spread his arms. "What about me hits you as subtle?[10]"

Fair point.[11] "She didn't come back to start up again."

"So she just wanted a fling[12]? To slum[13] for a couple hours? That sucks." Then thinking more about it, Fester said, "But hell, I'd take it[14]."

"She didn't come back for that either."

"Then what did she come back for?"

Ray shook his head. "It's not important. She's gone. She won't be back."

"So she just came back to mess with your head[15]?"

Ray played with his napkin[16]. "Something like that."

"Cold.[17]"

Ray did not reply.

"But you know what's interesting, Ray?"

"No, Fester, why don't you tell me what's interesting?"

1. *Plus tu bois, plus la fille a l'air canon.*

2. *des lunettes de chagrin d'amour*

3. *du grand amour*

4. *divin*

5. *mal de crâne*

6. *un martèlement sourd et régulier*

7. *laisser tomber*

8. *levant*

9. *de façon exagérée*

10. *Qu'est-ce que tu vois de subtil en moi ?*

11. *Effective-ment.*

12. *une aventure*

13. *S'encanailler*

14. *je dirais pas non*

15. *serait juste revenue pour te mettre la tête à l'envers*

16. *sa serviette*

17. *Un peu salaud.*

"Jennifer broke my heart, sure, but she didn't break me. You know what I mean? I still function. I got a business.[1] I got a life.[2] I moved on. Yeah, I drink sometimes, but I didn't let it destroy me."

"Again with the subtle," Ray said.

"I know there are few things worse than a broken heart, but it is nothing that you shouldn't be able to recover from[3]. Do you know what I'm saying?"

Ray almost laughed. He knew. And he didn't. A broken heart is bad, but there are indeed things worse. Fester thought that a broken heart had crushed Ray. It had, no question about it[4]. But you do recover from a broken heart[5]. Ray would have, if that had been all. But as Fester had noted[6], there are a few things worse, more scarring[7], harder to get over, than a broken heart.

Blood, for example.

BROOME didn't like confiding in[8] Megan.

He still didn't believe that she was coming totally clean[9], but that just made it more important, not less, to hit her with the full horrible, awful facts[10] of the case. So on the drive down to[11] Atlantic City, he told her enough to scare the crap out of her[12]—how he believed that many men, not just Stewart Green and Carlton Flynn, went missing on Mardi Gras, how none of them had ever been seen again[13].

When he finished, Megan said, "So are these men dead or did they run away or did someone kidnap them or what?"

"I don't know. We only know of the fate of one[14]—Ross Gunther."

"And he's dead."

"Yes. A man is serving time[15] for his murder."

"And you think that man is innocent?"

"Yes."

She thought about it for a moment. "So how many men have you found that fit this Mardi Gras pattern[16]?"

Marginal notes (French):

1. J'ai ma propre boîte.
2. J'ai ma petite vie.
3. on s'en remet
4. aucun doute là-dessus
5. on s'en remet en effet
6. l'avait fait remarquer
7. qui vous marquent davantage
8. faire des confidences à
9. qu'elle ait été tout à fait honnête avec lui
10. de lui asséner les faits dans toute leur horreur
11. durant le trajet vers
12. la faire flipper
13. et qu'on n'avait jamais revu aucun d'eux
14. ce qui est arrivé à l'un d'eux
15. purge une peine
16. qui correspondent à ce schéma de Mardi gras

"We are still working on it[1], but for now we have fourteen."

"No more than one a year?"

"Yes."

"And always around Mardi Gras."

"Yes."

"Except, well, now you have another body in Harry Sutton. He doesn't fit the pattern at all."

"I don't think he's part of the Mardi Gras group."

"But it has to be connected[2]," she said.

"Yes," Broome said. "By the way, does that holiday[3] mean anything to you[4]? Mardi Gras, I mean."

Megan shook her head. "It was always a wild night[5], but other than that[6], nope, nothing."

"How about to Stewart Green?"

"No. I mean, not that I know about anyway[7]."

"Stewart Green is the only one we have a possible sighting of[8]. You get now why I need to talk to anyone who might have seen him?"

"Yes," Megan said.

"So?"

She thought about it, but in truth[9], there was no option but the truth here[10]. "Lorraine saw him."

"Thank you."

Megan said nothing. Broome explained how he didn't want Megan to give her a heads-up[11], that he'd visit her soon[12].

"I've known Lorraine a long time," Broome said.

Megan smirked, remembering how Lorraine said she'd thrown him a one-timer. "Yeah, I know."

Broome parked the car and brought her into the precinct through the side[13] door. He didn't want Goldberg or anyone else to know she was here. He set her up[14] in a storage room[15] on the ground level[16]. Rick Mason, the sketch artist and all-around computer weenie[17], was there.

"What's with the secrecy?[18]" Mason asked.

"Think of it as[19] witness protection."

---

1. On est toujours dessus

2. il y a forcément un lien

3. ce jour de fête

4. a une signification particulière pour vous

5. une nuit de folie

6. à part ça

7. pas que je sache, en tout cas

8. qui a peut-être été vu

9. à dire vrai

10. elle n'avait plus le choix : elle devait lui dire la vérité

11. la prévienne

12. qu'il irait la voir bientôt

13. sur le côté

14. l'installa

15. cagibi

16. au rez-de-chaussée

17. petit génie de l'informatique

18. Pourquoi toutes ces cachotteries ?

19. Prenez ça comme

"From your fellow cops[1]?"

"Especially from them. Trust me on this[2], okay?"

He shrugged. Once Megan settled in, Broome headed back to[3] his car. He quickly called Erin. Earlier he had asked her to check for any surveillance cameras[4] around Harry Sutton's office, see if they could get an image of this young couple. She told him now that she was still working it. He had also asked her to find the whereabouts of[5] Stacy Paris, the girl Mannion and Gunther had battled over[6].

"Stacy Paris's real name is Jaime Hemsley. She's living near Atlanta."

"Married?"

"No."

Atlanta. He wouldn't have time to get down there[7]. "Maybe you can reach her by phone, see what she can tell us about the night Gunther died."

"I already called. No answer, but I'll keep working on it. Broome?"

"What?"

"If Mannion is innocent," Erin said, "I mean, if he's spent eighteen years in jail for the work of a serial whatever … man, that would really blow[8]."

"You got a way with insight[9], Erin."

"Well, you didn't just fall for me because of my hot bod[10]."

"Yeah, I did," he said. "Talk to Stacy. See what she knows."

He hung up. The ride to La Crème was a short one.[11] The lunch crowd was pouring in[12], many lining up for the[13] suspect[14] buffet before ogling[15] the girls, begging[16] the question, "How hungry were[17] these guys?"

Lorraine wasn't at her customary post[18] behind the bar. There had been a night many years ago when the two of them had a textbook[19] one-night stand[20]. It had been fun and empty[21], the kind of thing that paradoxically made you feel alive and wishing it had never happened—the way all one-nighters do, Broome thought, even by the most jaded of participants[1]. Still, when you sleep with someone, even when drunk and stupid and with no desire for a repeat[2], there was a bond[3]. He hoped to use that now[4].

Broome headed to the back of the club. Rudy's door was closed. Broome opened it without knocking. Rudy was trying to pull his too-tight shirt[5] over his thick[6] head and then past down the bowling-ball gut[7]. There was a girl in the office, helping him. She was young. Probably too young. Rudy shooed her out the side door[8].

"She's legal[9]," Rudy said.

"I'm sure."

He invited Broome to sit. Broome shook him off.

"So," Rudy said, "you're here two days in a row[10]."

"I am."

"What, you got a thing for[11] one of my girls?"

"No, Rudy, I got a thing for you. Excessive shoulder hair turns me on.[12]"

Rudy smiled and spread his hands. "I do have the kind of body that appeals to all persuasions[13]."

"Right, exactly. Where's Lorraine?"

"She should be back any minute[14]. What do you want with my best employee?"

Broome pointed with his thumb. "I'll wait out front.[15]"

"I'd rather you just left.[16]"

"Or I can start carding[17] all the girls."

"Go ahead[18]," Rudy said. "I run a legitimate establishment[19]. You think I need that kind of trouble?"

"Whatever. Like I said, I'll wait out front."

"You didn't hear me. I don't want trouble."

"You won't get any if you cooperate."

"That's what you said yesterday. You remember yesterday, don't you?"

"Yeah, what about it?"

"You threatened one of my girls. Tanya."

"Tawny."

---

1. même les plus blasés

2. sans aucune envie de recommencer

3. ça crée des liens

4. espérait bien tabler là-dessus

5. chemise trop serrée

6. grosse

7. sa grosse bedaine

8. la chassa par la porte de service

9. Elle a l'âge légal

10. de suite

11. vous avez le béguin pour

12. Les épaules poilues, ça m'excite.

13. en a pour tous les goûts

14. d'une minute à l'autre

15. Je vais attendre dehors.

16. J'aurais préféré vous dire au revoir.

17. à ficher

18. Allez-y

19. Tout est en règle

"Whatever.[1]"

"I didn't threaten her. I talked to her."

"Right. And you didn't follow up on that[2] conversation and get a little more persuasive[3]?"

"What are you talking about?"

Rudy had a huge bowl[4] of M&Ms on his desk. He reached[5] his catcher-glove paw[6] into the bowl. "Tawny called me last night. She quit[7]."

"And you think I had something to do with that?"

"You didn't?"

"Maybe my conversation opened her eyes. You know, that and the beatings your client Carlton Flynn laid on her[8] and this toilet of a workplace[9], stuff like that[10]."

"I don't think so."

"Why not?"

"One of my other girls lives with her. Said Tawny threw her stuff in a suitcase[11] and ran out. Said she looked like someone had given her a fresh tune-up[12]."

"Who?"

Rudy poured the M&Ms into his mouth. "I figured that it was you."

Broome frowned. "Where is Tawny now?"

"Gone. She hopped on a bus[13]."

"Already?"

"Yep, last night. Tawny called me from the bus station to quit."

Broome tried to think it through. It could have been just what he originally said. These girls—they were not exactly the most stable columns in the Forum[14]. She had been hurt already. Her finger had been broken. Her abusive[15] quasi-boyfriend[16] had gone missing. A cop had interrogated her. She had probably just decided to cut her losses[17] and head home.

"This girl Tawny lived with," Broome said.

"Not here. And she knows nothing."

"Rudy, this isn't a time to get cute[18] with me."

Rudy sighed. "Calm down, you know me, I'm a model citizen. I'll get her in, but in the meantime"—he gestured over Broome's shoulder and out the door—"my best employee just arrived. On time[1], as always. She's never late."

Broome turned and saw Lorraine heading toward her post behind the bar.

"Hey, Broome."

He turned back to Rudy. His face was different now. Whatever human mask Rudy normally wore for cops[2], it was gone.

"She's special. Lorraine, I mean. You get that, right?"

"What's your point, Rudy?"

"If whatever you do here ends up hurting that woman"—Rudy gestured again toward where Lorraine was now cleaning off the bar—"I don't give a crap what kind of[3] badge you got. There won't be enough of you left for a DNA match.[4]"

25

EARLIER that day, Ken had made his way to[1] Megan Pierce's sliding glass door[2] off the wooden deck[3]. Barbie had gone through the garage—backup in case the door was locked[4]. It wouldn't be necessary. The sliding glass door was unlocked. Ken quietly opened it. He was about to step inside when the doorbell rang.

He slipped back outside[5] and ducked low[6]. The cop Broome entered the house.

Ken wanted to curse[7], but he never cursed. Instead he used his favorite word for such moments: "setback[8]." That was all this was.[9] The measure of a man isn't how many times he gets knocked down.[10] It is how many times he gets back up again.[11]

He texted Barbie to stay put[12]. He tried to listen in[13], but it was too risky. No matter.[14] Ken stayed down and out of sight. The Pierces' backyard[15] had plush[16] Brown Jordan furniture[17]. There was a corner fountain and a full-size soccer goal[18] and a cedar swing set[19] that had definitely seen better days[20].

It was really a very nice house. Ken wondered how this seemingly ordinary[1] woman and mother fit into the disappearance of Carlton Flynn, but that was indeed his job.

He waited. He thought about Megan Pierce's kids. He could almost see them kicking the ball into that soccer goal[2], lounging on the furniture[3], having a burger grilled on the Weber.

He thought about what that life must be like[4] for the father of the house. Kids. Family dinners. Barbecues. Church on Sunday. His beautiful wife smiling through this sliding glass door as he taught his son to play catch[5]. Ken wanted that life. He wanted that for himself and, he realized, he wanted it for Barbie. He could almost see her through that window now, smiling at him, filled with love[6]. He could see them getting their children to bed, making sure they all brushed their teeth and said their prayers[7], and then he could see the two of them disappearing into their own bedroom hand in hand. He could see Barbie closing the door and turning toward him.

What more could any man want?

He knew, of course, that it wouldn't be that[8] simple. He had compulsions[9], but even those[10] he could share with his beloved[11].

What was he waiting for?

He turned back toward the house. He didn't relish[12] making these children motherless[13], but right now he saw no other alternative. Fifteen minutes passed. Megan Pierce accompanied Detective Broome to his car. After they drove off, Ken and Barbie met up by the rented Miata[14].

"What do you think that police officer was doing here?" Barbie asked.

"I don't know."

"We should have come up last night."

"It was too risky."

"So now what?"

---

1. qui semblait si ordinaire

2. envoyer le ballon dans le filet

3. se prélasser sur les fauteuils

4. la belle vie que ça devait être

5. à taper dans un ballon

6. débordante d'amour

7. dit leurs prières du soir

8. aussi

9. des pulsions

10. ça aussi,

11. bien-aimée

12. n'était pas enchanté

13. de priver ces enfants de leur mère

14. se rejoignirent devant la Miata de location

They drove off, back to the Garden State Parkway heading[1] south. Ken wasn't all that concerned[2]. Chances were excellent that[3] Broome and the Pierce woman were heading back to Atlantic City. Ken picked up speed[4]. Three miles down the parkway, he spotted[5] Broome's car. He stayed way back[6], not really bothering to follow[7]. No question[8] now. They were going back to Atlantic City.

Two hours later, Broome parked in the lot[9] at the police precinct. Broome took Megan Pierce in through a side entrance.

"Now what?[10]" Barbie asked.

"I love you," Ken said.

"What?[11]"

He turned toward her. "I never told you. But you know."

She nodded. "I love you too."

He smiled and took her hand.

"Why did you tell me now?" Barbie asked.

"I will do anything to protect you. I want you to know that."

"I know that too."

He took out his cell phone and dialed the number[12]. It was answered on the third ring.[13]

"Goldberg."

Ken said, "Hello, Deputy Chief Goldberg."

Silence on the other end of the phone[14].

"I remembered that you didn't want me to call you Mr. Goldberg," Ken continued. "You said that you preferred Deputy Chief Goldberg."

"Yeah," he said in the wariest of voices[15]. "What do you want? I'm kinda busy here.[16]"

"I don't mean[17] to disturb you[18], Deputy Chief Goldberg, but this is a matter of some urgency[19]."

"I'm listening."

"Your colleague Detective Broome just entered your precinct[20]."

"So?"

"He is with a woman named Megan Pierce."

Silence.

"We will need to talk to her."

"The same way you talked to Harry Sutton?"

"That isn't your concern[1]."

"Like hell it's not. Why do you think I'm so busy?"

"Deputy Chief Goldberg, please find a way for us to reach her[2]."

"Reach her?"

"Let us know how and when she'll be leaving.[3] It might be best to encourage her to leave alone."

Silence.

"Mr. Goldberg?"

No "Deputy Chief" this time. The slip had been intentional.[4]

"Got it," Goldberg said before hanging up[5].

Ken took Barbie's hand. "Should we get married?" he asked.

"That's hardly an appropriate proposal.[6]"

But she smiled when she said it, and his heart soared[7]. He sat with this woman who meant so much to him[8], his partner in everything really, his soul mate[9] like no other, and just let his heart soar. "You're right. I'll prepare a proper[10] proposal."

"And I'll prepare a proper way to say yes."

They held hands and watched the door and just enjoyed[11] the moment. A few minutes later, Detective Broome exited[12] without the woman. Barbie let go of his hand. "We should split up[13]," she said.

"But we just got engaged[14]," he said with a small chuckle[15].

"Not officially, mister. But you know I'm right. You take the car and follow the detective. I will keep an eye on[16] the precinct."

"Don't take her on yourself[17]," he said.

She shook her head and dazzled him with a smile[18].

"What?"

---

1. ne vous regarde pas

2. arrangez-vous pour que nous puissions la contacter

3. Dites-nous quand et comment elle repartira.

4. L'oubli était délibéré.

5. raccrocher

6. Ce n'est pas une demande dans les règles.

7. son cœur fit un bond

8. avait tant d'importance pour lui

9. âme sœur

10. en bonne et due forme

11. savourèrent

12. ressortit

13. On devrait se séparer

14. on vient à peine de se fiancer

15. petit rire

16. Je surveillerai

17. Ne t'occupe pas d'elle toute seule

18. lui fit un sourire éblouissant

"We aren't even married yet and already you're bossing me around[1] like a husband. Go."

LORRAINE was pulling the handle[2] for a draft beer[3] when Broome approached. She looked up and gave him that crooked smile[4]. "Well, well, as I live and breathe[5]."

"Hey, Lorraine."

"You want a drink, or are you going to give me that classic line[6] about being on duty[7]?"

Broome sat down. "I am on duty. And, yeah, pour me[8] two fingers."

She finished with the draft and sauntered[9]—Lorraine never walked, she sauntered—toward the corner of the bar where they kept the good stuff[10]. Broome spun around on the stool[11]. There was a line at the buffet. An actual line for the food[12]. On the stage[13] a girl danced with the enthusiasm of a coma patient[14]. The old Neil Diamond classic "Girl, You'll Be a Woman Soon" played through the speaker system[15].

Lorraine handed him the drink. "Something I can do for you, Detective?"

"Do you have a guess?[16]"

Lorraine arched an eyebrow[17]. "I assume you're not back for a second round[18]."

"I wish.[19]"

"Liar."

Broome didn't know how to take that one[20], so he pressed on. "I talked to your old friend Cassie or Megan or whatever you want to call her."

"Uh-huh."

"The situation is bad. Did you hear about Harry Sutton?"

Lorraine nodded as a shadow crossed[21] her face. "Did you know him, Broome?"

"A little."

"He was just the best. Harry had this way about him[22], I mean, everyone loved Harry. Even you cops.

You know why? Because he was genuine[1]. And he always cared. Biggest heart I ever saw.[2] He believed in everyone. There were some girls in here I couldn't stand[3]. Obnoxious pains in the ass[4], sure, but some were just plain bad[5]. But Harry, he'd still try to find the good. He'd still want to help and not just to get in their pants[6], though, hell, he sometimes did that too. Who could resist a guy who looked at you like that—like you really mattered, you know?" Lorraine shook her head. "Why would anyone hurt someone like Harry?"

"That's what I'm here to find out," Broome said.

"It's corny[7]," she said, working[8] the bar with a dishrag[9], "but the world is a little crappier today without him in it[10]. You can just feel it."

"Then help me, Lorraine. For Harry."

"What, you think I know something about it?"

"It's all connected," Broome said. "Harry's death is just one part. I got a guy in jail for eighteen years who may be innocent. Carlton Flynn is missing, and there are a lot of other men missing or dead."

He stopped.

"Including[11]," Lorraine said, clearly seeing the light[12], "Stewart Green."

"Yes."

Lorraine cleaned the bar a little more. "So Cassie told you I was the one who saw him."

"I sort of forced her[13] to give up the name[14]."

Lorraine gave him the grin again[15]. "You're such a tough guy[16], Broome."

"She wanted to call you first, but I wanted to tell you myself."

"Because of our past?[17]"

Broome shrugged and took a deep sip[18]. "Did you see Stewart Green?"

"I can't be sure."

He just looked at her a little longer.

"Yeah, okay," Lorraine said. "I saw him."

---

1. sincère
2. Un cœur gros comme ça.
3. que je ne pouvais pas sentir
4. Des petites garces
5. de la mauvaise graine
6. pour se les faire

7. C'est bête à dire
8. essuyant
9. torchon
10. un petit peu plus merdique maintenant qu'il n'est plus là

11. Y compris
12. voyant où il voulait en venir

13. Je l'ai plus ou moins obligée
14. à cracher le morceau
15. lui sourit de nouveau
16. T'es un vrai dur

17. À cause de ce qui s'est passé entre nous ?
18. avala une grande lampée

1. lui fit un clin d'œil
2. comme d'hab
3. pas vrai ?
4. hésitèrent un moment à se rebiffer
5. pour jouer les durs
6. se ravisèrent
7. clients les plus généreux
8. Tu te feras pardonner plus tard.
9. le crâne rasé
10. un bouc
11. des anneaux dans les oreilles
12. tatouage
13. sur l'avant-bras
14. moulant
15. manifestement fait de la muscu
16. calvitie naissante
17. masquer en plaquant quelques cheveux
18. bouffi
19. d'entrain
20. C'est-à-dire ?

Two gray-haired men came up to her bar. The taller one leaned forward, winked[1], and said, "Hey, Lorraine, the usual[2]."

"Use the other bar," Broome said.

"Huh?"

"This bar is closed."

"You're sitting here, ain't ya?[3]"

Broome replied by showing them his badge. The two men considered taking it further[4], just to look tough[5], but then thought better of it[6]. They turned and walked away.

"Those are two of my best tippers[7]," Lorraine said.

"You'll make it up to them.[8] You said you saw Stewart Green."

"Yeah," she said. Lorraine pushed the hair off her face. "But he looks different."

"Different how?"

"Different all over. He's got a shaved head[9] and a goatee[10]. He wears hoop earrings[11] and got a tattoo[12] on his forearm[13]. He was in jeans and a tight[14] T-shirt, and he's clearly been working out[15]."

Broome frowned. "Stewart Green?"

Lorraine didn't bother replying.

Broome thought about those photographs on Sarah Green's fireplace mantel. In these photographs Stewart dressed in either polo 'n' khakis or a business suit. He had a bald spot[16] he'd started to cover up with a wispy comb-over[17]. He looked soft and puffy[18].

"When did you see him?" he asked.

Lorraine started cleaning a glass with too much gusto[19].

"Lorraine?"

"I've seen him more than once."

That surprised him. "How many times?"

"A few."

"What's a few?[20] More than twice, more than five times?"

"I don't know," Lorraine said. All hints of that playfulness[1] were gone now. She looked frightened. "Maybe once a year, once every two years, something like that. I don't keep track.[2]"

"Once every year or two?"

"Yeah."

Broome's head was spinning[3]. "Wait, so when was the first time you saw him?"

"I don't know. A while ago.[4] Ten, fifteen years maybe."

"And you never thought to[5] contact the police?"

"Huh?"

"You saw a guy who'd gone missing. You never thought to tell us?"

"Tell you what exactly?" Lorraine put her hands on her hips[6], her voice rising[7]. "Was he a criminal you were after?"

"No but—"

"And, what, do you think I'm an informant[8] or something? I've worked in this business for twenty years. You learn quick that nobody sees nothing[9], you know what I'm saying?"

He did.

"I wouldn't be talking to you now only ..." Lorraine suddenly seemed depressed[10] and deflated[11]. "Harry. How could someone hurt Harry? Look, whatever[12], I don't want more people to die. When you're a customer in here, I don't much care what you do. Break whatever commandment.[13] But if people are starting to die ..."

She turned away.

"When was the last time you saw Stewart Green?"

Lorraine didn't answer.

"I asked—"

"A few weeks back."

"Can you be more specific[14]?"

"It might have been around the time that[15] that Flynn guy disappeared."

237

---

1. Toute trace de malice

2. Je n'ai pas pris de notes.

3. en eut le vertige

4. Il y a un bail.

5. songé à

6. sur les hanches

7. haussant le ton

8. tu me prends pour un indic

9. On apprend vite que personne voit jamais rien

10. déprimée

11. abattue

12. Bon, écoute

13. Tu peux enfreindre le commandement que tu veux.

14. précise

15. C'était à peu près au moment où

1. se figea

Broome froze[1].

"Lorraine, I need you to think hard about this: Was he here on Mardi Gras?"

"Mardi Gras?"

"Yeah."

She thought about that. "I don't know, it could be. Why?"

2. son pouls s'accélérer

Broome could feel his pulse start to pick up pace[2]. "In fact, when you saw him over the years, could it have been during other Mardi Gras?"

3. la grimace

She made a face[3]. "I don't know."

"It's important."

4. tu veux que je me rappelle un truc pareil ?

"How the hell would I remember something like that?[4]"

5. Chez vous, on distribue

"Think. You guys give out[5] beads on Mardi Gras, right?"

"So?"

6. essaie de te rappeler

7. Représente-toi la scène.

"So think back[6]. You remembered Stewart had hoop earrings. Close your eyes now. Picture when he was here.[7] Was he wearing Mardi Gras beads maybe?"

"I don't think so. I mean, I don't know."

"Close your eyes and try."

8. Tu te paies ma tête ?

"Are you kidding me?[8]"

9. Allez

"Come on[9], Lorraine, this is important."

10. s'emplissaient de larmes

"Okay, okay." He could see now that her eyes were welling up[10]. She quickly closed them.

"Anything?"

"No." Her voice was soft now. "I'm sorry."

"You okay?"

11. se reprit et ouvrit les yeux

She blinked open her eyes[11]. "I'm fine."

"Is there anything else you can tell me about Stewart Green?"

12. Je dois me remettre au boulot.

Her voice was still soft. "No. I gotta get back to work.[12]"

"Not yet."

13. les images de vidéosurveillance

Broome tried to think it through, then he remembered: Erin had the security footage[13]. That was how they had realized the Mardi Gras connection. Erin could look through them[1] now and search for[2] the man Lorraine described. He debated dragging Lorraine in[3] for Rick Mason to sketch[4], but Mason was also an expert on age-progression software[5]. He could work that with what he now knew—shaved head and goatee?—and then bring it back to show Lorraine.

"I don't understand," Lorraine said. "Why did you ask about Mardi Gras?"

"We see a pattern."

"What kind of pattern?"

He quickly figured, why not?[6] Maybe she'd remember something. "Stewart Green went missing on Mardi Gras. So did Carlton Flynn. A man named Ross Gunther was murdered on Mardi Gras. Other men too."

"I don't understand."

"Neither do we[7]. I have pictures that I want to show you—of missing men. Maybe you'll recognize one." He had the file with him. No other patrons[8] had come over to this corner[9]. They sat by the main stage while a stripper dressed as[10] Jasmine from Disney's *Aladdin* started to dance to[11] "A Whole New World." The act[12] gave a whole new meaning to[13] the phrase[14] "magic carpet ride[15]."

Broome took out the photographs and started to spread them[16] on the bar. He watched Lorraine's face. She took her time with the most recent one, the one that had been sent anonymously to his office.

"That's Carlton Flynn," she said.

"That one we know."

Lorraine put it back and went through the other pictures. The tears were back in her eyes.

"Lorraine?"

"I don't recognize any of them." She blinked, turned away. "You should go."

"What's the matter?"

"It's nothing."

Broome waited. For a moment Lorraine said nothing. He had always seen her upbeat[17], always with

1. les visionner
2. chercher à repérer
3. hésita à emmener Lorraine au poste,
4. que Mason dresse un portrait-robot
5. un expert du logiciel de vieillissement
6. hésita un moment, mais pourquoi pas ?
7. Nous non plus
8. Aucun autre client
9. ne s'était approché de ce coin du bar
10. déguisée en
11. sur
12. Le numéro
13. donnait un tout autre sens à
14. l'expression
15. « voyage en tapis volant »
16. les étaler
17. optimiste

that sideways[1] smile, the smoky voice[2], the throaty laugh[3]. She had always been the dictionary definition of the good-time party girl[4].

"I'm dying[5]," Lorraine said.

Broome felt something in his chest dry up and blow away[6].

"I just came from the doctor."

He finally found his voice[7]. "What's wrong?"

"Cancer. It's already pretty far along[8]. I have a year, maybe two."

Broome could feel his throat tightening up[9]. "I don't know what to say."

"Don't tell anyone, okay?"

"Okay."

Lorraine tried to give him the crooked grin[10]. "Believe it or not, you're the only one I've told. Pathetic, right?"

Broome reached his hand across the bar[11]. For a moment she didn't move. "I'm glad you told me," he said.

She put her hand on his. "I've made choices people don't understand, but I don't have regrets. I was married once, and yeah, true, he was an abusive son of a bitch[12]. But even if he wasn't, that life just wasn't for me. This one was. I've loved it here. It's been a lot of laughs[13], you know what I mean?"

Broome nodded, met her eye.

More tears came to her eyes. "But this is the part that sucks about having no one[14], you know? I wish … oh man, I sound like such a baby … I want someone to care. I want someone to be crushed when I go. I want someone to hold my hand when I die."

Again he wasn't sure what to say. He didn't want to sound patronizing. He wanted to do something, anything. Broome liked to be detached[15]—emotions were messy[16]—but he hated feeling helpless[17].

"I'll be with you, if you want. I'll hold your hand."

"You're sweet[18], but no."

Margin notes:
1. en coin
2. cette voix rocailleuse
3. ce rire de gorge
4. le parfait exemple de la fille qui aime faire la fête
5. Je vais mourir
6. sentit quelque chose se briser dans sa poitrine
7. retrouva enfin la parole
8. C'est déjà bien avancé.
9. se serrer
10. lui faire son sourire en coin
11. tendit la main à travers le bar
12. une brute et un salopard
13. On a bien rigolé
14. c'est là que ça craint d'avoir personne
15. avoir l'air détaché
16. les émotions, c'est le souk
17. détestait ce sentiment d'impuissance
18. gentil

"I mean it.[1]"

"I know you do, but that's what I meant. Sure, I could find some people who pity me enough[2] to be with me at the end. But the kind of thing I'm talking about, you only get that through commitment[3]. You only get that through being with someone during good times and bad[4], over years, in a real relationship. You don't just get to ask for it in the end[5], you know what I'm saying?"

"I guess I do."

"It's okay. Like I said, I wouldn't change a thing. That's life. You can find joy and be happy—but you don't get to have everything[6]."

The simple wisdom that is the truth[7]. She smiled at him. He smiled back.

"Lorraine?"

"Yeah."

"You're beautiful, you know."

"You hitting on me?[8]"

"Maybe."

She arched an eyebrow. "Would it be a pity screw?[9]"

"For you or for me?"

She laughed. "Maybe both."

"Even better[10]," Broome said. "I got this case right now, but as soon as it's done ..."

"You know where to find me."

Her hand slipped out of his then.[11] She started down[12] toward the other end of the bar. Broome was about to leave when Lorraine said, "I assume Cassie is helping you out[13]?"

"She is. She may have even gotten a look at[14] Harry's killers."

"How?[15]"

"She went back to his office last night."

"Alone or with Ray?"

Broome stopped. "Ray?"

1. Sincèrement.

2. auraient assez pitié de moi

3. c'est seulement après des années d'engagement

4. après des années à partager les bons et les mauvais moments

5. Ça se demande pas à la fin

6. on peut pas tout avoir

7. La vérité est parfois dans la sagesse toute simple

8. Tu me fais du gringue ?

9. Ce serait baiser par compassion ?

10. C'est encore mieux

11. Elle retira sa main de la sienne.

12. partit

13. te donne un coup de main

14. Il se pourrait même qu'elle ait aperçu

15. Comment ça ?

1. écarquilla les yeux
2. s'en mordait la langue
3. s'en fichait

Lorraine's eyes widened a bit[1]. He could see that she wanted to take it back[2], but Broome was having none of that[3].

"Who the hell is Ray?"

26

1. d'abord pensé
à la sécurité

2. quelques—unes
des mères au
foyer

3. éveiller de
soupçons

4. par orienter
la conversation

5. sur les
banalités de la
vie bourgeoise

6. l'entraîneur
parent d'élève

7. penchait en
faveur de son
gosse

8. de commande
en ligne pour la
cantine

9. un service

10. seraient pris
en charge après
l'école

11. insinua
qu'ils pourraient
rester dormir

12. de conduire
les enfants à
leurs activités
du week-end

13. ne serait pas
rentré avant
plusieurs heures

NATURALLY, Megan's first worry had been for the safety[1] of her family.

Before she let Broome start going into details, she'd called a few of the stay-at-home mothers[2]. She didn't want to raise suspicions[3], so she started chatting[4] about the usual suburban inanities[5]: kid sports, the father-coach[6] who favored his own kid[7], the teachers who gave too much/too little homework, the new online school-lunch ordering[8] system. Broome just shook his head. Eventually Megan got around to asking the mom for a favor[9], making sure that both Kaylie and Jordan had after-school coverage[10] and even encouraged sleepovers[11], so they'd be safe and away from the house. She promised to do all the weekend driving[12] in exchange.

That done, Megan tried calling Dave again. Still no answer. She texted, "Stay in the office until you talk to me"—no reply but even under the most pessimistic of scenarios, he wouldn't be home for hours[13].

1. qui ne tournait déjà plus très rond

2. fut à nouveau secoué

3. sans fenêtre

4. qu'elle avait à peine aperçues

5. se concentrer

6. montra des exemples

7. esprit

8. quel que soit l'angle par lequel elle abordait le sujet

9. relier

10. chaque année

11. autour de

12. s'était produite

13. plus fin

14. Les « et si... » dardaient toujours leurs têtes hideuses.

15. avait fait front

16. disparu corps et biens

17. trop horrible à envisager

Then Broome started talking, and her world, already tilted off its axis[1], took another hit[2].

Now here she was, sitting in a windowless[3] room in a police station, trying to give descriptions of two people she barely saw[4] to a sketch artist. She tried to focus[5]. Rick Mason gave her prompts[6] that helped her see that young couple clearer in her mind's eye[7].

Megan tried to sort through what Broome had told her, but in the end, no matter how many different ways she tried to approach it[8], none of it made sense. Broome was trying to connect[9] three seemingly different events. One, a murder from eighteen years ago. Two, a group of men, like Stewart Green and Carlton Flynn, who had vanished annually[10] on or around[11] Mardi Gras over a seventeen-year period. Three, last night's torture death of poor Harry Sutton. If he was right, if they were somehow linked, Megan couldn't imagine what part the young couple, for example, could possibly play. They'd have been kids when the first murder and Stewart's disappearance had occurred[12].

"His nose was thinner[13]," she said to Mason.

He nodded and went back to work.

The what-ifs kept raising their hideous heads.[14] What if Megan hadn't run away all those years ago. What if she had stayed and faced the music[15] and seen what really happened to Stewart Green. Would this all be behind her now? Would all those "Mardi Gras Men"—men who had seemingly vanished off the face of the earth[16], never to be seen again—from Stewart Green right up to Carlton Flynn, would they still be here and with their families and living their lives?

What if she had just stayed with Ray.

There were no regrets—only what-ifs. There couldn't be regrets once you had children—it would be too monstrous to contemplate[17]. Would Megan's life have been happier or sadder with any of these what-ifs? That no longer mattered because any what-if led to[1] a world without her children, without Kaylie and Jordan even being born[2], and there was no way any parent could ever entertain that existence being preferable[3]. In the end, whether her life had ended up being exciting or not, fast paced[4] or not, joyful or not, the one scenario she could never embrace[5] would be one without Kaylie and Jordan.

A mother can't go there[6].

The door flew open[7], and a big man with steel-wool gray hair and a dress shirt a couple of sizes too small burst in[8]. The man was beefy[9] and red faced[10]. "What the hell is going on?" he shouted.

Rick Mason jumped up[11]. "Chief Goldberg …"

"I said, what the hell is going on?"

"I'm sketching two possible suspects."

"Why would you be doing that down here?"

Mason said nothing.

"You have an office, don't you?"

"Yes."

"So why are you down here?"

"Detective Broome suggested that I work here."

Goldberg put his hands on his hips. "Did he now[12]?"

"He said that he didn't want this witness compromised[13]."

Goldberg turned his attention to Megan. "Well, well. If it isn't Janey from the diner. Another friendly visit?"

Megan said, "I'd rather not say[14]."

"Excuse me? Who are you really?"

"Am I compelled[15] to give you my name?"

That caught him off guard.[16] "Legally[17], I guess not—"

"Then I'd rather not. I'm here of my own free will[18] and at the request of[19] Detective Broome."

"Oh, really?" Goldberg bent down in her face[20]. "I happen to be Detective Broome's immediate superior[21]."

"That doesn't change anything."

"Doesn't it, Ms. Pierce?"

1. auraient débouché sur

2. soient seulement nés

3. que pour un parent c'était tout bonnement inenvisageable de préférer une vie sans ses enfants

4. à 100 à l'heure

5. le seul scénario impossible à imaginer

6. ne peut concevoir ça

7. s'ouvrit avec fracas

8. fit irruption

9. corpulent

10. rougeaud

11. se leva d'un bond

12. Tiens donc

13. mettre son témoin en danger

14. Permettez-moi de ne pas répondre

15. Suis-je dans l'obligation

16. La question le déstabilisa.

17. Légalement

18. de mon plein gré

19. à la demande de

20. se pencha tout près d'elle

21. le supérieur hiérarchique

Megan closed her mouth. Goldberg had already known her name. That couldn't be a good thing. He moved toward the sketch pad[1]. Rick Mason tried to block the view[2], like a fourth grader[3] who didn't want to get copied off[4] on a test[5]. Goldberg nudged him aside[6] and put on a pair of glasses. When his gaze landed on[7] the sketches of the young couple, his body convulsed[8] as though he'd been zapped with a stun gun[9].

"Who the hell are these two?"

No one said anything.

Goldberg turned his attention to Mason. "Did you hear what I asked?"

"I don't know. I was just told to get the sketch."

"For what case?"

He shrugged.

Goldberg turned back to Megan. "Where did you see these two?"

"I'd rather wait for Detective Broome."

Goldberg looked at the sketches again. "No."

"No?"

"You tell me now. Or you get the hell out of here."

"Are you serious?"

"I am."

This Goldberg guy was giving Megan a serious case of the willies[10]. She would indeed get out of here. She'd take a walk, maybe go to the diner, and then she'd call Broome and regroup[11]. There was a reason why Broome wanted to keep her hidden—and maybe it had to do with more than just protecting her identity. Maybe it had to do with his charging rhino of a boss[12], Goldberg.

She pushed back her chair. "Fine, I'm out of here."

"Don't let the door hit your ass on the way out[13]."

Goldberg turned away, troubled[14]. His rudeness[15] surprised her. It was almost as though he wanted her out[16]. This was probably some kind of power play[17] with Broome, but she didn't like it. Still, it would be

246

best to get out of here now so she didn't tell him anything she shouldn't[1].

Megan stood. She had just grabbed her purse[2] when once again the door burst open.

It was Broome.

When Broome first pushed through the door[3], she could see something odd on his face: anger—even before he saw Goldberg. The anger, weirdly enough[4], seemed directed at her[5]. She had a second to wonder what that was about[6], if something had gone wrong with his visit with Lorraine, but before Broome could act upon it[7], he spotted[8] Goldberg. When he did, Broome's face fell[9].

For a moment the two men just stared at each other. Both were making fists[10] and for a split second, Megan wondered if one of them was going to take a swing[11]. Then Broome took a step back, shrugged, and said, "Busted.[12]"

That opened the floodgates[13]. "What the hell is going on, Broome?" Goldberg demanded.

"This woman, who shall remain anonymous, may have seen Harry Sutton's killers."

Goldberg's mouth dropped open[14]. "She was at the scene[15]?"

"She saw these two walking out when she was walking in. We have no reason for them to be in the building at that hour. I'm not saying they did it, of course, but they are people of interest[16]."

Goldberg thought about it. He flicked his gaze toward[17] Mason. "The sketch done?"

"Just about.[18]"

"Finish it up. You"—he pointed at Broome—"I want to see in my office in five minutes. I got a call to make[19] first."

"Okay."

Goldberg left. When he was gone, the anger returned to Broome's face. He glared down at Megan[20].

"What?" she asked.

1. avant de lui dire quelque chose qu'elle risquait de regretter
2. venait de récupérer son sac à main
3. passa la porte
4. bizarrement
5. dirigée contre elle
6. juste le temps de se demander pourquoi
7. puisse expliquer sa colère
8. remarqua
9. son visage se décomposa
10. serraient les poings
11. flanquer un coup de poing à l'autre
12. On est pris en flag.
13. Ce fut assez pour faire exploser Goldberg
14. en resta bouche bée
15. sur place
16. pour nous, ils sont à rechercher
17. se tourna vers
18. Presque.
19. J'ai un appel à passer
20. fixa Megan avec colère

Still staring at her, "Mason?"

"Yeah?"

"Give us five minutes."

"Uh, sure."

Rick Mason started to leave. Broome's eyes were still locked on hers[1], but he held up his hand toward Mason[2]. "Actually, I need you to do something."

Mason waited.

"We have an age progression on[3] Stewart Green, right?"

"Right."

"Add a shaved head and give him a goatee and a hoop earring. Can you do that for me?"

"Sure, yeah, okay. When do you need it by[4]?"

Broome just frowned.

"Got it," Rick Mason said. "Yesterday."

"Thanks."

Broome was still staring at her. As soon as Mason left, Megan decided to take the offensive. "Stewart Green shaved his head and grew[5] a goatee? Did Lorraine tell you that?"

Broome kept glaring.

"What's your problem?" she asked.

He leaned[6] a little closer to her and waited to make sure that she was looking directly into his eyes.

"Do you want to keep lying to me," Broome said, "or do you want to tell me about your old beau[7], Ray Levine?"

DEL Flynn brought pink roses, Maria's favorite, to her room. He brought them[8] every day. He showed them to his former wife[9] and kissed her cold forehead[10].

"Hey, Maria, how you feeling today?"

The nurse[11]—he could never remember her name—gave him flat eyes[12] and left the room. In the beginning, when Maria had first been wheeled into this room[13], the nurses had looked upon Del Flynn with respect and admiration. Here he was, the ex-husband

1. restaient rivés sur les siens
2. arrêta Mason d'un geste
3. On a bien fait une simulation de vieillissement pour
4. Il vous faut ça pour quand ?
5. s'est fait pousser
6. se pencha
7. votre ancien galant
8. en apportait
9. ex-femme
10. son front glacé
11. infirmière
12. le regarda d'un air indifférent
13. été amenée dans cette chambre pour la première fois

of this comatose[1] woman, and look at the sacrifices he was making for her. What a man, they'd thought. What a devoted[2], dedicated[3], loving, understanding[4] hero of a man[5].

The staff[6] had left an empty vase already filled with water. After all this time, they knew his routine[7]. Del slipped the bouquet into the water and sat next to Maria's bed. He glanced toward the door and made sure that no one was in earshot[8]. They weren't.

"Maria?"

For some reason he waited for her to answer. He always did.

"I should have told you this before, but I got some bad news."

He watched her face for the smallest change[9]. There wasn't. There hadn't been in a very long time. Del let his eyes wander around the room[10]. If appearances meant anything, you'd never guess that they were in a hospital. Sure, there was that constant beeping[11] from the medical equipment and the dull hospital background noise[12]. But Del had transformed this room. He brought in all Maria's old favorite things—the stuffed bear[13] he'd won for her at Six Flags when Carlton was six, the ornate Navajo rug[14] they'd bought on that vacation to[15] Santa Fe, the dartboard[16] they'd hung up in the basement of[17] that old house on Drexel Avenue.

Del had surrounded[18] Maria with[19] old photographs too—their wedding picture[20], their first Christmas with Carlton, Carlton's graduation[21] from Parkview preschool[22]. His favorite photograph had been taken at Atlantic City Mini Golf, right on the Boardwalk by Mississippi Avenue. He and Maria had gone there often. There were bronze statues of children at play throughout the course[23]. Maria had liked that—like it was a visit to a museum and mini golf place all in one. Maria had made a hole-in-one[24] on the last hole, and the cashier[25], the same guy who'd asked them what

1. dans le coma
2. attentionné
3. dévoué
4. compréhensif
5. homme admirable
6. Le personnel
7. ses habitudes
8. personne n'était à portée de voix
9. à l'affût du moindre changement
10. laissa son regard errer à travers la pièce
11. les bips incessants
12. le bourdonnement feutré de l'hôpital
13. l'ours en peluche
14. le tapis navajo à motif sophistiqué
15. pendant des vacances à
16. le jeu de fléchettes
17. au sous-sol, dans
18. entouré
19. de
20. photo de mariage
21. la fête de fin d'année
22. la maternelle
23. le long du parcours
24. fait un trou en un
25. le type de la caisse

color ball they wanted to use, came out and took this photograph, and the way the two of them were smiling you'd think they won a trip to Hawaii rather than a free game[1].

Del stared at that picture now and then slowly turned back to Maria. "It's about Carlton."

No response.

Eighteen months ago, a drunk driver[2] had run a red light[3] and smashed into[4] Maria's car. It had been late at night. She had been driving alone to pick up a prescription[5] at the all-night pharmacy[6] for Carlton. That was what single[7] women did, he guessed. If she'd still been married to Del, if she hadn't been so damned stubborn[8] and forgiven him[9], she would have never been out that late[10] driving and she'd be fine and they'd be fine and they'd still be going to that mini golf place and then playing a few hands[11] at Caesars or getting a steak at Gallagher's or splitting a funnel cake[12] on the Boardwalk. But he'd blown it[13] a long time ago.

"He's missing," Del said, tears coming to his eyes. "No one knows what happened to him. The cops are on it[14], but you know that's not enough. So I hired[15] some people. You know the kind. You probably wouldn't approve, except when it came to[16] your boy, you'd kill, right?"

Again no answer. The doctors had explained that there was no hope. She was brain-dead[17]. They had encouraged him to let her go. Others had done the same in both gentle and forceful tones[18]. Maria's sister had even tried to sue[19] to become medical proxy[20], but Maria had named him and so she lost. Everyone wanted to pull the plug[21]. Making her live like this, day after day, month after month, heck, maybe year after year, was cruel, they claimed.

But Del couldn't let her go.

Not yet. Not until she forgave him. He begged her[22] every day for forgiveness[23]. He begged her to come back to him, to let them be what they were, what they always should have been. In short[1], he said all the things he should have said before the accident.

Some days Del actually thought that redemption was possible[2]. Some days he thought that Maria would open her eyes and she would see all that he'd done for her, all the sacrifice, all the devotion. She would have heard all the words he'd said during his visits to her bedside, and she would forgive him. But most days, like right now, he knew that would never be. He knew that what he was doing was indeed cruel[3] and that he should let her go, and move on with his life. He and Maria had been divorced now for longer than they were married. Del had been married twice since. He was with Darya now.

Then other days—rare days but they were there—Del wondered whether he intentionally held on to her[4] out of spite[5]. Maria had never forgiven him and that ruined everything[6]. Maybe, subconsciously[7], he was angry with her. Maybe keeping her alive was payback[8]. God, he hoped not, but some days he couldn't shake the feeling[9] this was all nothing but a grand selfish gesture[10].

Del wasn't good at letting go. He couldn't let go of the only woman he ever loved.

And he couldn't—would never—let go of his son.

"I'm going to find him, Maria. I will find him and I will bring him here and when you see him, I mean, really, when your boy is back home and safe ..."

There wasn't more to say. He sat next to her and fingered the Saint Anthony medal[11]. He loved this medal. He never took it off[12]. A few weeks back, he'd noticed that Carlton wasn't wearing his. His son had replaced it with some crappy[13] two-bit[14] dog tags[15] like he'd really been in the military[16] or something, and, man, when Del saw that he hit the roof[17]. How dare he? The idea of his son replacing his Saint Anthony medal, the one his sainted mother[18] had giv-

1. Bref

2. qu'il y avait une chance de rédemption

3. cruel, en vérité

4. il se cramponnait à elle

5. par rancune

6. ça avait tout gâché

7. qu'inconsciemment

8. en représailles

9. s'empêcher de penser

10. que son geste n'était qu'une forme suprême d'égoïsme

11. caressait du doigt sa médaille de saint Antoine

12. ne la quittait jamais

13. à la con

14. en toc

15. plaques d'identité militaire

16. comme s'il avait vraiment fait l'armée

17. il était sorti de ses gonds

18. sa sainte mère

en him, for those poser[1] dog tags, had enraged Del. When Carlton shrugged and countered[2] that he liked the dog tags, that his friends all wore them, that they looked "cool," Del had come close to hitting his son[3]. "Your grandfather wore dog tags while storming Normandy[4], and believe me, he never thought they were cool!" Del's real name was, in fact, Delano, named for[5] Franklin Delano Roosevelt, his parents' hero. Carlton walked away then, but when he went out that night, Del noticed with some pride[6] that the Saint Anthony medal was back around his neck—along with the dog tags.

The kid was learning the art of compromise[7].

When Del's cell phone rang—Darya had recently made[8] the Black Eyed Peas' "I Gotta Feeling" his ringtone[9]—he snatched it up quickly[10]. The song, with its famed[11] "Tonight's gonna be a good night" chorus[12], felt particularly obscene[13] in here. He put the phone to his ear and said, "Flynn."

"It's Goldberg."

Del Flynn heard something strange in the cop's tone[14]. Normally Goldberg was strictly seen-it-all bored[15], but he seemed strangely agitated now. "You got news?"

"Do you know what those two lunatics of yours[16] did?"

"That's not your concern."

"The hell it's not. It's one thing to rough up a whore[17], but this guy was a—"

"Hey," Flynn said, cutting him off[18]. "You really want to share your concerns over a phone line[19]?"

Silence.

"It's a mess[20]," Goldberg said.

Flynn didn't much care. He only cared about one thing: finding Carlton. "Don't worry about that. I'll clean up the mess."

"That's what I'm afraid of. That couple you hired—they're psychos[21], Del. They're out of control[22]."

252

"Let me worry about them," Del Flynn said, taking his wife's hand in his. She felt cold as stone[1]. "Just help us find our son."

There was a brief pause. "About that," Goldberg said.

The agitation was gone from his voice. What replaced it sent a chill straight through Del's heart[2]. "What?"

"The blood we found in that park. You remember?"

"I remember."

"We don't have a firm DNA test or anything. That can take weeks. And really it might not mean anything at all. I mean that. So let's not get ahead of ourselves[3]."

The knot[4] that had been in Del Flynn's stomach since Carlton vanished tightened. "But?"

"But based on the preliminary findings[5]," Goldberg said, "I believe the blood at the park belongs to[6] your son."

1. froide comme la pierre

2. frappa Del en plein cœur

3. ne nous emballons pas

4. nœud

5. d'après les premières constatations

6. appartient à

27

1. Vous avez perdu votre langue

2. Quand il avait nommé Ray

3. avait senti son cœur tressauter

4. Ça alors

5. je m'attendais pas à celle-là

6. À mon tour de vous surprendre

7. repensa à la soirée de la veille

8. qui semblait les protéger de son ombre

9. posa brutalement quelque chose

BROOME leaned in closer. "Cat got your tongue[1], Megan? I asked you about your old beau, Ray Levine."

At the mention of Ray's name[2], Megan felt her heart tumble down[3].

"Hello?"

"It's not what you think," she said.

"Gee[4], I didn't expect that line[5]. Let me come back with an unexpected one of my own[6]: What's not what I think?"

Megan didn't even know what to say, how to explain it. She flashed back again to last night[7], to how she felt in Ray's arms, to Lucy looming above them almost protectively[8].

"How could you lie to me like that?"

"I didn't lie."

Broome slapped something down[9] on the table. "Did Ray Levine take this picture?"

It was the anonymous picture of Carlton Flynn in the park.

"I know your old squeeze[1] used to be a big-time[2] photojournalist—and I saw your face when I first showed this to you. So let's stop with the lies[3], okay? Ray Levine took this picture, didn't he?"

Megan didn't reply.

"Answer me, damn it. If he's innocent, he's got nothing to worry about[4]."

"Right, sure," Megan said. "Just like that Ricky Mannion guy you told me about. How long has he been in prison?"

Broome sat next to her. "Eighteen years for something he didn't do. You want to help him get out[5]?"

"By having him trade places with[6] another innocent man?"

"Hey, Megan, I know he used to be your boyfriend and all, and, man, that's just so sweet[7], but this is a hell of a lot bigger[8] than you guys[9] or your summer romance[10] or whatever game[11] you two were playing with Stewart Green."

"Game?"

"Yeah, Megan, game. The night Stewart Green disappeared—Ray Levine was there, wasn't he?"

She hesitated just long enough[12].

"Damn," Broome said. "I knew you were holding something back[13]—I just didn't know what. So let's follow this through[14], shall we? Ray Levine was at the park the night Stewart Green vanished and—lo and behold[15]—seventeen years later he's there again when Carlton Flynn vanishes. That about sum it up?[16]"

She couldn't protect Ray, at least not by lying. "It's not what you think."

"Yeah, you said that already. Was Ray there the night Stewart Green disappeared or not?"

Megan tried to think how best to put this[17]. "We were supposed to meet there[18], yes, but Ray showed up late[19]."

"Late when?"

"After I ran."

---

1. votre vieux copain
2. à succès
3. on arrête les mensonges
4. il n'a rien à craindre
5. l'aider à en sortir
6. En laissant sa place à
7. c'est mignon tout plein
8. tout ça dépasse de loin
9. vous deux
10. votre amourette
11. le petit jeu
12. quelques secondes de trop
13. que vous me cachiez quelque chose
14. allons jusqu'au bout
15. devinez quoi
16. C'est un bon résumé ?
17. formuler ça le mieux possible
18. On était censés se retrouver là-bas
19. est arrivé en retard

Broome made a face. "After you ran?"

"Yes."

"I don't get it. How would you know what happened after you ran?"

"He told me."

"Ray?"

"Yes."

"When?"

"Last night."

"You're kidding, right?" Broome couldn't have looked more incredulous[1] without plastic surgery[2]. "Let me get this straight[3]: Ray Levine told you that he showed up after you saw Stewart Green lying there."

"Yes."

Broome shrugged. "Well, heck, that's enough for me[4]. I might as well close the book on him.[5] He's clearly innocent."

"Very funny."

"He told you this last night."

"Yes."

"And you, what, just believed him?[6]"

"Yes, but …" Megan again wondered how to put this so he'd understand. "Do you want the truth?"

"No, no, really, I mean, now that Harry's dead and Carlton Flynn's blood was all over that park[7], what I really want from you, Megan, is more lies."

She tried to slow herself down[8]. Her heart raced in her chest[9], her mind pulled in a hundred different directions[10]. "I told you the truth about the night in the woods. I saw Stewart lying there by that boulder[11]. I thought he was dead."

Broome nodded. "And you were supposed to meet Ray?"

"Yes."

"But you didn't see him?"

"That's right."

"Go on."

1. n'aurait pu avoir l'air plus incrédule

2. sans l'aide de la chirurgie esthétique

3. Récapitulons

4. ça me suffit

5. Pas la peine de chercher plus loin.

6. paf, vous l'avez cru ?

7. qu'on a retrouvé le sang de Carlton Flynn partout dans le parc

8. de reprendre son calme

9. battait la chamade

10. partait dans tous les sens

11. à côté de ce rocher

Megan took a deep breath. "Well, I'd been pretty badly abused by Stewart[1]. I told you about that too."

"Did Ray know?"

"I guess he did. But that's not the point[2]."

"What is?"

"Stewart Green was a bad combo[3]: a violent bully[4] and a real citizen. I mean, if he was just a run-of-the-mill[5] degenerate[6], would you still care about his whereabouts[7], after all these years? Would you still visit his wife on the anniversary of his disappearance? If some, I don't know, working stiff[8] with no wife and kids went missing instead, would you cops care this much[9]?"

The answer was obvious: No. That hit home for Broome.[10] It explained why no one had seen the Mardi Gras connection. Berman's wife hated him. Wagman was a truck driver passing through[11]. Her accusation was true[12]—and yet it was also, for the sake of Ray Levine's possible role in these cases[13], totally irrelevant[14].

"We cops play favorites[15]," Broome said, folding his arms. "Big news flash.[16] So what?"

"That's not my point[17]."

"So what is your point?"

"When I saw Stewart Green lying there, when I thought he was dead, it naturally crossed my mind that Ray had something to do with it[18]."

"You were in love with Ray?"

"Maybe."

"Don't give me maybe."

"Okay, suppose I was."

Broome started pacing. "So you didn't just run away to protect yourself. You ran away to protect the man you loved."

"The cops would put it on one of us[19], that was for sure," Megan said. "If I stayed, one of us—or hell, maybe both of us—would have ended up in prison. Like Ricky Mannion."

---

1. Stewart me maltraitait régulièrement

2. ce n'est pas la question

3. mix

4. tyran

5. quelconque

6. dépravé

7. à ce qu'il est devenu

8. vulgaire pékin

9. autant

10. Sa remarque fit mouche.

11. de passage

12. Ses accusations étaient fondées

13. quant au rôle éventuel de Ray Levine dans ces affaires

14. absolument pas pertinentes

15. Nous, les flics, on a des chouchous

16. Quel scoop.

17. ce que j'essaie de dire

18. était impliqué

19. auraient accusés l'un de nous deux

Broome smiled now.

"What?"

"That all sounds great and dramatic, Megan, except for one thing: You thought Ray did it, didn't you? He was protecting you, and part of you was relieved to get this creep off your back[1]. Plus, really, when you stop and think about it[2], Stewart Green had it coming[3], right?"

She didn't reply.

"So that night, you see Stewart Green. You think he's dead. You're relieved, but you also think your boyfriend, Ray Levine, killed him. You ran so he wouldn't get caught[4]."

She wasn't sure how to reply so she went with[5], "I'm not denying that[6]."

"And"—Broome held up his hand—"you ran because you really didn't want to stay with Ray or marry him or whatever, because now, justified or not[7], you viewed[8] Ray Levine as[9] a killer. You ran away from that too, didn't you?"

Broome stepped back. He could see that he had hit the mark[10]. For a moment, they sat there in silence. Broome's phone buzzed. He looked down and saw it was Goldberg paging him up to his office[11].

"All these years," Broome said, "you thought Ray killed Stewart Green."

"I thought it was possible."

He spread his arms. "So that leads up to[12] the big question: What made you change your mind?[13]"

"Two things," she said.

"I'm listening."

"One"—she pointed to the table—"Ray sent you that picture."

Broome waved it off[14]. "To toy[15] with me. Lots of serial killers do."

"No. If he'd been killing men all these years, he'd have started toying with you years ago. You didn't have a clue[16] that Carlton Flynn had ever been

---

1. d'être débarrassée de ce taré
2. on y pense
3. ne l'avait pas volé
4. pour qu'il ne se fasse pas prendre
5. opta pour
6. Je ne dis pas le contraire
7. à tort ou à raison
8. avez pris
9. pour
10. mis dans le mille
11. qui le convoquait dans son bureau
12. Ce qui nous amène à
13. Qu'est-ce qui vous a fait changer d'avis ?
14. balaya l'argument
15. jouer
16. ne saviez même pas

258

to the park[1]. Without that photograph, you'd know nothing. He sent it in[2] to help you find the real killer."

"So he was, what, being a good citizen[3]?"

"In part, yes," she said. "And in part because he, like me, needs to know the truth about that night. Think about it.[4] If Ray hadn't sent you that picture, you'd still be at square one[5]."

"And pray tell[6], how did he happen to take that picture?"

"Think about that too. Why this year? Why not last year or the year before? If Ray was the killer, he could have sent you a new one every year, right? He would have sent them on Mardi Gras. But you see, for Ray, the big day[7] was February eighteenth. That's the last time we were together. That's when it all ended so horribly for us[8]. So Ray goes there—on the anniversary, not Mardi Gras. He takes pictures. That's what he does. That's how he processes[9]. So he wouldn't have pictures of your other victims—because he wasn't there on Mardi Gras, except when it overlapped[10] with February eighteenth. He'd only have pictures of Carlton Flynn."

Broome almost chuckled. "Wow, you're really reaching[11]."

It was, Broome knew, outrageous[12] and full of holes[13], and yet, as he had learned over the years, the truth has a more unique stench than[14] lies. Still, he didn't have to rely on intuition[15]. Would Ray have pictures from every February 18? That might back[16] her crazy claim[17].

But more important: If Ray snapped a photograph of the victim, maybe, just maybe, he took a photograph of the killer.

"You said two things," Broome said.

"What?"

"You said there were two reasons you changed your mind about Ray killing Stewart Green. You just gave me one. What's the other?"

1. était allé dans ce parc

2. vous l'a envoyée

3. faisait son devoir de citoyen, c'est ça

4. Réfléchissez.

5. en seriez encore à la case départ

6. dites-moi, je vous prie

7. la date importante

8. tout a fini de façon si terrible pour nous

9. C'est comme ça qu'il fonctionne

10. ça coïncidait

11. faites vraiment tout pour l'aider

12. tiré par les cheveux

13. bourré de failles

14. une odeur caractéristique par rapport aux

15. de se fier uniquement à son intuition

16. confirmerait

17. thèse extravagante

"The simplest reason of all," Megan said. "Stewart Green isn't dead."

DEPUTY Chief Samuel Goldberg wanted to cry.

He wouldn't, of course; couldn't even remember the last time he had, but suddenly the desire was there. He sat alone in his office. The office was really a glass partition[1], and everyone could see in[2] unless he closed the blinds[3] and whenever he did that, every cop in the precinct, a naturally suspicious group by nature, got extra-antsy[4].

Goldberg closed his eyes and rubbed his face[5]. It felt as though the world were closing in on him, preparing to crush him like in that Star Wars[6] trash compactor scene[7] or that old *Batman* TV episode where Catwoman's spiky wall[8] nearly skewers[9] the Dynamic Duo. His divorce cost him a fortune. The mortgage payments[10] on his and his ex's properties were ridiculous. His oldest daughter, Carrie, the greatest kid any guy could ever hope to have, wanted to become a tennis phenom[11] and that was so damned expensive. Carrie was training down in Florida with some world-famous[12] coach, and it was costing Goldberg more than 60K[13] a year, which was nearly his take-home salary[14] after taxes[15]. Plus, okay, Goldberg had expensive taste in women, and that was never a good thing for the bank account[16].

So Goldberg had to be creative[17] to make ends still not meet[18]. How? He sold information. So what? For the most part, the information didn't change a damn thing. For that matter, neither did law enforcement[19]. You get rid of the Italians, the blacks take it over[20]. You get rid of the blacks, you got the Mexicans and the Russians and so on. So Goldberg played both sides[21]. Nobody got hurt except those who deserved to get hurt. Criminal-on-criminal crime[22], so to speak[23].

As for this new situation—providing information on the Carlton Flynn case—well, that seemed even more basic. The father wanted to find his kid. Who couldn't get that? The father believed the cops could only do so much[1] and that he could help them out. Goldberg doubted it, but sure—why not?—go for it[2]. At worst[3], the father feels like he did the most he could. Who wouldn't understand that? And at best, well, the cops did have limits. They had to follow certain rules, even the dumb-ass ones[4]. Someone outside of law enforcement circles[5] didn't have those restraints[6]. So maybe, who knows, this could be a good thing for everyone.

Plus, yep, Goldberg gets money.

Win-win-win.[7]

During his marriage, Goldberg's now ex-wife, one of those beautiful women who wanted you to take them seriously[8] but the only reason you'd bother is because they're beautiful, had thrown a lot of yoga-Zen-Buddhist crap at him[9], warning him about the danger of his extracurricular moneymaking activities[10]. She talked about how bad deeds[11] could enter the soul[12] and the slippery slope[13] and that it would color his chakra red[14] and all that. She talked this way until, of course, he pointed out that if he listened to her they'd have to move into a smaller house and skip[15] the summer vacations and forget about Carrie's tennis lessons.

But maybe there was something to[16] all that slippery-slope mumbo jumbo[17]. A stripper gets hurt a little—big deal, right? But maybe it is. Maybe it just snowballs from there[18].

And where does it end up?

Megan Pierce, wife and mother of two, who could now identify Del Flynn's two psychopaths—that's where. She needed to be silenced.[19] That's the problem with crossing the line[20]. You step over it for a second, but then that line gets blurry[21] and you don't know where it is anymore and next thing you know,

1. qu'il y avait une limite à ce que les flics pouvaient faire

2. qu'il essaie

3. Au pire

4. même débiles

5. ne faisant pas partie de la police

6. contraintes

7. Tout le monde y gagne.

8. qu'on les prenne au sérieux

9. lui avait sorti un tas d'âneries du yoga et du bouddhisme

10. ses agissements extra-professionnels lucratifs

11. actions

12. pénétrer l'âme

13. la pente savonneuse

14. teinterait de rouge son chakra

15. faire une croix sur

16. de vrai dans

17. charabia

18. qu'après, ça fait boule de neige

19. Il fallait la faire taire.

20. quand on franchit la ligne

21. devient floue

you're supposed to help two maniacal Talbots-catalogue models[1] kill a woman.

Goldberg's cell phone rang. He looked at the caller ID and saw it was the psycho chick[2].

"Goldberg," he said.

"Is she still in your precinct, Deputy Chief Goldberg?" Her upbeat voice[3] reminded him of the hot[4] cheerleader[5] captain from his high school days. "Yes."

The young woman sighed. "I can wait."

And then Goldberg said something that surprised even him: "There's no need.[6]"

"Pardon?"

"I'm getting all the information on her, and then I'll pass it on[7]. There's no need for you to, uh[8], discuss anything with her. You can just let her be[9]."

Silence.

"Hello?" Goldberg said.

"Don't worry, I'm here," she said in a singsong voice[10].

Where the hell had Flynn found these two? He decided to push it a bit[11].

"Plus there is a lot of heat[12]," Goldberg said.

"Heat?"

"People are watching her.[13] Cops. You'd never have a chance to get her alone for more than a minute or two. Really, it's best to leave this one to me[14]."

Silence.

Goldberg cleared his throat and tried to move her off this topic[15]. "The blood by those ruins belongs to Carlton Flynn, just so you know[16]. So what other angle are you two working on? Anything I can help with?"

"Deputy Chief Goldberg?"

"Yes."

"When will Megan Pierce be leaving the precinct?"

"I don't know, but I just told you—"

"She saw things, Deputy Chief Goldberg."

He flashed onto[1] Harry Sutton's dead body[2]—the poor guy's pants[3] down around his ankles[4], the burn marks[5], the incisions, the horrible things done to him. Beads of sweat[6] popped up[7] on Goldberg's brow[8]. He hadn't signed on for this.[9] It was one thing to sneak[10] a little information to a worried father. But this?

"No, she didn't."

Again the young woman said, "Pardon?"

"I was just with her[11]," Goldberg said, realizing that he was talking too quickly[12]. "She said she saw a black man at the scene, that's all."

Silence.

"Hello?"

"If you say so[13], Deputy Chief Goldberg."

"What's that supposed to mean?"

But the call had already been disconnected.

1. revit brusquement
2. le cadavre
3. pantalon
4. aux chevilles
5. les brûlures
6. Des gouttes de sueur
7. perlèrent
8. front
9. Ça n'était pas compris dans le deal.
10. refiler
11. Je viens de la quitter
12. se rendant compte qu'il en avait trop dit
13. Si vous le dites

28

WALKING toward Goldberg's office, Broome debated the pros and cons[1] and quickly deduced[2] that he had no choice. Goldberg was finishing a phone call. He gestured for Broome to sit.

Broome glanced at his boss's face and then did a double take[3]. Goldberg hadn't been a beauty who radiated good health[4] to begin with, but right now, sitting behind his cluttered desk[5], he looked like something pulled out of the bottom of the laundry hamper[6]. Something that maybe the cat coughed up first.[7] Something that was pale and pasty and shaky[8] and maybe in need of an angioplasty[9].

Broome took a seat. He expected to be chewed out[10], but Goldberg seemed too exhausted. Goldberg hung up the phone. He looked at Broome through eyes with enough baggage[11] to work a pole[12] at La Crème and said in a gentle voice that surprised Broome, "Tell me what's going on."

The tone threw him[1]. Broome tried to remember the last time Goldberg had been anything but[2] piss-contest hostile[3]. He couldn't. It didn't matter. Broome had already decided that he had to come clean[4] and tell Goldberg his suspicions. It would be impossible to move ahead[5] without his immediate superior's okay[6]. They probably had enough now to go to the feds[7]—probably had enough yesterday but Broome didn't want to rush it[8]. He didn't want to look like a fool[9] if he was wrong, didn't want to lose the case[10] if he was right.

Broome started with the murder of Ross Gunther, then moved on to[11] the missing Mardi Gras Men—Erin had so far come up with[12] fourteen disappearances in seventeen years that fit—and then he segued into[13] Carlton Flynn. He ended with his suspicion that last night's murder of Harry Sutton was connected, but he had no idea how[14].

"Still," Broome said, finishing up, "our witness gave us a good description of two people near Harry Sutton's office at the time of his death. We'll get the sketches out[15] as soon as we can."

Goldberg roused himself from[16] whatever stupor he'd sunken into[17] and said, "By witness, you mean the woman I just met downstairs[18]?"

"Yes."

"And you're hiding her because … ?"

"She's the Cassie I told you about before," Broome said. "The one who came forward[19] yesterday."

"Stewart Green's ex?"

"Not ex, but, yes, the girl Green stalked[20] or whatever. Now this Cassie has a new identity—husband, kids, the works[21]—and she asked me to protect it. I promised her I would try."

Goldberg didn't push it. He picked up a paper clip[22] and began to bend it back and forth[23]. "I don't get something," he said. "Every Mardi Gras, some guy goes missing?"

---

1. le prit au dépourvu
2. que Goldberg n'avait pas été
3. hargneux
4. le mettre au parfum
5. d'aller plus loin
6. sans l'accord de son supérieur
7. pour faire appel au FBI
8. précipiter les choses
9. passer pour un imbécile
10. qu'on lui retire l'enquête
11. passa aux
12. avait jusqu'ici trouvé
13. enchaîna avec
14. du comment
15. On va diffuser les portraits-robots
16. sortit
17. de sa torpeur
18. que je viens de rencontrer en bas
19. Celle qui s'est présentée
20. que Green harcelait
21. tout le toutim
22. un trombone
23. le plier dans tous les sens

"Right."

"And we haven't found any bodies[1]?"

"Not one," Broome said. "Unless you include[2] Ross Gunther."

Goldberg twisted[3] the paper clip until it broke. Then he picked up another. "So this Gunther guy gets murdered in this park eighteen years ago on Mardi Gras. And this other guy, what was his name?"

"Ricky Mannion."

"Right, Mannion. He goes down for it[4]. They had a solid case[5]. Mannion still claims innocence[6]. The next year on Mardi Gras, Stewart Green vanishes. We don't know it at the time[7], but he was in that same remote part of the park and he was, what, bleeding?"

"That's right."

"But someone has seen him recently?"

"We think so, yes."

Goldberg shook his head. "Now we skip ahead[8] seventeen years. Another man, Carlton Flynn, vanishes on Mardi Gras—and the preliminary labs[9] tell us that he too was bleeding up at the same spot?"

"Yes."

"Why am I just hearing about this now?[10]" Goldberg put his hand up before Broome could say anything. "Forget it, we don't have time for that now." He drummed the desk with his fingertips[11]. "Three men bleeding in the same spot," he said. "We should send the lab boys back up there[12]. They need to go over every inch of the area[13], see if they can find any other blood samples[14]. If—I don't know, this whole thing is so crazy—but if some of the other Mardi Gras Missing were also cut up[15] there, maybe we can find old traces of blood."

It was a good idea, Broome thought.

"What else do you need?" Goldberg asked.

"A warrant[16] to search[17] Ray Levine's apartment."

"I'll work on it.[18] Should we put an APB[19] on him?"

1. on n'a retrouvé aucun corps

2. Sauf si on compte

3. tortilla

4. a été coffré pour ça

5. un dossier en béton

6. clame toujours son innocence

7. à l'époque

8. faisons un bond de

9. les premières analyses

10. n'ai-je pas été mis au courant plus tôt ?

11. pianotait sur le bureau

12. renvoyer l'équipe médico-légale là-bas

13. Il faut qu'ils passent la zone au peigne fin

14. échantillons

15. ont aussi été découpés

16. Un mandat de perquisition

17. pour fouiller

18. Je m'en charge.

19. avis de recherche

266

"I'd rather not," Broome said. "We don't have enough yet for an arrest, and I don't want to spook him[1]."

"So what's your plan?"

"I'm going to see if I can find him. I want to talk to him alone before he thinks about lawyering up[2]."

There was a knock on the door. Mason entered. "I got the age progression on Stewart Green." He passed one copy[3] to Goldberg, one copy to Broome. As promised it was Stewart Green, seventeen years after he vanished, with a shaved head and goatee.

Goldberg asked, "Have you finished those sketches for the Harry Sutton case?"

"Just about."

"Good, give them to me." Goldberg turned to Broome. "You go after Ray Levine. I'll take care of[4] getting the sketches out."

KEN found a quiet booth toward the back of La Crème, one that gave him a pretty poor view of[5] the dancers but a great view of the older barmaid who'd brought Detective Broome to this den of sin[6].

Earlier Ken had managed to get close enough to hear snippets[7] of the conversation between Detective Broome and the barmaid he called Lorraine. She clearly knew a lot. She was clearly emotional about it[8]. And, he thought, she clearly was not telling all.

Ken was so happy, nearly giddy with joy[9] over his upcoming nuptials[10]. He considered various ways to pop the question[11]. This job would pay well, and he'd use the money to buy her the biggest diamond he could find. But the big question was: How should he pop the question? He didn't want anything cheesy[12] like those men who propose on stadium[13] scoreboards[14]. He wanted something grand yet simple[15], meaningful yet fun[16].

She was so wonderful, so special, and if any place could hammer that fact home[17], it was here at this alleged[18] gentlemen's club. The women here were gro-

---

1. le faire flipper

2. à appeler un avocat

3. un exemplaire

4. Je m'occupe de

5. ne donnait pas une bonne vue sur

6. dans cet antre du Mal

7. des bribes

8. en était visiblement toute remuée

9. presque ivre de joie

10. à l'idée de son prochain mariage

11. de faire sa demande

12. ringard

13. dans un stade

14. le tableau d'affichage [des scores]

15. de magnifique et de simple à la fois

16. d'éloquent et de drôle à la fois

17. en faire la démonstration

18. soi-disant

1. malades
2. artificielles
3. le même pouvoir de séduction
4. qu'un défilé de grosses têtes pour le carnaval
5. la choper pendant une pause
6. la fin de son service
7. la ligoter
8. sa bien-aimée
9. diriger les opérations
10. pensa qu'il avait une chance folle

tesque. He didn't understand why any man would want any of them. They looked dirty and diseased[1] and fake[2], and part of Ken wondered whether men came here for other reasons, not sexual, to feel something different or because this club had perhaps the same appeal as[3] a carnival freak show[4].

Ken wondered how long the barmaid Lorraine would work, if he could snatch her on a break[5] or if he'd have to wait until her shift was done[6]. If it was at all possible, Ken wanted to tie her up[7] and wait for his beloved[8] to join him. She loved to be in charge[9] when they hurt women.

He felt the vibration from his cell phone. He looked down and saw it was from the love of his life. He thought of her face, her body, her cleanliness, and never felt so lucky in all of his life[10].

He picked up the phone and said, "I love you."

"I love you too. But I'm a little worried."

"Oh?"

She filled him in on her conversation with Goldberg. When she finished, he asked, "What do you think?"

"I think our friend Deputy Chief Goldberg is lying."

"I do too."

"Do you think I should take care of it?" she asked.

"I don't see any other way."

11. avait hâte de rentrer chez elle
12. s'expliquer avec lui
13. que je vous fasse raccompagner
14. un véhicule de notre parc
15. venir le récupérer
16. demain matin
17. qu'il faut que j'interroge
18. Partez sans a priori

MEGAN finished with the sketches. She was anxious to get home[11] and talk to Dave and figure this whole mess out[12]. When Broome came back into the room, he said, "Do you want me to have someone drive you home[13]?"

"I'd rather just rent a car and drive myself."

"We can give you one from the pool[14] and get it picked up[15] in the morning[16]."

"That'd be fine."

Broome crossed the room. "You know I need to question[17] Ray Levine, right?"

"Yes. Just keep an open mind[18], okay?"

"I'm nothing if not open-minded[1]. Any idea where I can find him?"

"Did you try his place[2]?" she asked.

"I had a patrol car stop by[3]. He's not home."

Megan shrugged. "I don't know."

"How did you find him yesterday?" Broome asked.

"It's a long story."

Broome frowned.

"From his boss," Megan said. "A guy named Fester."

"Wait, I know him. Big guy with a shaved head?"

"Yes."

"He owns some fake[4] paparazzi company or something." Broome sat by a computer screen[5] and started typing[6]. He found the telephone number for Celeb Experience on Arctic Avenue in Atlantic City. He dialed the number, spoke to a receptionist, and was patched through to[7] Fester. He identified himself as a police officer[8] and told him that he needed to speak with Ray Levine.

"I'm not sure where he is," Fester said.

"He's not in any trouble.[9]"

"Uh-huh. Don't tell me. He came into[10] a lot of money, and you want to help."

"I just need to talk to him. He may have witnessed[11] a crime."

There was noise in the background. Fester shushed someone[12]. "Tell you what. I can call his cell for you[13]."

"Tell you what," Broome countered[14]. "How about you give me his cell number and I call him directly?"

Silence.

"Fester or whatever the hell your name is, you don't want to mess with this[15]. Trust me here. Give me his number. Don't call and warn him or any of that. You won't be happy with how it all turns out[16], if you screw this up[17]."

"I don't like being threatened."

"Deal with it.[18] What's Ray's number?"

Sidebar glossary:

1. Si quelqu'un n'a pas d'a priori, c'est bien moi.

2. chez lui

3. J'ai envoyé une voiture de police sur place

4. bidon

5. s'assit devant un ordinateur

6. commença à tapoter sur le clavier

7. on lui passa

8. dit qu'il était officier de police

9. On ne lui reproche rien.

10. est entré en possession de

11. a peut-être été témoin d'

12. dit à quelqu'un de se taire

13. l'appeler sur son portable

14. répliqua

15. ne vous mêlez pas de ça

16. Vous n'aimerez pas ce qui risque de se passer

17. si vous faites tout foirer

18. C'est votre problème.

Fester postured[1] for another minute or two, but eventually he gave it up[2]. Broome wrote it down, warned Fester one more time not to say a word, and then hung up.

DAVE couldn't think straight[3].

He took a break from[4] the labor dispute[5] he'd been working on and moved into his office.

"Do you need anything, Mr. Pierce?" the young associate[6] asked him.

She was a recent Stanford Law grad[7] and gorgeous and chipper[8] and full of life, and you wondered when life would beat it out of her[9]. It always did in the end. That kind of enthusiasm wouldn't last[10].

"I'm fine, Sharon. Just finish up those briefs[11], okay?"

It was amazing what we could hide when we try, he thought. No one—neither his clients nor opposing counsel[12]—had any idea that as he sat through the depositions, jotting notes[13] and giving counsel, he was completely devastated by his wife's lie. The lawyerly façade[14] never gave way[15]. He wondered now if we were all like that, all the time, if everyone in the other room was just putting on a mask to hide some internal pain, that all of them, everyone in that room, had also been crushed[16] this morning and was as good at hiding it as he was.

Dave looked at his wife's panicked text. She wanted to explain. Last night he had been so forgiving[17]. He loved her. He trusted her. Whatever else there was in her or his life, well, everybody has something, right? No one is perfect. That core would always be there.[18] But when morning came, despite the night's bliss[19], that whole rationale[20] had just felt wrong.

Now he felt adrift.

He would have to talk to Megan eventually, hear her explanation. He wondered what it would be and if he'd believe her. Dave was tempted to call her back now, but he'd let her stew[21] another few hours. Why not, right? No matter what the explanation, she had lied to him.

Dave glanced at the computer monitor. Eventually, he guessed, Megan would want to know how he'd known about her visit to Atlantic City. He wasn't sure he wanted to tell her. Last night he had detested tracking the GPS in her cell, but suddenly he liked the idea of being able to know where she was at his whim[1]. That was the problem with crossing lines. That was the problem with losing trust[2].

He clicked the link to her phone's GPS and waited for the map to load up[3]. When it did, he couldn't believe what he was seeing. Megan wasn't home, crying or stewing[4] or feeling bad about what she'd done.

She had gone back to Atlantic City.

What the … ?

He took out his smartphone and made sure that he could see the GPS map on the app[5]. He could. That meant that if Megan moved, he'd be able to see. Fine.

Maybe it was time to see for himself[6] what she was doing.

Dave grabbed his car keys. He rose, pressing his office intercom button[7]. "Sharon?"

"Yes, Mr. Pierce?"

"I'm not feeling well. Please cancel the rest of my day.[8]"

MEGAN was pacing while Broome wrote down Ray's cell phone number. She hadn't asked for the number last night—hadn't wanted it—but she casually[9] glanced over Broome's shoulder and memorized it. She debated calling Ray, warning him about Broome's upcoming[10] visit, but a voice inside her told her to leave it be[11].

Let the investigation take its natural course[12], she thought.

She didn't believe that Ray was guilty of … of what anyway? Assault? Kidnapping? Disappearances? Mur-

---

1. quand ça lui chantait

2. quand on n'avait plus confiance

3. que la carte s'affiche

4. en train de ruminer

5. l'application

6. d'aller voir par lui-même

7. et appuya sur son interphone

8. Merci d'annuler mes derniers rendez-vous de la journée.

9. discrètement

10. imminente

11. une voix intérieure lui souffla de ne pas s'en mêler

12. suivre son cours

1. s'était
montrée
persuasive

2. dans les
arguments
qu'elle avait
présentés à

3. de son mieux

4. qui la
rongeait encore

5. Tant
d'éléments

6. ne collaient
pas

7. ce qui
l'obsédait

8. ne lui avait
pas tout dit

9. avant tout

10. intelligent

11. Se faire
plaquer par
une femme qu'il
aimait

12. l'aurait
blessé

13. maison de
retraite

14. Entre deux
sanglots

15. On aurait
dit une enfant
apeurée

16. la vieillesse
ne progresse pas
en ligne droite

17. La vieillesse
est une boucle

18. qui nous
ramène en
enfance

19. pas avec ses
bons côtés

20. cette chaîne
de télé-achat

der? She had been persuasive[1] in her arguments to[2] Broome, defending Ray as best she could[3], but there was something that still gnawed at her[4]. So much of this[5]—Stewart Green, Carlton Flynn, the Mardi Gras Missing—didn't add up[6], but the one thing she couldn't shake[7] was the feeling that Ray was keeping something from her[8].

There was more to what happened to him, more to what crushed him, than a girlfriend running away. Yes, they were lovers and all that and who knows what they might have been. But Ray was also first and foremost[9] a photojournalist. He'd been independent and sarcastic and smart[10]. A lover running out on him[11] would hurt, sting[12], break his heart. But it wouldn't do this.

Her cell phone rang. She could see from the caller ID that it was her mother-in-law calling from the nursing home[13]. "Agnes?"

She could hear the old woman crying.

"Agnes?"

Through the tears[14], her mother-in-law said, "He was back last night, Megan."

Megan closed her eyes.

"He tried to kill me."

"Are you okay?"

"No." She sounded like a scared child[15]. It was obvious and a bit of a cliché, but we don't really age in a straight line[16]. We age in a circle[17], curving back to childhood[18], but in all the wrong ways[19]. "You have to get me out of here, Megan."

"I'm a little busy—"

"Please? He had a knife. A real big one. The same one you keep in your kitchen, you remember, the one I got you for Christmas from that Home Shopping Network[20]? It's the same kind. Check your kitchen. Is the knife still there? Oh God, I can't stay here another night…"

Megan didn't know what to say. Another voice came on the phone. "Hi, Mrs. Pierce, this is Missy Malek."

She ran[1] the nursing home. "Please call me Megan."

"Right, you've told me that, sorry."

"What's going on over there?"

"As you know, Megan, this behavior is nothing new[2] for your mother-in-law."

"It seems worse today."

"This isn't a disease[3] that improves with time[4]. Agnes will continue to get more and more agitated, but there are things we can do to help in these situations. I've spoken to you about this before, am I right?"

"You have, yes."

Malek wanted to move Agnes to the third floor, out of "independent living"[5] to the "reminiscent floor"[6] for those with advanced Alzheimer's. She also wanted authorization to use heavier sedatives[7].

"I've seen this kind of thing before," Malek said, "though rarely this acute[8]."

"Could there be something to it[9]?"

"Pardon?"

"To what Agnes is claiming[10]. She still has plenty of moments of clarity. Could there be something to it?"

"Could a man be breaking[11] into her room with your kitchen knife and threatening to kill her? Is that what you're asking me?"

Megan wasn't sure how to respond[12]. "Maybe, I don't know, maybe someone on your staff is playing a prank[13] or she's misinterpreting[14] something …"

"Megan?"

"Yes?"

"No one is playing a prank. It is the cruelty[15] of her disease. We understand when it is something physical—losing a limb[16], needing a transplant[17], whatever. This is similar. It is not her fault. It is something chemical[18] in her brain[19]. And sadly, as I've tried to stress[20], this isn't a problem that will get better. Which is why

1. dirigeait

2. n'est pas nouveau chez

3. une maladie

4. s'arrange avec le temps

5. la faire passer de la zone « autonome »

6. à « l'étage du souvenir »

7. des sédatifs plus forts

8. mais rarement de façon aussi aiguë

9. une part de vérité

10. prétend

11. entrer par effraction

12. ne sut que répondre

13. lui fait une farce

14. interprète mal

15. le côté cruel

16. la perte d'un membre

17. la nécessité d'une greffe

18. un phénomène chimique

19. cerveau

20. comme je l'ai déjà souligné

1. revoir comment organiser au mieux la vie d'Agnes

2. pesa brusquement plus lourd

3. de nouveau à l'appareil

4. ne bouges pas

you and your husband really need to seriously reeval-uate Agnes's living arrangements[1]."

Megan's phone felt suddenly heavy[2]. "Let me speak to Agnes please."

"Of course."

A few seconds later, the scared voice was back[3]. "Megan?"

"I'm on my way, Agnes—and I'm taking you home. You just stay put[4], okay?"

29

WHEN you first get to the Atlantic City boardwalk, you are pretty much stunned by[1] the seedy albeit lively predictability of it all[2]. Skee-ball[3] arcades[4], funnel cakes, hot dog stands[5], pizza stands, time-share salesmen[6], mini-golf, suggestive T-shirt shops, souvenir stands—all perfectly blended in[7] among giant casino hotels, the Ripley's Believe It or Not! Museum (this one featured a "penis sheath[8]" from New Guinea used, according to the caption[9], "as decoration and protection against insect bites[10]," not to mention a heck of a conversation starter[11]), and upstart new malls[12]. In short, Atlantic City's boardwalk is exactly what you expect and probably want: total cheese[13].

But every once in a while, the boardwalk threw you a surprise[14]. If you've played the board game Monopoly, you know the geography, but there, tucked in an alcove[15] where Park Place meets[16] Boardwalk, with the tacky[17] Wild Wild West-themed façade of Bally's Hotel and Casino looming as its backdrop[18], was a

1. ce qui frappe surtout, c'est

2. que le quartier est à la fois aussi minable mais aussi vivant qu'on s'y attendait

3. de jeux

4. galeries

5. vendeurs de hot dogs

6. agences immobilières [pour apparts en multi-propriété]

7. qui se fondent parfaitement

8. étui pénien

9. d'après l'étiquette à côté

10. les piqûres d'insectes

11. mais qui était génial à lancer dans la conversation

12. de tout nouveaux centres commerciaux

13. très kitsch

14. réserve une surprise

15. dans un recoin

16. croise

17. ringard

18. en toile de fond

Korean War memorial that, for a few moments anyway, had the ability to strip away[1] the kitsch and make you reflect.

Broome spotted Ray Levine standing next to the memorial's almost supernaturally dominant figure[2]—a twelve-foot-high[3] statue of *The Mourning*[4] *Soldier* sculpted by Thomas Jay Warren and J. Tom Carillo. The soldier had his sleeves rolled up[5], his helmet[6] in his right hand, but what struck you, what gave you pause[7], was the way the bronze figure looked down, clearly grieving, at the[8] too-many dog tags dangling from[9] his left hand. You could see the devastation on his brave, handsome face as he stares at his fallen[10] comrades' tags, the rifle[11] still strapped to his back[12], the dagger[13] still on his hip. Behind him, a group of weary[14] soldiers seem to materialize from a wall of water, one carrying a wounded[15] or perhaps dead comrade. Next to that, under an eternal flame, the names of 822 New Jerseyans killed or missing are engraved[16].

The effect would normally be sobering and reflective[17], but here, shoehorned among[18] the flotsam and jetsam[19] of the Atlantic City boardwalk, it was profound[20]. For several moments, the two men—Broome and Ray Levine—just stood there, staring up at the dog tags clutched[21] in the mourning soldier's hand, and said nothing.

Broome moved a little closer to Ray Levine. Ray sensed him[22], knew he was there, but didn't turn toward him.

"You come here a lot?" Broome asked.

"Sometimes," Ray replied.

"Me too. Kinda puts it in perspective somehow[23]."

Tourists walked mere feet away[24], checking out[25] the casino signs for jackpots and cheap buffets. Most never saw the memorial or if they did, they cast their eyes away[26] as though it were the homeless begging for change[27]. Broome got it. They were here for other reasons. Those guys on the wall, the ones who had fought or died for such freedom, would probably get it[1] too.

"Heard you were in Iraq during the first war," Broome said.

Ray frowned. "Not as a soldier."

"As a photojournalist, right? Dangerous work. Heard you took shrapnel in your leg."

"No big deal[2]."

"That's what the brave[3] always say." Broome noticed Ray's backpack[4] and the camera in his hand. "You take pictures here?"

"I used to."

"But not anymore?"

"No. Not anymore."

"Why not?"

Ray shrugged. "It's stone and bronze. It never changes."

"As opposed," Broome said, "to something like, say, nature. Or like something growing[5] near ruins. Those are better places to take pictures, right?"

Ray turned and faced him[6] for the first time. Broome could see that Ray hadn't shaved[7]. His eyes were glassy[8] and bloodshot[9]. Megan had told him that she'd met up with her former beau last night for the first time in seventeen years. Clearly he had reacted by hitting the bottle[10], something, according to those who knew him, Ray Levine did with a fair amount of regularity[11].

"I assume, Detective Broome, that you didn't call to ask me my theories on photographic subjects[12]."

"Maybe I did." Broome handed him the anonymous photograph of Carlton Flynn at the park. "What can you tell me about this?"

Ray glanced at it, said nothing. "It's amateurish[13]." He handed it back to Broome.

"Ah Ray, we're always our own toughest critics[14], aren't we?"

---

1. comprendraient sans doute aussi

2. Pas grave

3. les gens courageux

4. le sac à dos

5. qui pousse

6. lui fit face

7. ne s'était pas rasé

8. vitreux

9. rouges

10. en se mettant à picoler

11. assez régulièrement

12. n'êtes pas venu me demander ce qu'il est bon de photographier

13. du travail d'amateur

14. on est toujours plus sévère envers soi-même

Ray said nothing.

"We both know you took this picture. Please don't bother with the denials[1]. I know you took it. I know you were at the ruins the day Carlton Flynn disappeared. And I also know you were there seventeen years ago when Stewart Green disappeared."

Ray shook his head. "Not me."

"Yeah, Ray, you. Megan told me everything."

He frowned. "Megan?"

"Oh, that's her name now. You know her as[2] Cassie. She's married, you know. Did she tell you that? Two kids?"

Ray said nothing.

"She didn't want to sell you out[3], if that means anything to you. In fact, she insists[4] you're innocent. She says you sent this picture to help us." Broome tilted his head[5]. "Is that true, Ray? Were you looking to[6] help us find the truth?"

Ray stepped away from[7] the statue and started[8] toward the dancing water[9] in the Fountain of Light. Sometimes the fountain, which had been there for nearly a hundred years, danced[10] high, but right now the water was barely visible, bubbling maybe two or three inches[11].

"There's two ways I can play this[12]," Ray said. "One, I lawyer up and[13] not say a word."

"You could do that, sure."

"Two, I can talk to you and cooperate and trust it will work out[14]."

"I confess that I prefer option two," Broome said.

"Because option two is dumb[15]. Option two is how a guy like me gets in a jam[16], but you know what? We're in Atlantic City, so I'm going to roll the dice[17]. Yeah, I took that picture. I go to that park once a year and take pictures. That's what I do."

"Hell of a[18] coincidence."

"What?"

---

1. n'essayez pas de le nier
2. sous le nom de
3. vous trahir
4. maintient que
5. inclina la tête
6. Cherchiez-vous à
7. s'écarta de
8. se dirigea
9. les jets d'eau
10. montait
11. ne bouillonnant qu'à 5 ou 6 cm du sol
12. Je peux réagir de deux façons
13. j'appelle un avocat et, en attendant,
14. espérer que ça ne m'attire pas d'ennuis
15. stupide
16. se fout dans le pétrin
17. tenter ma chance
18. Une sacrée

"You being there the same day Carlton Flynn gets grabbed."

"I was there February eighteenth. I go there every February eighteenth, except when I spent a little time out west[1]."

"What's so special about February eighteenth?"

Ray frowned. "Now who's playing games?[2] You talked to Cassie, so you know."

Fair enough[3], Broome thought. "It's like a pilgrimage or something[4]?"

"Something like that. I go, I sit, I take pictures, I contemplate."

"Contemplate?"

"Yep."

"All because your girlfriend ran off on you there?"

Ray didn't reply.

"Because, if you don't mind me saying[5], Ray, you sound like a pussy-whipped[6] pansy[7]. Your girl left you—so what?[8] Grow a pair[9] and move on with your life. Instead you go back to where she dumped your pathetic ass[10] and take pictures?"

"She didn't dump me."

"No? So Megan has been biding her time[11] under a pseudonym with the rich husband and two kids, just waiting for your career as a fake paparazzo to take off[12]?"

Ray actually smiled at that.[13] "Does sound kind of pathetic."

"So?"

"So I'm pathetic," Ray said with a shrug. "I've been called worse.[14] Anything else I can help you with, Detective?"

"Let's go back seventeen years to that night by the ruins."

"Okay."

"Tell me what happened."

1. j'ai habité un temps sur la côte ouest

2. Qui est-ce qui joue au plus malin maintenant ?

3. Bon, d'accord

4. une sorte de pèlerinage

5. sans vouloir vous vexer

6. que sa gonzesse mène par le bout du nez

7. chochotte

8. et alors ?

9. Montrez que vous avez des couilles

10. vous a laissé tomber comme une merde

11. attendait son heure

12. décolle

13. Cela fit sourire Ray.

14. On m'a traité de pire.

1. faisait pré-
enregistrée
2. me suis cassé

3. super
altruiste

4. D'un côté
5. j'ai eu envie de
danser la java
6. très bon
mobile
7. Je ne suis pas
allé vérifier son
pouls
8. voulez savoir
9. réfléchit
longuement

10. Quel métier
fascinant
11. L'inaugu-
ration
12. concession-
naire
13. sorti un
tapis rouge
14. marchait
forcément
dessus
15. alors on
accourait et on
le ou la prenait
en photo
16. me suis fait
agresser
17. Vous avez
porté plainte ?
18. perdre une
nuit à

Ray's voice sounded canned[1]. "I was supposed to meet Cassie. I saw Stewart lying there. I figured that he was dead, so I took off[2]."

"That's it?"

"Yep."

"You didn't call an ambulance or help him?"

"Nope."

"Wow, Ray, you're quite the humanitarian[3]."

"Did Cassie tell you what Stewart Green was like?"

"She did, yes."

"So you get it then. Half of me[4] wanted to do the Snoopy happy dance[5] when I saw him." Ray held up a hand. "And, yes, I know that gives me a great motive[6], but I didn't kill him."

"You sure he was dead?"

Ray turned to him. "I didn't go over and check vital signs[7] if that's what you're asking[8]."

"Then you weren't sure?"

Ray mulled it over[9]. "There's something else you might want to know. Not about that night, but about this February eighteenth."

"Go on."

"I worked a job that night. After I took the pictures in the park."

"A job?"

"Yeah, a bar mitzvah, as a hired paparazzo."

Broome shook his head. "Glamour profession[10]."

"You have no idea. Do you know what job I just came from? Grand opening[11] of a Ford dealership[12]. They had a red carpet out[13] and anyone who stopped by got to walk it[14] and we crowded them and took pictures[15], and then they tried to sell them a Focus or an Escort or whatever. Anyway, when I was leaving the bar mitzvah, I got jumped[16]. Someone stole my camera."

"Did you report it to the police?[17]"

"Right, like I wanted to waste a whole night on[18] that. But that's not my point. At first, I figured it was

280

just a routine mugging[1], but then I wondered how come[2] the guy only took my camera and didn't at least try to grab my wallet."

"Maybe he felt rushed[3]."

"Maybe. But when I got home, I saw Carlton Flynn on the TV. That's when I realized I had a picture of him. See, the pictures were still on my camera, but I have a Wi-Fi connection that automatically uploads them to[4] my home computer every ten minutes or so. But the mugger wouldn't know that[5]."

Broome saw where he was going with this[6]. "So you think the mugger may have been after the picture[7]?"

"It's possible."

"So you sent it to me anonymously?"

"I wanted to help, but I wanted to keep my name out of it[8] for obvious reasons. Like you say, the fact that I was there for both disappearances was suspicious. I can see from your face[9] that it still is. But that's why."

"You get a look at the guy who jumped you?"

"No."

"Height[10], weight[11], white, black, tattoos, anything?"

"Nothing. I got hit with a baseball bat. I went down[12]. I mean, I tried to hold on to[13] the camera, but sorry, that's all I know." Ray filled him in on[14] the whole incident, how he took more than one blow[15], how he fought for his camera, how the attacker finally ran[16].

"Were you drunk?"

"What? No."

"Because you drink a lot, right?"

"I'm also of legal age[17]. So what?"

"I hear you have blackouts[18]. That true?"

Ray didn't bother responding. Broome reached into his pocket[19] and took out the age-progression picture of Stewart Green with the shaved head and goatee. "Could this have been the guy?"

---

1. une agression banale
2. pourquoi diable
3. qu'il était pressé
4. les télécharge sur
5. ne pouvait pas le savoir
6. voulait en venir
7. essayait peut-être de récupérer la photo
8. voulais pas être impliqué
9. à la tête que vous faites
10. Taille
11. corpulence
12. Je me suis écroulé
13. ne pas lâcher
14. lui narra
15. plusieurs coups
16. que son agresseur avait fini par partir en courant
17. je suis majeur
18. des pertes de conscience
19. fouilla dans sa poche

When Ray Levine saw the image, the bloodshot eyes widened. He looked as though someone had whacked him anew with that baseball bat[1]. "Who the hell is that?"

"Do you recognize him or not?"

"I ... No. I mean ... no, he's not the guy who attacked me."

"I thought you didn't see your attacker."

"Don't be cute[2], Broome. You know what I mean."

Broome lifted[3] the picture higher, nearly shoving it in Ray's face[4]. "Have you ever seen this guy before?"

"No."

"So why the startled face?"

"I don't know. Who is he?"

"Don't worry about it."

"Cut the crap[5], Broome. Who is he?"

"A suspect. You either know him or you don't."

"I don't."

"You sure?"

"Yes."

"Cool." Broome put the picture away[6], wondering what to make of the[7] reaction. Had Ray seen Stewart Green? He'd go back to it[8] later. Time to change direction a bit, keep him off balance[9]. "Now earlier, you stated[10] you go up to the iron-ore ruins every February eighteenth."

"No, I didn't. I said, most[11]."

"Right, okay, forgetting the years you were away[12]. Do you have proof[13]?"

"Proof that I was up there on various February eighteenths?"

"Yes."

"Why would I need that?"

"Humor me."

"You're investigating[14] murders and disappearances. I don't think I'm much in the mood to[15] humor you."

"Who said anything about murders?"

Marginal notes (footnotes):

1. lui avait re-flanqué un coup avec la batte de base-ball
2. Faites pas le malin
3. leva
4. la collant sous le nez de Ray
5. Arrêtez vos conneries
6. rangea la photo
7. comment interpréter sa
8. y reviendrait
9. pour continuer à le déstabiliser
10. avez déclaré
11. presque tous [les 18 février]
12. à part les années où vous n'étiez pas dans les parages
13. pouvez le prouver
14. enquêtez sur
15. être trop d'humeur à

Ray sighed. "Wow, did someone just buy you a boxed set[1] of old *Columbo* episodes? You don't think I know that Cassie—or what did you call her? Megan? You don't think I know she visited Harry Sutton? He was murdered, right? It's in all the papers[2]."

"Oh. Fair point. So let's stop with the games. Can you prove you were taking pictures at the park"—Broome made quote marks with his fingers[3]—" 'most' February eighteenths?"

Ray thought about it. "Actually, I think I can."

"How?"

"The photographs I take. They're date stamped[4]."

"Can't you fix that?[5] Like make it look like another date?"

"I don't know, frankly. You can have your experts look for themselves. You can also check weather reports[6] maybe, see if it was raining or snowing or what that day. I still don't get it. What difference does it make what day I was there?"

Simple, though Broome wouldn't say it now. If Ray Levine could show he went up on February eighteenths—and not Mardi Gras—it would back[7] his story. Of course, Broome would subpoena[8] all the photographs and see what other dates he was[9] in that section of the park. But it would be a start[10].

It was coming to an end.[11] Broome could feel it. After seventeen years of hunting[12], searching[13], never letting go, he was so damn close[14] to breaking this case open[15]. Odd when you thought about it. Every February eighteenth—well, "most"—Ray Levine visited that park and reflected on[16] a certain incident. Meanwhile, on that same day, Broome visited Sarah Green and reflected on the very same incident. Except "reflected" wasn't really the right word, was it? Broome had been obsessed with[17] the Stewart Green case from day one. While all the other cops in town dismissed it as[18] yet another philandering creep[19] who ran off with a stripper, Broome had held on with

---

1. vient de vous offrir un coffret

2. journaux

3. dessina des guillemets en l'air

4. horodatées

5. Mais ça peut se bidouiller, non ?

6. les bulletins météo

7. ça confirmerait

8. ferait saisir

9. quels autres jours il était venu

10. un début

11. Les choses se précipitaient.

12. passées à chercher

13. fouiller

14. sur le point de

15. résoudre l'affaire

16. repensait à

17. obsédé par

18. ne l'avaient pas prise au sérieux,

19. convaincus qu'il s'agissait encore d'un tordu coureur de jupons

a ferocity that surprised even him. Yes, getting to know the family Stewart left behind—Sarah, Susie, and Brandon—had helped him focus[1], but even back then, he recognized that Sarah was somewhat deluding herself[2], that all would not be well in that sad, lonely house if her beloved husband were returned safely[3].

In truth, even way back then[4], Broome had believed that Stewart Green's disappearance was more than it seemed, much more, something dark and horrible and almost beyond his comprehension[5]. Now he was sure of it.

"Are we done here, Detective?"

Broome checked his cell phone. Goldberg was going to text him when he got the subpoena[6] and had it served[7]. He didn't want Ray Levine heading home before then, perhaps tampering with[8] or destroying evidence[9].

"That picture you sent me anonymously—that wasn't the only one you took that day, right?"

"No, of course not."

"Where are the rest of the pictures?"

"On my hard drive[10] at home, but I back them up to a cloud[11]."

"A cloud?"

"That's what they call it[12]. For safe storage.[13] It's like a disk in the sky. Think of it as e-mailing stuff to yourself.[14] I can access them from any computer with the proper codes[15]."

Whoa, Broome thought. "I have a laptop in my car," he said. "Would you mind?[16]"

"What, now?"

"It could really help. My car is right around the corner[17]."

Broome had parked on South Michigan Avenue near Caesars. While the computer booted up[18], Ray said, "I sent you the last picture I took. Once someone else came on the scene[19], I figured it was time to go."

---

1. à rester concentré
2. se mentait à elle-même
3. lui était rendu sain et sauf
4. à l'époque
5. qui le dépassait
6. le mandat
7. le faisait remettre à l'intéressé
8. car il risquait de falsifier
9. de détruire des éléments de preuve
10. disque dur
11. je les sauvegarde aussi sur un « cloud »
12. comme ça que ça s'appelle
13. C'est une sécurité.
14. Un peu comme si on s'envoyait un mail à soi-même.
15. si on a le bon mot de passe
16. Si ça ne vous ennuie pas...
17. à deux pas
18. s'initialisait
19. Quand quelqu'un d'autre est arrivé

"So that's the only picture of Carlton Flynn?"

"That's right."

"And there was no one else in any of the other pictures?"

"Right. Before that, I had the place to myself[1]."

The computer came to life. Broome handed it to Ray. The sun was bright[2], putting glare on the screen[3], so they slipped into the car. Broome watched the people exiting the[4] casinos. They always did it the same way—with a stumble[5], a shade of the eyes with one hand[6], big-time blinking[7].

"Did you see anyone on your way back down[8] from that spot?" Broome asked.

"No, sorry."

Ray got on the Internet and went to a Mac Web site. He typed in a user name[9] and password[10] and clicked on some folders[11] and then he handed the laptop back to Broome. There were eighty-seven photographs. He started with the last, the photograph Ray had sent anonymously. Something struck Broome right away[12]. The first few were all what one might call picturesque landscapes[13], except something in the composition brought on feelings of[14] melancholy. Most times, landscape scenes make you yearn for[15] the great outdoors[16] and that solitude. But these were stark[17], lonely, depressing—interesting because that was clearly the photographer's mood and intent[18].

Broome continued to click through the photographs. For some reason that dumb line from[19] that song "A Horse with No Name" came to him: "There were plants and birds and rocks and things." That pretty much summed it up[20]. Broome had hoped to find, what exactly? He didn't know. Clues.[21] But all he saw were bland[22] yet creative and moving[23] photographs of the scene where one man lost his heart—and others lost ... again what?

"You're good," Broome said.

Ray did not reply.

1. j'étais tout seul

2. radieux

3. d'un éclat aveuglant sur l'écran

4. sortant des

5. un temps d'arrêt

6. une main en visière

7. obligés de cligner des yeux

8. en redescendant

9. un identifiant

10. un mot de passe

11. répertoires

12. frappa immédiatement Broome

13. des paysages pittoresques

14. provoquait

15. vous donne des envies de

16. grands espaces

17. austères

18. l'humeur et l'intention

19. une phrase idiote de

20. C'était à peu près tout

21. Des indices.

22. fades

23. émouvantes

Broome could almost feel the foreboding[1] now, the cumulative impact of Ray's work starting to wear him down[2]. He was nearly finished going through the photographs when something snagged his gaze[3].

Broome stopped.

"Can you zoom in[4]?"

"Sure. Just click the command and plus buttons."

The photograph was one of the first Ray had snapped[5] that day, taken from a different viewpoint[6], so maybe that explained it. There were trees, of course, and the big rock and the old furnace chimney[7], but from here, Broome thought he could see something else, something behind the ruins of that old chimney in the background[8]. He clicked, zooming closer and closer. The picture quality, fortunately[9], was excellent, so there was very little pixilation[10].

Broome felt his heart rise to his throat[11].

Ray looked over his shoulder. "What is that?"

Broome moved in closer[12]. Something was jutting out[13] behind the chimney. It was green and metallic with a black rubber end[14]. Broome could only make out maybe six inches of it[15]. But that was enough. He'd spent the summer after high school graduation[16] working for a moving company[17], so, even though he could only see the handle[18], he had a pretty good idea what it was.

"It's a hand truck[19]," Broome said. "Someone hid a hand truck near where these guys disappeared."

30

MEGAN started the journey to[1] her mother-in-law.

Her thoughts were with poor Harry Sutton. There was, of course, the possibility that the timing of his murder[2] was a coincidence. She had returned to Atlantic City over a[3] seventeen-year-old incident. The young couple being sought[4] by the police would have been, what, five, maybe ten years old back in those days. So perhaps, if those two were the ones who did it, Megan and her past had absolutely nothing to do with what happened to Harry.

Her mind continued to nimbly do this denial dance step[5], but in the end, the truth seemed pretty obvious: She had dragged[6] danger and death to Harry Sutton's door[7]. She couldn't figure out how yet. But in her heart, Megan knew that once again, she had messed up[8].

Two weeks ago, she had returned to Atlantic City for the first time for that mundane trade show[9]. Part of her had convinced herself that it was no big deal, that

1. se mit en route pour aller voir

2. la date de son meurtre

3. à cause d'un

4. recherché

5. persistait dans le déni allègre

6. conduit

7. jusque chez Harry Sutton

8. merdé

9. salon professionnel

the visit was strictly for career opportunities[1]. She had truly believed the gritty[2] city she still missed[3] hadn't been calling to her. But that was more self-delusion[4]. She could have stayed at the seminar, for example. Some other real-estate wannabes[5] had even planned a group dinner[6] at the Rainforest Café, but Megan had passed[7]. Instead, she had gone to La Crème.

Who could blame her[8]? Who doesn't visit old haunts[9] when they return to a city that meant so much to them[10]?

She decided to try Dave again. When her call went to voice mail[11], she started to feel the first wave of anger. After the beep, she said, "Enough of this. We have to talk. Your mother is having serious issues[12]. Grow up[13] and call me."

Megan hung up, nearly hurling[14] the phone across the front seat. On the one hand, of course she understood his behavior. She was the one in the wrong[15]. But maybe that was the problem. In a sense, she had always been the one in the wrong. Over the years, she had let the guilt of her deception[16] color everything in their relationship[17]. Her fault? Sure. But maybe Dave had taken advantage of it. Her guilt had made her acquiesce too many times. She didn't resent the kids for any of it[18]. She wouldn't trade it[19] but …

But why wasn't Dave calling her back?

All those years he had been working, yes, providing[20], putting food on the table and all the rest of the crap men use to justify what they do—but Dave liked his work. He thrived on late hours[21] and travel and golf on Sunday mornings and then coming home to his hot, willing[22] wife. She had been all that for him, even when she didn't want to be. Don't get her wrong.[23] Dave had never bullied[24] her. He had never been mean[25] or deceptive, but then again, why would he be? He had the perfect wife. She had given up on finding a career of her own. She paid all the bills[26], took care of all the shopping, drove all the carpools, made sure the household[1] was in order. She took care of his mother, cared about her more than he ever could, and after all that, all the sacrifices she'd made, how did he treat her?

He was ignoring her calls—and he'd somehow been spying on her[2].

Not that she didn't deserve that[3]. But still[4]. Here she wanted to talk to him, tell him about her past and inner demons[5] and let him know that the wife he had sworn to protect[6] was in danger, and he wouldn't even return her desperate calls, choosing instead to act like a petulant[7] child.

She reached for her phone again. She had already put Ray's number in so she'd remember it. She hit the dial button, but before it could even start ringing, she saw the sign for[8] the Sunset Assisted Living Home.

Don't be an idiot, Megan, she told herself.

Megan hung up the phone, parked, and with the anger still seething[9], she headed inside.

***

BARBIE stayed two cars back.

She wasn't overly concerned about being spotted[10]—Megan Pierce hardly seemed like an expert in noticing tails[11]—but you never knew. The fact that this seemingly simple housewife[12] was somehow caught up[13] in all this indicated that she was not merely[14] what she appeared to be. The same, of course, could be said about Barbie herself.

As Barbie drove, her mind kept slipping back to Ken's sudden proposal[15]. It was sweet and cute, sure, but it was mostly disturbing[16]. She had always assumed that Ken saw past the illusions cast upon us[17], that their relationship had opened his eyes to a new and different reality. But it hadn't. Even he could not

---

1. que la maison

2. trouvé moyen de l'espionner

3. Elle le méritait sans doute

4. quand même

5. les démons qui la rongeaient

6. qu'il avait fait serment de protéger

7. qui boude

8. le panneau indiquant

9. bouillant encore de colère

10. spécialement inquiète de se faire repérer

11. semblait peu douée pour voir qu'elle était filée

12. femme au foyer

13. impliquée

14. seulement

15. la demande en mariage inattendue

16. perturbant

17. au-delà des conventions factices

289

see past the bill of goods[1] we are sold from our first days on this planet[2].

We are told, for example, by our unhappy, miserable[3] parents, that the way to find joy in life is to live and do exactly as they have. Barbie never understood that logic. What do they say about the definition of insanity[4]? It is doing the same thing over and over[5] and expecting different results. Generationally[6] the world seemed to do just that. Barbie's father, for example, had hated trudging off to work[7] in that tired suit and tie[8] every morning, coming home at six P.M. feeling angry and defeated and finding classic solace[9] in a bottle. Her mother had detested being a housewife—forced into a role her mother had played and her mother before her—and yet, in the ultimate life blind spot[10], what did Mom want for her own daughter?

To find a man and settle down[11] and have children of her own—as though resentment[12] and unhappiness were a legacy she hoped to pass down[13].

What kind of subversive logic was that?

Now Ken wanted to marry her. He wanted to have the house and the picket fence and of course, the children, even though Barbie had long ago accepted that she did not have a maternal bone in her body[14]. She looked out the windshield[15] and shook her head. Didn't he get it? She loved this life—the rush, the excitement, the danger—and she firmly believed that it was God's plan for her. He had made Barbie this way. Why would He do that if she was meant to be yet another brain-dead[16] housewife, wiping kid snot[17] and cleaning up poop[18]?

She would help Ken see that they had been brought together for a reason. She loved him. He was her destiny. Her role, she knew, was to pull the blindfold off his eyes[19]. He would understand. He would even feel relief that he would not have to simply do the expected[20].

Megan signaled right[1] and took the exit ramp[2]. Barbie followed. She dismissed thoughts about the proposal and focused on her feelings about what she had to do to Megan. On the one hand, she didn't relish killing this woman. If she had believed Goldberg—and she hadn't—but if she believed that the woman held no threat[3] to her and Ken, so much the better[4]. She would let her get back to that pathetic house and that husband and those kids without a second thought[5]. But that couldn't be[6] now. It had to be done. In this line of work[7], you don't last long if you allow loose ends[8].

Up ahead Barbie saw Megan park her car and enter a place called Sunset Assisted Living. Hmm. Barbie parked farther down the lot. Then she reached under the car seat and pulled the blade into view[9].

STILL in a daze[10], Ray started for home.

Broome had called his crime-scene people, and without another word, rushed back[11] to the ruins in the park. Ray stayed where he was for another five minutes, seemingly unable to move[12]. None of this made any sense. He tried to sort through it, but that only led to more confusion.

As Ray stumbled down[13] Danny Thomas Boulevard past the tacky-to-the-point-of-classy[14] Trump Taj Mahal, he felt his phone vibrate. He reached for it, his hands feeling too big for his pocket, and clumsily withdrew it[15]. The vibrations had stopped, and the missed call icon[16] appeared. He checked the caller ID. When he saw the call had come from a "Megan Pierce," his heart sped up[17].

Cassie.

Should he call her back? He wasn't sure. She had called him, which was certainly a sign of some sort, but then again she had also hung up. Or been disconnected. But if she'd been disconnected, wouldn't she call back when she was back in range[18]? Right, okay,

1. mit son clignotant à droite

2. emprunta la bretelle d'accès

3. ne représentait pas une menace

4. ça aurait été pour le mieux

5. sans hésiter

6. impossible

7. Dans ce métier

8. si on ne fait pas le ménage derrière soi

9. en sortit un couteau

10. Encore sonné

11. avait filé à nouveau

12. comme pétrifié

13. marchait cahin-caha dans le

14. si ringard qu'il en devenait presque classieux

15. l'en sortit tant bien que mal

16. l'icône « appel manqué »

17. s'emballa

18. aurait de nouveau du réseau

wait for the return call. He shook his head. What the hell was wrong with him? All of a sudden he was a clammy-handed[1] adolescent trying to interpret the signals of his first crush[2].

Ray wondered how she had gotten his phone number. Didn't matter. What mattered was that she had called. Why? He had no idea. He kept the phone in his hand, willing it to vibrate[3], checking the battery to make sure it had enough juice[4], checking the bars to make sure he had enough coverage[5]. Pathetic. Stop it. Cassie would call back or she wouldn't.

And what if she didn't?

Was he willing to go back to … to what? More booze and blackouts?

When he made the final turn toward his basement home[6]—a grown man renting out[7] a basement, for crying out loud[8]—Ray pulled up short[9]. There, in front of the dwelling[10], were four police cars.

Uh-oh.

He ducked[11] behind a telephone pole[12]. More pathetic. He debated making a run for it[13], but what good would that do[14]? Plus, if they wanted to arrest him, Broome could have done it ten minutes ago. He took another look. His Pakistani landlord[15], Amir Baloch, stood in front of the house, his arms crossed. Ray approached tentatively[16], waiting for the cops to grab him. They didn't. They entered and left the house with boxes[17].

Amir shook his head. "Like I'm back in the old country."

"What happened?" Ray asked.

One of the cops spotted Ray and approached. His name tag[18] said Howard Dodds. "Raymond Levine?"

"Yes."

"I'm Officer Dodds." He handed him a sheet of paper[19]. "We have a subpoena to search these premises[20]."

Marginal glossary:

1. aux mains moites
2. premier amour
3. priant pour qu'il se remette à vibrer
4. qu'elle n'était pas à plat
5. qu'il avait du réseau
6. tourna enfin dans la rue menant à son appart en sous-sol
7. un adulte qui loue
8. quelle tristesse !
9. pila
10. l'immeuble
11. se cacha
12. poteau téléphonique
13. envisagea de se faire la malle
14. ça servirait à quoi
15. propriétaire
16. prudemment
17. des cartons
18. plaque d'identité
19. une feuille de papier
20. qui nous autorise à fouiller les lieux

"He only lives in the basement," Amir said with a whine[1].

"The search is for the entire property," Dodds said.

Ray didn't bother reading the order[2]. "Can I help you find something?"

"No."

"I can give you passwords to my computer, if that makes it easier."

Dodds smiled. "Nice try.[3]"

"Excuse me?"

"Certain passwords are designed[4] to destroy or delete[5] files[6]."

"I didn't know."

"Just looking to be helpful[7], hmm?"

"Well," Ray said, "yes."

"Just let us do our job." He turned and started back into the house.

Ray looked at his ashen[8] landlord. "I'm sorry, Amir."

"Do you have any idea what they want?"

"It's a long story."

Amir turned to him. "Will I get in any trouble?"

"No."

"You're certain?"

"Positive.[9]"

"I got in trouble in Karachi. They held me in prison for six months.[10] It is why we moved[11] here."

"I'm sorry, Amir."

"What will he find?"

"Nothing," Ray said. And he meant it. They would pore through[12] his photographs, but they wouldn't find anything. He flashed again to that night, to all that blood. That was the one[13] image he'd never been able to kill with[14] the alcohol—the one image that wouldn't let up[15] or even fade[16].

That was not entirely true. Cassie would never fade either.

Ray thought now about that strange photograph Broome had shown him, the one of the man with the

---

1. d'un ton plaintif
2. mandat

3. Bien tenté.
4. conçus
5. supprimer
6. des fichiers

7. pour rendre service

8. livide

9. Sûr et certain.
10. J'ai fait 6 mois de prison.
11. pour ça que nous sommes venus nous installer
12. éplucheraient
13. seule
14. noyer dans
15. persistait
16. sans même s'estomper

shaved head and goatee. He didn't get it, but it felt as though the walls were closing in on him[1]. His chest began to hitch.[2] He walked away, leaving Amir alone in front of his own home. For a moment Ray thought that he might cry. He tried to remember the last time he did that, really cried[3] the way he wanted to right now[4]. There were only two times in his adult life. The first was when his father died. The second was seventeen years ago, in that park.

He headed down the block[5]. His favorite pub was there, but he didn't enter, didn't have a craving even[6]. Rare. What he craved—what he'd always craved, he now realized—was to unburden himself[7]. That sounded so hokey[8], so new age and therapist-like[9], but maybe, in the end, telling someone the truth about that night would, if not set him free,[10] at least get him off this destructive path[11].

Maybe that was why he had sent Broome that photograph in the first place.

The question now was, who should he tell? The answer, as he stared down at the phone in his hand, was obvious.

The phone still hadn't vibrated again, but so what? She had made a move[12]. Now he should[13].

Ray hit the dial button, saw the name Megan Pierce pop up[14], and put the phone to his ear.

31

MEGAN was down the hall from Agnes's room when her cell phone sounded[1].

The Sunset Assisted Living facility tried like hell[2] to be something other than what it was[3]. The exterior aimed for[4] Second-Empire Victorian B and B[5] but landed more like[6] prefab[7] motel with the aluminum siding[8] and fake ferns[9] and wheelchair ramps[10] on the lemonade porches[11]. The interior too had lush green carpeting[12] and too-bright reproductions of Renoir and Monet, but even the artwork came across as[13] something you'd pick up at a bad yard sale[14] or one of those clearance showrooms[15].

She passed by Missy Malek, who gave her the practiced, concerned face[16] and said, "Perhaps we should talk soon?"

"After I see Agnes."

"Of course," Malek replied with something close to a bow[17].

1. sonna

2. mettait le paquet

3. se donner un autre look

4. visait une apparence

5. de bed and breakfast

6. ressemblait plutôt à

7. en préfabriqué

8. son revêtement en alu

9. ses fougères artificielles

10. ses rampes pour fauteuils roulants

11. vérandas

12. une belle moquette verte

13. avait un faux air de

14. qui peut s'acheter aux puces

15. aux fins de soldes d'un dépôt-vente

16. la regarda avec une sollicitude étudiée

17. en faisant presque une petite révérence

1. venait de
tourner dans

2. qu'elle
reconnut comme
étant celui de
Ray

3. se figea

4. qu'elle n'avait
pas le choix

5. que tu te fais
appeler

6. Je dirais bien

7. dans notre
histoire n'était
authentique

8. as bien fait de

9. À peu près
10. J'en doute.
11. sont en train
de fouiller

12. Si ça peut te
consoler

13. avait un
timbre étrange

14. fut reprise
d'un frisson

So Megan had just made the turn down[1] Agnes's corridor when the phone number she recognized as Ray's[2] popped up on her mobile's screen. She froze[3], unsure what to do, but in the end, she knew there was only one choice here[4]. She hit the answer button and put the phone to her ear.

"Hello?"

"I hear they call you[5] Megan now," Ray said.

"It's my real name."

"I'd make the obvious comment[6] that maybe nothing about us was real[7]—"

"But we both know that would be a lie," she said.

"Yeah."

Silence.

"Did Broome find you?" she asked.

"He did."

"Sorry about that."

"No, you made the right move[8] telling him."

"What did you say to him?"

"Pretty much[9] the same thing I told you."

"Did he believe you?"

"I doubt it.[10] The police are searching[11] my apartment."

"Are you okay?"

"I'm fine."

"If it helps[12]," Megan said, "I believe you."

There was no reply.

"Ray?"

When he spoke again, his voice was different, softer and with a strange timbre[13]. "Are you still in Atlantic City?"

"No."

"Can you come back down?"

"Why?"

More silence.

"Ray?"

"I didn't tell you the truth," he said.

Megan felt the chill[14]. "I don't understand."

"Come back down."

"I can't. I mean, not now anyway[1]."

"I'll wait inside Lucy. I don't care how long it takes[2]. Please come."

"I don't know."

But he had already hung up. She stood there, staring down at the phone, until a sound[3] snagged[4] her attention. She looked up and saw Agnes wander out[5] of her room, confused and blank eyed[6]. Her gray hair was a complete mess[7]. The skin of her face was pale past the point of translucent[8], the blue of the veins too visible.

When a nurse intercepted her[9], Agnes cried out[10], "Don't hurt me!" and pulled away[11].

"I would never hurt you, Agnes. I'm just trying—"

"Stop!" Agnes cringed now[12] as though she expected[13] the nurse to strike her[14]. Megan hurried down the hall and nudged the nurse out of the way[15]. She looked her mother-in-law in the eyes, her hands on her shoulders, and said, "It's okay, Agnes. It's me. It's Megan."

Her eyes narrowed. "Megan?"

"Yes. It's okay."

Agnes cocked her head to the left[16]. "Why are you here? Why aren't you at home with the babies?"

"They're not babies anymore. They're teenagers. I'm here because you called me."

"I did?" Fear crossed[17] Agnes's face. "When?"

"It's not important. It's okay now. I'm here. You're safe."

The nurse looked on sympathetically[18]. Megan took Agnes in her arms and led her back into the room[19]. Behind them, Missy Malek appeared, but Megan shook her off[20] and closed the door. It took some time, but Megan got Agnes to calm down[21], to stop shaking and whimpering, and then, as had happened before, clarity came back[22] to her mother-in-law's eyes.

"Are you okay?" Megan asked her.

Side notes:

1. en tout cas
2. d'avoir à attendre longtemps
3. bruit
4. capte
5. sortir
6. l'air égaré
7. en pagaille
8. d'un pâleur extrême
9. l'arrêta
10. s'écria
11. se dégagea
12. eut alors un mouvement de recul
13. craignait
14. ne la frappe
15. repoussa doucement l'infirmière
16. pencha la tête vers la gauche
17. La peur se lut sur
18. avec compassion
19. la reconduisit dans sa chambre
20. la repoussa d'un geste
21. réussit à calmer Agnes
22. la lucidité revint

Agnes nodded. "Megan?"

"Yes."

"Who were you on the phone with?[1]" Agnes asked.

"When?"

"Just now.[2] When I came out of my room. You were down the hall talking on the phone[3]."

Megan wasn't sure how to respond. "Just an old friend."

"I didn't mean to pry[4]."

"No, that's okay, it's just ..." She stopped, fought back the tears[5]. Agnes looked at her with such concern[6] that Megan could actually feel something inside of her give way[7]. "My whole life has been a lie."

Agnes managed a smile[8] and patted her hand[9]. "Oh, I wouldn't say that."

"You don't understand."

"Do you love my Davey[10]?"

"Yes."

"Megan?"

"What?"

"I know," Agnes whispered in a voice that chilled[11] the room.

"What?"

"Last week."

"What about last week?"

"The day after Davey brought you to our house, I called Emerson College. You said you went there. But, well, something didn't add up. So I called them. They never heard of you[12]."

Megan didn't know what to say.

"I won't tell." The voice was a whisper[13] again. "It's okay, really. I lie about my age to Roland[14]. I am three years older than him, but he doesn't know. The truth is, you love my Davey. I know. You're good for him. Not like those snotty[15], rich girls from town. Your secret's safe with me[16], honey. I just ask one thing."

A tear had escaped and ran down Megan's cheek[17]. "What?"

Marginal glossary notes:

1. Tu étais avec qui au téléphone ?
2. À l'instant.
3. étais au téléphone dans le couloir
4. être indiscrète
5. essaya de refouler ses larmes
6. d'un air si inquiet
7. sentit quelque chose se briser en elle
8. esquissa un sourire
9. lui tapota la main
10. petit Dave
11. glaça
12. n'avaient jamais entendu parler de toi
13. n'était qu'un murmure
14. J'ai menti à Roland sur mon âge
15. prétentieuses
16. Je ne trahirai pas ton secret
17. coula le long de la joue de Megan

"Give me some grandchildren[1]. You're going to make a wonderful mother."

Agnes knew, Megan thought. All these years, this whole time, Agnes had known about the lie[2]. The realization[3] was almost too much to bear[4].

"Megan?"

"I promise."

"No, not that." Agnes's eyes flickered[5]. She looked toward the door. "They want to move me to the third floor, don't they?"

"Yes. But you don't have to go if you don't want to."

"It won't help.[6]" She lowered her voice[7]. "He will find me. Even there. He will find me and he will kill me."

"Who?"

Agnes looked to her left, then to her right. She leaned in closer and locked eyes with Megan[8]. "The bad man who comes at night."

It was then[9] that Megan remembered the spy camera in the digital clock. "Agnes?"

"Yes?"

"Was the bad man here last night?"

"Of course. That's why I called you."

Sometimes it was like dealing with a human TV set[10] that kept changing channels[11]. Megan pointed toward the clock. "Do you remember when I was here yesterday?"

Agnes started to smile. "The spy camera!"

"Yes."

"So you can see him? You can see the bad man?"

"We can look.[12]"

Megan had set[13] the spy camera's timer[14] to run from nine P.M. until six in the morning. It didn't record everything—it worked by motion detector—so it wasn't as though they'd have to go through[15] nine hours of material[16]. Megan checked the back of the clock[17] and saw the light was flashing[18]. That meant there was something in the digital hard drive[19].

1. des petits-enfants

2. savait qu'elle avait menti

3. L'idée

4. insupportable

5. clignèrent nerveusement

6. Ça n'arrangera pas les choses.

7. baissa la voix

8. regarda Megan droit dans les yeux

9. C'est alors

10. comme si elle était face à une télévision humaine

11. qui changerait de chaîne sans arrêt

12. On peut vérifier.

13. réglé

14. minuterie

15. elles n'auraient pas à visionner

16. d'enregistrement

17. l'arrière du réveil

18. que le voyant lumineux clignotait

19. dans la mémoire interne

"I'll be right back[1], Agnes."

She hurried down the corridor and back to the front desk[2]. She borrowed[3] a laptop and came right back to the room. Agnes was still on the bed. The clock/camera worked via a USB port[4]. She moved the camera to the bed and plugged it into[5] the laptop. Agnes moved closer. The spy camera icon came up. Megan moved the cursor over it[6].

"If he was in your room," Megan said, "we should see it now."

"What's going on here?"

They both looked toward the door. Missy Malek had entered, her hands on her hips, her lips pursed[7]. She took in[8] the whole scene—the two women on the bed, the clock/camera plugged into the laptop—and her eyes opened. "What is this?"

"It's a surveillance camera," Megan said.

"Excuse me?"

"A hidden camera.[9] It's built into[10] the digital clock."

Malek's face reddened[11]. "You can't have that in here."

"I already did."

"We have privacy rules[12]. When Agnes first joined here[13], your husband as her guardian[14] signed an agreement[15]. It specifically stipulated[16]—"

"I never signed it," Megan said.

"Because you have no legal standing[17]."

"Exactly. And this is Agnes's room. She wanted the camera in here, didn't you, Agnes?"

Agnes nodded. "Yes, I did."

"I don't understand," Missy Malek said. "You taped us?[18]"

"I guess I did."

"Do you know what a violation of trust that is[19]?"

Megan shrugged. "If you have nothing to hide …"

"Of course we don't!"

"Terrific[20]," Megan said. "Would you like to watch with us?"

Malek shot a glance at Agnes, then back to Megan. "This is a mistake."

"Then it's our mistake," Megan said.

The images were grainy[1], not so much because the camera had a poor resolution[2] but because it was set to film in the dark. The first thing to pop up was a still frame[3] of Agnes sitting up in the bed. The camera's night-vision setting[4] gave[5] the room a spooky green haze[6].

Though the lens was set on wide[7] to take in the entire[8] room, you could still make out[9] the frightened expression on Agnes's face. The night vision made her eyes glow white[10].

There was a play arrow[11] on the still frame. Megan looked back at Missy Malek. Malek looked resigned[12]. Megan clicked the icon.

The video began to run[13]—and it did indeed solve the[14] mystery, but not in the way Megan expected.

No sound was recorded, but maybe that was merciful[15]. On the screen, Agnes was sitting up. You could see that she was screaming, crying. She was clearly terrified. She picked up her pillow for protection[16]. She cowered into the far corner[17] of the bed, trying to escape, pulling her knees up to her chest[18]. She stared up at her assailant, her right hand shielding[19] her face.

But there was no one there.

Megan felt her heart sink. She sneaked a glance at Missy Malek. Her face was still resigned, but not out of[20] guilt or fear. She had known. Megan looked at her mother-in-law. Agnes watched the screen with her mouth opened. At first she looked confused, but through the fog[21], Megan could see clarity. Agnes could see what was happening. Part of her mind could accept it, but a bigger part simply would not. It was like suddenly telling someone that up was down and left was right.

"He made himself invisible," Agnes said.

But her heart wasn't in it[22].

1. granuleuses

2. n'avait pas une bonne résolution

3. image fixe

4. Le mode de prise de vue de nuit

5. plongeait

6. dans une inquiétante brume verdâtre

7. sur la position grand angle

8. de façon à prendre toute

9. on distinguait pourtant

10. faisait briller ses yeux dans le noir

11. une flèche pour lancer la lecture

12. avait un air résigné

13. démarra

14. donna bien la clé du

15. était-ce une bonne chose

16. pour se protéger

17. se blottissait au bout du

18. les genoux remontés contre le menton

19. protégeant

20. ce n'était pas dû à

21. le brouillard

22. elle dit cela sans conviction

1. *accourut*
2. *gobelet*
3. *tenait des comprimés*
4. *dont Megan supposa qu'il contenait de l'eau*
5. *la borda délicatement*
6. *sortit sur la pointe des pieds*
7. *Il faut reconnaître que*
8. *ne s'anima à nouveau qu'*
9. *pour mieux voir*
10. *qui vérifiait qu'Agnes allait bien*

11. *s'éclipsa*
12. *d'une voix extrêmement frêle*
13. *de nouveau accablée*
14. *au fond d'elle-même*

15. *Ce qui s'appelle prendre ses rêves pour la réalité.*
16. *à quel point elles avaient été proches*
17. *si ce n'est la vérité, quelque chose qui s'en approchait*

After what seemed like an hour—in truth, it was maybe two minutes—a nurse rushed[1] on-screen and began to calm Agnes. Megan could see that the nurse had a cup[2] in one hand. With the other, she produced pills[3]. Agnes swallowed them using the cup of what Megan assumed was water[4]. Then she leaned back. The nurse gently tucked her in[5], waited a moment, and then tiptoed out the door[6].

A minute later, the recording stopped.

To her credit,[7] Malek didn't say a word. Agnes stared at the screen, waiting for something else to happen. The screen came alive only[8] one more time. According to the digital clock in the corner, it was about an hour later. Agnes and Megan leaned forward for a better look[9], but all they saw was a nurse checking up on Agnes[10].

On the screen, Agnes remained asleep.

That was it.

"You saw him, right?" Agnes said, pointing at the screen. "With the knife? One time he came in with a coyote and a bottle of poison."

Malek slipped out of the room[11] without saying another word.

"Megan?" Agnes said, her voice so frail[12].

"It's okay," Megan said, feeling a fresh wave of devastation[13]. Damn. What an idiot she was. Hadn't she known in her heart of hearts[14] what the surveillance would show? Had she really believed a man with a knife (not to mention the occasional coyote and bottle of poison) came in at night to terrorize an old woman? Talk about wishful thinking.[15] Agnes had been the closest thing a woman like Megan—a woman living a lie for almost her entire adult life—had to a confidante and best friend. Today she had learned just how close they had been[16]—that for all these years Agnes had known, if not the truth, something close to it[17]. She hadn't cared.

Agnes had known Megan better than anyone, and she had loved her anyway[1].

"You should go home now," Agnes said in a faraway voice[2]. "You need to take care of the baby."

The baby. Singular.[3] The human TV had changed channels or at least time zones[4] again. But either way, Agnes was right. Enough. Enough chasing the past.[5] Enough living with lies. Her father-in-law—the late, lied-to-about-age Roland Pierce[6]—had often said, "Youth is but a breath[7]." True, but so is[8] your twenties[9] and middle age[10] and every stage[11]. It's pretty much life's only guarantee.

When had Agnes started to fade away[12]? When would Megan?

She didn't want to live one more day with the lies.

Megan kissed her mother-in-law on the forehead, holding her lips there[13] and closing her eyes. "I love you so much," she said softly. "I won't let anything bad happen to you. I promise."

She pulled away and started down the corridor. Missy Malek was there, looking a question at her[14]. Megan nodded and said, "I'll talk to my husband, but let's start making arrangements for the move."

"She'll be happier. I'm certain."

Megan kept walking through the overdone lobby[15] and passed the cafeteria. The doors slid open. Megan welcomed the cool air[16], especially after the stifling heat[17] inside. She closed her eyes for a second and took a deep breath.

There was still no message from Dave on her cell phone. She felt sad and angry and exhausted[18] and confused. Ray was waiting for her at Lucy. She didn't want to go. He was part of her past. Opening that door could only lead to unhappiness[19]. It was time to move on.

Ray's words came back to her: *I didn't tell you the truth.*

1. malgré tout

2. d'une voix lointaine

3. Au singulier.

4. de fuseau horaire

5. Plus question de courir après le passé.

6. feu Roland Pierce, celui à qui Agnes avait menti,

7. La jeunesse est éphémère

8. c'est pareil

9. vers les 20 ans

10. la cinquantaine

11. stade de la vie

12. décliner

13. y gardant longuement les lèvres

14. l'air interrogateur

15. dans le hall d'entrée prétentieux

16. apprécia un peu d'air frais

17. la chaleur étouffante

18. épuisée

19. ne pourrait que mal finir

1. Est-ce qu'elle ne lui devait pas bien ça ?

2. l'avait attirée ici

3. sa jeunesse perdue

4. reprendre pied

5. lui arriver dessus

Could she just let that go? And his tone, the desperation in his voice … could she really walk away from that? Didn't she owe him something[1]? And maybe, in the end, that was what had brought her down[2]. Maybe it wasn't the chance to relive some bygone youth[3], but the chance to help someone else find his footing[4].

She arrived at her car door. As she reached for the handle, something caught her eye.

Megan turned quickly and saw the knife heading toward her[5].

32

BROOME'S heart sunk. "It's not here anymore.[1]"

He was back at the old furnace ruins with Samantha Bajraktari and the young tech. Cowens had declined to join them[2] this time, so Broome figured that he'd struck out with[3] Samantha.

"What did you think you saw in the photo?" she asked.

"A hand truck."

"A hand truck? You mean, like for moving boxes[4]?"

"Or bodies," Broome said. He put his hand on the old brick[5]. When you took a step back[6], the ruins from the iron-ore mill were actually pretty cool. Broome remembered his and Erin's honeymoon[7] in Italy. They'd done two weeks in Naples, Rome, Florence, and Venice. The art was incredible, sure, but what fascinated Erin and him—two old-school cops at heart[8]—were the ruins. Something about the remnants[9] of death, the clues to something missing called out to them[10]. They'd been fascinated by the Roman

1. Il n'est plus là.

2. refusé de se joindre à eux

3. fait un flop avec

4. un truc pour déplacer les cartons

5. vieilles briques

6. Si on prenait un peu de recul

7. lune de miel

8. tous deux flics de la vieille école

9. dans ces vestiges

10. les interpellait

305

Forum, by the Coliseum, and most of all, by Pompeii, an entire city buried[1] by a volcano. Two thousand years ago, Mount Vesuvius[2] erupted[3], covering the city and its inhabitants[4] in about twenty feet of ash[5]. For seventeen hundred years[6], Pompeii stayed that way—the crime scene totally vanished, hidden from view—before it was accidentally unearthed[7] and its secrets were painstakingly[8] and slowly revealed[9]. Broome thought now about walking through the perfectly preserved[10] streets holding the hand of his beautiful new wife, and because he was a total moron[11], he had no idea at the time that this would be the single greatest moment of his life[12].

"You okay?" Bajraktari asked.

Broome nodded. The Pine Barrens, he knew, were loaded with[13] ruins from the eighteenth and nineteenth century. They weren't tourist spots[14], except for the major ones in Batsto and Atsion. Most were, like this one, hard to find and required trekking[15]. All that was left now were crumbling relics from a bygone era[16], but at one time, here in the woods of New Jersey, they were flourishing villages[17] for paper mills[18] or glass factories[19] or iron-ore mills. Eventually, the natural resources dried up[20] and so then did most villages. But in some cases, you really didn't know what happened. One day the people were there, living their lives and raising their families[21]. The next, or so it seemed, they were gone, maybe waiting to one day be unearthed like something in Pompeii.

Bajraktari studied the brick from a furnace that had been built in 1780. "You thought you saw a hand truck, right?"

"Yes."

She rubbed the brick.

"What?"

"There's a little scraping[22] here. It could even be a little rust[23]. I can't know for certain without running[24] a test."

"Like maybe a hand truck was resting against it[1]?"

"Could be."

Samantha bent down to the ground[2]. She rubbed her hand on the dirt[3]. "What's your theory with this hand truck?"

"Right now?" Broome said. "The most obvious."

"Which is?"

"It was used to transport something."

"Like, say, a dead body?"

Broome nodded. "Let's say once a year—on Mardi Gras—you were killing or, I don't know, incapacitating[4] men up here. Knocking them unconscious[5], for example. Let's say you wanted to move them[6]."

She nodded. "You might use a hand truck."

"Right."

"If that were the case[7]," Samantha said, "there'd be marks of some kind[8]. Indentations[9] in the ground. I don't know how big they'd be. The ones from years ago would be long gone[10], of course, but maybe if Carlton Flynn was moved that way just a few days ago, we'd still see something."

She moved back down toward the giant boulder where she'd found the blood. Broome followed. Bajraktari got down on her hands and knees now[11], moving her face to within an inch of the dirt[12] like a tracker[13] in an old Western. She started crawling around[14], moving faster now.

"What?" Broome asked.

"Do you see this?"

She pointed to the ground.

"Barely."

"It's an indentation. There are four of them, making a rectangle. I'd estimate it being about two feet by four.[15]"

"And what does that mean?"

"If you wanted to get the body on a hand truck, you'd lay the truck down on all fours[16]. When the body was initially dropped on it[17], that would be the

---

1. avait été appuyé contre le mur

2. se pencha sur le sol

3. passa la main sur la terre

4. d'immobiliser

5. En les assommant

6. les déplacer

7. Si c'était le cas

8. il y aurait des marques

9. Des rainures

10. auront disparu depuis longtemps

11. se mit à quatre pattes

12. le visage au ras du sol

13. un traqueur

14. à ramper

15. Il ferait en gros 60 cm sur 120.

16. il faut poser le diable à plat

17. on laisse tomber le corps dessus

heaviest point[1]." She looked up at him. "In short, it would make indentations like this.[2]"

"Whoa."

"Yep."

"Will you be able to, I don't know, follow the tracks[3]?"

"I don't think so," she said. "The ground is pretty hard, but …" Her voice trailed off.[4] She turned her head and, now like a tracking dog[5], she started back up the path[6]. She stopped and bent down.

"It went that way?" Broome asked.

"Nothing conclusive[7], but look at the way this shrub[8] is broken."

Broome came over. He squatted down[9]. It did indeed appear as though something heavy, perhaps a body-laden[10] hand truck, had run over the area. He tried to find a trail[11], but there wasn't one. "Where could he have gone?"

"Maybe not that far. Maybe to bury the body."

Broome shook his head. "It's been too cold the past few weeks."

"There are broken branches over here. Let's follow them."

They did. They were getting deeper into the woods[12], farther off the[13] path. They started down a hill[14]. Now, in an area where no one would have any reason to roam[15], they found even more broken branches, more signs that something substantial[16] had, if not bulldozed[17], gone through[18] at a faster pace[19].

The sun was setting[20], the night growing cold[21]. Broome zipped up[22] his windbreaker[23] and kept moving.

The brush thickened[24], making it more and more evident that someone had come this way. Broome knew that he should slow down, that he should be careful not to trample[25] a potential crime scene, but his legs kept moving. He took the lead[26] now. His pulse quickened. The hairs on the back of his neck stood up.[1]

He knew. He just knew.

"Slow down, Broome."

He didn't. If anything[2] he moved faster now, pushing the branches to the side, nearly tripping[3] on the thick roots[4]. Finally, less than a full minute after starting down the hill, Broome broke through to a small opening[5] and stopped short.

Samantha Bajraktari came up behind him. "Broome?"

He stared at the broken structure in front of him. It was a low wall, no more than three feet high, nearly covered with vines[6]. That was how it worked out.[7] When man abandoned, nature moved in[8] and took back what was rightfully hers[9].

"What is that?" Bajraktari asked.

Broome swallowed. "A well.[10]"

He hurried over and looked down into the hole. Blackness.

"Do you have a flashlight[11]?"

The echo of his voice told him[12] that the hole was deep. A knot formed in his stomach.[13]

"Here," she said.

Broome took the flashlight and flicked it on[14]. When he aimed it straight down the hole[15]—when the beam first hit[16]—the sight[17] stopped Broome's heart for a second. He may have made a sound, some kind of groaning[18], but he couldn't be sure. Samantha came up next to him, looked down, and gasped[19].

KEN sat on the last stool and watched the barmaid.

Her name was Lorraine, and she was good at her job. She laughed a lot. She touched the men on the arm. She smiled, and if it was an act[20], if underneath it all she detested what she was doing, you never saw it[21]. The other girls, yes, they tried. They smiled but it never reached beyond the lips and often, too often,

---

1. Il avait les poils de la nuque hérissés.

2. Au contraire même,

3. manquant trébucher

4. grosses racines

5. clairière

6. de vigne vierge

7. C'était normal.

8. regagnait du terrain

9. reprenait ses droits

10. Un puits.

11. une torche

12. L'écho de sa propre voix lui indiqua

13. Son estomac se noua.

14. l'alluma

15. la pointa vers le fond du trou

16. le faisceau éclaira le fond

17. la vision

18. grognement

19. poussa un petit cri

20. si c'était du cinéma

21. ça ne se voyait pas

---

you could see the blankness on their faces[1] and the hate in their eyes.

The regulars[2] called the older barmaid Lorraine. Regulars at a strip club—Ken tried to imagine anything more pitiable[3]. And yet he understood. We all do, really. We all feel the pull.[4] Sex, of course, had one of the biggest. It didn't hold a candle to control[5], but most of these men would never know that. They'd never get to experience it and so they'd remain naive to what could really tear at a man's soul[6].

But Ken had learned that the secret to combat anything that pulled you[7] like this was to understand that you really could not stop it. Ken considered himself a disciplined man, but the truth was, human beings were not built for self-denial[8]. It was why diets[9] rarely worked in the long run[10]. Or abstinence.

The only way to beat it[11] was to accept that it was there and thus channel it[12]. He looked at Lorraine. She would leave eventually[13]. He would follow her and get her alone and then … well, channel.

He swiveled[14] on the stool[15] and leaned his back against the bar. The girls were ugly. You could almost feel the diseases emanating from their very pores[16]. None of them, of course, held a candle to[17] Barbie. He thought about that house on the end of a cul-de-sac, about children and backyard barbecues and teaching his kid to catch a baseball and spreading out the blanket for July Fourth[18] fireworks[19]. He knew that Barbie had serious reservations[20]. He understood her pessimism all too well, but again there was the unmistakable draw[21]. Why, he wondered, if family life leads to unhappiness, are we all still drawn to it? He had thought about that and realized that it wasn't the dream that had gone wrong[22] but the dreamers[23]. Barbie often claimed that they were different and thus not meant for[24] that life. But in truth, she was only half right[25]. They were different, yes, but that gave them a chance to have that life. They wouldn't enter that domestic world like mindless drones[1].

It wasn't that the life people longed for was inherently[2] bad or unworthy[3]—it was that the life for most of them was unobtainable.

"What can I get you, handsome?"

He spun around. Lorraine was standing there. A beer rag[4] was draped over her shoulder. She had dangling earrings[5]. Her hair had the consistency and color of hay[6]. Her lips looked as though there should be a cigarette dangling from them. She wore a white blouse[7] intentionally buttoned too low[8].

"Oh, I think I've had enough," Ken said.

Lorraine shot him the same half-smile he'd seen her give the regulars. "You're at a bar, handsome. Gotta drink something. How about a Coke at least?"

"Sure, that'd be great."

Without taking her eyes off him[9], Lorraine threw some ice[10] in a glass, picked up a soda gun dispenser[11], and pressed[12] one of the buttons. "So why are you here, handsome?"

"Same as any guy."

"Really?"

She handed him the Coke. He took a sip.

"Sure. Don't I look like I belong?[13]"

"You look like my ex—too damn good-looking for your own good[14]." Lorraine leaned in[15] as if she wanted to share a secret. "And you want to know something? Guys who look like they don't belong," she said, "are our best customers[16]."

His eyes had been drawn to the cleavage[17]. When he looked back up, she met his eye. He didn't like what he saw, like this old barmaid was somehow able to read him[18] or something. He thought about her tied down[19] and in pain[20], and the familiar stirring came back to him[21]. He maintained eye contact[22] and tried something.

"I guess you're right about me," he said.

---

1. comme de stupides parasites
2. intrinsèquement
3. indigne
4. torchon
5. des pendants d'oreilles
6. la texture et la couleur du foin
7. chemisier
8. volontairement très décolleté
9. le quitter des yeux
10. des glaçons
11. un pistolet à soda
12. appuya sur
13. Ne me dites pas que j'ai pas l'air comme tout le monde ?
14. trop beau pour ton bien
15. se pencha vers lui
16. clients
17. par son décolleté
18. lire dans ses pensées
19. ligotée
20. en train de souffrir
21. cette pensée l'excita comme d'habitude
22. ne la lâcha pas des yeux

1. *C'est-à-dire ?*

2. *pleurer quelqu'un*

3. *L'éclair*

4. *Oh ça oui*

5. *d'important*

"Come again.[1]"

"About my belonging. I came here, I guess, to reflect. And maybe to mourn[2]."

Lorraine said, "Oh?"

"My friend used to come here. You probably read about him in the paper. His name is Carlton Flynn."

The flick[3] in her eyes told him that she knew. Oh my, oh my[4], she knew. Yes, now it was his turn to look at her as though he could see inside and read her every thought.

She knew something valuable[5].

33

MEGAN saw the knife arching toward her[1].

She didn't have any martial arts training[2], and even if she had, it probably wouldn't have helped. There was no time to duck out of the way[3] or block the wrist[4] or whatever would be appropriate for a situation like this.

They say that in moments like this, when violence and destruction are upon you[5], that time slows down[6]. That wasn't really true. For that brief moment, as[7] the point of the blade got closer[8] to the hollow of her throat[9], Megan became something other than an evolved human[10]. Her brain suddenly worked at only its most base.[11] Even an ant[12], if you step near it, somehow knows to run the other way. We are, at our core[13], all about survival[14].

That was what was working here. The primordial part[15] of Megan, the part that existed long before cognitive thought, took over[16]. She didn't really think or plan or any of that. There was no conscious thought,

1. lui fondre dessus
2. n'y connaissait rien en arts martiaux
3. d'esquiver le coup
4. de bloquer le poignet
5. vous tombent dessus
6. ralentit
7. à mesure que
8. s'approchait
9. du creux de sa gorge
10. un être humain évolué
11. Son cerveau devint primaire.
12. une fourmi
13. au fond de nous
14. mus par l'instinct de survie
15. Le côté primitif
16. prit le dessus

not at first, but certain defense mechanisms come pre-baked into[1] our nervous systems.

She snapped her arm up[2] toward her neck[3] in an attempt to stop the blade from[4] penetrating her throat and ending[5] her life.

The blade sliced deep[6] into her forearm[7], traveling freely through the flesh[8] until it banged up against the bone[9].

Megan cried out.

Somewhere again in the deep recesses[10] of her brain, Megan could actually hear the grating sound of metal scraping bone[11], but it meant nothing to her. Not now anyway.

It was all about survival.

Everything else, including reason, was taking a backseat to[12] man's most primitive instinct. She was literally fighting for her life[13], and so one calculation dominated all others: If the attacker pulled the knife free[14], Megan would end up dead.

All her focus now[15] was on that knife, but somewhere, in the corner of her mind, Megan spotted the blond hair and realized that her attacker was the same woman who'd killed Harry Sutton. She didn't bother wondering why—that, if she lived, would come later—but there was a fresh surge of anger[16] now mixed in with the fear and panic[17].

Do not let her get the knife back.

No, time still hadn't slowed down. Only a second, maybe two, had passed since Megan first caught sight of the knife heading toward her. Again, working purely on instinct, with the blade deeply embedded in her muscle tissue[18], Megan did something that would normally be unthinkable[19]. She used her free hand to cover the knife, slapping her palm[20] against her own forearm—trapping[21] the razor-sharp[22] blade in her own flesh.

She didn't think about this—about how she was actually trying to *keep* a knife in her arm. She only knew that whatever happened, whatever hell or fury was about to rain down on her[1], there was no way she could let[2] this woman have the knife back.

When the blonde tried to pull the blade free, the blade running against the bone, a searing[3] pain shot through Megan, nearly buckling her knees.

Nearly.

That was the thing with pain. Part of you wants to stop, but if you care about your life—and what person doesn't?—then that desire can override the network[4] that controls your behavior. It may be something chemical, like adrenaline. It may be something more abstract like will[5].

But the pain meant nothing to Megan right now.

Survival and rage—they were all that mattered now. Survival, well, that was obvious, but she was also pissed off at[6] everything—at this killer who harmed poor Harry, at Dave for abandoning her, at Ray for giving up on everything[7]. She was furious at whatever deity[8] decided that old people like Agnes should be rewarded[9] at the end of their lives with[10] the torture and indignity[11] of losing their minds[12]. She was livid with[13] herself for not appreciating what she had, for needing to poke at[14] the past, for not understanding that a certain amount of dissatisfaction was part of the human experience—and mostly, she was pissed off that this stupid blond bitch[15] wanted to kill her.

Well, screw that.[16]

Megan let out a scream—an unnerving[17], primordial, high-pitched[18] shriek[19]. With the blade still trapped in the meat[20] of her forearm, she twisted hard at the waist[21]. The blonde made the mistake of trying to maintain her grip[22], but Megan's sudden move knocked her off balance[23]. Just a little.

Just enough to make her stumble forward.

Megan snapped her elbow straight up. The pointy bone landed square on[24] the bottom of the blonde's nose, jamming it up[25] toward the forehead. There was

1. quelles que soient les atrocités qui allaient pleuvoir

2. il était hors de question de laisser

3. fulgurante

4. neutraliser le réseau [nerveux]

5. la volonté

6. en rogne contre

7. d'avoir tout laissé tomber

8. envers le dieu, quel qu'il soit, qui

9. récompensées

10. par

11. le scandale

12. que c'était de perdre la raison

13. furieuse contre

14. d'aller réveiller

15. salope

16. Et puis merde.

17. déconcertant

18. perçant

19. hurlement

20. gras

21. fit brutalement pivoter sa taille

22. ne pas lâcher prise

23. lui fit perdre l'équilibre

24. en plein sur

25. l'enfonçant

a cracking sound[1]. Blood spilled down the blonde's face.

But that didn't end it.

The blonde, now in pain too, found new strength. She got her balance back[2] and pulled at[3] the blade with all her might[4]. The blade scraped along[5] the bone as though it were whittling it down[6]. Megan still tried to stop it, but the blonde had the momentum[7] now. The blade slid out, popping free from the muscle with an audible, wet sucking sound[8].

Blood poured[9] from the wound[10], bubbling out geyserlike[11].

Megan had always been squeamish[12]. When she was eight, one of her "stepfathers[13]" wanted to see the latest installment of[14] *Friday the 13th*, and since he couldn't find a babysitter, he dragged Megan with him. The experience had been scarring[15]. Since then—even now—she had trouble sitting through[16] any R-rated[17] film that contained violence.

None of that mattered now. The sight of blood—both her own and the blonde's—didn't make her cringe[18]. In fact, she almost welcomed it.

For a moment, there was no pain in her arm—and then it came in a powerful gush[19], as though that nerve ending had been blocked like a bend in a garden hose[20] that is suddenly let go[21].

The pain blinded[22] in a white-hot fury[23].

With an animal-like snarl[24], the blonde raised the knife and came at her again.

Again working on instinct, Megan thought, keep the vital organs safe[25]. The throat, the heart, the softest tissue. Megan ducked[26] her chin, closing down[27] access to her neck and chest. She turned her shoulder toward the blow. The point of the blade hit flat[28] on the top of her shoulder bone[29].

Megan cried out again.

The pain grew, but the knife did little more than penetrate the skin.

Megan unleashed a kick[1] that landed[2] on the blonde's bent knee, forcing it back the wrong way[3]. The leg bowed[4] and crumbled[5]. The blonde fell and immediately started scrambling to her feet[6].

For a moment Megan debated running. But no. The blonde wouldn't stay down. She was, in fact, almost back up on her feet. The blonde was younger and probably stronger and faster, but no matter what— no matter how this was going to end—Megan would be damned if she'd die with a knife in her back while she ran away.

No friggin' way.[7]

Megan leapt[8] toward her attacker, that one thought back in her head[9]:

Get. The. Knife.

The two women toppled to the pavement[10]. Megan focused on getting the knife. She grabbed the blonde's wrist with both hands. Blood was everywhere now, coating them both in crimson[11]. In some distant part of her brain, Megan realized that she would have to move fast. She was losing blood, too much of it. If this continued, she would simply bleed out[12].

Megan pushed down on the wrist, but the blonde would not let go of the knife. Megan angled[13] her fingers so that her nails dug into the thin skin[14] on the inner[15] wrist. The blonde cried out, but her grip didn't loosen[16]. Megan dug deeper now. She tried to use the end of her nail to scrape the skin off the spot[17] below the thumb where you check for the pulse. Wasn't that an artery?

The blonde cried out again, leaned her head forward, and then she sank her teeth[18] into Megan's wounded arm.

Megan howled in pain[19].

The blonde chomped down through[20] the flesh, her teeth nearly meeting. The bite, too, had drawn blood—the blonde's pearly white[21] teeth were

1. lança un coup de pied
2. atterrit
3. l'enfonçant dans le mauvais sens
4. céda
5. s'écroula
6. de se relever

7. Hors de question, bordel !
8. bondit
9. de nouveau cette seule idée en tête
10. roulèrent sur le trottoir
11. les couvrant toutes deux de rouge vif
12. c'est bien simple, elle allait se vider de son sang
13. plia
14. ses ongles se plantent dans la peau fine
15. de la face interne du
16. ne lâcha pas prise
17. lui arracher la peau
18. planta les dents
19. hurla de douleur
20. enfonça encore les dents, déchirant
21. blanc nacré

1. en étaient maculées

splattered with it[1]. Megan dug her fingernail into the wrist even deeper.

The knife dropped to the pavement.

And that was when Megan made a mistake.

She was so focused on possessing the knife, in picking it up and stabbing this blonde until there was nothing left of her, that she forgot all the other tools[2] in a human being's arsenal.

2. armes

3. lâcher

4. en tirant sur un morceau de peau

5. le détachant

6. le recrachant

In order to get the knife and make it her own, Megan had to release[3] the wrist. The blonde, realizing exactly that Megan was solely focused on the knife, reacted. First, she finished her bite by tearing back on the flesh[4], ripping it off[5], and spitting it out[6] on the ground.

The fresh wave of pain made Megan's eyes roll back.

7. se balança sur une jambe

8. la tête la première

9. qui amortisse sa chute

With Megan still reaching for the blade, the blonde shifted her weight[7]. Megan tumbled off balance. She fell headfirst[8] to the right, unable to get her hands in a position to break her fall[9].

10. cogna fort

11. pare-chocs

The side of her skull banged hard[10] against the bumper[11] of her car.

Stars exploded in her head.

Get. The. Knife.

12. s'approcha rapidement

13. shoota dans

14. en plein dessus, lui écrasant le crâne

15. se sentit partir

The blonde scampered closer[12] and threw a stomping kick at[13] Megan's head. It landed flush, crushing her skull[14] against the bumper again. Megan could feel consciousness slipping away[15] now. For a moment she really didn't know where she was or when it was or any of that. She didn't even know about the blonde or feel the next kick. Only that one thought remained.

Get. The. Knife.

16. dans les côtes de Megan

17. de part et d'autre du corps

18. était tombée de très haut

The blonde stood and threw a kick to Megan's ribs[16]. She fell forward, confused, dazed. Her cheek felt pavement. Her eyes closed. Her arms were splayed to the sides[17], as though she'd been dropped from a great height[18].

Megan had nothing left.

A beam of light[1] passed over her[2], maybe from a flashlight, maybe from an oncoming[3] car. Whatever it was, it made the blonde hesitate just long enough. With her eyes still closed, Megan's hand ran along the pavement[4].

She still knew where the knife was.

The blonde screamed and jumped down to finish Megan off.

But Megan had the knife now. She flipped over onto her back[5], the handle of the knife against her sternum, the blade up in the air.

The blonde landed on the sharp point[6].

The blade dug deep into the blonde's belly. Megan didn't let it go at that. She pulled up, slicing through[7] the stomach, until the blade stopped at the ribcage[8]. She could feel the sticky warmth on her[9] as something poured out of the wound[10].

The blonde's mouth opened in a silent scream. Her eyes widened and then they locked on[11] Megan's. Something passed between the two women, something deep and profound and base and beyond rational explanation[12]. Megan would think about that look for a very long time. She would replay it in her head[13] and wonder what she saw, but she would never be able to voice it to anyone[14].

The blonde's eyes opened a little more and then, with Megan watching[15], something in the blonde's eyes dimmed[16], and Megan knew that she was gone for good[17].

Megan heard footsteps[18] as she began to collapse back to the pavement. Her head was nearly down when she felt hands grab her, hold her gently, and then cradle her to the ground[19].

She looked up and saw his fear.

"Megan? Oh my God, Megan?"

She almost smiled at Dave's beautiful face. She wanted to comfort him, say that she loved him, that she would be fine—even her base instinct, she'd re-

1. faisceau de lumière

2. au-dessus de sa tête

3. qui passait

4. sonda le trottoir à tâtons

5. roula sur le dos

6. arriva sur la pointe

7. lui tranchant

8. cage thoracique

9. sur elle la chaleur gluante

10. de quelque chose qui coulait de la plaie

11. fixèrent

12. d'irrationnel

13. repasserait cet instant dans son esprit

14. d'en parler à qui que ce soit

15. sous les yeux de Megan

16. se voila

17. pour de bon

18. des bruits de pas

19. la poser délicatement par terre

1. impossible
d'émettre le
moindre son

member later, was to love and comfort this man—but no words would come out[1].

Her eyes rolled back. Dave disappeared, and there was only darkness.

34

BROOME shivered in the cold[1].

There were six more cops by the well now. One offered him a blanket. Broome frowned and told him to buzz off[2].

There were bodies in the well.

Lots of them. One piled on top of the other.[3]

The first one they brought up[4] belonged to Carlton Flynn.

His corpse[5] was the freshest[6] and, ergo[7], most horrid. It reeked[8] from decay[9]. Small animals—rats and squirrels[10], maybe—had gnawed on[11] the dead flesh. One of the officers turned away[12]. Broome didn't.

The ME[13] would try to find a time and cause of death, but despite what you see on television, there was no guarantee he'd find either. What with the outdoor temperatures[14] and the animals feasting on[15] vital organs, there would be tons of room for confusion[16].

1. grelottait
2. d'aller au diable
3. Empilés les uns sur les autres.
4. qu'ils remontèrent
5. cadavre
6. le plus récent
7. donc
8. empestait
9. la chair en décomposition
10. des écureuils
11. grignoté
12. détourna la tête
13. médecin légiste
14. Entre la température extérieure
15. qui s'étaient repus
16. il y avait largement de quoi s'y perdre

Of course, Broome didn't need scientific evidence to know the timing. Carlton Flynn, he was certain, had died on Mardi Gras.

For a few moments, when the body was brought up with a pulley[1] and rope[2], they all just stood there solemnly[3].

"The rest are little more than skeletons[4]," Samantha Bajraktari said.

That didn't surprise Broome. After all these years, after all the twists and turns[5] and new developments and sightings[6] and rumors, it all came down to this. Someone had killed these guys and dumped them[7] down[8] this well. Someone had gotten the men to come to this remote site, murdered them, and then used a handcart[9] to drag them to[10] a well about fifty yards off the beaten path[11].

There was no doubt anymore. This was the work of a serial killer.

"How many bodies?" Broome asked.

"Hard to say yet. At least ten, maybe twenty."

The Mardi Gras Men hadn't run off or taken on new identities or traveled to some remote island[12]. Broome shook his head. He should have known. He'd always believed that JFK was killed by the lone gunman[13]. He'd scoffed at[14] UFOs[15], at Elvis sightings[16], at fake moon landings[17], at pretty much every dumb-ass conspiracy theory. Even as a cop, he always suspected the obvious: the spouse[18], the boyfriend, the family member, because in nearly all matters[19], the shortest distance between two points is a straight line[20].

Stewart Green would probably be near the bottom of the pile.

"We have to tell the feds," Samantha said.

"I know."

"You want me to handle it?[21]"

"It's already done."

He thought about Sarah Green, sitting in that house all these years, not able to move on, not able to mourn,

1. une poulie
2. une corde
3. solennellement
4. des squelettes
5. toutes les péripéties
6. des gens qu'on dit avoir vus
7. les avait balancés
8. au fond de
9. un diable
10. les traîner jusqu'à
11. à moins de 50 m du sentier principal
12. partis sur une île déserte
13. par le tireur isolé
14. Il n'avait jamais cru aux
15. ovnis
16. gens qui disent avoir vu Elvis
17. au fait qu'on n'a jamais marché sur la Lune
18. conjoint
19. presque toujours
20. ligne droite
21. Vous voulez que je m'en charge ?

and all this time her husband had probably been dead in the bottom of a well. Broome had gotten too involved. That had clouded his vision.[1] He had wanted to rescue the[2] Greens. He had convinced himself there was a chance to do that; that despite the odds[3], he would find Stewart Green whole[4] and bring him back.

Dumb.

There were still questions, of course. Why hadn't Ross Gunther's body been dumped down the well too? There were a few possibilities, but Broome didn't love any of them. The bodies in the well also didn't answer the question about who had killed Harry Sutton and why, but perhaps the timing had indeed been a coincidence. As for Lorraine seeing Stewart Green alive, that was an easy mistake to make[5]. Even she had admitted[6] that she had her doubts[7]. It was probably someone who looked like Stewart. What with the shaved head and goatee and seventeen years of aging[8], even Broome could hardly say for sure[9] that age progression was based on him.

Unless, of course, Lorraine hadn't been wrong. Unless Stewart Green hadn't been the first victim but the perpetrator[10] ...

He didn't think so.

Another skeleton was brought up.

"Detective Broome?"

He turned.

"I'm Special Agent Guy Angiuoni. Thanks for calling us."

They shook hands[11]. Broome was too old to play territory games[12]. He wanted this crazy son of a bitch caught[13].

"Any clue who's down there?"

"My wi"—he almost said wife—"My partner, Erin Anderson, is still making up[14] a list of men who vanished on or around Mardi Gras[15]. We can get you that

1. Ça lui avait embrouillé l'esprit.

2. venir au secours des

3. contre toute probabilité

4. indemne

5. facile de se tromper

6. Elle-même avait admis

7. ne pas être sûre

8. plus vieux

9. aurait du mal à affirmer

10. l'auteur

11. se serrèrent la main

12. se chamailler pour des histoires de territoire

13. qu'on chope ce taré

14. est en train de compiler

15. le jour de Mardi gras ou autour de cette date

1. pour que vous puissiez comparer avec

2. redescendre

3. aider mon équipe à prendre le relais

4. Ça prendrait des heures

5. son équipe

6. découvert

7. si tant est qu'ils aient découvert quelque chose

8. qu'on ait vraiment

9. ce serait dans tous les médias

10. l'apprenne par

11. sans scrupules

12. de quelqu'un d'ici

13. à votre disposition

14. un enquêteur de la police judiciaire

15. Erin y avait mis le temps

16. que Ross Gunther et Ricky Mannion s'étaient disputée

information so you can match it to[1] the victims in that well."

"That'd be very helpful."

The two men watched the pulley and rope head back down[2].

"I hear you may have a suspect," Angiuoni said. "A man named Ray Levine."

"He's a possibility, I guess, but there's not much evidence yet. We already have a warrant being served on his place."

"Great. Maybe you could help coordinate with our people taking over that[3]?"

Broome nodded and turned away. It was time to get out of the woods. There was nothing he could do here right now. It'd be hours[4], maybe days. In the meantime he'd find out what his people[5] had uncovered[6], if anything[7], in Ray Levine's basement. He thought about Sarah Green and if he should wait until they had firm[8] confirmation that he was in that well, but, no, the media would be all over this[9]. He didn't want Sarah to hear about it from[10] some pushy[11] reporter.

"I can meet your guys at Levine's," Broome said.

"I appreciate that. I want to keep you involved in this, Detective. We do need a local guy[12] to coordinate with us."

"I'm at your disposal[13]."

The two men shook hands. Using his flashlight, Broome started back down the path toward his car. His cell phone buzzed. He saw that it was from Megan Pierce.

"Hello?"

But it wasn't Megan Pierce. It was a homicide investigator[14] from Essex County telling him that someone had just tried to murder Megan Pierce.

IT took Erin a while[15], but she'd finally found the home number for Stacy Paris, the exotic dancer Ross Gunther and Ricky Mannion had fought[16] and, in

324

Gunther's case at least, died over[1]. Stacy Paris had changed her name to Jaime Hemsley. She was single[2] and owned a small clothing boutique[3] in the tony[4] suburb of Alpharetta, Georgia, half an hour from Atlanta.

Erin debated making the call but not for very long. Despite the hour[5], she picked up the phone and dialed.

A woman with a light Southern drawl[6] answered the phone. "Hello?"

"Jaime Hemsley?"

"Yes, may I help you?"

"This is Detective Erin Anderson from the Atlantic City Police Department. I need to ask you a few questions."

There was a brief silence.

"Ms. Hemsley?"

"I don't see how I can help you."

"I hate to call you out of the blue[7] like this, but I need your help."

"I don't know anything."

"Well, Jaime, or should I say, Stacy, I do," Erin said. "Like, for example, your real name."

"Oh my God." The Southern drawl was gone. "Please. I'm begging you.[8] Please let me be[9]."

"I don't have any interest in[10] harming you[11]."

"It's been almost twenty years."

"I understand that, but we have a new lead[12] in Mr. Gunther's murder."

"What are you talking about?[13] Ricky killed Ross."

"We don't think so. We think someone else did it[14]."

"So Ricky is going free[15]?" There was a sob[16] in her voice. "Oh my God."

"Ms. Hemsley—"

"I don't know anything, okay? I was a punching bag for both of those psychopaths. I thought ... I thought God did me a favor[17]. You know—two

---

1. à cause de laquelle Gunther au moins était mort

2. célibataire

3. boutique de vêtements

4. chic

5. Malgré l'heure tardive

6. qui parlait avec un léger accent du sud

7. à l'improviste

8. Je vous en supplie.

9. laissez-moi tranquille

10. Je n'ai pas du tout l'intention de

11. vous faire du mal

12. piste

13. Qu'est-ce que vous racontez ?

14. que c'était quelqu'un d'autre

15. va être relâché

16. un sanglot

17. m'avait rendu un service

birds, one stone[1]? He got both of them out of my life[2] and gave me a fresh start[3]."

"Who gave you a fresh start?"

"What do you mean, who? God, fate[4], my guardian angel[5], I don't know. I had two men fighting over[6] which one would eventually[7] kill me. And suddenly they were both gone."

"Like you were saved[8]," Erin said, as much to herself as[9] the witness on the phone.

"Yes. I moved away. I changed my name. I own a clothing store. It's not much, but it's all mine. Do you know what I mean?"

"I do."

"And now, what, Ricky is going to get out[10]? Please, Detective, please don't let him know where I am."

Erin pondered[11] what she was hearing. This situation again fit a certain profile[12] that had been emerging[13] in connection with the missing men—that is, most of these men were not exactly model citizens. Several of the wives or girlfriends[14] had been equally up front[15], begging Erin not to find their missing partners[16].

"He won't find you, but I need to ask: Do you have any idea who may have done this?"

"Killed Ross, you mean?"

"Yes."

"Other than Ricky, no."

Erin's cell phone sounded. It was Broome. She thanked Jaime Hemsley and told her that she'd call her if she needed anything else. She also promised to let her know if Ricky Mannion was released[17] from prison.

After they both hung up, Erin picked up the cell. "Hello?"

"They're dead, Erin," Broome said in the strangest monotone[18]. "They're all dead."

Erin felt a cold stone form in her chest[19]. "What are you talking about?"

He told her about the photograph of the hand truck, the trip back to the ruins, the bodies in the well. Erin sat unmoving[1].

When Broome finished, Erin said, "So that's it? It's over[2]?"

"For us, I guess. The feds will find the guy. But there are parts that still don't fit[3]."

"No case is a perfect fit, Broome. You know that."

"Yeah, okay, but here's the thing. I just got a call from an investigator up in Essex County. Megan Pierce was attacked tonight by a young blond woman who matched[4] her description of the woman who was in Harry Sutton's office."

"Is she okay?"

"Megan? She has some injuries[5] but she'll live[6]. But she killed her assailant. Stabbed her in the gut.[7]"

"Wow."

"Yeah."

"Definitely self-defense?[8]"

"That's what the county cop[9] told me."

"Do they have an ID on[10] the blond woman?"

"Not yet."

"So how do you think it fits?"

"I don't know. Maybe it's unrelated[11]."

Erin didn't think so. Neither, she knew, did Broome. "So what do you want me to do?" she asked.

"Not much we can do about the Megan Pierce situation. When the local cops come back with an ID on this blond attacker, maybe we can go from there[12]."

"Agreed.[13]"

"I also think we still need to figure out how exactly this Ross Gunther's murder is tied into all this[14]."

"I just talked to Stacy Paris."

"And?"

Erin filled him in on her conversation.

"That doesn't help much," he said.

"Other than it fits a loose pattern.[15]"

"Abusive[16] men."

1. resta sans bouger

2. fini

3. encore des choses qui ne collent pas

4. correspond à

5. est blessée

6. rien de mortel

7. Elle l'a poignardée dans le ventre.

8. C'est sûr que c'était de la légitime défense ?

9. le flic du comté

10. On a l'identité de

11. que ça n'a pas de rapport

12. qu'on aura un point de départ

13. D'accord.

14. s'insère là-dedans

15. À part que ce serait encore le même schéma.

16. qui maltraitent leur nana

"Right."

"So look harder at that angle[1]. Abusive boyfriends or spouses or whatever. Mardi Gras is linked into this somehow[2]. That day set this whole thing off.[3] So widen the scope a little[4], see if there are any other Mardi Gras cases we missed."

"Okay."

"More important, though, the feds are up at the ruins right now gathering[5] the bodies. They're going to need your help with the IDs."

Erin had figured as much[6]. "No problem. Let me work up[7] the details and get the names to them. What about you?"

"I'm going to stop by Ray Levine's, but then I have to talk to Sarah before the media contacts her."

"That's going to suck[8]," Erin said.

"Maybe not. Maybe she'll welcome the closure[9]."

"You think?"

"Nope."

Silence.

Erin knew him well enough. She moved the phone from one ear to the other[10] and said, "You okay, Broome?"

"Fine."

Liar. "You want to come by[11] when you're done[12]?"

"No, I don't think so," he said. Then: "Erin?"

"Yes?"

"Remember our honeymoon in Italy?"

It was a curious question, totally out of the blue[13], but something about it, even in the midst of all this death[14], made Erin smile. "Of course."

"Thank you for that."

"For what?"

But he'd already hung up[15].

35

LUCY the Elephant was closed for the night. Ray waited for the last guard to leave. Ventura's Greenhouse, a rather happening restaurant and bar[1], was in full swing[2] across the street from Lucy. It made entering from that side particularly difficult. Ray circled around to[3] the usual spot by the gift shop and hopped over it[4].

Years ago, when Cassie had lifted a key off an ex-boyfriend[5], she had made him a copy. He had kept it all these years. He already knew that it didn't work anymore, but that didn't worry him much. Lucy had doors in both thick hind legs[6]. The visitors used one. The other had a simple padlock[7] on it. Ray picked up a heavy rock[8] and broke the lock with one swing[9].

Using his key ring flashlight[10] to guide him[11], Ray headed up the spiral staircases and into the belly of the mammoth beast[12]. The "innards[13]" were a vaulted chamber that gave off[14] the feel of a small church[15]. The walls had been painted a strange shade of pink

1. un café-restaurant assez branché

2. noir de monde

3. fit le tour de l'autre côté pour atteindre

4. sauta par-dessus

5. piqué une clé à un ex-petit ami

6. pattes arrière

7. cadenas

8. une pierre bien lourde

9. brisa le cadenas d'un seul coup

10. Se servant de la lumière sur son porte-clé

11. pour voir son chemin

12. du pachyderme

13. entrailles

14. dégageait

15. une atmosphère de chapelle

that was purported to be[1] the anatomically correct hue[2] for an elephant's gastrointestinal tract[3]. Ray would take their word for that[4].

In the day, he and Cassie had hidden a sleeping bag[5] in the bottom of the closet. It looked like[6] the closet had been taken out[7] during a renovation. Ray wondered if someone had stumbled across[8] the old sleeping bag and what they'd made of that[9] and what they ended up doing with it[10]—and then he wondered why, when the world was caving in on him again[11], he was thinking of something so asinine[12].

Silly to come back here.

He hadn't been inside this six-story[13] pachyderm in seventeen years, but if this stomach lining[14] could talk… He let the smile hit his face[15]. Why not? Why the hell not? He had tortured himself long enough. That horrible night was all coming back now. There was no way to stop it. He was about to face some really bad times[16], so why not remember the glorious nights? As his father had always reminded him, you can't have an up without a down[17], a left without a right—and you can't have good times without expecting bad.

Here he was, in the belly of the beast, waiting for the only woman he'd ever truly loved, and he realized that there had been virtually[18] no good times in the past seventeen years. Just the bad. Pathetic. Pathetic and stupid.

What would his father have thought?

One mistake. One mistake made seventeen years ago and he—the intrepid photojournalist who had no issue with[19] working the frontlines[20] during firestorms[21]—had let that mistake cripple him[22]. But that was how life worked, wasn't it? Timing. Decisions. Luck.

Crying over spilled milk.[23] How attractive.[24]

Ray took the spiral staircase up to the canopy/observatory[25] on Lucy's back. The night air was brisk[26] now, the wind coming in hard off[1] the ocean. It smelled wonderfully of salt and sand. The sky was clear, and the stars glistened off[2] the Atlantic tonight.

The sight, Ray thought, was breathtaking[3]. He took out his camera and started snapping pictures. It was amazing, he thought, what you could live with and what you could live without.

When he finished with that, Ray sat out[4] in the cold and waited and wondered—another what-if—how telling Megan the truth would change things all over again[5].

WHEN the doctor put the bandage[6] on Megan's arm he muttered something about working[7] for a butcher[8] in his youth and wrapping ground chuck[9]. Megan got it. The arm was, to put it kindly[10], a mess.

"But it'll heal[11]," the doctor said.

The arm still throbbed its way through[12] the morphine. Her head ached too, probably from the aftereffects[13] of a concussion[14]. She sat up in bed.

Dave had been made to[15] stay in the waiting room while Megan was interviewed bedside[16]. The cop— she had introduced herself as County Investigator Loren Muse—had been surprisingly reasonable[17]. She had let Megan patiently explain what happened, never so much as raising an eyebrow[18], even though the story sounded crazy: "Yes, see, I was leaving an old folks' home[19] when this preppy blonde jumped me with a knife. ... No, I don't know her name. ... No, I don't know who she is or why she tried to kill me, except, well, I saw her hanging around Harry Sutton's office last night. ..."

Muse had listened with a straight face[20], interrupting rarely. She didn't ask condescending questions or look dubious[21] or any of that. When Megan was finished, Muse called Broome down in[22] Atlantic City to confirm the story.

---

1. un vent violent arrivant de
2. brillaient sur
3. à couper le souffle
4. s'installa
5. pourrait à nouveau tout changer
6. pansement
7. grommela qu'il avait travaillé
8. un boucher
9. qu'il emballait du hachis de bœuf
10. pour dire les choses poliment
11. ça finira par guérir
12. la lançait, malgré
13. le contrecoup
14. commotion
15. dû
16. on interrogeait Megan à son chevet
17. restée très modérée
18. ne levant pas même un sourcil
19. maison de retraite
20. le visage impassible
21. ni semblé dubitative
22. là-bas, à

Now, a few minutes later, Muse slammed closed[1] her notebook[2]. "Okay, that's enough for tonight. You must be exhausted."

"You have no idea."

"I'll try to get an ID on the blonde. Do you think you'll be up for talking[3] again tomorrow?"

"Sure."

Muse rose. "You take care of yourself, Megan."

"Thanks. Would you mind doing me a favor?"

"Name it.[4]"

"Could you ask the doctor to let my husband come down now?"

Muse smiled. "Done."

When she was alone, Megan lay back on[5] the pillow. On the nightstand[6] to her right was the cell phone. She thought about texting Ray that she wouldn't show up[7]—wouldn't ever show up, in fact—but she felt too weak[8].

A moment later, Dave rushed[9] into the room with tears in his eyes. A sudden hospital memory surged through[10] Megan, taking her back[11], making it hard to breathe[12]. Kaylie had been fifteen months old, just starting to walk, and they'd taken her to Thanksgiving dinner at Agnes and Roland's house. They had all been hanging[13] in the kitchen. Agnes had just handed Megan a cup of tea when she turned and saw the stumbling Kaylie lean hard[14] against the baby gate[15] at the top of the basement stairs. Roland, she would later learn, hadn't set up the gate[16] correctly. As she watched in mounting horror[17], the gate gave way[18], and Kaylie began to tumble[19] down the concrete steps[20].

Even now, thinking about it some fourteen years later, Megan could still feel that maternal panic. She remembered that in that split second[21], she could foresee[22] the inevitable: The basement steps[23] were steep[24] and dark with jagged edges[25]. Her baby would land headfirst on the concrete. There was nothing Megan could do to stop it—she was too far away—but sit there, teacup in her hand, frozen, and watch her baby fall.

What happened next would stay with her always.[1] Dave, sitting next to her, dived[2] toward the open door. Dived. As if the floor were a pool[3]. Without any hesitation or even time for conscious thought. Dave was not a great athlete nor did he possess lightning[4] reflexes. He was not particularly quick or agile, and yet he dived across that linoleum floor with a speed he could never duplicate if he trained for ten years. As Kaylie started to fall out of sight, Dave slid across toward the open door, stretched his arm out[5], and grabbed[6] the falling Kaylie by her ankle[7]. He couldn't stop his momentum[8], couldn't stop himself from falling down those harsh steps, but somehow he managed to throw Kaylie back[9] toward the kitchen floor, saving her. Dave had no way to break his own fall now. He crashed to the bottom of the steps, breaking two ribs[10].

Megan had heard about such heroics[11] before, those rare spouses or parents who sacrificed themselves without thought. She read about shootings[12] where husbands naturally stepped[13] in front of their wives, saving them. They weren't always good men, by[14] classic definition. Some were drunks or gamblers or thieves. But they also were on some base level congenitally brave[15]. There was a selflessness within them[16], a purity of action. They made you feel safe and cared for and loved. You couldn't teach it. You had it or you didn't.

Even before that, Megan knew that Dave had it.

He sat next to her and took her hand—the hand of the good arm—in his. He stroked[17] her hair gently, as though she were suddenly made of porcelain[18] and might break[19].

"I could have lost you," Dave said, and there was a terrible sense of awe in his voice[20].

---

1. Elle n'oublierait jamais ce qui s'était passé alors.

2. avait plongé

3. une piscine

4. fulgurants

5. avait tendu le bras

6. saisi

7. par la cheville

8. stopper son élan

9. renvoyer Kaylie

10. se cassant deux côtes

11. de tels exploits

12. fusillades

13. s'étaient placés

14. selon

15. fondamentalement courageux

16. en eux une forme d'altruisme

17. caressa

18. en porcelaine

19. risquait de se casser

20. sa voix avait des accents d'épouvante

1. terriblement pragmatique
2. indicible
3. garde
4. Plus que tu ne le sauras jamais.
5. La vérité m'est bien égale.
6. qu'il finirait par changer d'avis
7. les regrignoteraient peu à peu
8. quittait lentement la sienne
9. chercha machinalement
10. jouer contre
11. encourageait
12. Le football américain
13. ce qu'il préférait
14. à se faire un max de blé
15. des abonnements
16. pour de très bonnes places
17. son père
18. de ne pas bosser au pub
19. d'assister à

"I'm okay," she said, and then because life can also be frighteningly practical[1] in moments of abject[2] horror, she asked, "Who's watching[3] the kids?"

"They're with the Reales. Don't worry about it, okay?"

"Okay."

"I love you," he said.

"I love you too," she said. "More than you can ever know.[4] But I need to tell you the truth."

"It can wait," he said.

"No, it can't."

"You're hurt. My God, you were nearly killed tonight. I don't care about the truth.[5] I only care about you."

She knew that at this very moment he meant that—and she also knew that eventually that thought would change[6]. She would heal and come home, and then life and questions would nibble around the edges again[7]. Maybe he could wait. But Megan couldn't.

"Please, Dave, just let me talk, okay?"

He nodded. "Okay."

And then while his hand slowly slipped off hers[8], Megan told him everything.

WHEN the doorbell rang, Del Flynn's hand automatically went for[9] the Saint Anthony medal.

Del sat at home watching the Celtics take on[10] the Sixers. He cheered for[11] the Sixers—they were his favorite basketball team—but the only team the Flynns truly loved was the Philadelphia Eagles. Football[12] was Del's game[13]. Three generations of Flynn men—Del's dad; Del; Del's son, Carlton—had been huge Eagles fans. Twenty plus years ago, when Del had finally started making some serious dough[14], he started to buy Eagles season tickets[15] right on the fifty-yard line[16]. It took him two years to persuade his old man[17] to skip working the pub[18] on just one Sunday and attend[19] a game. It had been a great day, the Eagles beating the Cowboys by three. Del's father died not long after that[1]—lung cancer[2], probably from all those years in that smoky[3] pub—his work literally killing him. But that game was a good memory, one Del kept with him and took out sometimes when he wanted to remember his old man before that damned disease[4] ate away at his insides[5].

Del remembered taking Carlton to his first game when he was only four. The Eagles had played the Redskins, and Carlton had wanted to buy a Redskins pennant[6], even though he hated the Skins. After that, it became something of a tradition—Carlton collecting pennants of the opposing team and hanging them on that wall above his bed. Del wondered when that stopped, when Carlton didn't want the pennants anymore, and when he eventually moved from that to taking them down[7].

From the TV, the Sixers' new center missed two straight free throws[8].

Del threw up his arms in disgust and turned as if to bemoan[9] the poor shooting[10] with his son. Carlton, of course, wasn't there. He wouldn't care anyway. He was all about the Eagles too. Man, that kid had loved going to the games. He loved everything about it—the tailgating[11], throwing a football in the parking lot[12], buying those pennants, singing the Eagles' fight song[13]. Of the eight Eagles home games[14] per year, Carlton usually got to go to only two or three, though he begged for more. For the others, Del took friends or business associates or gave them to some guy he owed a favor[15].

Man, what a dumb, stupid waste[16].

Of course, as Carlton had gotten older, he didn't want to go with Del either. Carlton wanted to go with his friends and hang out and party[17] afterward[18]. That was how it was, right? Dad and son can't get on the same page[19]—like that old song "Cat's in the Cradle[20]" or whatever. Del wondered where Carlton had started

1. peu après
2. un cancer du poumons
3. enfumé

4. cette putain de maladie
5. ne commence à le ronger

6. fanion

7. il avait fini par les décrocher
8. coups francs
9. déplorer
10. mauvais lancer
11. les hot dogs avant le match
12. les petits foots dans le parking
13. l'hymne de combat
14. jeux à domicile
15. pour renvoyer l'ascenseur à quelqu'un
16. quel stupide gâchis
17. faire la fête
18. après
19. ne sont plus sur la même longueur d'onde
20. son berceau

to slip off the tracks[1]. There was an incident his senior year of high school where a girl accused Carlton of rape[2] and assault after a date[3]. Carlton had told Del that she was just pissed off because he'd dumped her ass after a one-night stand[4]. Del believed him. Who raped someone on a date? Rapists hid in bushes and jumped out and stuff. They didn't get invited back to a girl's place, like Carlton. Still, there were bruises[5] and some bite marks[6], but Carlton said that was how she liked it. Del didn't know, but in the end, he didn't care about thin lines[7] and all that she-said, he-said stuff. No way was his son going to jail for some misunderstanding[8]. So Del made some payments, and it all went away.

That was the way it worked. His son was a good kid. It was a stage he was going through[9] maybe. He'd grow out of it.[10]

But still, something had changed in his boy, and now, with so much time on his hands, Del tried to figure out what. It could very well have been football. When he was really young, Carlton had been a great running back[11]. Even in eighth grade[12] he broke all the town records[13] for yardage[14] in a season. But then Carlton stopped growing[15]. This frustrated the hell out of him[16]. It wasn't Carlton's fault. It was genetics[17], plain and simple[18]. Nothing you can do about it. When Carlton got demoted to[19] second-string[20], he started lifting[21] more and, Del suspected, started taking steroids. That was where it started. Maybe. Who knew for sure?

Del tried to concentrate on the Celtics and Sixers, and, surprising himself, he could. Funny how life worked. He actually gave a crap[22] if the Sixers won. Still. Despite what was going on in his life. Maria, of course, would laugh her ass off[23] when she saw him get so involved in watching a game[24]. She'd point at the TV and say, "You think these guys would go to your job and cheer you on[25]?" She had a point, but so what? And as if to show she didn't mean any harm, Maria would always bring out a snack for him then, potato skins[1] or nachos[2] or something.

It was at the moment, sitting on his white couch and thinking about his sweet Maria, with the Sixers on an eight-to-zero run, that Del heard the doorbell ring.

His hand immediately landed on the medal of Saint Anthony of Padua. You were supposed to invoke his name[3] in the memory of lost things, including, Del knew, lost people. When he was younger, Del found such stuff total nonsense[4], but he'd grown superstitious[5] over the years.

He pushed himself off the white leather[6] and opened the front door. Goldberg, the cop, stood there in the cold. He didn't say anything. He didn't have to. Their eyes met, and Goldberg gave him the smallest, most devastating nod[7] one man could give to another[8]. Del felt something in his chest crumble into dust[9].

There was no denial. Not at first. At first, there was only a crushing clarity[10]. Del Flynn understood completely what this meant. His boy was gone forever. He'd never be back. His son was dead. His young life was over. There would be no reprieve[11], no miracle, nothing to save him. Del would never hold him or see him or talk to his boy again. There'd be no more Eagles games. Carlton was gone, no more, and Del knew that he would never recover[12].

His legs gave way[13]. He began to collapse to the ground—wanted to actually—but Goldberg caught him in his strong arms. Del sagged[14] against the big cop. The pain was too great, unfathomable[15], unbearable[16].

"How?" Del finally asked.

"We found him near where we found his blood."

"In the woods?"

"Yes."

Del pictured Carlton there—alone, outside, in the cold.

1. des pommes de terre au four [garnies]

2. [chips de maïs au fromage fondu]

3. l'invoquer

4. pensait que c'était de la foutaise

5. devenu superstitieux

6. se leva du sofa en cuir blanc

7. hochement de tête

8. que puissent échanger deux hommes

9. se briser dans sa poitrine

10. une terrible évidence

11. pas de sursis

12. ne s'en remettrait jamais

13. se dérobèrent

14. s'affaissa

15. insondable

16. insupportable

"There were other bodies too. We think it might be the work of a serial killer."

"A serial killer?"

"We think so."

"So you mean, like, there was no reason? It was just random[1] that he killed my boy?"

"We don't know yet."

Del tried to push away[2] the pain, tried to concentrate on what Goldberg was saying. That was what you did in times of agony.[3] Some people used denial.[4] Some used the need for vengeance. Whatever, you didn't concentrate on what it all meant to you because that would be too much to bear[5]. You diverted with the irrelevant[6] because you couldn't change the awful truth, could you?

With the tears starting to flow[7], Del asked, "Did my boy suffer?"

Goldberg thought about it for a second. "I don't know."

"Have you caught the guy?"

"Not yet. But we will."

From the TV, Del could hear the home crowd cheering[8]. Something good had happened for the Sixers. His son was dead, but people were cheering. No one cared.[9] The electricity in the house still worked. Cars still drove by.[10] People still cheered for their favorite teams.

"Thank you for telling me in person," Del heard himself say[11].

"Do you have someone who can stay with you?"

"My wife will be home soon."

"Do you want me to stay with you until then?"

"No. I'll be fine. I appreciate you coming by.[12]"

Goldberg cleared his throat[13]. "Del?"

He looked up at Goldberg's face. There was genuine compassion there[14], but there was something else too.

Goldberg said, "We don't want any more innocents hurt. You know what I'm saying?"

338

Margin glossary:

1. au hasard
2. chasser
3. C'est ce qu'on fait quand on souffre.
4. Certains se réfugient dans le déni.
5. trop dur à supporter
6. On s'intéresse à des points sans importance
7. Tout en pleurant
8. les acclamations des fans
9. Tout le monde s'en fichait.
10. Les voitures continuaient à passer dans la rue.
11. s'entendit dire
12. Merci d'être venu.
13. s'éclaircit la voix
14. Il y vit de la compassion

Del did not reply.

"Call those psychos off[1]," Goldberg said, handing him a cell phone. "There's been enough death for one night."

Through the blinding agony[2], there was indeed the crushing clarity. Goldberg was right. Too much blood had been spilled[3]. Del Flynn took the phone from Goldberg's hand and dialed Ken's number.

But no one answered.

BROOME called Sarah Green. "Will you be home in an hour?"

"Yes."

"Can I come by?"

"Something new?[4]"

"Yes."

There was a brief pause. "It doesn't sound like good news.[5]"

"I'll be there in an hour."

The streetlights[6] in front of Ray Levine's residence were too bright and too yellow, giving everything a jaundiced feel[7]. Four Atlantic County squad cars were parked in front of the modest dwelling. As Broome approached, he saw the feds pull up[8] in a van[9]. He hurried inside[10] and found Dodds.

"Anything?" Broome asked.

"Nothing surprising, if that's what you mean. No murder weapons.[11] No hand trucks. Nothing like that. We already started going through the photographs on his computer. On that score[12], at least[13], the guy was telling the truth—the pictures by the old iron-ore mill were taken on various February eighteenths, not Mardi Gras."

That backed[14] Ray Levine's story in a pretty big way[15].

Dodds looked out the window. "That the feds?"

"Yep."

---

1. Dites à vos cinglés d'arrêter
2. À travers sa souffrance aveuglante
3. versé
4. Il y a du nouveau ?
5. Ça n'a pas l'air d'être une bonne nouvelle.
6. L'éclairage public
7. baignant toutes choses d'une atmosphère déplaisante
8. se garer
9. fourgon
10. se précipita à l'intérieur de la maison
11. Pas d'arme du crime.
12. Sur ce point
13. du moins
14. Cela confirmait
15. brillamment

1. prennent la relève
2. C'est eux qui vont gérer
3. de s'attarder
4. hocha pensivement la tête
5. juifs
6. cet appart de merde
7. se font beaucoup de fric
8. Je voulais pas donner dans le stéréotype.
9. pas grave
10. rien de compromettant
11. sachet pour éléments de preuve
12. le contenu
13. il comprit enfin
14. fut pris d'un vertige
15. chancelant
16. reçut une autre secousse
17. difficile de tenir debout
18. ressentit un coup à l'estomac

"They taking over[1]?"

Broome nodded. "It's their baby[2] now." He looked at his watch. There was no reason to hang[3] here. He could get to Sarah's and start to explain. "If there's nothing else ..."

"Nope, not really. Just one thing I found weird."

"What's that?"

"Ray Levine. That's the guy's real name?"

"It is."

Dodds nodded more to himself[4]. "You know any other Levines?"

"A few, why?"

"They're Jewish[5], right? I mean, Levine is a Jewish name."

Broome looked around this dump of a basement[6] and frowned at Dodds. "Not all Jews make a lot of money[7]. You know that, right?"

"That's not what I meant. I'm not stereotyping or nothing like that.[8] Look, just forget it, okay? It's no big deal[9]."

"What's no big deal?" Broome asked.

"Nothing. But, okay, like I said, we didn't find anything incriminating[10]. It's just that, well"—he shrugged—"what would a Jewish guy be doing with this?"

He handed Broome a small plastic evidence bag[11]. Broome looked down at the contents[12]. At first he didn't comprehend what this was, but a few seconds later, when he did, when it finally registered[13], Broome felt a sense of vertigo[14], like he was falling and falling and couldn't stop. His world, already teetering[15], took another sudden, jarring turn[16], and it was almost hard to stay upright[17].

"Broome?"

He ignored the voice. He blinked, looked again, and felt his stomach drop[18], because there, inside the plastic bag, was a medal of Saint Anthony.

FROM his spot across the street, Ken watched Lorraine leave La Crème by the back[1] door. It took her a fair amount of time[2] to get through the lot[3]. Her departure seemed to be something of an event[4]. Every girl who worked in that cesspool called out to the older barmaid and gave her a long hug[5]. Lorraine in turn accepted the embrace and then seemed to give each one of them something they craved—a sympathetic ear[6], a crooked I-get-it smile[7], a kind word.

Like she was their mother.

When she was finally through the crush of girls[8] and headed for home, Ken followed at a safe distance. The walk to her place wasn't far. The barmaid lived, of course, in some two-bit dump, a house that one might kindly say[9] had seen better days[10], though it was probably grimy[11] from day one.

Lorraine used a key to open the door and disappeared inside. Two lights went on toward the back. Before that there was no illumination in the house. That seemed to indicate that she was here alone. Ken circled the house, peeking in through[12] the windows. He found Lorraine in the kitchen.

She looked, he thought, exhausted. Her high heels had been kicked off[13], her bare[14] feet up on a chair. She warmed her hands on a cup of tea, gently sipping it[15] and closing her eyes. In this harsher light[16], she was far less attractive, far older, than she had looked in the dim[17] light of that strip joint.

That made sense[18], of course.

Some life this barmaid had made for herself[19], Ken thought. He'd be doing her a favor[20] if he just put her out of her misery[21]. Ken felt that itch return[22] in full force. His hands tightened into fists. He looked at that kitchen table and thought, Yes, it would probably be sturdy enough[23] to do the job.

Time to get to work.

As Ken approached Lorraine's door, his phone vibrated. He checked the number, saw it wasn't Barbie,

1. de derrière
2. un bon bout de temps
3. traverser le parking
4. être l'événement
5. la serrait longuement dans ses bras
6. une oreille compatissante
7. un sourire en coin compréhensif
8. eut traversé la foule des filles
9. pour dire les choses élégamment,
10. connu des jours meilleurs
11. crasseux
12. en jetant un regard par
13. Elle avait envoyé promener ses talons hauts
14. nus
15. en le sirotant délicatement
16. lumière crue
17. tamisée
18. C'était logique
19. Quelle vie elle s'était fait là, cette serveuse
20. Il lui rendrait service
21. s'il mettait fin à son supplice
22. Ça le démangeait de nouveau
23. suffisamment solide

1. se tapota les cheveux

2. un bruit de pas traînant

3. glisser le verrou du haut

4. le nombre de gens qui faisaient pareil

5. ne lui claqua pas la porte au nez

6. beau mec triste

7. Un soupçon de peur parcourut

8. buriné

9. hésitante

10. du genre à

11. grand format

12. entra

13. amortirait le choc

14. s'il pouvait la ramener à cette époque et à cet endroit

15. ça l'aiderait à comprendre

decided not to answer it. He knocked, patted down his hair[1], and waited. There was a shuffling sound[2], and then Ken could hear the top lock's deadbolt sliding open[3]. Odd how many people just did that[4]. You have the most expensive lock and yet you just open the door to any knock.

Lorraine's eyes widened a little when she saw Ken, but she didn't slam the door closed[5] or anything like that. "Well, well. If it isn't the handsome mourner[6] who looks like my ex."

She tried to give the crooked smile, the one he'd seen in the club, but it wasn't quite working. Ken spotted... fear maybe? Yes, fear. The tiniest trace rippled across[7] her weather-beaten[8] face, and that excited him.

Ken offered up his most gentle expression. "I need to talk to you about something."

Lorraine looked reluctant[9]—maybe scared too—but she wasn't the type to[10] make a scene or turn someone away.

"It's really important," he said. "May I come in?"

"I don't know," Lorraine said. "It's kinda late."

"Oh, don't worry." He gave her the smile with all the teeth[11]. "This will only take a second, I promise."

And then Ken pushed his way in[12] and closed the door behind him.

IT was getting cold outside, so Ray took the stairs back down into the vaulted "stomach room" of Lucy. It had been a dumb idea to come here. What, really, was the point? Yes, he had wonderful memories here. Maybe he thought that Cassie would too. But so what? Did he think bringing her here would somehow soften the blow[13]? Did he think that if he could get her to go back to that time and place[14] it would help her see[15] why he did what he did?

Dumb.

Yes, some things could be made better by setting and context[1], but was he really naïve enough to think, what, that there would be a hormonal rush[2] just being[3] inside this edifice, and that that rush would somehow make what he had done more palatable[4]? He suddenly felt like a bad real estate[5] agent believing location, location, location[6] could somehow make his confession that much better[7].

Ray looked at his cell phone. No text messages from Cassie or Megan or whatever the hell her name was. He debated calling her again, but what was the point of that? He'd wait another hour, maybe two, and then he'd leave. Where would he go? The cops were probably finishing up[8] at his place, but did he really want to go back to that dingy[9] basement?

No.

It was time to move on. If Cassie—that would always be her name to him, not Megan—didn't want to hear what he had to say, well, he'd just have to find a way to deal with that[10]. But staying here, with the world around him falling apart[11], made no sense. It was too risky, and while he certainly had had no trouble[12] finding ways to wreck his life[13] over the years, he wasn't overtly suicidal[14].

When Ray started for the stairs in Lucy's hind leg, he heard a noise below. He stopped and waited.

Someone had opened the door.

"Cassie?"

"No, Ray."

His heart deflated[15] when he recognized the voice. It belonged to Detective Broome.

"How did you find me?" Ray asked.

"Your cell phone signal. It's easy when someone leaves their phone on[16]."

"Oh. Right."

"It's over, Ray."

He said nothing.

"Ray?"

---

1. en contexte
2. une poussée hormonale
3. rien qu'en étant
4. plus acceptable
5. immobilier
6. que, si c'est bien situé
7. ses aveux en seront tellement plus convaincants
8. en avaient sans doute terminé
9. miteux
10. il faudrait qu'il se fasse une raison
11. pendant que le monde s'écroulait autour de lui
12. bien qu'il n'ait eu aucun mal
13. à trouver des moyens de foutre sa vie en l'air
14. franchement suicidaire
15. Son espoir fut douché
16. quand on laisse son portable allumé

1. Inutile d'essayer de fuir.

2. L'endroit est cerné.

3. opta pour

4. soyez gentil

5. Facilitez-moi les choses

6. Mettez-vous à genoux

7. Je vais vous passer les menottes

8. vous lire vos droits

"I hear you, Detective."

"There's no point in running.[1] The place is surrounded.[2]"

"Okay."

"Are you armed?"

"No."

"I'm here to arrest you, Ray. Do you understand?"

Not sure what to say to that, Ray settled for[3]: "Yes, I understand."

"Then do both of us a favor[4]," Broome said. "Make it easy and safe[5]. Get down on your knees[6] and put your hands on top of your head. I'll cuff you[7] and read your rights[8]."

36

AT eight a.m. the next morning, Megan opened her eyes and felt a world of hurt[1]. It had been a long night on so many levels[2]—not the least of which had been[3] the emotional toll of telling[4] Dave the entire truth about her past—and now every part of her body was experiencing a fresh adventure in pain[5]. The arm was the worst of it; it felt as though it'd been mangled[6] by a tiger and then jammed[7] into a blender[8] set on pulverize[9]. A blacksmith[10] was mercilessly using her skull as an anvil[11]. Her tongue and mouth had the dryness of both the Sahara and the worst hangover imaginable.

Megan opened her eyes slowly. Dave sat at the end of the bed, his head lowered into his hand[12]. He, too, looked in pain, albeit not the throbbing kind[13]. His hair stuck up in all different directions[14]. He had, she surmised[15], stayed by her side all night.

She tried to remember what time she had finished talking—Dave had barely spoken—but couldn't. She

1. des douleurs intenses
2. par bien des aspects
3. le plus dur ayant été
4. contrecoup émotionnel d'avoir dit à
5. découvrait des douleurs jusqu'ici insoupçonnées
6. déchiqueté
7. enfoncé
8. dans un mixeur,
9. position purée
10. Un forgeron
11. comme d'une enclume
12. se tenant la tête
13. même si c'était moins physique
14. Il était tout ébouriffé
15. supposait-elle

had talked past exhaustion[1], not so much falling asleep as passing out from[2] the combination of weariness[3], pain, and morphine. If Dave had commented on her confession, she didn't remember it.

Megan had never been so thirsty. When she reached for the cup of water on the nightstand, her entire body screamed in protest[4]. She let out a small cry[5]. Dave snapped his head up[6] and said, "Let me get that for you[7]."

He moved to the nightstand and carefully lifted the glass[8] toward her, easing the straw[9] between her lips. She sipped[10] greedily[11]. The water was pure ambrosia[12]. When she finished, Dave put the water back on the nightstand and sat next to her.

"How are you feeling?" he asked.

"Like I kissed a bus.[13]"

He smiled and stroked her forehead. "Let me get the doctor."

"Not yet." His hand felt cool against her skin. She closed her eyes and enjoyed his touch[14]. A tear ran down her cheek. She wasn't sure why.

"I've been running through[15] everything you told me," Dave said. "I'm still trying to process.[16]"

"I know. But talk to me, okay?"

"Okay."

She opened her eyes and looked at him.

"It's hard," Dave said. "I mean, on the one hand, it doesn't really matter, I guess, what you were in the past. Do you love me?"

"Yes."

"Are your feelings for me a lie?"

"No, of course not."

"Then what else matters? We all have pasts. We all have secrets. Or something." He shifted in his seat.[17] "That's the one hand. That's the part I get."

"And the other hand?"

Dave shook his head. "I'm still processing."

"Processing," she said, "or judging[18]?"

---

1. sans tenir compte de son épuisement

2. mais plutôt abrutie par

3. lassitude

4. protesta bruyamment

5. poussa un gémissement

6. leva la tête d'un coup

7. Laisse, je vais le prendre

8. leva le verre doucement

9. plaçant délicatement la paille

10. but

11. avidement

12. avait un goût divin

13. Comme si j'étais passée sous un bus.

14. savourant sa caresse

15. J'ai repensé à

16. Je n'ai pas encore bien assimilé.

17. Il gigota dans son fauteuil.

18. de me juger

346

He looked confused. "I'm not sure I get what you mean."

"If my secret past was that I'd been, I don't know, a rich princess and a virgin[1] before we met, do you think you'd have as much trouble[2] processing?"

"You think I'm that shallow[3]?"

"I'm just asking," she said. "It's a fair question.[4]"

"And if I said, yes, that scenario would be easier to process?"

"I'd understand, I guess."

Dave considered that. "Do you want to hear an odd truth?"

She waited.

"I never fully trusted you[5], Megan. No, wait, that's not really true. What I mean is, I never really believed you. I trusted you. Implicitly[6]. I made you my wife and I loved you and I know you loved me. We shared a life and a bed[7] and had children together." Dave swallowed hard[8], looked away, turned back to her. "I would trust you with my life.[9] You know that."

"I do."

"And yet I didn't always believe you. You can trust someone and know there is something else there. Do you know what I mean?"

"Yes."

"Was it hard lying to me all those years?"

"Not just you. Everyone."

"But mostly me."

She didn't argue[10].

"Was that hard?"

Megan considered that. "Not really, no."

He sat back[11]. "Wow, that's honest."

"The truth wasn't really an option[12]. I didn't see any point in[13] telling you about my past. The truth could only make things worse."

"Had to be hard though, right?[14] On some level.[15]"

"I guess I got used to it[16]."

---

1. vierge

2. que tu aurais autant de mal à

3. que je suis aussi superficiel que ça

4. Ce n'est que justice.

5. Je ne t'ai jamais fait complètement confiance

6. Implicitement

7. avons partagé notre vie et notre lit

8. avala sa salive

9. Je mettrais ma vie entre tes mains.

10. n'insista pas

11. se radossa dans son fauteuil

12. envisageable

13. l'intérêt de

14. Ça a dû être dur quand même, non ?

15. D'une certaine façon.

16. que je m'y suis faite

1. sinon

2. je ne pourrai pas m'empêcher d'imaginer

3. Je n'ai pas d'excuses à faire.

4. Elle eut de nouveau les larmes aux yeux.

5. pas après avoir tant souffert

6. sortiez avec les unes et les autres

7. de l'herbe

8. de voir le rapport

9. une époque révolue

10. l'air ébahi

11. se frotta le visage

12. Ils nous éloignaient l'un de l'autre.

13. sonna avec fracas

14. On ne devait pas te déranger.

15. tendit son bras indemne vers le téléphone

16. Il paraît que votre soirée a été un peu mouvementée.

He nodded. "Part of me wants to know details because otherwise[1] my imagination won't let it go[2], you know what I mean?"

She nodded.

"But most of me knows it's better to just let it go."

"It was a long time ago, Dave."

"But it's part of you."

"Yes. Just as your past is part of you."

"Do you miss it?"

"I won't apologize for it.[3]"

"That's not what I asked. I asked if you miss it."

More tears came to her eyes.[4] She was not going to lie again, not after she had gone through so much[5] to tell the truth. "When you were in high school, you were into that theater group, right?"

"So?"

"You guys hung out and hooked up[6] and smoked dope[7] together. That's what you told me."

"I'm not sure I see the point[8]," Dave said.

"You miss that, don't you? You wouldn't go back. It's a time that's over and gone[9]. Do I have to hate my past in order for you to accept me?"

Dave sat back as though startled[10]. "You really think it's the same thing?"

"How is it different?"

He rubbed his face with his hands[11]. "I don't know. That's what I need to process." Dave tried to smile. "I think the lies were harder on us than you know. They gave us distance on some level.[12] They had to. So it will be different now. But maybe it will be better."

The phone on the nightstand jangled[13].

Dave frowned. "You weren't supposed to be disturbed.[14]"

Megan reached for the phone with her good arm[15]. "Hello?"

"I heard you had a rough night.[16]"

It was Detective Broome

"I'll be fine."

348

"Have you turned on the television yet[1] this morning?"

"No, why?"

"Carlton Flynn is dead. So are a bunch of other men[2]. We found their bodies in a well near the old furnace."

"What?" Megan managed to sit up[3] this time. "I don't understand. Stewart Green too?"

"Probably. They're still going through the bodies."

Talk about trying to process. "Wait, so someone murdered them all?"

"I'll give you the details later, but right now I need your help."

"How?"

"I know you're in a lot of pain[4] so if you can't handle it[5]—"

"What do you need, Detective?"

"Last night, we arrested Ray Levine for the murders." She opened her mouth, but for a moment no words could come out. Her world flipped upside down all over again.[6] "Is this some kind of joke?[7]"

"No—"

"What's wrong with you?[8] Are you out of your mind?[9]"

Dave looked at her quizzically[10]. She ignored him.

"Broome," she shouted.

"I'm here," Broome said.

Megan started to shake her head, ready to tell him that it simply wasn't possible[11], but then she thought back to last night[12], to the last thing Ray had said to her: *"I didn't tell you the truth."*

"No, no, it's a mistake," she said, feeling a tear slip down[13] her cheek. "Do you hear me? What evidence[14] do you have?"

"I don't want to get into that right now[15], but I need your help."

"How?"

---

1. allumé la télé

2. Un tas d'autres types aussi

3. réussit à s'asseoir

4. vous souffrez beaucoup

5. si vous n'avez pas la force

6. Son univers fut à nouveau chamboulé.

7. C'est une plaisanterie ?

8. Qu'est-ce qui vous a pris ?

9. Ça va pas la tête ?

10. d'un air interrogateur

11. c'était tout bonnement impossible

12. repensa à la nuit précédente

13. couler sur

14. Quelles preuves

15. expliquer là maintenant

1. en garde-
   à-vue
2. refuse de
   nous parler
3. en tête-à-tête
4. dans votre
   état actuel
5. jusqu'à ce
   que vous soyez
   d'attaque
6. attentivement
7. zone de
   détention
   provisoire
8. portait la
   combinaison
   orange des
   détenus
9. menottés
10. une salle
    d'interrogatoire
11. du comté
12. avait fait le
    nécessaire pour
    qu'
13. avocat
14. avec de
    bons effets de
    manches
15. dont le
    costume lavande
    était un peu
    trop voyant
16. un bain
    moussant
17. rétorqua
    Flair en agi-
    tant les mains
    comme des
    marionnettes
18. hélas
19. un conciliabule
20. ouste
21. Ça valait le
    coup d'essayer.
22. Même
    escortée par la
    police

"We have Ray in custody[1]," he said. "He won't talk to any of us[2]. He'll only talk to you face-to-face[3]. I know it's a lot to ask, in your current condition[4], and it can certainly wait a few days until you're up for it[5]—"

"What's the address?" she asked.

Dave just stared at her.

Megan listened closely[6]. Then she hung up the phone and turned to her husband. "I need you to drive me to a prison."

AFTER Broome hung up with Megan, he headed back into the holding area[7]. Ray Levine was dressed in prison-garb orange[8]. His hands and legs were both shackled[9]. They were in an interrogation room[10] at the Atlantic County[11] jail. Ray had called his one friend in the area, his boss, Fester, and Fester arranged for[12] an attorney[13] named Flair Hickory to represent Ray. Hickory was known for being very good and very flamboyant[14].

When Broome entered the room, Flair Hickory, whose lavender suit was a bit much[15] at eight in the morning, said, "Well?"

"She's on her way."

"Wonderful."

"I'd still like to ask your client a few questions."

"And I'd like to take a bubble bath[16] with Hugh Jackman," Flair countered with a double hand wave[17]. "But alas[18], we can dream, can't we? My client made it clear. Before he says a word to you, he wants a private powwow[19] with Megan Pierce. Now, shoo[20]."

Broome left the room. Special Agent Angiuoni shrugged and said, "It was worth a shot.[21]"

"I guess."

"Even with the police escort[22], it will take at least an hour for her to get down here. Why don't you get some air or something?"

"I have to go back to La Crème."

"The nightclub? Why?"

Broome didn't bother explaining. He headed outside to his car. There were still loose ends to tie up.[1] It had indeed been a long night. The feds were still tearing apart[2] Ray Levine's residence, searching for other trophies[3]. Twelve bodies had so far been taken out of the well, though, as they got deeper into the hole, it became harder to immediately classify whose bones belonged to whom. The bodies had been broken down into a heap[4] over the years, the well becoming the ultimate boneyard[5].

After Broome arrested Ray Levine last night, he headed to that doomed house that had once been the family home of Stewart and Sarah Green. He told Sarah what he knew, that all evidence pointed to the fact[6] that Stewart was in the bottom of the well, the victim of a serial killer. Sarah had listened intently[7] as always. When he finished, she said, "I thought you said someone saw Stewart recently."

So that was where Broome was headed now—to La Crème's Saturday Brunch 'n' Munch. They opened for breakfast just about now and shockingly did a pretty brisk business[8]. He didn't think that this particular trip[9] would produce anything tangible. Lorraine, Broome was certain, would shrug her shoulders and say, "I told you I wasn't sure. You just wouldn't listen."

But the truth was—a truth he could maybe start admitting to himself[10]—he wanted to see Lorraine. It had been a horrible night, filled with too much blood and too many dead bodies. Sure, he had a professional excuse for visiting her[11], but maybe he just wanted to be with her, to see a familiar, pretty face looking back at him[12], one that wasn't married to another man. She had that way about her, Lorraine, another wounded veteran[13] of this city, and it felt good to be around her. Maybe that was all he wanted. Maybe he wanted to disappear into that comforting, crooked smile and throaty laugh for a little while. And may-

---

1. Il restait des détails à régler.

2. en train de démanteler

3. à la recherche d'autres trophées

4. étaient devenus un tas d'ossements

5. un parfait ossuaire

6. tout tendait à prouver

7. attentivement

8. étonnamment l'endroit était déjà bondé

9. cette petite visite

10. qu'il pouvait peut-être enfin s'avouer

11. un prétexte professionnel pour passer la voir

12. voir un minois familier le regarder

13. elle aussi une sorte d'ancien combattant rescapé

1. ne serait plus là

2. rater une occasion

3. une fois de plus

4. commencé à faire la queue

5. d'ailleurs, selon où ils avaient été durant la nuit

6. veillé

7. Quoi qu'on dise,

8. la conclusion évidente restait

9. qu'ils étaient vraiment désespérés

10. vêtus de noir

11. fond

12. fonçant vers

13. le poussa par-derrière

14. l'envoyant à terre

15. grassouillet

16. Des filles comme ça, y en a à la pelle.

17. plus forte

18. se mit à tourner

19. Ne me racontez pas de craques.

be the fact that she was dying, that maybe in a few months she wouldn't be here at all[1] … maybe that made him realize how badly he didn't want to miss out[2] yet again[3] in his life.

Was that so wrong?

The bouncers at La Crème were just opening the doors when he arrived. Some patrons had actually lined up[4] early, probably coming straight from the casinos or whatever nighttime activity had kept them out[5]. That was the breakfast clientele—not people who had just woken up for a morning meal but those who had stayed up[6] all night and needed to start the next morning with a strip show. You could spin that any way you want, but[7] it was hard not to conclude[8] that they were, at best, pretty freaking desperate[9].

Broome nodded at the black-clad[10] bouncers as he entered. He headed inside the dark confines[11], making a beeline for[12] Lorraine's bar. But she wasn't there. He was about to turn around and ask where she was when someone shoved him from behind[13], sending him flying[14].

It was a red-faced Rudy.

"What the hell, Rudy?"

Rudy pointed a beefy[15] finger at him. "I warned you."

"What are you talking about?"

"First you talk to Tawny. Okay, no big deal. A dime a dozen.[16] Fine." He shoved Broome again. "But I warned you, right?"

"Warned me about what?"

"I told you Lorraine was different. That she was special. I told you what I'd do if something happened to her."

Broome froze. The music seemed suddenly louder[17]. The room began to spin[18]. "Where is she?"

"Don't give me that where-is-she crap.[19] You know very well—"

Broome grabbed him by the lapels[1] and threw him against the wall[2]. "Where is she, Rudy?"

"That's what I'm asking you, asswipe. She never showed up for work this morning."

1. par les revers
2. le plaqua au mur

37

1. à la fois
quelconque et
surréaliste

2. face à

3. Le trajet en
voiture s'était
déroulé en
silence.

4. incompréhen-
sible

5. de parler de
la pluie et du
beau temps

6. de son côté

7. tout ça devait
être difficile
pour lui

8. trop sidérée

9. Ça
attendrait.

10. été passée
au détecteur de
métal

11. soigneuse-
ment fouillée

12. d'être
autorisée à
entrer dans

13. l'avait
accueillie

IN some kind of nondescript yet surreal[1] interrogation room, Megan sat across from[2] Ray.

The car ride down had been subdued.[3] A federal
agent named Guy Angiuoni called and gave her details on the murders and the arrest. It was beyond
comprehension[4]. When she hung up, Dave tried small
talk[5]. She didn't respond. Dave knew now about her
past relationship with Ray—not the details, of course,
but enough. She, in turn[6], knew that this couldn't
be easy on him[7]. She wanted to comfort and assure
him. Dave deserved that and more. But she was too
stunned[8].

It would have to wait.[9]

Megan had gone through a metal detector[10] and
thorough body search[11] before being allowed to enter[12] the holding room. There were five men inside:
Special Agent Guy Angiuoni; two police guards; Ray's
attorney, Flair Hickory, who greeted her[13] with a
warm smile; and of course, Ray.

Flair Hickory held up a small stack of papers[1]. "These are sworn affidavits[2] that state[3] that your conversation with my client will not be eavesdropped upon[4] or recorded[5] or used in any way," he said. "Everyone in this room has signed one."

"Okay."

"I'd be oh so grateful if you could[6] sign one promising not to divulge anything[7] that my client tells you[8] during this conversation."

"That's not necessary," Ray said.

"It is for her benefit as well[9]," Flair explained. "Even if you trust her, Ray, I'm trying to make it more difficult for them to compel her[10] to speak."

"It's okay," Megan said.

The fingers on her bad arm still functioned enough for her to hold the pen[11] and scrawl a signature[12].

Flair Hickory collected the papers[13]. "Okay, everyone, time to leave."

Special Agent Angiuoni started for the door. "Someone will be watching[14], Mrs. Pierce. If you're in any danger, just raise your good arm over your head if you need us."

"My client is trussed up[15] like an S-and-M prop[16]," Flair countered. "She's in no danger."

"Still."

Flair rolled his eyes[17]. Guy Angiuoni was first to leave, followed by the two guards. Flair was last. The door closed behind him. Megan took the seat across the table from him[18]. Ray's ankles were shackled to[19] the chair, his arms to the table.

"Are you okay?" Ray asked her.

"I was attacked last night."

"Who?"

She shook her head. "We're not here about me[20]."

"Is that why you weren't able to show at Lucy last night?"

Megan wasn't sure[21] how to answer that. "I wouldn't have shown up anyway.[22]"

1. pile de papiers

2. des déclarations sous serment

3. stipulant

4. ni écoutée

5. ni enregistrée

6. Je vous serais terriblement reconnaissant de bien vouloir

7. de ne rien divulguer

8. de ce que mon client vous aura dit

9. C'est pour son bien à elle aussi

10. de la forcer

11. pour qu'elle arrive à tenir le stylo

12. à gribouiller sa signature

13. ramassa les documents

14. aura l'œil sur vous

15. est ficelé

16. accessoire sado-maso

17. leva les yeux au ciel

18. prit le siège de l'autre côté de la table

19. enchaînées à

20. pour parler de moi

21. ne savait trop

22. Je ne serais pas venue de toute façon.

He nodded as if he understood.

"Did you kill all those men, Ray?"

"No."

"Did you kill Stewart Green?"

He didn't reply.

"You found out he was hurting me[1], didn't you?"

"Yes."

"You cared about me. You even ..." She stopped, started again. "You even loved me."

"Yes."

"Ray, I need you to tell me the truth now."

"I will," he said. "But you first[2]."

"What?"

When Ray met her eyes, she felt it everywhere[3].

"Cassie," he said. "Did you kill Stewart Green?"

BROOME didn't bother to ask Rudy follow-up questions[4].

He tried not to panic, but it wasn't working. He told Rudy to stay at the club and call if Lorraine arrived. Without another word Broome ran back to his car, grabbed his gun[5], and hurried toward Lorraine's house.

Please no, please no, please no ...

He called his dispatcher for backup[6], but there was no way he'd wait[7]. He sprinted all out[8] now. His lungs burned.[9] His breath reverberated in his own ears.[10] His eyes grew wet[11] in the morning air.

None of that mattered. Only one thing mattered.

Lorraine.

If something happened to her, if someone hurt her...

There were people out on the streets, all stumbling in the sun after a night basking in artificial light[12]. Broome didn't even glance at them[13].

Not Lorraine. Please, not Lorraine ...

Broome veered to the right[14] at the corner. Up ahead, he saw Lorraine's house. He remembered the

---

1. avais découvert qu'il me faisait du mal

2. toi d'abord

3. frissonna de tout son corps

4. poser d'autres questions à Rudy

5. attrapa son revolver

6. le standard pour avoir des renforts

7. il n'allait pas les attendre

8. fonçait

9. Ses poumons le brûlaient.

10. Il entendait l'écho de sa propre respiration.

11. en pleuraient

12. une nuit passée à la lumière électrique

13. ne leur accorda pas un regard

14. tourna à droite

other time he'd been there, when he stayed for the night. Funny[1], how you miss the obvious[2]. It had meant little to him, probably less to her, and now he cursed[3] his stupidity.

With a surge of adrenaline[4], Broome picked up his pace[5], hopping the steps on the front stoop[6] two at a time[7]. He almost crashed into her door[8], ready to take it down with his shoulder[9], but he pulled up.

You don't just crash in. He knew better than that[10]. But he wasn't about to wait either. He calmed himself and tried the front doorknob.

It was unlocked.[11]

His heart skipped a beat[12]. Would Lorraine be stupid enough to leave her front door unlocked in this neighborhood[13]?

He didn't think so.

He swung open[14] the door slowly, the gun at the ready[15]. The door squeaked[16] in the morning air.

"Police!" he shouted. "Is anyone here?"

No reply.

He took another step into the house. "Lorraine?"

He could hear the fear in his own voice.

Please no, please no, please no ...

His eyes took in the front room. It was completely unremarkable. There was a couch with matching[17] love seat, the kind you could find in pretty much any highway furniture store[18]. The TV was modest size by today's standards[19]. In true Atlantic City style, the clock on the wall had red dice[20] instead of numbers.

There was a coffee table with three ashtrays[21] showing old scenes of the Atlantic City Convention Hall on the Boardwalk. There was a small bar to the right with two barstools. Bottles of Smirnoff Vodka and Gordon's London Dry Gin stood guard[22] like two soldiers. The coasters[23] were the same disposable[24] ones used at La Crème.

"Anyone here? This is the police. Come out with your hands up.[25]"

---

1. Bizarre
2. comme on ne fait pas attention aux choses les plus évidentes
3. maudissait
4. Mû par une poussée d'adrénaline
5. accéléra
6. du porche
7. deux par deux
8. faillit forcer la porte
9. la défoncer d'un coup d'épaule
10. que ça ne se faisait pas
11. La porte n'était pas verrouillée.
12. s'arrêta de battre une seconde
13. quartier
14. poussa
15. revolver au poing
16. grinça
17. qui va avec
18. pratiquement n'importe quel magasin de meubles à prix discount
19. pour le goût moderne
20. des dés rouges
21. cendriers
22. montaient la garde
23. Les dessous-de-verre
24. jetables
25. Sortez les mains en l'air.

1. illustrations
2. comprenaient
3. d'anciennes affiches de revues déshabillées
4. Chez Lorraine,
5. ce n'était ni très grand ni très sophistiqué
6. ça lui ressemblait tellement
7. atteignit
8. en désordre
9. un vestiaire
10. voyantes
11. sur des mannequins
12. des cintres
13. couleur vert avocat
14. couvert de petits aimants souvenirs
15. s'arrêta net
16. couvert de sang
17. les yeux dans ceux de Cassie
18. si elle trahissait un mensonge
19. rien, la question l'étonnait, c'est tout
20. avec insistance

Still nothing.

The artwork[1] on the walls featured[2] spectacular reproductions of vintage burlesque posters[3]. There was one from the Roxy in Cleveland, one for the Coney Island Red Hots, and right up front, in bright yellow, one that featured "Miss Spontaneous Combustion," Blaze Starr appearing at the Globe in Atlantic City.

Lorraine's place[4] wasn't very big or fancy[5], but it was so her[6]. Broome knew that her bedroom was to the left, the bathroom to the right, the kitchen in the back. He hit[7] the bedroom first. It was, he thought, something of a mess[8], looking more like a dressing room[9] than a place to sleep. Lorraine's flashy[10] work clothes were mostly on dress dummies[11] rather than hangers[12], but it almost seemed like a conscious design choice.

The bed, however, was still made.

Broome swallowed and moved back into the main room. There was no more time to waste. He hurried over to the kitchen. From a distance he could see the avocado-green[13] refrigerator loaded with souvenir magnets[14]. When he reached the door, Broome stopped short[15].

Oh no …

He looked down at the linoleum under the table and started shaking his head. He stared harder, hoping that something would change, but of course it didn't.

The kitchen floor was drenched in blood[16].

"CASSIE, did you kill Stewart Green?"

Ray looked up, finding Cassie's gaze and holding it[17]. He wanted to see her reaction to what he was about to say, to see, in the jargon of this damned city, if he could spot a "tell."[18]

"No, Ray, I didn't kill him," she said. "Did you?"

Ray watched her beautiful face, but there was nothing, just surprise at the question[19]. He looked at her hard[20], and he believed her.

"Ray?"

"No, I didn't kill him."

"Then who did?"

Ray had to get to it now[1]. He had to tell her the truth. The trouble was, now that he knew for sure that she hadn't been the one, how should he word this[2]?

A little late to worry about that[3].

"That night," Ray began, "you trekked up[4] to that spot. You saw Stewart Green lying by that big rock, and you thought he was dead."

"We went over this[5], Ray."

"Just bear with me.[6]"

"Yes," Cassie said. "I saw him and thought he was dead."

"So you ran, right? You were scared. You thought you'd be blamed[7]."

"Or you."

"Right," Ray said. "Or me."

"I don't understand, Ray. Why am I here? What did you want to tell me?"

He wondered how to make her understand. "Why were you there that night?"

She looked confused. "What do you mean?"

"Why did you go to the park that night?"

"What do you mean, why? I got your message. It gave me pretty specific instructions on how to get there.[8]"

Ray shook his head. "I never left you a message."

"What? Of course you did.[9]"

"No."

"Then how did you know to go there[10]?"

Ray shrugged. "I followed you."

"I don't understand."

"I knew what you'd been going through with Stewart Green[11]. I even asked you to run away[12] with me. I wanted us to start fresh[13], remember?"

A sad smile crossed her face. "You were dreaming."

"Maybe. Or maybe if you'd listened to me—"

1. en venir au fait

2. comment le formuler

3. pour s'en inquiéter

4. es montée à pied

5. On l'a déjà dit

6. Un peu de patience.

7. qu'on t'accuserait

8. Il m'indiquait très précisément comment y aller.

9. Bien sûr que si.

10. tu as eu l'idée d'y aller

11. ce que Stewart Green te faisait endurer

12. t'avais même demandé de t'enfuir

13. nous offrir un nouveau départ

"Let's not go down those roads[1], Ray."

He nodded. She was right. "I followed you that night. You parked at that lot[2] in the Pine Barrens and started up the trail. I couldn't imagine why or who you were meeting[3]. I guess I was jealous[4], I don't know. It doesn't matter anymore.[5] You started up the path. I didn't follow. If you wanted to be with another man, well, really, that had nothing to do with me[6]. We weren't exclusive.[7] That was part of the fun, right?"

"I don't understand," she said. "You didn't leave that message to meet you?"

"No."

"Then who did?"

"I've had a lot of time to think about that over the last twenty-four hours. The answer is pretty obvious, I guess. It had to be Stewart Green. He was setting you up[8], trying to get you alone[9]."

"But when I got up there[10] …"

"Stewart Green was dead," Ray said.

"At least, that's what I thought."

Ray took a deep breath. The blood filled his head[11]. "And you were right[12]."

She looked confused. "What?"

"Stewart was dead."

"You already killed him?"

"No. I told you. I wasn't the one.[13]"

"Then what happened?" she asked.

"You went up that path," Ray said. "You saw his body. You thought that he was dead, so you ran back down[14]. I saw you. In fact, I was going to stop you, make sure you were okay. Another one of those what-ifs. If I had just stopped you there. If I had asked you what happened …"

His voice drifted off.[15]

She leaned forward. "What happened, Ray?"

"I thought … I don't know … I thought Stewart had hurt you or something. I was confused[16] and angry, so I hesitated. And then, well, you were gone. So I ran up the path. Toward the ruins."

Megan studied his face. She was curious, sure,[1] but she also cared[2]. He could see that[3]. He was coming to it now[4], and maybe, finally, she was starting to see the truth.

"When I got up there, I saw Stewart Green lying there. He was dead. His throat had been slit.[5]" Ray leaned closer[6], wanted to make sure that she could see his eyes now—see what he had seen that night. "So picture it[7], Cassie. Picture me running up there and finding Stewart's throat slit."

She could see it now. All of it. "You thought ... You thought I killed him."

He didn't bother nodding. He lowered his head.

"What did you do then, Ray?"

Tears started flowing down his face.[8] "I panicked..."

"What did you do?"

The blood. All that blood.

"... or maybe it was just the opposite[9]. Maybe I suddenly grew too logical[10]. I'd seen you run away. I drew the most obvious conclusion[11]: You'd had enough of his abuse[12]. He was a real citizen. No one would help. So you did what you had to[13]. You arranged to meet him in that remote spot so you could kill him, and then something made you run. Maybe you freaked out[14]. Maybe someone spotted you[15]. I don't know. But you left clues. There were other cars in that lot. Someone might remember you. They'd find the body and the police would start investigating and they'd trace him back to La Crème, and in the end, well, it would all come back to[16] you."

She saw it now. He could tell by the expression on her face.

"So I did the only thing I could do to help you. I got rid of the body.[17] No body, no case.[18]"

She started shaking her head.

1. voulait savoir, bien sûr,

2. était aussi inquiète pour lui

3. le voyait bien

4. Il était sur le point de tout lui dire maintenant

5. On lui avait tranché la gorge.

6. se pencha vers elle

7. Alors, essaye de t'imaginer

8. Il se mit à pleurer.

9. que c'était l'inverse

10. que j'ai tout d'un coup fait preuve de trop de logique

11. J'en ai tiré la conclusion la plus évidente

12. tu en avais eu assez qu'il te maltraite.

13. avais fait la seule chose à faire

14. que tu avais paniqué

15. que quelqu'un t'avait vue

16. on remonterait de toute façon jusqu'à

17. Je me suis débarrassé du corps.

18. Sans cadavre, pas d'enquête.

"Don't you see? If there was no body, people would assume Stewart ran away. Someone might suspect you, but with no body, I knew you'd be safe."

"What did you do, Ray?"

"I dragged him[1] deeper in the woods. Then I went home and got a shovel to bury him[2]. But it was February. The ground was too hard. I tried, but the dirt wouldn't give way[3]. Hours passed.[4] Daylight was coming.[5] I had to get rid of the body. So I went home and got my chain saw[6]. ..."

Her hand went to her mouth.[7]

The blood, Ray thought again, his eyes closing. So much blood.

He had wanted to stop, but once the chain saw started, Ray had no choice. He had to finish the job. He didn't bother telling her the rest, what it felt like[8] to saw through[9] human flesh and bone, to put pieces of a human being, even one as deplorable as Stewart Green, into black plastic garbage bags[10]. The only thing that got him through[11] was the thought he was doing it to save the woman he loved. He took the bags and weighed them down[12] with rocks[13] and drove down to a spot he knew near Cape May. He threw the bags into the water. Then he went home and expected to find Cassie. But she wasn't there. He called her. She didn't reply. He spent the night shivering in his own bed[14], trying to get those images out of his head[15]. They wouldn't leave. He looked for Cassie the next day and the next. She still wasn't there. The days turned to weeks[16], to months, to years. But Cassie was gone.

And all Ray had left was the blood.

ERIN Anderson hit pay dirt[17].

She had spent most of the evening working with the feds on the IDs. It was too early for anything firm, but she had already gathered[18] enough information about clothing[19] and watches[20] and jewelry[21] to get

1. l'ai traîné
2. une pelle pour l'enterrer
3. impossible de casser la croûte de terre
4. L'heure tournait.
5. Il allait faire jour.
6. ma tronçonneuse
7. Elle mit la main à la bouche.
8. ce que ça faisait,
9. de scier de la
10. des sacs poubelles en plastique noir
11. qui l'avait fait tenir
12. les avait lestés
13. des pierres
14. à trembler dans son lit
15. s'enlever ces images de la tête
16. étaient devenus des semaines
17. tapa en plein dans le mille
18. recueilli
19. les vêtements
20. les montres
21. les bijoux

362

an idea of what bones might belong to what missing man. The rest would be up to DNA.[1] That might take some time.

When Erin got a free second, she hit the precinct computer[2]. Broome had told her to spread out the search[3], look for any other violence that might connect to Mardi Gras. A few minutes later, she found one case that might fit, though it wasn't really a direct hit[4].

At least, not at first.

Erin had been searching for murdered or missing men. That was why this particular case had slipped through the cracks[5]. In the end, this particular death had been ruled self-defense[6] rather than a homicide. Because no one was charged with a crime[7], the case had not been widely reported[8]. A man named Lance Griggs was stabbed to death[9] in his home in nearby Egg Harbor Township—not Atlantic City itself. Griggs had a long history of spousal abuse[10]. That was why the case had now caught her eye. No, he hadn't vanished. He hadn't been dumped down[11] a well. But Griggs, like so many others involved in this case, was a serial abuser.

According to the report, his wife had been hospitalized repeatedly[12]. The neighbors reported hearing beatings[13] over the years. The cops had visited the residence plenty of times. Erin shook her head. She had dealt with plenty of cases of spousal abuse. She had heard all the justifications, but she still, in her heart of hearts, never got why the women stayed.

Griggs had, it seemed, attacked his wife with a tire iron[14], breaking her leg and then pressed the bar against her throat. His wife finally broke away[15], grabbed a knife, and stabbed him. With Griggs's long arrest record, there were plenty of mug shots[16] for her to bring up[17]. She did that now. The wife had also been arrested when the body was first discov-

---

1. Pour le reste, il faudrait attendre les tests ADN.

2. se logua dans le système informatique du commissariat

3. d'élargir ses recherches

4. le même cas de figure

5. était passé inaperçu

6. considéré comme un cas de légitime défense

7. il n'y avait pas eu de mise en examen

8. on n'avait guère parlé de l'affaire

9. avait été tué à coups de couteau

10. un lourd passé de violence conjugale

11. jeté dans

12. plusieurs fois

13. avaient déclaré avoir entendu que quelqu'un se faisait tabasser

14. démonte-pneu

15. s'était dégagée

16. photos d'identité judiciaire

17. à consulter

ered. Erin brought up her picture too and put them side by side.

Some happy couple.[1]

"What are you working on?"

She turned to see Goldberg. Great, just what she needed. He, too, looked drawn[2] and exhausted, his tie[3] loosened to the point where it could almost double as a belt[4]. It had been a long night for all of them.

"Probably nothing important," Erin said, reaching for the monitor dimmer[5]. "I was doing a little more investigating on Mardi Gras crimes."

"Stop."

"What?"

"Turn that back up[6]," Goldberg said.

Erin grudgingly[7] did as he asked.

Goldberg stared at the screen. "And these two are involved?"

"Yes. She killed him years ago."

He shook his head. "This doesn't make any sense."

"How's that?"

Goldberg pointed to the screen. "I know that woman."

THE sight of the blood on the kitchen floor worked like a punch deep in Broome's gut[8].

He gripped his gun tighter[9] and started making all kinds of prayers and promises[10], hoping against hope[11] that Lorraine was still alive. Broome cursed himself for talking to her, especially in a place where anyone could see. Hadn't he learned anything from Tawny and Harry Sutton? There were dangerous people involved in all this.

How could he have been so careless[12]?

His heart pounded against his chest[13], but there was no time to waste. He had to get to her[14], had to try to stop the flow of blood[15]. Broome ducked down, rolled to his right[16], and once again, he met up with a shock[17].

Notes in margin:

1. Tu parles d'un couple !
2. avait les traits tirés
3. la cravate
4. si desserrée qu'elle pouvait servir de ceinture
5. se penchant pour réduire la luminosité de l'écran
6. Rallumez
7. à contrecœur
8. fit à Broome l'effet d'un coup de poing dans le ventre
9. serra son arme
10. de promesses
11. espérant malgré tout
12. si imprudent
13. battait la chamade
14. devait la trouver
15. le sang
16. fit un roulé sur sa droite
17. mais un nouveau choc l'attendait

It wasn't Lorraine's dead body he saw.

It was the body of a man. Looking closely, Broome remembered the description Megan had given of the guy by Harry Sutton's office. Could be the same guy.

This man was definitely dead.[1] His throat was slit.

Broome was about to turn around when he felt the gun press against his neck[2].

"Drop the gun[3], Broome," Lorraine said.

1. Il ne faisait aucun doute que l'homme était mort.

2. revolver sur sa nuque

3. Lâche ton arme

38

IT broke Megan's heart in a thousand ways.[1]

She had wondered why Ray had been so surprised by the sightings of[2] Stewart Green. Now she understood. Ray knew that Stewart had been dead all these years. He had made the huge sacrifice, too huge really[3], a sacrifice and then a secret that had gnawed at him[4], kept him down[5] and troubled, probably cost him a bit of his sanity[6]. Some people can live with that kind of thing. They do what they have to do. But Ray was too sensitive[7]. He couldn't. Especially when you added on[8] being abandoned[9] by the woman you loved. Especially when you added on that you wouldn't see that woman—the woman you made this huge sacrifice to save[10]—or even know what became of her[11], not until seventeen years later.

The last thing Megan told Ray before she left the interrogation room was that she would do everything in her power to make sure he was freed[12]. She meant it.[1] She owed him that. She would help him, and then fair or not[2], she'd be gone for good[3].

But the first thing she said when she walked out[4] of the room was, "Where's my husband?"

"He's down the hall on the left."

She hurried toward him. When she got to the room, Dave looked up, startled, and Megan felt her heart swell with genuine love[5]. She rushed over to him as he stood, collapsing[6] into his arms.

It was then, being held by her husband[7], that she felt safe enough to wonder about how she ended up on that path[8] that night.

Wasn't it Lorraine who had passed on that[9] message to meet Ray up at those ruins?

Wasn't it Lorraine who started the rumor that[10] Stewart Green was still alive—even though they now knew for certain he was dead?

Wasn't it Lorraine who claimed to know where Megan had been over the past seventeen years—even though it was impossible?

She ran back toward Special Agent Angiuoni[11].

"Where's Detective Broome?"

"I don't know. He said something about[12] a club called La Crème?"

GOLDBERG pointed over Erin's shoulder at the computer screen[13]. "That's Lorraine, the barmaid at La Crème. What the hell happened?"

"She killed her abusive husband."

"What?"

"It was declared self-defense. Open and shut.[14]"

"Where the hell is Broome?" Goldberg snapped[15]. "He needs to know about this."

LORRAINE said, "Drop the gun."

"What are you talking about? I'm here to help you, Lorraine."

1. Ce n'étaient pas des paroles en l'air.

2. qu'il le mérite ou non

3. elle disparaîtrait pour de bon

4. sortit

5. s'emplir d'un amour sincère

6. s'écroulant

7. dans les bras de son mari

8. pour se demander comment elle s'était retrouvée sur ce chemin

9. lui avait passé le

10. avait lancé la rumeur disant que

11. retourna voir Angiuoni en courant

12. a vaguement parlé d'

13. montrait l'écran du doigt au-dessus de l'épaule d'Erin

14. Affaire classée illico.

15. aboya Goldberg

"Please, Broome." She pushed the gun harder against his head[1]. "It's been a long night.[2] Drop the gun."

Broome did as she asked[3].

"Now call your dispatcher. Tell them you don't need backup, that it's all clear[4]."

Still stunned[5], Broome did as she asked. Then he pointed to the body on the floor. "Who is that?"

"Someone Del Flynn hired."

"What did he want?"

"To torture me into giving him[6] information on Carlton's whereabouts. Funny though.[7] He was the type who could dish it out[8] but couldn't take it[9]. So many men are like that."

Broome looked at her. She met his eyes and nodded, as if encouraging him to see what was now so obvious[10].

"My God … it was you?"

"Yep," she said.

"You killed all of them?"

"You got it. One per year. Always on Mardi Gras, but I didn't think anyone would ever figure out that pattern[11]. Most of these scumbags[12] had no one who cared enough to report that they were missing. I'm impressed you picked up the Mardi Gras connection[13]."

"It was my partner," Broome said.

"She's your ex-wife, right? Smart[14] woman, I bet[15]. Kudos to her.[16]"

He said nothing.

"Oh, don't worry, Broome. I'm not going to kill you and go after her or any of that." Lorraine gave him a crooked smile and stared at the gun as though it had suddenly materialized in her hand[17]. "I imagined a hundred different ways this might end, but me holding a gun on you and explaining?" She shook her head. "It's all so … I don't know … meh[18]. Are you going to try to stall for time[19] hoping someone will rescue you?"

"Not my style."

"Good, because it would really be gauche[1]. Don't worry, though. It'll all become clear soon enough."

"What will become clear?"

"My plan. And I need to tell it my way[2]. I need you to listen, Broome. If you ever had any feelings for me, you'll try to open your mind a little here[3], okay?"

"Do I have a choice?"

"I guess not, what with me having the gun and all[4]. But I'm tired, Broome. It's been a good run[5], but it's coming to an end[6]. I just want … I want you to listen to me. That's all. Let me start at the beginning and maybe you'll see where I'm going with this[7], okay?"

Lorraine seemed so sincere. She waited for him to answer, so he said, "Okay."

"You know I used to be married, right?"

"I do, yes."

"Got hitched[8] right out of high school[9]. I won't bore you with my early years[10] in a small town with an alcoholic dad. It's an old story, and we've seen the results on these streets a hundred times, haven't we?"

Broome thought the question was rhetorical[11], but again Lorraine stopped, the gun still in her hand. "We have," he said.

"I was going to be different though. I had a man who loved me. We eloped[12] and he got a job, and then he lost the job and started beating the crap out of me[13]. Broome, it was bad. You have no idea. He'd hit me once or twice before, you know, when we first got together. Nothing serious, you know how it is. Happens to every woman where I grew up[14]. So I shrugged it off.[15] But men can grow so little so fast[16], you know what I mean?"

Broome nodded, not sure what else to do.

"Life started pissing on my husband like he was the only urinal in the club.[17] And how does my little man react? He pounds the hell out of[18] the one person who still cares about him. Ironic, don't you think?"

Sidebar notes:

1. très maladroit
2. le raconter à ma façon
3. d'être un peu compréhensif
4. vu que c'est moi qui tiens le flingue
5. La promenade a été bonne
6. elle touche à sa fin
7. je veux en venir
8. Je me suis passé la corde au cou
9. à peine sortie du lycée
10. Je te passe les détails de mon enfance
11. pour la forme
12. On s'est enfuis
13. à me frapper comme un malade
14. là où j'ai grandi
15. Alors j'ai minimisé.
16. rapidement devenir mesquins
17. Mon mari s'est mis à en chier comme c'est pas permis.
18. tabasse

Broome said nothing.

Lorraine's hair fell over her face. She pushed it away[1] with one finger. "So guess what happened to me next, Broome? Come on, you're a smart guy. What always happens in cases like this?"

"You got pregnant[2]," Broome said.

"Ding, ding, ding, correct answer[3]. And for a few months while I was prego, peace ruled the land[4]. All the experts were wrong, I thought—a baby can and will improve a marriage[5]. Then one night, my future baby's daddy complains[6] that the steak is too chewy[7]. He gets all pissed off[8] and I say something stupid and he kicks me[9] in the stomach and I fall down and then he starts stomping on me so bad[10] I lose[11] the baby."

Broome stared down at the dead man on the floor, still unsure what to say.

"He stomps on me so bad, the crazy psycho, he actually ruptures my uterus[12]. You know what that means, Broome? Do I need to spell it out for you[13]? No kids. Not ever." Tears came to her eyes. She blinked them away[14], seemingly angry at herself[15]. "I wanted them[16], you know. I act otherwise[17] and maybe now, well, I'm a girl who's learned to make the best of my lot in life[18]. But back then, my whole dream was to have a couple of kids[19] and a little yard. Pathetic, right? I wasn't asking for a mansion[20]. Just a husband and some kids and a place we could call our own[21], you know?"

Broome inched closer[22] to her, trying to find an angle where he could make a move. "I'm sorry about that, Lorraine. I'm sorry you had to go through that."

"Yeah, it's a sad story, right?" She raised the gun, and her tone changed. "Please don't get cute, Broome. My intention here is to make the guy on the floor my final victim, not you."

Broome stopped.

"Anyway, let's skip ahead a few months[23]. To Mardi Gras night. Mr. Wonderful Hubby gets pissed drunk[24] and takes a tire iron to me. So I killed him. Just like that. And you know what, Broome?"

"What?" he said.

"It was the best thing I ever did. I was free and happy."

"No remorse?[1]"

"Just the opposite, Broome. What's the opposite of remorse?" Lorraine snapped her[2] fingers when the answer came to her[3]. "Pure satisfaction. That's what I felt. I moved into the city[4], got a job at La Crème, and well, every Mardi Gras, I celebrated my freedom[5], if you will[6], by helping another girl go free[7]. You know the rest."

"Not really."

"Oh?"

"I don't know the part where you decided to celebrate your freedom and pure satisfaction by turning into a serial killer[8]."

Lorraine chuckled at that. "Serial killer. Ooo. Sounds so … I don't know … Hannibal Lecter[9] or something. But it's a fair point. I could remind you[10] that every guy I killed deserved it. They were all scum, beating girls at the clubs, ruining lives[11]. So, yeah, that was part of it. I could also remind you that by killing those losers[12], I gave many girls a second chance. No one missed these guys.[13] A couple of the wives even pleaded with you not to find their husbands, didn't they?"

"That doesn't excuse what you did."

"No, it doesn't, does it? I mean, I use it as a justification[14], certainly. We kill innocent animals, right? These guys were worse. I had my outlet.[15] But you're right. It's not really an excuse. I can only tell you this, Broome. You'll think it's odd, but maybe you'll get it. You called me a serial killer before, but my theory is, and, yeah, this will sound strange"—her voice became a whisper[16]—"but there are a lot of us out there[17]."

1. Aucun remords ?

2. claqua des

3. lui vint à l'esprit

4. suis venue m'installer en ville

5. fêtait ma liberté

6. en quelque sorte

7. en libérant d'autres filles

8. en devenant une tueuse en série

9. [du film le Silence des agneaux, 1991]

10. te rappeler

11. fichant des vies en l'air

12. ces paumés

13. Ces types n'ont manqué à personne.

14. ça me permet de me justifier

15. Ça me défoulait.

16. murmure

17. il y en a plein des comme moi

The temperature in the room dropped a few degrees.

"Think of them as sleepers[1], Broome. Millions of them, I bet. A lot of people are natural-born[2] killers, serial or otherwise[3]. They just don't know it.[4] I mean, how would you ever know, if you never did the deed[5]? I had no idea, see, and then I killed Mr. Wonderful and it was like opening a floodgate[6]. It felt so good. Not just because he deserved it. But the very act itself.[7]"

Police sirens shattered the morning air[8].

Lorraine sighed. "We don't have much time, Broome. I guess the rest of the answers will have to wait."

"Wait for what?"

She didn't reply. Broome wondered what that meant—what she planned on doing[9]. Surrounding[10] her house with police cars would not be helpful. Broome glanced down at the dead body.

"Why, Lorraine?"

"Weren't you listening?"

"Because they deserved it."

"Yes. And because I liked it. They needed killing.[11] I needed to kill."

It was, in the end, as simple as that.

A bullhorn sounded.[12] "Lorraine Griggs? This is the police."

Lorraine gestured toward[13] the window. "Our time is up.[14]"

"So what are you going to do now?"

"Do?"

"What's your plan?" Broome spread his arms. "Are you going to, what, enjoy one more kill[15] before they arrest you?"

"Ah, Broome," Lorraine said, giving him a smile that shattered his heart anew[16]. "I'd never hurt you.[17] Not in a million years.[18]"

He looked at her, confused.

The bullhorn again: "Lorraine Griggs. This is the police. ..."

Marginal glossary notes:

1. Des dormants, en quelque sorte
2. nés
3. ou non
4. Mais ils n'en savent rien.
5. si on ne l'a jamais fait
6. ça a été comme une porte qui s'ouvrait
7. Mais aussi l'acte en lui-même.
8. Des sirènes de police éclatèrent dans l'air matinal.
9. ce qu'elle avait l'intention de faire
10. L'encerclement de
11. Il fallait que quelqu'un les tue.
12. Une voix retentit dans un mégaphone.
13. désigna
14. C'est l'heure de nous quitter.
15. t'offrir un dernier petit meurtre
16. qui, une fois de plus, lui déchira le cœur
17. Je ne pourrais jamais te faire de mal.
18. Jamais de la vie.

"I got it all planned out[1]," she said to him. "This is where it ends. I told you yesterday. I'm dying. I don't want to spend my last days on the lam[2]."

She spun[3] the gun on her finger. The barrel[4] was now pointed at her.

Broome said, "Don't."

"What?" She looked down at the barrel. "You thought I was going to kill myself? Oh, that's sweet, Broome, but, no, that's not my plan."

Lorraine handed him the gun and held up her hands. "Arrest time."

"So that's it? You're just going to surrender[5]?"

"Yep, hon[6], that's it." She once again gave him the crooked smile. "Stick a fork in me, I'm done.[7]"

Broome just looked at her. "I don't know what to say, Lorraine."

Her eyes flicked[8] to the door then back to him[9]. "Remember how you said you'd be there when I die?"

Broome nodded. "Yeah, sure."

"So here's your big chance to prove you're not a liar[10]." There were tears in her eyes now. "Promise me you won't just leave me. Promise me you'll stay close[11]."

1. J'ai tout prévu
2. en cavale
3. fit tourner
4. canon

5. te rendre
6. chéri
7. Tu peux me cueillir, je suis mûre
8. Elle tourna les yeux
9. de nouveau vers lui
10. c'est le moment de prouver que tu n'es pas un menteur
11. que tu resteras auprès de moi

373

Epilogue

1. retira la perfusion
2. débrancha l'appareil respiratoire
3. resserraient leur étau
4. perdu tout ce qui avait de l'importance
5. ne lui lâcha pas
6. dès lors
7. en évoquant leur premier rendez-vous
8. s'était cassé la figure en se dépêchant pour sortir
9. lui ouvrir la portière
10. lui raconta
11. qu'il avait failli s'évanouir

Two weeks later

"ARE you ready?" the doctor asked.

Del Flynn nodded. He held his beautiful Maria's hand. The doctor pulled out the feeding tube[1] and disconnected her breathing apparatus[2]. Del knew that somewhere outside this room, the cops were steadily closing in[3] on him and Goldberg, but that was okay. He had already lost whatever really mattered[4]. This— what was going on right here, right now—was all that mattered now.

Del never left Maria's side. He never let go of[5] the hand. For eight hours, he talked to Maria about the first time he had ever seen her, how he knew even then[6] that they were destined to be together. He laughed about their first date[7], how he stumbled jumping out[8] of the car to open the door for her[9]. He recounted[10] every second of the day Carlton was born, how he had nearly fainted[11] at the sight, how he had never seen her look more beautiful than when she held her little boy. And in the end, when there were only scant minutes left in Maria's life[1], he started to sob[2]. He begged her to forgive him[3]. He pleaded for her not to[4] leave him all alone. He ranted and raved[5], but he never told her what had happened to Carlton.

Maria died with Del holding her hand.

BEFORE Ray Levine was released from prison, he agreed to help the authorities try to find the remains of[6] Stewart Green. His lawyer, Flair Hickory, drew up the papers[7]. In exchange for his help, Flair demanded[8] that no charges be filed[9] against his client. The county prosecutor's office[10] quickly agreed. In the end, Ray Levine would only be guilty of disposing of a dead body[11] anyway, a crime where the statute of limitations had long since passed[12].

At the request of Sarah Green, Stewart Green's widow[13], Broome was put in charge of the search party[14]. Ray Levine led them down yet another hidden path—so many hidden paths in this case—to the remote cliff[15] where he had hurled[16] the bundled and bagged body parts[17] into a lake.

In something of a final shock, the divers[18] found a few of them still intact.

So now they were all at the cemetery, lowering the remains of Stewart Green into the earth[19]. Sarah, officially widowed[20] now, stood between her daughter, Susie, and her son, Brandon. Broome watched their faces and wondered what next[21]. Sarah had been living in that state of suspended animation[22] for so long he worried that she wouldn't be able to move out of it[23].

For others, life had moved on. Ricky Mannion, for example, had been exonerated[24] of the murder conviction and released from Rahway. When he walked out of the gates, no one was there to meet him.

1. alors que Maria n'avait plus que quelques minutes à vivre
2. sangloter
3. la supplia de lui pardonner
4. la supplia de de pas
5. tempêta tout ce qu'il pouvait
6. de trouver la dépouille de
7. rédigea les accords
8. exigea
9. qu'aucune accusation ne soit retenue
10. Le bureau du procureur
11. d'atteinte à l'intégrité du cadavre
12. infraction pour laquelle il y avait largement prescription
13. veuve
14. chargé de mener les recherches
15. falaise
16. d'où il avait balancé
17. les sacs de débris humains
18. plongeurs
19. pour la mise en terre de la dépouille de Green
20. veuve
21. ce qu'ils allaient devenir
22. comme en suspens
23. de passer à la suite
24. disculpé

1. cercueil

2. la règle qu'elle avait imposée

3. à quoi elle jouait

4. même s'il avait du mal à l'admettre

5. relations difficiles

6. faisait de son mieux pour y répondre

7. C'est le premier que j'aie tué

8. en tenue pénitentiaire orange

9. ça a marché

10. battue

11. Tu n'as pas idée de ce qu'il lui faisait subir.

12. un taré ne suffit pas

13. initial

14. n'a pas marché

15. regarda ailleurs

16. le désir retombe un peu

17. lui mettre le meurtre sur le dos

18. drôle de

The casket[1] hit the bottom of the hole.

Broome had just come from yet another visit/interrogation with Lorraine. She would only talk to him—that was her rule[2]—but then he was free to discuss what he learned with others. At first, he wondered what her game was[3], why, other than exhaustion and not wanting to be on the lam, she had so easily surrendered and what all that talk about a "plan" was.

It took some time, but eventually he got it.

Broome had become Lorraine's confidant and confessor, and while he hated to admit it[4], he still liked being with her, which, of course, might explain his troubled relationships[5] with women.

Lorraine knew that he had questions still, so she tried her best to answer them[6]. During their last private meeting, he said, "Tell me about Ross Gunther."

"He was my first kill[7]," Lorraine, now garbed in that federal-pen orange[8], told him. "After my husband, of course. I was a little too ambitious, but it paid off[9]."

"What do you mean, ambitious?"

"See, I liked Stacy. She was a nice kid who'd been battered down[10] by men her whole life. She had this horrible boyfriend named Ricky Mannion. You wouldn't believe what he would do to her.[11] And then, because sometimes one creep isn't enough[12], Stacy ends up attracting the attention of a second total psycho named Ross Gunther. So my original[13] plan was to kill both."

"What went wrong[14]?"

Lorraine smiled and looked off[15]. "Killing can be a little, well, like sex for most men I know. After you do it once, you kinda lose the urge[16] for a little while. So I killed Gunther and instead of killing Mannion, I found it more interesting to just pin the murder on him[17]. Truth was, killing Gunther alone wouldn't have freed Stacy. I needed to get rid of both of them. It's a funny[18] logic, I admit that, but it works."

"So that was year one?"

376

"Yes."

Then Broome got to the real heart of it[1]. "And Stewart Green was year two?"

"Yep. Here's the thing. I never knew what happened to him. I mean, I knew I killed him. I sent Cassie up there because I wanted her to know she was free. I didn't think she'd freak[2]. I should have known[3]. That was a mistake on my part, and I learned my lesson[4]. Anyway, when nobody ever found Stewart's body ... well, I never really knew what happened either. It kinda freaked me out.[5] I figured that Cassie hid the body or something[6]. But then she vanished too. I even wondered for a bit if maybe Ray Levine had killed her and hidden both bodies, especially after I spotted him by the ruins a few weeks ago just before Carlton Flynn showed up[7]."

"Wait, you saw him?"

Lorraine nodded. "I almost called the whole thing off[8], but I figured[9], I wouldn't be alive by next Mardi Gras, so what the hell[10]."

"So it was you who attacked Ray with the bat and stole the camera. You wanted the pictures he took."

"Guilty[11]," Lorraine said. "You're not going to charge me with assault[12], are you?"

"We can let it slide[13]."

"Wouldn't look like much next to[14] all those dead bodies, would it? Anyway, where were we[15]? Cassie, right?"

Broome nodded.

"I didn't want to mess up her life or anything[16], but I needed to know what happened. It haunted me.[17] I tried to find her, but she really managed to vanish. Meanwhile I watched you, Broome, chase your own tail[18] trying to find what happened to Stewart Green. You had no idea what happened. Without a body, you really had no case. See, I learned from that[19]. All that confusion. So I decided to change my MO[20]."

"You decided to hide the bodies," Broome said.

1. en vint au cœur de l'affaire

2. qu'elle allait paniquer

3. m'en douter

4. j'ai retenu la leçon

5. Ça m'a fait un peu flipper.

6. un truc comme ça

7. l'arrivée de Carlton Flynn

8. J'ai failli tout annuler

9. je me suis dit

10. qu'est-ce que ça pouvait bien faire

11. Je plaide coupable

12. m'accuser de coups et blessures

13. fermer les yeux

14. Ça paraîtrait peu de chose, à côté de

15. où en étions-nous

16. foutre le bordel dans sa vie

17. Ça me tourmentait.

18. tourner en rond

19. ça m'a appris un truc

20. procéder autrement [MO=modus operandi]

"Yep."

"You made it look like maybe the men had gone missing or run away."

"Exactly. If I kept leaving dead bodies up there, the cops would be all over it[1]. I'd have to find new spots every year. It'd be too much[2], you know what I'm saying? But with disappearances, well, in many cases there was nothing to go on[3]."

"There's one thing I still don't get."

"Then ask away[4], handsome."

Broome shouldn't be enjoying this[5]. "You told Megan—Cassie—that you always knew where she was. How?"

"Oh, that was a lie," Lorraine said. "I had no idea until recently."

That surprised him. "I don't get it. How did you finally find her?"

"The truth is, Cassie—let's not call her Megan, that's not how I knew her—Cassie was the best[6]. I loved her. Truly.[7] And she loved the life[8]. That's the part they don't talk about, Broome. You hear about the drugs and the prostitution and the abuse, but that's not the whole picture[9]. You've seen the clubs, Broome. For some of the girls, this is the best they'll ever get[10]. It's fun and exciting. It's a party every night and in this miserable drone of a life[11], what's wrong with that[12]?"

"And Cassie was one of those girls?"

"Oh, she was indeed[13]. I knew she'd be missing the life. So, that's why, even after seventeen years, I wasn't surprised when she came back to the club for a visit. She told you about that, right?"

Broome nodded. "She did."

"She pretended to come down to[14] Atlantic City for some stupid convention, but of course she ended up back in La Crème."

"And you recognized her?"

"Yep. So I followed her back to the[15] Tropicana. I got friends at the front desk[16]. They gave me her real

---

Marginal notes (left column):

1. s'en mêleraient
2. Ça deviendrait trop compliqué
3. il n'y avait aucune piste
4. pose-moi toutes les questions que tu veux
5. n'était pas censé apprécier ces échanges
6. la plus chouette
7. Profondément.
8. adorait cette vie
9. il n'y a pas que ça
10. ce qu'elles trouveront de mieux
11. vie pourrie
12. quel mal à ça
13. ça oui
14. a fait semblant de venir à
15. l'ai suivie jusqu'au
16. qui travaillent à la réception

name and address. I went up to her place and figured a way to get her back down here[1]."

"You pretended that you saw Stewart. You acted like maybe he had something to do with[2] Carlton Flynn."

"Right. And when I saw her reaction, I knew that she didn't know what happened to the body either. So now it's your turn, Broome." Lorraine leaned forward. "Tell me about Stewart Green. That's always been the big mystery to me[3]. Tell me what happened to his body."

So he did. He told her the whole story about Ray Levine cutting up the corpse. Lorraine listened intently.

"Poor, sweet Ray," she said.

"Which begs yet[4] another question," Broome said. "How did Carlton Flynn's Saint Anthony medal end up[5] in Ray Levine's apartment?"

"I put it there[6]," Lorraine said. "How else?"

"How did you get in?"

"You're kidding, right? Ray lived in a basement with narrow windows. I opened one and tossed the medal into the middle of the room. Simple as that. Funny thing, though, about Ray cutting up the body."

"What about it?"

"It's like the opposite of what I said[7]."

"I'm not following.[8]"

"When I experienced[9] violence, I found out I had a taste for it[10]. When poor Ray did, he found out the opposite. It brought me to life.[11] It crushed him. It's all in how we're hardwired[12], Broome. He was too soft[13]. It wasn't Cassie leaving that destroyed him. It was that he couldn't live with all that blood ..."

Broome wanted to ask more, but she said, "Enough for[14] today, hon. I got a TV thing[15]."

And that was what Broome had realized. That was her plan.

She was close to getting caught[16]. They had found the bodies. They had found out about her killing[17] her

---

1. j'ai imaginé un moyen de la faire revenir

2. à voir avec

3. resté un grand mystère pour moi

4. Ce qui m'amène à

5. s'est-elle retrouvée

6. C'est moi qui l'y ai mise

7. le contraire de ce que je viens de dire

8. Je ne te suis pas.

9. j'ai découvert

10. que j'aimais ça

11. Ça a changé ma vie.

12. Ça dépend comment on est faits

13. sensible

14. C'est tout pour

15. J'ai une émission de télé qui m'attend.

16. sur le point de se faire choper

17. qu'elle avait tué

1. La police fédérale était sur le coup.
2. il lui en restait très peu
3. une star était née
4. fit sensation partout dans le monde
5. Les tueuses en série
6. encore plus rares
7. susciter l'intérêt
8. il suffit d'ajouter un peu de piment de com'
9. comme l'avaient surnommée les médias
10. vengeur
11. se manifestèrent
12. Les gens, fascinés, en redemandaient.
13. Elle attirait la sympathie
14. ça ne s'apprend pas
15. déconcerter
16. brouiller les pistes
17. gagner du temps
18. n'avaient pas de problème
19. de juger une mourante
20. l'attention médiatique qu'elle susciterait
21. Tu n'es que poussière...
22. les membres de l'assistance baissèrent la tête
23. cher disparu
24. un rang

husband on Mardi Gras. The feds were involved.[1] It was only a question of time, and she didn't have much of that left[2] anyway. But the moment she surrendered, well, a star was born[3].

Lorraine's case became an international sensation[4]. That was what Broome hadn't expected at first. Serial killers are rare. Female serial killers[5] are rarer still[6]. That would have been enough to garner attention[7], but then you add some professional spin[8] and voilà. Lorraine's lawyer was the famed Hester Crimstein, an expert in manipulating the media. Suddenly, Lorraine wasn't a murdering monster, as per her media nickname[9], but an abused woman who became the "Avenging[10] Angel." The wives and girlfriends of her victims came out[11], each telling a terrifying tale of abuse, of living in agony and fear, of being saved by the only woman who would help them.

Lorraine.

So now Lorraine did TV interviews. The fascination with her was endless.[12] Her natural likability came out[13] because you simply can't teach that[14]. Hester Crimstein's strategy was a simple one: confuse[15], deflect[16], stall[17]. The federal prosecutors were pretty much fine[18] with that last point. They didn't relish trying a dying woman[19] who many viewed as a hero.

Broome thought about that crooked smile Lorraine had given him before he arrested her. She had known. She had known exactly how it would play out in the media[20].

"Ashes to ashes[21]..."

Back at the funeral of Stewart Green, a man murdered by Lorraine, the mourners bowed their heads[22].

"We say our final good-bye to our dearly departed[23] ..."

Sarah Green moved toward the open ground with a rose in her hand. She tossed it down on the casket. Susie followed. Then Brandon. Broome didn't move. Erin, looking beautiful in black, was in the row[24]